The Alpha Promise

ISBN: 1-4392-1184-1
ISBN-13: 9781439211847

Visit www.booksurge.com to order additional copies.

The Alpha Promise

Hayat Ali

Part One
Mating Season

Chapter 1
Wounded Stranger

PEOPLE HAVE ALWAYS TALKED about things that go bump in the night. Adina Carr knew the stories. She had even read the books and watched the shows. But like everyone else, she took the stories with a grain of salt. Creatures of the night were flights of fancy to scare others into acting like they had more sense when they went out at night. They were not things to believe in, now or ever.

As she walked to her flat, oblivious to all the dark things that might harm her, Adina wished she could have just told Redman, her boss, that he had a great idea. But she just couldn't say that to him, especially not when his hand kept *accidentally* touching her butt. Rolling her eyes, she stormed to her apartment, wishing she knew what the hell she was going to do for money now that she'd been fired.

She had come to London on a whim with her then-boyfriend. Within three weeks, though, he had dumped her for the perky little fake blond posing at his art studio. Three days later, he moved back to the States with all the money, leaving her stuck in London. Thankfully, she was able to get a work visa, but that was going to expire in a week. She had planned to try for another but now that she was unemployed, it was going to be a lot harder to win anyone over to her cause. At least she had managed to save enough money to go back home and face her parents' I-told-you-so looks.

It was a Friday evening and the sun had just faded into the background, leaving a strange orange-brown hue in the sky. Adina wondered what she could do to lift her spirits, other than finding the nearest pub and drinking until she was too blind to notice the company she might take home. Since her boyfriend had gone, she'd been busy trying to keep from being homeless and helpless in a foreign city and had no one in her life. But given the way things had changed, she wanted to at least try to enjoy the city before she had to leave.

Adina didn't have any real friends in London, but that was nothing new; she'd spent the last twenty-three years cultivating her "loner" persona. It wasn't that she didn't like people, but she tended to be on the strange side, always a little too free in thought, and that usually made her lose friendships instead of keeping them. The one friend she had, Carol, she'd left back in the States so she could follow the man she had deemed her soul mate.

Her block was a street with rows and rows of walk-up flats without elevators or air conditioners. It was just a working-class neighborhood, not too far from the Queen's Palace, and just a quick train ride on the tube. It had been an okay place to live—not too many screams at night or hoodlums roaming the street—and for that reason she'd never felt threatened.

When she got to her apartment building and was fumbling with her keys, a creepy feeling made the hairs on the back of her neck stand up. She stopped and turned, looking for a clue as to what had set off her internal alarms. Seeing nothing, she slowly extended her arm to unlock the door. She was still wary, having learned a long time ago not to ignore any bad feelings. And right now she was having a major bad feeling. But seeing nothing, she cautiously continued her routine. The key slid into the lock and with a push, the door opened. A heavy wind came in after her. She secured the door and walked over to her mailbox.

The foyer and stairs were dimly lit, the superintendent having failed once again to change the dying or dead light bulbs. After checking for her mail, she slowly walked towards the stairs. A soft brushing sound made her jerk around but she saw nothing. Her eyes searched frantically for the thing that had freaked her out. She wanted to call out to whoever was following her, but she didn't dare. It could just be rats. But then she heard the sound again. Not a scratching, but a stomping, dragging limp.

Like a shot, she raced up the steps to her fifth floor flat. The eerie lighting and shadows only added to her nervousness. She swore silently to herself. Her pace might cause her to trip and break her neck. She tried to slow down at the third flight, but she heard footsteps right behind her. Her eyes widened in terror as she took off again, this time taking the stairs in twos.

The stomping behind her grew louder, even as she reached her landing. She raced down the hall to her apartment and wrestled with her keys. The sound was getting closer and she was starting to doubt she would make it. But she found the right key and placed it into the lock just as the sound faded into silence. Breathing heavily, she spun around, but saw nothing.

Facing the door again, she started to turn the knob when a voice whispered to her. Her breath caught as she strained to hear the words. When nothing happened, she released the air in a relieved rush. "Stop scaring yourself, Adina."

With her lips in a firm line, she pushed her door open. It spoke again, this time louder. "Help me," it said. Adina jerked around but saw nothing in the hallway. She stared into her apartment, fearing that the intruder could already be in there. She was backing towards the stairs when the voice came from directly behind her.

"Please," it said with a cough.

Jumping, her head jerked left and right. She squinted, trying to find the source of the voice. She was just about to dismiss the possibility of anyone being there when her eyes connected with radiant green ones. The eyes seemed to glow in the semi-dark corner of the stairway. There was something wholly unnatural about those eyes, frightening. At the same time she was transfixed, as if held in place by a supernatural force.

Every fiber in her being wanted to run, but her feet were glued to the floor. In the blink of an eye, the person was closer to her. She felt her breath quickening as her mind screamed for her to act, to get away, but she couldn't move. She was trapped in the gaze of those eyes.

"I won't hurt you. I just need your help. Please help me," the pained voice said from the shadows.

Adina felt herself about to say "yes," like she was a puppet, or worse, like an insect caught in a spider's web. The eyes were coming closer and she was still unable to move. Feeling a rage building inside her, she screamed, "NO!!!!!"

Whatever connection she had with those eyes shattered and she backed away with a body that finally responded to her command. Part of her wondered why her neighbors didn't come, but she remembered that her nearest neighbor had moved and the others were probably at the pub. Knowing she was on her own, Adina raced back to her door, but froze again.

"Please…I need your help…"

A heavy thump echoed in the hall.

Again she waited, all the while cursing herself. After taking a few deep breaths for courage, she turned towards the stairs and saw someone laid out on the floor. She stood there staring at the body, wanting to leave the person there and pretend that she hadn't seen or heard anything, but another part of her refused to do that. What if the situation was reversed? She would want someone to help her.

"Adina, you know if you do this, your life will forever change," she said to herself. She'd promised herself she wouldn't act impulsively after what had happened with her last boyfriend. "Screw it," she sighed, rolling her eyes.

She took tentative steps towards the person on the floor. As she got closer, a metallic smell hit her. Frowning, she walked even closer, bending as she approached.

Lying on the floor was a man in a torn black silk shirt, and what looked like leather pants. His long dark hair was splayed everywhere and blood was pooling around him. Gasping, she walked around him and noticed numerous injuries on his body. He appeared to have been in a bad fight with a wild beast. She glanced at his pale hand and focused on a huge ring on his index finger. It had a ruby set in an artfully engraved band. Adina's curiosity almost overtook her until the flowing blood made her regain focus.

Taking several deep breaths, she reached out slowly. It seemed like eternity passed before her hand touched his shoulder. She pushed him slightly, trying to determine if he was awake. She noted how cool he felt. After a pause, she pushed him again, forcing him over slightly. What she saw made her jump.

His face was badly bruised, several deep scratches were on his chest, and his shirt was practically in tatters. But what really threw her were his teeth. He had hissed when she turned him over, and she could have sworn she saw fangs in his mouth.

She struggled to think carefully about what she was about to do, because she had the weirdest, most dreadful feeling that a vampire was lying half-dead, if that was possible, on the hallway floor. And if that was true, did she really want to be involved in anything that could bring more of these creatures into her life? Based on the way he looked, she knew that if his problems followed him, she would not have any real defense against them.

"Damn, Adina, you just had to look."

* * *

Dragging the man—vampire, whatever—was more than a chore for Adina. He was not only heavy, but tall. He had to be at least six foot three and two hundred pounds. She felt the pulling all in her back but finally dragged him into her flat and left him on the floor.

Deciding that he would be all right until she finished forming a plan, she went into her kitchen to grab a mop. She filled her bucket with water and walked out of the kitchen, carefully stepping around whatever was on the floor, then went into the hallway.

There, she began cleaning up the blood on the floor and stairs, going all the way down to the second landing before resting. Satisfied that she had hidden any evidence, she went back to her apartment. She secured all the locks before facing the man on the floor. Placing the bucket and mop by the door, she thought about what she must do, already dreading the work it would take to get his blood out of the worn carpet.

Sighing, she pushed off the wall and headed into her bathroom. She had a small three-room flat, a bedroom, with a small bath attached, a kitchen dining area and a living room. The living room was furnished sparingly with a worn out couch and a television. Straight across the living room from the front door was the kitchen and to the right of the living room, the bedroom, which had a small window that faced the street.

Walking through her bedroom, she kicked off her shoes. Going into the bath, Adina let the water run until warm then filled the bathtub. Turning, she opened the medicine cabinet above the sink, pulling out antiseptic, cotton balls, and she set them on the counter. Finding that she really didn't have anything else, she closed the cabinet.

Turning back to the tub, she stopped the water and returned to her bedroom. She found some long scarves that weren't made of wool and pulled them out, already grimacing at how they would have to be used. Tossing them on the bed, she closed her closet and faced a body-length mirror on the other side of the door.

"You're crazy, Adina," she said, eyeing her image before walking away.

Creeping back into the living room, she was almost afraid that the vampire-man might have moved, but he hadn't. Walking over to him, it took a moment before she realized that his chest wasn't moving. In a panic, she began CPR but stopped when she saw him shift.

"There is a vampire in my house. I just invited a vampire into my house!" The words echoed through her apartment—or so she thought—but her reaction was utter calm.

Adina shook her head as she digested what she was doing, fascinated by the truth of her words. She had an honest-to-God vamp lying on her floor. She should be concerned, but she wasn't, at least, not yet. Her more practical side screamed that she should at least find a cross or something, just in case the TV shows were right. Instead, she shrugged it off. The vampire was helpless in her hands and until proven otherwise, she wasn't going to consider him a threat.

With firm resolve, Adina began the lengthy process of hauling the vampire to her bathroom. Pulling him with every ounce of her strength, she managed to get him into the bathroom, making only three stops for rest. Once there, she was able to get a better look at him under the harsh light.

His face was strong, nice square jaw, almond shaped eyes, a straight nose, and high cheekbones. There was an almost aristocratic, Asiatic appeal to his features. His skin was pale, almost white, which contrasted deeply with his dark hair and eyebrows. Even with the bruises, he had a handsome face that she thought didn't deserve to be marred by violence. The cuts on his chest were bad, but not as bad as she had thought. Removing what remained of the shirt as carefully as possible, she stared at his well-toned chest and stomach, pale like the finest marble and just as strong.

Adina swallowed and counted to ten—twice—before reaching for his pants. She had to do it. Everything had to go if she was to truly access the damage. Moreover, she knew that she needed to clean him. Yet, her skin felt hot and flushed at the idea of removing this vampire's pants. From what she had seen of the upper body, she had a strong feeling that she would be impressed by what was below. With a quivering hand, she told herself to stop acting like a child and unbuttoned his pants.

The leather was like a second skin and he wore nothing underneath, probably because of it. Once she'd undone the buttons, she removed the black, square-toed boots from his feet. Again she paused to collect herself.

"Stop acting like a punk. It's not like you ain't seen a naked man before," she muttered to herself. But she knew that it was more than that. She had never seen a naked man this fine in person. Even her "ex" didn't have a body as tight as this vampire's.

It was a slow process. She grabbed the top of his pants and started to pull it. As she did, her fingers dragged against his cool, firm skin. Her eyes closed as she fought off the dirty thoughts and slowly revealed his manhood. Her eyebrows arched in appreciation of its length and size before she returned to the task of removing the second skin.

She started to pull the pants when they'd reached mid-thigh. At first nothing happened. Going back to top, careful not to touch his penis, she dragged them down a bit further. Returning to the ends, she pulled again and this time, a good jerk got the pants off. She fell backwards and banged her head against the bathroom door.

Standing and rubbing her head, she couldn't help but stare at him. Again, she was impressed by the muscular, yet hurt, being on the floor. She glanced at the tub to keep her mind from sinking into the gutter. She had to figure out the best way to get the vampire into the tub. She didn't want to put him in face first, though it probably wouldn't harm him. Still, she didn't want to climb in the water herself.

"What to do, what to do." She scratched her head, tilting it slightly before rolling up her boot-cut jeans.

Once she had them rolled to her knees, she approached him from behind. Placing her hands under his arms, she dragged him closer to the tub. Taking a tentative step into the tub, she found the water warm, not scalding. She silently prayed that she wouldn't slip and break her neck in trying to get the vampire into the water. Putting her other foot in, she backed away from the faucets and heaved with all her might, letting out a harsh grunt.

It took four tries and three near-slips to finally get his upper body into the tub. Water had splashed all over the floor, but at least he was finally in. Carefully, she propped his head against the wall and stepped out of the tub. Once out, she lifted his legs into the water before sitting on the stool to take a breather. Adina kept her eyes on the form in the tub, making sure he didn't slip or move. After her breathing returned to normal, she went to work washing all of his wounds with antiseptic and soap. She removed as much grime from the rest of his body as she could, desperate to avoid his most private parts. She even washed his hair, letting her fingers massage the silken strands. By the time she finished, the water had cooled and darkened, and as it drained, she thought of the tub as one more thing she would have to clean. When the water was gone, she grabbed a towel and dried him off as much as she could while he was still in the tub.

Then came more heaving, to pull him out and drag his heavy body to her one luxury in the apartment, her queen-size bed. After she finally got him onto the mattress, she had to stop because piercing waves of pain were running down her spine.

I'm really gonna feel it in the morning, she thought, but went about the task of binding as many wounds as possible. When she finished, she covered him up and stood there, watching him do whatever he was going to do while resting. A part of her wondered if he was still alive, but instinctively she knew that he was. Like most wounded people, he just needed time to heal.

Why did he seek my help?

Now that he was stable, she could consider the question that had been with her since the moment she saw him. Why her flat and why her? What happened? How had he got there and who did that to him? And finally, what the hell was going on?

She knew that the answers wouldn't be revealed until the vampire recovered. More importantly, she knew that she probably wouldn't like the answers too much. Yet, she couldn't help staring at this handsome creature in her bed and thinking about the consequences of her choice. She had a vampire in her house. A creature, which prior to falling out, had a hold over her that took all her will to break. A creature, that prior to being fired today, she didn't think even existed. She didn't know what was true and what wasn't. She didn't know if she should run to the church for holy water or find a wooden stake. She just wasn't sure.

The only thing she could be sure about was that her life was about to change. She only hoped that it would be for the better.

Chapter 2

Failure

THE PRINCE OF TENHAR, Lars, sat in a private car on the train from Denmark heading towards Switzerland and reading a novel. He was very fair-skinned, even for a vampire, with white blond hair to his shoulders, piercing blue eyes and a taste for eighteenth century clothes. Lars' rise as Prince was secured through subtle politicking and assassination. He was ruthless enough to kill anything and anyone he deemed a threat to his power. Lars' singular goal was to usurp the throne of the vampire council and have Tenhar dominate all Vampires.

His private car was elegant in its simplicity. The furnishings were lush, the walls a soft blue that blended with exposed metal, and four chairs sat in the room. Lars sat closest to the window. The table in front of him bore a glass of warm brandy and a smaller one of blood. He relaxed while waiting for the news that would change everything.

For the past fifty years, Lars had plotted to eliminate Jin, the High Prince son of Danpe and Hinghou lineage. It was necessary in order for the Tenhar to reclaim their power and prove to the other tribes that they deserved to be the supreme rulers of all the clans. Lars was trying to work the plan by using Jin, but his parents were proving to be efficient at thwarting him, including keeping his clan away from the planned event in London. When it became apparent that Eldon, Prince and Grand Master of Danpe, and Father of Jin, would not allow Tenhar to participate in the ritual, Lars went to see the Kinlye.

The Kinlye was a barbaric tribe of vampires who were keen on the baser ways of existence. Their dark fetishes had kept most vampires at bay, including Tenhar, but they could be of some use. Most didn't know Kinlye's capabilities, but Lars did, and he requested a small pet. He asked them for a hellhound. It was a simple potion that anyone could access. However, if a vampire was brave enough to go to a Kinlye stronghold, they could ask directly…for a small price. A few humans were all it cost and the potion was his.

Lars had one of his kin obtain something with Jin's scent and let his plan fall into place. If all worked out, Jin would be torn to tatters and the vampire council would be in deep disarray. A war would break out, and then Lars would show the full strength of Tenhar power. He closed his book, smiling wickedly at the thought. He could almost taste the victory. The idea actually made him gleeful. The cell phone vibrating in his jacket pocket interrupted his bliss. He listened awhile, then his handsome pale features turned to stone.

"What did you say to me?" He said in a cool voice.

"He escaped. We have the hellhounds on his scent as we speak."

"How did that untrained brat manage to escape the hellhounds?"

"He morphed, my Lord, and disappeared into the night."

"I see."

The vampire on the line, nervous, began babbling rapidly.

"Sir, he was hurt pretty badly. Like I said, the hellhounds are able to track him."

"So you've said, and for your sake, you better hope they find him. What of the others?"

"They're dead."

"Well, that impetuous ass called the High Prince had better be dead by morning, or the hellhounds will feast on your innards."

He slapped his phone shut with a sneer. The plan had become a disaster. Now he had to make alterations to insure he and his tribe wasn't implicated in any way. He couldn't believe that the Prince had managed to elude the hounds. Lars had assumed that the Prince would not know how to defend himself. It was a well known fact that the Prince had been kept ignorant of all his power so his parents could control him more effectively. But it was a mistake to assume anything and Lars was determined not to make that mistake again.

"At least I prevented one of their plans for him," he mumbled with a small amount of satisfaction. Then he opened his phone to begin the process of covering his tracks.

* * *

Eldon was walking amongst his guests, trying to keep everyone calm. Thankfully, he hadn't seen his wife. She would no doubt riddle him with questions about why Jin hadn't made it to the Gathering. Several women were standing about dressed in elegant gowns. The men were stoic, trying to keep themselves neutral, but coming over to Eldon to discuss the attributes of their tribes. They were all jittery waiting for Jin to arrive, craning the necks for the chance to be the first to catch his eye. Eldon rolled his eyes. He hated the need for a Gathering at all, but he understood.

Thirty minutes later, the Grand Master and Prince of Danpe sat in an oversized chair made of tightly knitted crimson fabric with a stiff high back and sides to obscure him as he brooded. He could feel it in his gut that something wasn't right. Jin and his entourage should have been there by now or called to explain the delay. But so far, neither had happened. Eldon had already sent a few of his people to find out anything. Now all he can do was wait.

He was on his second glass of wine, his green eyes growing dark with worry when he sensed one of his trackers next to him. He tilted his head to hear the news.

"Sire, the Prince has been attacked. Although there's no trace of the car, we did find blood and tests indicate that it belong to the Prince's bodyguard. Sire…" the tracker hesitated before speaking again, "Sire, we believe the hellhounds were set loose on your son and his bodyguards."

Eldon's eyes brightened until reaching a florescent green. The wine glass in his hand shattered before he stood with a roar.

"Everyone out!"

Within minutes, all were ushered out and the Grand Master was storming down the halls to find the Prince's mother.

Chapter 3
Dreaming of a Dark Angel

IN'S MIND SLOWLY BEGAN to return from the fog that his pained body had dragged him into. He was becoming aware that he was resting on a soft palate and his wounds, though still painful, had lost a bit of their sting.

Taking a moment, he expanded his senses to understand his surroundings without having to open his tired eyes. From the smell, he was in a home, a woman's home. There was a distinct spicy, floral scent permeating the room.

Obviously, he was lying on a nice-sized bed. The person who had taken him in had also cleaned him up. He could still smell antiseptic faintly, feel the bindings over his wounds. Without the treatment he still would have healed, but much slower. As it was, he was wounded badly enough that he needed to remain in a dormant state if he was going to heal completely. With blood, the process would go faster, but he doubted that his savior would have any lying around to feed his kind.

How had he gotten into a situation where he had to reveal himself to a human? That was the highest violation of the Order's rules and it bothered him. It would definitely not do if the son of the Grand Master of Danpe, as well as the next in the line, was the one violating it, particularly not with an inter-tribal war on the horizon. He was the son that was supposed to unite the Danpe with the Hinghou. Marriage had ended the last war between the two major vampire tribes. This arrangement would elevate the vampires to another level.

Some who were lead by the Tenhar resented the alliance between the tribes. They were the ones who despised Jin because he was to become leader at the end of the moon cycle. Jin's many enemies felt threatened by his power, especially his insistence that humans never know of vampires and that vampires never feed on humans. As a result, Jin had been heavily guarded against possible assassination attempts.

Then tonight, on a clear evening, Jin's guards were struck down and Jin himself was attacked by vicious hellhounds. They had been conjured because it would be impossible to trace the summoning vampire's signature if Jin was killed. Jin had barely managed to escape by morphing into a jaguar and racing away. Hellhounds were vicious, but not very fast, as their large bodies were made more for power than speed. Once he lost his attackers, he morphed back into his human form, bloody and disorientated. He knew it would be a matter of time before he was caught again. He needed a place to hide, heal, and plan. But he knew nothing of the area he found himself in.

Frantically looking around while hiding in the shadows, he tried to spot a way out but found nothing. Just when he was about to give up, he spotted a young woman walking quickly up the street. She was human, that much he knew, but at the moment it was the best he could do. His ears perked and he picked up the sound of the hounds in the distance, gaining on his location. Making a decision to violate the very code he was sworn to uphold, he followed her.

She sensed him when she reached her door, which made him to pause. He didn't want her to know about his presence before they entered the building. He waited until she felt secure enough to open the door, and with his last bit of strength, moved like the wind past her into the building. The woman hardly noticed him, closing the door securely behind her. Changing back, he stood and tried not to pass out from the blood loss. He took a step and landed harder than he'd intended, scaring her.

"Aaa," he snarled before following the woman up the stairs as fast as he could. When he heard her keys entering the lock, he knew he had to stop her and called out for help. He sensed her hesitation. Jin hoped she would overcome her fear and come to him. As he asked, he continued the arduous climb up the stairs, using the banister to pull himself up.

Glancing up, he caught her eye. Seeing this as the best opportunity, he used his thrall to hold her in place and calm her, promising not to harm her. But she was strong-willed and it was a struggle. She broke the hold so sharply that it left him with a piercing headache. Desperation took a hold as he tried to catch up with the woman, begging for her help until all that had happened overwhelmed him and caused him to pass out on the floor.

Now in a room belonging to a woman, rather *the* woman that he sought, he couldn't help but wonder what had changed her mind. After being so frightened that she'd broken his thrall to get away, why was she helping him now? In fact, how had she even managed to get him into the bed he was in now? Did she seek assistance? When he opened himself up more, he realized that no one else had been in the room with her. But he didn't know what had happened and the idea that he couldn't remember troubled him. What if she was a spy? What if Tenhar had managed to recruit her? He let the thought turn over in his mind, then dismissed it. If that had been the case, he'd already be dead. No, this woman chose to have mercy, exposing herself to a world beyond her comprehension.

A tightening in his belly told him that he needed to feed. He must have really lost a lot of blood. If he didn't get blood soon, he would slip into a deep coma that only his people could wake him from. He needed to communicate this to the woman without scaring her. But how do you ask a human, "Hey, you got blood?" Most likely, the only blood she had was in her own body and he refused to take a drop from her. But still, he had to have it.

He heard movement coming towards him. He had heard her moving further in the apartment but now she seemed to be coming closer. He knew that it was now or never, but he didn't know the best way to tell her to get him blood. Then he smelled something familiar. Blood! He smelled freshly heated blood!

The bed shifted from her weight next to him. He heard the mug placed on the night table. After a moment, he felt a hand on his forehead, palm first, then on the back on his cheek.

"Hey, can you hear me?" her voice was smoky and low.

Straining slightly, Jin opened his eyes to gaze into her brown orbs. There was a frown on her face, perhaps concern. She studied him a moment.

"None of that. I've already decided to help you, no need to try and hypnotize me."

Jin was confused until he realized that she thought he was trying to use his thrall.

"My eyes…" His throat hurt but he tried to talk again. In a stronger voice he said, "My eyes are naturally this way, especially in the dark."

She arched an elegant eyebrow before standing up. Walking over to the wall, she flicked a switch, instantly brightening the room. Jin squinted. The lights were turned off again.

"Sorry. I didn't know light could hurt your eyes…"

"Normally, it doesn't. It's just that I'm very sensitive right now. Please turn them back on if it brings you comfort."

He heard nothing, but sensed the lights coming back on. Slowly, he opened his eyes. When they finally stopped stinging, he captured his first good look at the woman.

Though he could see her in the dark, under the light, the shadows that surrounded her features had disappeared. She wasn't a very tall woman, at the most five foot six. Her face was oval shaped, with full generous lips, a medium nose, and dark brown eyes. Her braided hair was tied back from her face in a loose tail. The shirt was bulky around her frame, but he could discern a full figure underneath, full breast, curvy waist, and round bottom. The jeans she wore hugged her shapely thighs and her exposed legs emphasizing the fact that she probably took good care of herself. Rich dark brown skin smooth and lush looked soft though he hadn't been able to touch it yet. She was beautiful, his dark angel. He never thought he would say so of any human.

She returned to his side, studying him, warily. He did nothing to startle her, wanting her to feel comfortable and in control. Though the smell of the blood was intoxicating, it wouldn't do to freak out his savior. So he waited for her to make the next move, content to remain still and watch his dark angel.

"Are you a vampire?" she asked softly.

A loaded question with an answer that is twice as lethal. The rule about human awareness of vampires is the death or if possible the conversion of the human and the punishment of death to the vampire.

For centuries, this rule has kept all vampires in check, not because they cared so much for human life but their own life. Jin had never exposed himself to humans before, though like many of his kind, he had lived among them. He just didn't really pay attention to them, their frailty making him uncomfortable. Yet the woman before him fascinated him with her strength and courage to help a creature she knows is a vampire despite questioning it.

"What is your name?" he countered avoiding her question.

She smiled brightening her face and his heart. The small laugh that left her lips entices his ears making him wish to hear it again and again.

"Adina. My name is Adina Carr. And you are?"

He smiled lightly, "Jin. My name is Jin."

"Jin the vampire?"

He turned his head away, not ready to acknowledge the truth of her words. He heard her sigh. Turning back to her he noticed that she has taken on a far away look; contemplative perhaps.

"I know you're a vampire but I guess I need to hear you say it to really believe it. Although," she moved to face him more directly, "you do have a reflection so maybe I'm wrong."

He couldn't help the annoyed grunt that emanated from him, "That stupid parlor trick. Dracula has forever cursed us with that bit of trickery."

She stared at him like he was crazy before smiling again, "So you are a vampire…" her voice turned wistful, almost as if she was glad he was a vampire rather than a mere human.

"Would it ease your mind to hear me say that I am?" he challenged.

"Well, at least I wouldn't think I was crazy."

Jin sighed before saying, "Then yes I am. And you're not supposed to know that we exist."

"But I do know because I helped you. You asked for my help." Tilting her head she studied him curiously.

Yes he did and it would be his fault when they came for her. It would be his fault when she was presented with a choice of damnation or death. And it would be his fault that her life has changed forever. It was his debt.

"I know," he whispered partly ashamed. To have to ask this weaker creature for assistance, jeopardizing her life was sinful.

"Why did you help me?" It was his turn to be curious.

"Because you asked. How could I leave you there helpless? What kind of person would that make me?"

What kind of person would that make her? And what kind of person was he for having brought death to her doorstep?

Chapter 4
Knowledge is Frightening

ADINA STARED AT THE guilty-looking vampire in front of her. She was still waiting for his answer, but he just looked at the ceiling. She wondered if she should have said anything. It seemed to put a weird type of distance between them.

When the silence was finally too much, she turned towards the blood she had warmed for him, wondering if it was what he needed. It had taken twenty minutes just to fill half a cup with the blood from her own hand.

After cleaning up the mess in her home, she sat on her couch, exhausted. She didn't even care that she was sweaty and stained with the vampire's blood, she just wanted to rest. Never in her life had she labored like that. Yet, she couldn't feel bad about it. In fact, she felt good about helping someone in need. She hoped that she was building a lot of good karma.

Once Adina sat for awhile, she began to wreck her brain for any tidbits of information that might help with her guest and her predicament. She considered the possibility that the vampire needed blood. That had to be true, right? Based on the movies and books, that's all vampires seem to want. The more she thought about it, the more she wondered if giving him blood would help him.

"Right, like you got blood just laying all over the place."

With a shake of her head, she tried to think of where to get blood. Finally, she stood and went into her kitchen. She opened the fridge and stared inside. There were a couple of steaks she had bought for a meal later this week.

"I guess they'll have to do," she mumbled, taking them out and heated them in the microwave.

Then she grabbed a mug to collect the blood she was able to squeezing from the meat. For twenty minutes, she pressed and pushed until both steaks were mangled wads, but still the mug wasn't even half full. She needed to get more blood. But where? There was only one choice: herself. She would have to provide the blood.

She was partly revolted by the idea, but it had to be done. She couldn't afford to go to the butcher and buy more meat and she sure as hell wasn't going to ask him for a bucket of blood. So she took her sharpest knife and held it over her wrist.

She said a prayer and cut quickly before she could think about it. The pain nearly made her drop the knife. She muffled a whimper and held herself upright. She kept her wrist over the mug and let her blood flow until it was half full. Feeling lightheaded, she grabbed a towel and wrapped her wrist tightly. When it bled through, she wrapped it even tighter with a second towel. After a while, the bleeding slowed, then stopped, though she still thought she might pass out. She remembered all the times she had donated blood, and went to swallow some milk, then juice in huge gulps. The combination made her gag, but she forced herself to drink anyway. Then she took some bread from the plastic bag and chewed slowly. Soon, she gained some sense of control.

She put the mug in the microwave for a few seconds. When it finished, she carried it to the bedroom. He seemed still asleep. But after she woke him she noticed his eyes darting toward the mug. *Unspoken questioned answered there.* Suddenly his tongue darted out in anticipation of the drink.

"So I take it you want this?"

He didn't answer. Instead, he slowly pushed himself to sit up. The effort seemed to pain him, but once he was up, he was able to reach for the mug. When he had it, he didn't drink though. He seemed uncomfortable suddenly. She waited before asking what was wrong.

"I'm not accustomed to feeding in front of humans," he said, keeping his eyes lowered. It felt strange to admit such a weakness.

"Oh, well I can go if you want…"

"No. It is silly of me to behave in this manner. You have seen everything else about me. Why not this."

Adina's cheeks flushed but she sat silently.

The first sip was stilted, but after that taste, he didn't stop until the container as drained. He grimaced, then froze.

"What did you feed me?" he demanded.

Adina quivered from the sudden intensity in his eyes.

"Nothing. Just blood."

"What kind of blood?" he asked harshly.

"Animal."

"Human? Did you give me human blood?"

His rapid movement made her gasp.

"Yes. I didn't have enough, so I gave you some of my blood."

He just stared at her and Adina wondered if she had just made the worst mistake of her life. A moment later, she was sure that she had. His bruises were fading right before her eyes and his pasty white skin became a softer cream color. Her heart began to race as she wondered if the beast she had awoken would not be satisfied with just a taste of her blood.

The air was tense as she waited. But Jin only blinked and backed away from her.

"You shouldn't have done that," he whispered.

The wary Adina hid her agreement. Jin leaned back against her headboard. They sat quietly until she couldn't take it anymore.

"Look, I was just trying to help. It's not like I have another ready source of blood here. Besides, you didn't seem to mind drinking it. I mean, can't you smell the difference, like on television?"

A faint smile came onto Jin's face. He studied her a moment before responding.

"It is not your fault, your ignorance of us. We deliberately made sure that you knew nothing about us, for your protection as much as our own," he sighed. "I appreciate your help. I did need the blood, more than I thought, but human blood is very potent. And I'd never had any before today. Those of us who have human blood either lived in a time when it was necessary, or are elders and can handle its effects. Most of us drink animal or synthetic blood."

Adina sat back in fascination. "Really? What does human blood do besides help you heal faster?"

"Human blood gives us more power because we are similar to humans. It carries traits that lie dormant in our systems. It enhances our abilities and is intoxicating in a way that animal blood is not. Some say it is highly addictive."

Adina leaned back further. "Are you saying that I have to worry about you trying to munch on me now?"

His laughter was deep and melodious. It was rich in tone, smooth as jazz. She liked how it engulfed her, even in her wary state.

"Not at all. I meant that it could be if you drank enough of it, or so I'm told. You have to understand we have all but stopped drinking human blood. We needed to, in order to prevent awareness of our existence. But the effects are real. Even now I feel stronger than before. More healed, clearer in mind."

"But I mixed it with animal blood. Did that have any effect?"

"Yes. The blood was not as pure, so I believe that the effects might have been dulled but I can't tell you how. Further, you did not give me a lot of blood. But it was enough to help me recover a lot faster than animal blood alone would have."

She nodded but didn't move any closer to him.

The discussion of his healing brought forth earlier questions. There was a burning need to know, but she wasn't too sure that she was ready for the answer. So she stood up and walked to the bathroom.

She picked up the clothes that had been pushed under the sink and checked to see if anything could be salvaged. The shirt, in tatters, was a waste. But the pants were okay. The leather was strong and had protected him. Then again, maybe his attackers had only targeted his upper body.

She balled up the shirt and tossed it in the trash, but carried the pants back to her room. She went into her closet to look for a shirt. While she searched, she could feel Jin's gaze boring into her back. It was a peculiar feeling that she wasn't sure she liked. She felt as though it was more than watching. It felt like an examination, like he was measuring her for something. She wanted to spin around and ask what he was looking at, but she found what she needed in the closet. It was a dark sweater that had belonged to her "ex." She turned to find Jin facing forward with his head cocked as if he heard something.

Suddenly the covers were in the air and Jin was on his feet, hissing with eyes glinting. Adina wasn't too nervous to stop and gawk at this fine specimen of a man. A living, naked vampire was even more enticing than a half-dead, naked one. Jin stood with muscles taut and ready for attack.

Adina gave herself a mental kick. If Jin was tense, something bad was happening and she needed to know what it was.

"Jin," she said softly.

A hand went up to signal silence. Adina was getting scared. What bad thing was about to happen? What bad thing might be coming to her house?

Maybe the bad thing that attacked him in the first place.

Adina moved towards him, but he stopped her with another hand motion. She breathed quietly to calm her throbbing heart. After an eternity, Jin relaxed.

He turned to her he said, "We have to go."

Adina shook her head. "No way. Tell me what's going on? What's out there?" Her imagination conjured all kinds of monsters out there. But what scared her more was the ones she couldn't imagine.

She shook her head furiously. "No. I'm not leaving my home."

"You are not safe here, Adina," he said calmly, facing her.

Adina looked away. She wasn't leaving. She didn't care what *he* did, but she was staying in her apartment where she'd always felt safe.

"Why am I not safe in my home?"

"Because you helped me," he replied, stepping closer.

Adina already knew that, since she'd already moped about it earlier. She'd known it could come to this but that didn't mean she wanted to deal with it. All of her bravado disappeared the second she faced the prospect of a real danger out in the night. For the first time since childhood, she was afraid of the dark. She didn't want to find out that there were even creepier monsters that made things go bump in the night. More than that, she didn't want to go anywhere with a vampire who had just admitted that he had a taste for her blood.

"Who's after you?" The words trailed off as she realized that Jin now stood before her in all his glory.

Her nearness was affecting him in ways that he did not understand but he couldn't move away. A part of him wanted to think it was because of her blood, but that didn't explain the need to possess the woman before him. He shook his head. They were facing more serious matters before them. He reached for her.

Adina almost flinched at his touch, but held steady. When he touched her face, a faint shudder went through her. His cool hands were gentle as he raised her chin to face him. His eyes had an intense glaze but she knew he wasn't trying to hypnotize her. He was being sincere.

"We have to leave because the things that attacked me are still hunting me. They have all night to find me and they surely will sense my blood here."

Shaking her head, she said, "But I mopped it up."

Smiling at her ingenuity, he said, "That was wise, but it is not enough. They will come here and search until they are satisfied that I was not here. Those who hunt me have no regard for human life and they wouldn't hesitate to hurt you. I cannot allow that and I will not. I asked for your help and you gave it, now let me help you."

Adina knew what he said was true. She had known that helping him would change her life. But now that the moment had arrived, she wanted to fight it. Running off with a vampire, even a handsome one, was not her idea of a good plan. It was worse than the idea to come to London in the first place.

"Look, take your clothes," she said, pushing them towards him. "You can keep the shirt. I'm not going. I'll just call the cops and they will—"

"I know you are afraid. I understand what I'm asking, but you had to know in your heart that it could come to this. Adina, please believe me when I say that if you don't come with me now, you will not live to see another day. Even knowing about my existence is a death sentence."

"Then why did you ask me to help you?!" she shrilled. "If you knew I'd be killed for knowing what you are, why did you do this to me?"

"I know, and I'm sorry. I was desperate. I needed help and you were the only one available—"

"So to hell with my life!"

"You didn't have to help me," he countered.

"So it's my fault! I'll die because I showed basic human compassion. You bastard!"

She shoved passed him to her living room and threw herself
on the couch.

Fantasy time's over Adina. You really stuck your feet into it this time.

But she was more scared than angry. The truth of the situation
had just crashed down on her. Before, it had been easy to ignore,
busy as she was working to help him. But reality was setting in now
and she just couldn't cope.

She felt Jin enter the room. She didn't look at him, just continued
to stare at her blank wall.

"I was wrong to blame you," he said softly. "I did pull you into
this selfishly, when all of your actions have been selfless."

He went over to her. Adina noticed that he wearing the pants
again and the sweater she had offered. It was loose in the waist and
tight around his broad shoulders. He squatted in front of her, slowly
extending his hand, then finally let it rest on her knee.

"Adina, I cannot change what happened. All I can do is prevent
anything bad from happening to you as a result. Please let me help
you."

Again, she was trapped in his gaze. After a while she placed her
hand over his.

"Tell me what happened tonight. Who or what attacked you?"

Jin dipped his head, his long dark hair shadowing his face.
Adina resisted the urge to let the silky threads glide through her
fingers. The urge was removed when Jin got up and sat on the couch.
He leaned back before speaking.

"I'll tell you only under the condition that you come with me.
No questions asked. No hesitation."

He was waiting for her answer. Adina nodded silently.

"I was attacked tonight because I am the future leader of the
vampire empire. It was agreed that the two major and most ancient
tribes would form an alliance and between them, the actions of all
vampires would be controlled. This purpose was to stop the warring
of vampires, a war fought primarily behind the scenes through
assassination.

"There was to be a marriage between the prince of one tribe and princess of the other. My father of the Tribe Danpe was that prince, and my mother of the Tribe Hinghou, the princess. Their child would become the ruler of all vampires. As you guessed, that child is me. I spent the first few years of my life between both families, learning culture, beliefs and practices. I was training for the day I would have to control all the madness of the vampire empire.

"Everything was fine until a few years ago. A small group came forward to voice their disapproval not just with the alliance, but with the idea that I would rule them. One tribe in particular, Tenhar, was particularly incensed because they were left out of negotiations. Not only that, they don't agree with the basic tenets of our laws. They want recourse for the insult of not being invited to the original negotiations even though they boycotted earlier efforts.

"Although many thought it was ridiculous, my parents and their respective tribes wanted to appease Tenhar, but Tenhar rejected every offer. Finally, when there was to be no hope of keeping the peace, Tenhar demanded that I marry a woman from their tribe. My parents refused to force me to do so. They didn't want Tenhar to have that kind of power and they knew Tenhar would just have me killed. Because of the marriage, they would be able to fill the power void that would obviously be made.

"The rejection spurred more infighting and I was placed under protective custody for fear of a Tenhar attack. The point of killing me would be to create the same scenario, a power void for the next in line. All of the tribes would fracture because I would represent both Danpe and Hinghou. With me gone, the vampires would be in the same old position, in chaos and dying out."

Adina sat calmly, letting it all soak in. She was sitting next to the future leader of all vampires. He was targeted for assassination. She couldn't believe what she just gotten herself into. She suddenly felt unbelievably tired. Her arms felt heavy and sleep was pulling at her.

"Adina, we have to go."

She didn't move.

"You agreed," he reminded. He stood, offering his hand. "Please, let's go. We have wasted too much time as it is. They are getting closer."

She looked up at him before taking his hand. He pulled her up and brought her close. Adina tried to find comfort in his closeness and was surprised that she really did. After a minute, though, she moved away from him.

"Just let me get changed."

She walked into her room and closed the door behind her.

Chapter 5

Escape

ADINA WAS GONE FOR such a long time that Jin almost went after her. But Adina came back in dark jeans and a dark button down shirt. A backpack was strapped to her shoulders and she carried a pair of boots. It took a moment for him to recognize the boots as his own. She silently offered them to him. Jin took the boots as she walked into the kitchen.

His guilt reared its ugly head again. He should have known better, but the need to survive had outweighed common sense. Now he had to hide this human while trying to prevent his own assassination. He had no idea where his family was, only that his guards were dead. He had lost his cell phone and all his numbers in the attack, not that it mattered. As long as Adina was with him, he couldn't contact his people. Jin hadn't been in London in thirty years and now he had to figure out how to maneuver around the city.

It also didn't help that he found himself increasingly attracted to Adina. There was something about her that he couldn't place. It went beyond her sacrifice in helping him, then serving her own blood. Indeed, part of it was that she was attractive. But then there was something else.

He watched her come out of the kitchen, regarding him with determination in her eyes. She was not happy about what was happening, but she'd made a decision. Jin was going to make sure that she didn't regret it—any of it. It was his turn to be the guardian. He wasn't at full strength, but the potency of her blood had made him stronger. In a matter of hours, he would have his full strength back.

"So where are we going?" she whispered when she entered the room. They both had been whispering since the incident in the bedroom. He did sense the hellhounds coming, but there really wasn't a need to whisper. He responded in kind anyway.

"Away from here. Further into the city."

She arched an eyebrow at him. Silently, she walked towards the door.

"Not that way," he said, before heading towards the kitchen. The window in there was too small for what they needed, though. He looked at her and asked, "Do you have a fire escape?"

"By the bedroom window."

Jin didn't like that idea, either. So it would have to be the door. Moving swiftly, he paused before opening it.

"We have to make haste. They are very close. I was hoping to go out another way…"

BOOM!

An exploding sound ripped through the building and made Adina jump. Jin picked up the scent of the hounds and he snarled in anger. Going to the fire escape would be suicide, as the hounds were definitely in the building.

"What the hell was that!?" Adina hissed.

"The reason we need to leave." Grabbing her hand, he quietly opened the door. He noticed that the stairs continued up a flight. "To the roof?" he asked. Adina nodded.

GRRRRR!! HEEEEAHHH SSSSSS!!!

The noise was unbearable and Jin could feel Adina's fear. She refused to move with him when he stepped out, her eyes widening as the thumping increased.

Jin lifted her hand and kissed it softly, making her focus on him.

"Trust me, Adina. Trust me."

They stared at each other briefly before there was another bang. She jumped and Jin moved, pulling her up the stairs. Climbing as quietly as possible, they'd just about made it to the top when they heard a shriek.

"Please!!! Help me, God! Don't hurt me! Ahhhhhhhhh!!" came a man's voice from below.

Adina panicked. "We're gonna die," she said, starting to hyperventilate. Jin grabbed her shoulders and shook her gently.

"What!" she snapped.

"We're not going to die."

He grabbed her hand and pulled her the rest of the way, just as another person screamed to his death. Jin tried the knob and put all of his weight behind the door. Nothing happened.

BANG!!!! SSSSSSSSSSSSSS!!!!

Adina's growing panic was making Jin feel helpless. There was nothing he could do to stop her from being terrified. She wasn't a fool; she knew those people were dead. He could smell their deaths. With the images of half-eaten people on his mind, he forced the door open.

BANG!

BANG!

Both noises happened simultaneously. Jin took that as a good sign and pulled Adina to the roof. Once there, he looked around. When he turned back, Adina was running to the edge of the building.

"Adina, no!"

He rushed to her.

"Why not? We have to get out of here!!!"

"Yes, but not that way. They will see us."

She stared at Jin in fright, but accepted his hand. He led her to the opposite side of the roof. Below was an alley. It wasn't very wide, but it was very dark. He looked across the way for another door. Seeing none, Jin turned to the left and right to make sure of the hounds' location. They were getting closer and soon they would find her apartment. He wanted to be long gone before that happened.

"I need you to hold onto me," he said.

Adina frowned at him, but complied. She placed her hands on his shoulders as he pulled her close, wrapping his arm around her waist. With their bodies pressed together, he whispered, "Don't panic."

Jin lifted her off her feet and she had to grip his neck tighter. He secured her legs around his waist before breaking into a full sprint. He leapt off the roof and took them sailing into the night.

Her stomach dropped. She had never imagined flying outside of a metal can. She didn't dare look down. Her eyes stayed squeezed shut and she concentrated on the strong man she was wrapped around. A short time later, it felt like they were descending. She dared to open her eyes in time to watch them land on another rooftop. Looking around, she saw nothing familiar and realized she didn't know how far they had traveled. He landed as gently as if he had been walking on the roof all along.

They looked around, then faced each other. Being this close to him was a little unsettling, especially with his eyes on her face like a soft caress. When he focused on her mouth, a tingle went through her. He used his tongue to moisten his lips, smirking when her breath hitched. The heat between them reminded Adina that it was time to get off of him, even though she liked the secure feeling of his arm around her waist. She was frightened out of her mind and the flight had left a lot to be desired, but the feeling of this strong man against her was nice. It didn't fade when she unhooked her legs from his waist and slid them down his body, either.

For his part, Jin let her down slowly so that he could feel her a little longer. Having her legs glide down his legs almost made him forget that they were running for their lives. Even as he chastised himself, he knew that he wanted more. When her feet finally touched down, the two didn't separate. They held each other's eyes, a longing starting to develop between them both. Jin broke the contact to look about for a door.

"We have to keep moving."

Adina swallowed hard and nodded. Her heart was thumping.

Where are we?" she asked.

"About a mile from where you live."

"Really?" She looked around again.

He nodded, walking towards the door. "Yes. We need to go further still."

"Okay." She followed him.

Her thoughts returned to the people who had been killed and she felt sick. *That was my fault. I should have left well enough alone.* But in truth, it wasn't really her fault. Even if she hadn't helped Jin, those animals would have murdered those people. The guilt made her heart hurt. But what made it worst was she safe on this rooftop thinking about how to get closer to the vampire who had started it all.

Jin pulled the door hard to pop the lock. He beckoned for Adina to follow when a howl froze them both in their tracks. Adina raced through the door with Jin on her heels, slamming the door behind him.

It was dark in the building, but Jin saw steps leading to another door. Taking Adina's hand, he led them down the stairs to a door. This time, he was able to jimmy the lock without creating a disturbance. Peering out and seeing no one, Jin and Adina walked out. They took the stairs and climbed until they reached the front door. Just as Jin was about to open it, Adina pulled him back.

"Are we safe?"

Jin gave her hand a reassuring squeeze. "Yes. For now. Let's go."

She nodded. They left the building and walked down a street (not unlike hers) until reached a tube station. They climbed down the steps to the concrete landing. A token station was located near the end of the stairs. Visible through the window, an elderly gentleman who looked bored out of his wits, manned the booth. A radio in the background emitted a blues tune. Jin studied the man first before going to the turnstile. He turned to Adina in confusion.

She said, "You mean to tell me you came down here and don't know how to get in?"

"I've never had to ride," he explained.

Adina rolled her eyes, then leaned in. "So why take it now? Why can't we fly?"

"Would you like to risk exposure? One of my kind would have noticed us if I'd stayed up there longer than I did. I only got us far enough from the hellhounds not to be caught."

Adina stared before turning to the man at the booth. From a small pocket on her backpack, she removed some money.

"Two, please."

The man hardly looked up when he took the money and slid the tickets at her. She thanked him anyway and returned to Jin. Using her card first as an example, she moved through. Jin followed and they were gone.

The walked down the illuminated tunnel until they reached the tiled landing. No one else was on the platform. Adina glanced at her watch, noticing that it was 7:00pm, one of those weird times when people on the tube are sparse.

"We got about fifteen minutes," she told Jin.

He acknowledged her with a thin smile. He walked close to a bench where he could look at a wall map. Adina followed and sat on the bench. A part of her was still trying to figure out if she was dreaming. She hoped that she was because if not, she really couldn't believe it. But one look at Jin made her pray that he was real because no one had ever made her feel like this.

Jin pointed to a particular stop on the map. "How do we get here?"

Adina stood up. "We have to take this train. Then we can catch this train," she indicated with her finger. "Okay?"

"Yes."

"Are we safe down here? Will we be safe where we're going?"

Jin turned to give her a meaningful gaze.

"I hope so," he responded.

His eyes glowed an intense green. Adina was scared and excited. He looked at her like he needed her, wanted her. She licked her lips slowly and his eyes followed the movement of her tongue. He leaned closer, making it hard for her to breathe.

"Why are you looking at me like that?" she asked.

"How am I looking at you?" he replied in a low voice.

His closeness and his voice was making her tingle. All she wanted at that moment was to feel his lips on hers.

She started to say, "Like you want—"

He stepped in. "Want what?"

"To kiss me," she murmured.

His devilish smile electrified her. *Please let him do it. Please.*

"Is that what you want?" he asked with his breath on her neck. His silky hair grazed her cheek. His smell was a combination of her soap and his own male scent.

"Do you? Hmm?"

His lips touched her neck like a whisper. Adina's eyes closed to absorb the feeling. His right hand slid around her waist while his left moved her head to expose more of her neck. Something in Adina was screaming that he was a vampire and he'd drink her dry, but... Those thoughts vanished as his cool tongue traced the length of her neck before his lips clasped her jugular vein with a powerful suck.

Adina gasped. She gripped his shoulders as he sucked deeply, never biting. One of his hands massaged her neck while the other stroked her back, and the sensations aroused her to no end. She felt her nipples hardening, the moisture developing below. If he kept doing what he was doing, he might take her over the brink. When he stopped, Adina's eyes were glazed with passion. Finally, she focused on the impassioned eyes of her vampire.

"Yes," he growled before his lips descended on hers in a searing kiss. Adina moaned into his mouth, allowing him full access. He felt so good, his hard, strong body holding her close. He pulled her up to make her body glide against his. Adina couldn't restrain a gasp of pleasure. He put her back against the wall while his hand wrapped around her thigh and pulled her leg around his waist so he could grind against her. Adina whimpered in need. Her passion built up as the kiss took her breath away. His tongue moved in for a sensual exploration, playing a lovers dance with her own. Her fingers flowed through his hair and she pulled closer to feel his hardness. She was rewarded with a rumbling groan. He pressed closer still, both of them seeking release but finding none. Adina swore she didn't know how much time passed before he pulled away, sucking lazily on her bottom lip, finally letting her breathe.

Wow, Adina thought.

The train's horn blared down the tunnel.

Chapter 6
Contemplative Journey

*W*HAT THE HELL AM I *thinking? We've no time for passion.*

But even as Jin had the thought, he was reliving the feeling of Adina's body against his. Her heat made him feel alive. The warm caress of her mouth felt like home. A force within him was drawn and connected to this woman. One kiss and he belonged to her. She had that power over him.

After fifteen years of living like a monk, a human woman, of all things, brought Jin back to life. Never before had he been attracted to her kind. But all he could think about was claiming her mind and her body over and over again. He would give anything to hear her sultry moan in his ear.

It amazed him that her nearness made him forget how they had met and the reason they were using a form of transportation that he had never even imagined going near. Leaning his head back, he kept his eyes closed to hide the fire within them. The smell of her arousal was driving him wild, testing his ability to focus on the immediate problem of getting to safety. As much as he tried, all he could think about was her.

Adina sat quietly, legs crossed as she fought the urge to squirm. The moment on the platform, in Jin's arms, had left her trying to catch her breath. He had ignited a flame deep within her that was begging to be fed. But she knew that it wasn't the time.

When the train came, they moved apart, hastily straightening their clothes. Adina almost walked off without her backpack, but remembered it just in time. They sat close to the door. They hadn't spoken on the train, but Adina's thoughts were racing. She evaluated everything that happened to lead to the passionate moment.

Why had it happened? Yes, he was attractive, but they had just met. The first part of the meeting had been scary, the middle, okay, and the last part, downright terrifying. It had been a weird experience, to say the least, but that didn't explain her need right now to have this man inside her.

Adina sat up straighter at the thought. Did she really want intimacy with this vampire? The heavy brakes screeched, causing the passengers to pitch forward. Adina brushed against Jin momentarily. They stared at each other before Adina jumped up and headed for the door.

"Our stop is coming up," she said in a shaky voice.

He said nothing, only standing close enough to inhale more of her scent. *This is crazy. She is human, Jin…destined to die in the blink of an eye. You have lived 135 years and never has a human had that effect on you. Why are you letting her?*

But no answers came to him. When the doors opened to the crowded platform, he forced his mind to the task ahead. They pushed through the few people trying to step on the train. Over a loudspeaker, a voice admonished them to "mind the gap." Adina was ahead of him, confidently striding to the next platform. Jin was about to call out to her when the feeling hit him.

It took all his control to keep his eyes from glinting. That would have been a dead giveaway of his unearthly nature. But his hackles were raised because he sensed another. Focusing his mind as he'd been taught, he tried to discern the tribe based on the vibe he was receiving. At first he came up with nothing, but then he felt the vampire getting closer. Not wanting to take a chance, he pressed forward, putting distance between them. He kept one eye on Adina, while the other searching for the vampire.

Adina turned to him, confused as to why he was lagging. He didn't dare respond to her. If any of his kind saw him interacting with a human, it could cause real problems...problems that he really needed to avoid. With a slight nod, he indicated that all was fine. He waited for her response, still walking in her direction. Thankfully, she just shrugged and kept moving forward.

The vibe he felt turned into a hum that had his senses screaming. Whoever the vampire was, he had friends, and he could feel that they sensed him. He moved faster, deciding that he and Adina would take a cab. The sense of urgency increased and he quickened his pace. He was within two feet of Adina when he heard the hiss. The hairs on the back of his neck lifted.

"Get us out of here," he whispered, making sure his voice carried only to her. It was a trick his mother had taught him.

Adina didn't need to be persuaded. She had seen the tension in Jin's face when she turned around. She tried to ignore it, but his comment only added to her sense of urgency. She gradually picked up the pace and moved towards the nearest exit.

She was just starting to climb the stairs when she heard a ruckus. Someone standing behind Jin was staring at her. The eyes glinted so quickly that she thought she had imagined it, but when the person disappeared into thin air, she was sure. She climbed the stairs quickly, her fear of being caught increased with every step. She almost ran up the last few stairs, and when she reached the landing, she sprinted towards the exit.

Jin moved quickly behind her but didn't come too close. He observed the expression on her face when she turned around. She had recognized one of his kind. He could only hope they wouldn't think she understood what she had seen. If they thought she knew of the existence of vampires, they would hunt her down and kill her.

Adina was nowhere in sight when Jin reached the landing. Tense, he spun around to find her. At the same time, he needed to see if his kind had caught up with him. The vibe in him had become an intense hum. He was just about to go back to the stairs when he spotted her on his left, beckoning him to the exit.

Jin met her at the top of the stairs. He grabbed her hand and yanked her away from the station exit. Thankfully, people were teeming about Piccadilly Circus's shops and restaurants, and the place was crawling with cabs.

Jin flagged down a cabby. He opened the door, pushed Adina in, and slid in beside her.

"What it'll be mate?" asked the cabby.

"Take us to Bayswater. Make it quick."

The cabby shifted gears and they were off. Jin pushed Adina down in the seat just as he felt the Vampires come close to the place they had just left. He didn't look back, only forward, as they headed off to the new location.

I've got to be more careful. Pausing a moment, he evaluated his feelings about what had happened in the train station. He realized who the vampires were just as Adina something about it.

"I mean…I think I saw…"

Jin placed a finger over her lips, stilling her instantly. Their eyes connected in a burning gaze and slowly, he withdrew his finger. Many emotions passed between them before Jin turned away. Adina turned too, looking out of her window.

Adina's thoughts were a swirl in her mind. She was confused about herself, the situation, and what she should be feeling. She was afraid of her reaction to Jin, unsure if he had a hold over her. She was eerily calm at the moment and she was afraid that she might not be afraid enough. Something told her that what she had seen and heard was just the tip of the iceberg.

Who was the vampire in the tube station? Was the vampire after Jin? Did the vampire think she recognized him? Did he know that she was with Jin? Adina didn't want her heart to start pounding again. *My heart can't take much more of this.* She rolled her eyes, thinking she really should have left Jin on the steps where she found him, but the thought left a sour taste in her mouth. Though he was a vampire, he hadn't done anything to her...besides get her all hot and bothered. She almost blushed at the thought. *I have truly lost my mind, making out with a vampire in the tube like he was some normal guy. After all that's happened...* But one question stuck in her mind: Why hadn't he bitten her neck like in the movies?

Sneaking a glance at him, she wondered if he was *hungry* again. She hadn't given him a lot of blood, just enough to help. And it had helped remarkably, but he still had to need more. She wasn't about to ask him about it. He didn't need to get the idea that she was offering more of hers. Adina glimpsed at her wrist. She had forgotten about it so completely that she no longer felt the throbbing pain. Still, she marveled at her daring.

I *have truly lost my mind.*

Jin watched the cab edge closer to a familiar neighborhood. He struggled to remember the exact location of his father's former dwelling. It took some time, but he remembered just as the cab came within two blocks of it.

"Stop here, please," Jin said in a hypnotic voice.

The driver stopped, then turned to Jin for the payment.

"You've decided that you needed to take a drive. You needed time to think, but now you want to go to the airport for a fare."

The cabby's eyes took on a glazed appearance. Slowly, he turned around and Jin opened his door, beckoning to Adina. He got out, with her following quickly behind. He waited until the cab pulled off before heading to the flat.

"How did you do that?"

"It's just influence. It's something we can do."

"Am I under your influence?" she murmured.

Jin laughed. "No. Or else you wouldn't have even asked. Come, let's talk after we are secure."

There was nothing Adina could do but follow him. Questions and fears still swirled in her mind like a tornado at maximum velocity. But he was right about needing to reach safety before having any long discussions.

They walked briskly, taking only one turn before they reached a building with a classical architectural design. It had glass doors and a doorman stood in front of them. It was the place that Jin had been looking for.

He walked past the door, continuing to a narrow alley. He looked about to make sure that there hadn't been any nocturnal activity of any kind recently. Taking Adina's hand, he led her halfway down the dark stretch. There was a door on their left that looked like it hadn't been used in years. Jin released her hand and placed it to the right of the door. A moment later, the door opened.

"Come. It is okay," he said, standing aside to let her go first.

On the other side of the door was an elevator, dimly lit, but bright enough for Adina to see that no threat was present. She stepped in and Jin came behind her. With a thud, the outside world was shut away, the elevator doors closed. Almost instantly, the box brightened.

"A precautionary measure," he said. "When the door is open to the street, the lights dim so as not to draw unwanted attention."

Adina was impressed but said nothing, just quietly wondered what to expect next.

45

Chapter 7
A Night of Exploration

THE ELEVATOR RIDE ENDED on the tenth floor, where the doors eased open to a dark room. Jin stepped out first. Thick carpeting muffled the sound of his boots. He reached for the left side of the wall and flipped a light switch. Illuminated, the room was magnificent.

On the right, the walls were deep, imported oak with marble columns spaced evenly between. A wall of tinted windows was on the left, affording a view of the city. White sheets covered several upholstered chairs. At the far end of the room, an archway led further into the apartment. Jin walked around, pulling off sheets and revealing wonderful antique furniture.

The next room was even more expansive. It contained an elegant table with six chairs. To its right was a comfortable, but expensive-looking sofa. Behind it, a bookshelf followed the wall until it reached the corner of another. In front of the sofa was a coffee table, with a television beyond that. At the far end of that room was another wall, with another archway that led to even more rooms. Off to one side, a kitchen contained long counters and stainless steel appliances.

Adina's eyes bulged at the space. She couldn't help wishing she had a place of even half this size. It must have cost a fortune.

"What is this place?" she asked.

Jin shrugged. "It's my father's. He used it more than thirty years ago but by the looks of the furniture, he must have updated it recently."

Adina took it all in before asking, "He doesn't use this place?"

"No, not really. He has a bigger place out of the city that he prefers. He comes into the city sometimes to entertain guests, but..." Again, he shrugged.

Adina threw her hands up and said, "Okay, that's it! You need to tell me what's going on here!" She held up a hand to halt his response. She said, "I heard you loud and clear at my apartment, but come on, Jin! All I've ever heard about vampires is that they drink blood, can't handle the sun, don't have reflections, and turn other people into vampires by making them drink their blood. What's real? What's not? Do I have to worry about you snacking on me? Can I trust you not to hypnotize me when you want to have your way? Who was that at the train station? What...what is all this?"

Jin studied her in silence. They stayed like that for a long time before Jin walked to the kitchen. He opened the fridge and took out one of many packs of blood. He opened the microwave, inserted the packet, and heated it for a few seconds. With his back to Adina, he bit into the pack and slowly emptied its contents. The feeling of hunger that he had kept hidden from Adina faded away. He dropped the empty bag on the counter before turning to Adina, whose eyes had been on him the whole time. He leaned against the counter, trying to think of the best way to explain all that she had asked.

Meanwhile, a frustrated Adina threw herself on the sofa. She stared at the blank television screen until she felt Jin's presence next to her. He touched her cheek softly and she leaned into the feeling in spite of herself. She reached up and took his hand.

"Please tell me, Jin."

Jin stood a bit longer before taking a seat next to her. Sighing heavily, he said, "Adina, there's so much I don't want to tell you. You know too much already. But I guess there's no harm in you knowing more." He leaned back before speaking again. "I know what you've heard about vampires, but the fact is, we let you write those idiotic ideas to keep you confused and ignorant. These are the facts: Vampires are a subspecies of humans, derived from a genetic mutation over two millennia ago. Our kind can breed, but only for a very short period of time in our lives. Vampires can live up to five hundred years, sometimes more, but most just stop living. Living forever gets old, so many vampires just end it all out of boredom. Others die because after while the blood can't sustain them.

"We do drink blood, but not as often as you think. We need it to stay healthy and strong. It enhances the abilities that we may or may not have, depending on the clan line. I'm a product of two powerful, ancient clans. I have the ability to fly, to use 'thrall,' and control some weaker-minded individuals. I can shape-shift, but that takes a lot of energy.

"I can walk in the sun if I have had blood recently, but as I get closer to five hundred, I'm less able to do so. Our bodies break down, too, Adina, just differently. We do have reflections, we have animalistic eyes. No, holy water doesn't work, no, I'm not afraid of crosses, and no, a stake in the heart won't kill us. The only way you can kill a vampire is to cut off his head or starve him, but that could take months.

"My parents had me one hundred thirty-five years ago. I am still considered very young by our standards, but old enough to rule. I already told you some of the reasons they want me dead, but one reason, the primary reason, is that as I get older, I will become more powerful. Practically invincible. That scares Tenhar because they would be weakened by my power. Their clans might start to look to me and they would lose their position."

He turned to her. "Adina, you can trust me. I would never feed on you, not even if you begged me. You gave me a precious gift, your blood. I can never repay you for that, but I can assure you that you will not become—my midnight snack," he smirked. "Okay?"

Adina smiled. "Really?"

"Yes, really."

"Okay," she said. Then her stomach growled audibly. "Oh, god, I'm sorry. I haven't really eaten and I bet you don't have any real food."

"As a matter of fact, I do. There are some canned goods in there. Take whatever you want. Obviously, we don't keep perishables here."

Adina got up and went to the kitchen. After opening three cabinets, she found two cans of soup. Then she found a pot and warmed the soup.

"Jin, you said you are a vampire because of genetic mutation, but earlier you said you can convert humans. How do you make people vampires? "

Jin sighed. "We would have to infuse our blood with yours. It would, in a sense, poison you and you would become a vampire."

"So if you bit me, I wouldn't get sick?"

Jin looked puzzled.

"I don't know, maybe," he said. "All I know is that it wouldn't make you a vampire. Well, I don't *think* it would, but you have to understand, we haven't fed off humans for a long time. No one discusses humans in that manner because biting them is forbidden. One thing I do remember is that a human is forever linked to a vampire who has fed on them. If several feed on the same human, he might be driven mad."

Adina stirred her soup. Then she asked, "So can you make me sick by kissing me?"

Jin shook his head. "I doubt that. When we bite something, an enzyme is released. That enzyme is what causes the problems. It is not released with a kiss."

She nodded. Her next question made her hot. She started to ask anyway, but at the last minute, switched to the incident at Piccadilly Circle. "Who was that at the train, Jin?"

Jin noticed her hesitation but let it go. He said, "They were from a lesser tribe, the Pinu. They are sewer dwellers as far as I know. They have a shaky allegiance to my father; they can be very fickle."

"Do you think they know about me? Or maybe they can help you ..."

"The Pinu are self-serving and can be very dangerous. They love following the law if it hurts their enemies. If they found out that you were with me, they would insist on your death without question. They are just loyal enough to stay in my father's good graces, but they do believe in testing him.

"As to helping me, they won't, unless there's something to be gained. And I won't place my father in the position of owing Pinu anything...unless it is absolutely necessary."

Adina found a bowl to pour the soup into. With it, she walked over to the dining room table. She sat only after Jin waved his hand in consent. She began to eat, all the while turning over the knowledge she had just acquired. There was a whole world out there, of which she and most humans were completely unaware. It was fascinating that it could be that way. A whole culture was walking unnoticed among them. It seemed impossible, yet, it had been happening. As she ate, she wondered if she could go back to the life she'd had before or if she would always have to wonder who was a vampire and who wasn't.

Jin joined her at the table, trying to discern if she was okay. Up until now, she had taken just about everything in stride. There were moments of panic, but they were quickly followed by calm. Her faith in him was making her dearer to him than he wanted to admit. He had asked for her trust and she had given it—something that would never happen in his world. He knew, on some level, that he had earned her trust by not harming her or failing her in any way, and that frightened him. He didn't want to fail her now. She was the most amazing person he had ever met and probably would ever meet.

So watching her calmly eat soup, he was again fascinated by the fact that she was in his life at all. He'd had no right to bring her into it, but here she was, willing to help him, concerned for his safety, and not bothered at all by the fact that there was a blood-sucking monster in her midst. He almost winced at his own description, but it was true. And what made it even crazier was that he was so damn attracted to her that at times like this, he wanted to get closer. He didn't just want to know her intimately. He wanted to know what her world was like. Why was she in London? Her accent was a dead giveaway that she was American. He had to ask.

"Who are you, Adina Carr?"

She stopped eating and stared at him like he was crazy. "What do you mean?"

"Who are you? Why are you in London? "

She laughed a little. "Oh, that. Well, the short version is like a fool, I followed a man here, got dumped, he stole my money, and I had to work to get more. As of next week, my visa expires and I'll be heading back home. Maybe even sooner if we get out this mess. Once again, I got into it by listening to a guy."

Jin frowned. "How could he leave you here?"

"Because as my friend told me but I wouldn't listen, he was a bastard." Embarrassed, she asked, "Can we talk about something else? I really hate thinking about how dumb I am, especially considering where I am right now."

"What does that mean?"

She sighed, pushing the bowl away.

"Jin, don't take it personally, but I shouldn't be here, and if I thought like a street-smart person, I wouldn't be here. Don't get me wrong, I think it was right to help you, but once again, I didn't think of the consequences. Now I'm in a situation that's completely foreign to me, and once again I have to put my trust in someone who can screw me over bad. So far, you've turned out better than the human, but..." She faltered when his hand covered hers.

"I'm not going to fail you. You will be safe from all this. I promise you that."

She smiled. "You know what's really sick? I believe you."

"What is sick about it?"

"Because from what I've heard about vampires, you're supposed to be evil and you don't seem to be and—"

She paused because what she said next might change the climate of their discussion. But she saw the amused expression on Jin's face and continued. "—I need to believe you because I am so very attracted to you. I like you, for whatever reason, and I really want to believe that you aren't an evil bastard, in spite of being a vampire. Crazy, right? I don't know you..."

His thumb stroked her cheek. "Would it help you to know that I am just as confused about my attraction to you?"

"No. It makes me more worried. I can't help but think it was my blood..."

He gently shook his head. "It's not the blood. It is your heart. We are taught that humans are cruel and unforgiving, more so than us. We are taught that humans would harm us more than help us, if given the chance. You have proven that there are always exceptions. It doesn't help that I think that you are very beautiful as well."

She swallowed hard. "Really? You're not too bad yourself. But Jin, we both know nothing can come of it."

"I know," he said, holding her eyes in a stare. "But it only makes me want you more."

"Me, too," she whispered.

Her heart was pounding at his nearness. He could hear it clearly. Its rhythm was drawing him nearer and nearer to her. Something was telling him to stop, but he captured the soft, warm contours of her lips, anyway. He deepened the kiss, slowly gliding his tongue over her lips. She parted them with a sigh. He began to absorb some her heat, igniting a fire deep within him.

He slowly removed his mouth from hers. Their eyes remained connected as he stood, pulling her up with him. With her body flush against his, he kissed her more fiercely than before. He just couldn't get enough of her taste, her warmth, or her essence. He lifted her onto the table and let his kisses travel along her jaw line while her hands gripped his hair powerfully. She threw her head back to expose the bruise that had already formed on one side of her neck, but this time he licked slowly as he went down the center. One hand slid under her shirt to feel her soft skin.

Adina sighed as his tongue worked along her neck and collarbone, kissing in a slow languishing pace. Her hands moved through his hair, down to his back, and over his shoulders before coming back to his face. Cupping it, she pulled his lips back to hers. She kissed him tenderly at first, then more intensely. She loved the power of his kisses. They sent a thrill down her spine and warmed her center. He loosened her hair from its binding as he kissed her even more deeply. His hand skimmed over her waist to her lace-covered breasts. He cupped them, squeezing gently, feeling her hardening peaks.

Adina moaned, leaning into the feeling. His hands moved over her breasts as his lips found the left side of her neck, kissing and licking the vein there. She didn't notice that he had opened her shirt and removed her bra to free her heavy breasts until his cool hands molded themselves over them again. Her eyes flew open, blinking rapidly. She thought they should probably slow down, but his cool mouth was already licking and tugging her nipple he massaged the other breast.

Adina's breathing quickened, her back arched and her left hand on the table was the only thing holding her up. Her other hand cradled Jin's head, keeping him close to her breast. He lapped at it, amazed at how different its softness was from a vampire lover's cool, tough skin. Adina's body was warm and responsive. He eased her onto the table, vaguely aware that they had knocked the bowl to the floor. He couldn't care about that, though, not with the feast of this woman before him. He found the hard peak and gently grasped it with his teeth, pulling a bit, hearing her hiss in response. Smiling, he took the whole of it into his mouth, sucking until she writhed beneath him. His other hand teased and twisted her other nipple as her panting grew. The smell of her arousal called him.

Adina knew that she should stop, but he felt so damn good. The only thing that could make it better was if he were to go lower, touch her, fill her until she could bear no more. She felt his mouth move from her breast, tongue glide over her belly, swirl at her navel before kissing it.

"Oh, God," she moaned.

He kept kissing her stomach as he opened her pants. Kissing further down, he slid the pants off and filled his nostrils with the most tantalizing scent he had experienced in his one hundred thirty-five years as a vampire. It was a distinctly female, distinctly human scent—of life, of energy—that only they could produce. He let his tongue drag over her panty line before kissing the cloth over her pelvic bone. He dipped his head further to find that she was moist. He buried his nose in her scent, memorizing it, before laying his tongue against her center.

Adina almost lost control in that moment. She bit her lip in anticipation, all thoughts of stopping him swept away by pleasure. She almost squealed with happiness when his mouth touched her there. She lifted herself to get him closer, wishing he would remove the barrier and really touch her. Jin, having always been a conscientious lover, knew he was driving her wild, but he also knew that this was a moment for them both to savor.

His lips massaged her folds through the panties, just enjoying the feel of her movement. But before long, it wasn't enough for him. She became wetter as he worked, and his own need to taste her fully made him move aside her panties and place his tongue against her flesh. He licked the folds of her vagina before inserting his tongue, taking his first taste of heaven. Adina bucked from the cool feel of his tongue inside her. She started grinding against his face and Jin, hungry for more, delved deeper, lapping and licking her, ripping the offending panties away for greater access. Adina lifted off the table, her moans and sighs, like music to Jin's ears. He moved away, kissing her folds until he reached her clitoris, taking the tiny bulb into his mouth and sucking it hard until Adina screamed in pleasure.

Oh my god, Oh my God, Oh. My. God! She could feel herself about to explode. She had never felt that good with a man. Jin was a pro, taking care to make sure that she was fully aroused. His fingers entered her, pumping in and out as his mouth worked her clitoris. She was grinding harder against him, and his pumping became faster until he curled his fingers, stroking her inner walls with a powerful suck on her clitoris.

Adina came with a scream from deep within. She shook as powerful waves of pleasure passed over her. Jin was still pumping into her, having added a third finger to prolong her orgasm. She was panting so hard, lost in pleasure, that she didn't notice when he moved away from her. When she opened her eyes, she watched him slowly lick his fingers of her essence, his eyes glinting a feral green. Slowly, he removed his sweater, revealing his powerful chest and strong stomach. The shirt hadn't made it to the floor before his pants were opened and sliding over his hips, released a straining erection. Adina smiled in appreciation, sitting up to take in the magnificent specimen before her.

Jin walked back to her, focusing on nothing but the conquest in front of him. He approached her like she was his prey, deciding on the best way to take her. He knew that she was fragile. He couldn't just dive into her and fill her womb with his seed.

Next, he had to completely remove her pants. With vampire quickness, he ripped away her shoes and pants with one swift movement. Adina jumped a little but didn't seem too nervous. She watched him slide his arm around her waist and lift her up so that their chests touched. She loved the way his body felt against hers, his skin cool to her warmth, his body hard and strong against her softness. They kissed again. Adina tasted herself, making the kiss even headier than before. They stroked each other, giving and taking pleasure from the skin to skin contact. But Jin wanted more, needed more, because he still felt the heat on his fingers from his exploration. Now he really needed to feel her.

He lifted Adina so that he could enter her. Her mouth opened in a slow moan as his coolness entered her. It was incredible. He filled her in every sense. She pressed against him as he laid her against the table, her legs opening to accommodate him. She didn't care about where they were, she just wanted him to move in her, to fill her, to keep bringing the passions she had been feeling.

Jin almost came just from the feel of her heat surrounding him. Calming himself to let her adjust before taking more, he finally moved in her. He took his time, slowly pulling out and then hammering back in. He kept the pace steady for a while, just to hear her sighs and whimpers. Before long though, it was not enough for him and he pushed harder, grinding against her before pulling out faster, going in harder. Adina gripped his shoulders to keep from sliding off the table. Jin placed her right leg over his shoulder, pulling her closer. He pumped into her faster and faster, panting and moaning. He could feel her tensing, ready to come again, and he moved even faster, pushing harder so that she would. He wanted to feel her come, needed to feel it.

Adina's body was abuzz with pleasure. As he thrust into her, he took her breast into his mouth, tugging it and kissing it again. Adina's cries turned to shrills of pleasure. She could feel her body turning into a tight bow, ready to spring. She felt as though she was being split in two, but the feeling was delectable. For every thrust, she grinded more into him, until the scream of her pleasure hollowed out into nothingness. She couldn't see or even think, could only experience waves of ecstasy.

Jin growled when he felt her coming, feeling those inner walls grip him, but he was not ready yet. He still needed more. He kept thrusting while she rode her wave of bliss. She felt so hot, so good. He could not believe that he had been denying himself this type of pleasure. The intensity of it was driving him mad, making his animal instincts come forth uncontrolled. His power in her was so great that she screamed from the sheer force of it.

Adina didn't think she could take much more. She was already spent, but she could feel the slow burn building in her stomach again; it was making her eyes water. His eyes were as bright as she had ever seen them when he kissed her passionately, taking her breath away. He placed her other leg over his shoulder and touched a place in her that she never knew existed. She threw her head back and cried in ecstasy.

Jin had almost reached his tipping point. He felt the change in Adina when he delved even deeper into her. Seconds later, she was coming again, this time harder than before and screaming his name. Jin lifted up, fangs bared at the passion he had been building, until it finally exploded. Adina's legs fell away from his shoulders as he spilled his seed deep within her. A loud growl emanated from him. He fought the instinct to bite her before lowering onto her slowly, breathing heavily.

Jin licked Adina's sweat, settling on kissing the pulsing jugular vein and wondered, *how will I ever be able to leave her?*

Chapter 8
More Passion, More Problems

T HEY SAT IN A huge Jacuzzi with warm, bubbly water. It was soothing for Adina, who was a little sore from her encounter from Jin. She hadn't noticed how tightly he had been gripping her waist, and she just needed to soak.

After they made love, they laid on the table while a fire stilled burn between them. Jin finally got up and walked deeper into the apartment. She felt insulted until she heard water running. Sitting up, she watched him come back to her with a sultry smile. He picked her up and carried her down a dark hallway to a peach bathroom deep within the sanctuary. He stepped down into the miniature Jacuzzi, sitting her down, before taking a seat next to her. Adina relaxed into the warm water, and let a lazy, satisfied smile come over her face. She leaned against him, resting her head on his shoulder.

Jin turned off the water but the bubbles kept coming while they enjoyed the steam. Jin stroked her arm, and Adina could feel her eyes becoming heavy. Jin kissed her forehead, pulling her closer, and tried to think about what the hell he was going to do next.

He needed to contact his people, but he had to get Adina to safety first. That could only happen if he got her out of the country. The idea of never seeing her again pained him and he couldn't believe she was having that effect on him, but it had to be done. He couldn't keep her with him, no matter how he felt. And his feelings for her had only grown when they'd made love.

Being intimate with her was the last thing he should have done. He knew that it was forbidden, but here he was ready to take her again. Already, his hands were moving lower to touch her center again, to make her scream his name in that sexy voice of hers. But he shouldn't. He had started something that he could never finish. She was human and would never live as long as he and he would not want her to become a vampire, anyway. To become one of his kind would not only change her, but take her away from the only world she had ever known. Besides, he was the High Prince of Vampires, and no tribe would take her or their heirs seriously. She would be looked upon as weak and unworthy. He snorted at the idea of her being weak. She had to be the strongest person he had ever met. It was her willingness to help others, her inner strength, that made he want her more.

From the edge of sleep, Adina heard the snort and woke.

"What is it, Jin?" she asked.

"Nothing," he said, his hand sliding lower.

Adina smiled. "Nothing? It doesn't feel like nothing," she sighed as his fingers began rubbing her already sensitive folds. "Jin, I don't think I can right now."

He kissed her slowly while his fingers continued to stroke her. She rocked against his hand, making him smile in their kiss. "Are you sure?" he asked in a deep voice.

She gasped as a finger entered her.

"You're so bad," she moaned. Her hand covered his as he worked. But she whimpered when he pushed another finger into her.

Jin heard her slightly pained voice. He removed his fingers, kissing her deeply. He placed her on his lap but did not enter her. Instead he kissed her and caressed her back. They continued kissing deeply, his hands gripping her buttocks, kneading them. Adina draped her arms around his neck, loving his kisses even as she wondered why she was so enraptured by this vampire. A moment later, she gasped in surprise.

"Relax," he whispered as his finger rubbed her anus in slow, circular motion. It was an interesting feeling, for no one had ever done that to her before. She felt him kiss her neck and shoulder when his finger entered her anus. She almost jumped from his lap. Jin laughed.

"Just relax, Adina," he said against her neck.

"I don't know, Jin," she said in a soft voice.

"Trust me. I won't hurt you," he responded.

She looked into his eyes. His hands had stilled until he received her answer.

"Okay," she said.

He kissed her again, kissed her jaw, let his kisses trail down her neck to the tops of her breasts. He continued to kiss her there before taking one breast into his mouth. Adina cradled his head, loving his attention. She had never felt so loved, never trusted so completely. She relaxed fully, allowing herself to experience and enjoy.

Jin's finger caressed her anus, slipping in slowly, and when her breath caught, he teased her breast until she relaxed. Slowly, he slid the finger out. He inserted it again, slowly letting her adjust to the feel. As he did this, his other hand slipped a finger into her vagina, feeling its wetness. As his fingers created delightful sensations in her body she found herself willing to engage in more. Eventually his fingers stopped, and he placed his hard penis in her vagina. Gripping her butt, kneading it, he lifted her up and down at a slow, languishing pace, until she found the rhythm he liked. They slowly made love in the water, eyes connected in a powerful stare.

Adina watched his eye flint with every shift and circular move she made. He held her eyes, seemingly drawing in her soul. She witnessed emotions she didn't understand passing through his face. They were more than expressions of passion, there was something else there, a need and a pain that seemed to have taken hold in the gleaming orbs. Her heart was so moved by the look that she leaned forward, kissing him gently, and then hugged him, holding him close until they reach their climax. They came together, gazing into each other's eyes. When they came down again, she rested her head on his shoulder.

"I can't get enough of you," she whispered in his ear.

Jin couldn't speak. He was fighting his need to mark her, to permanently claim her as his own. Though he had said he would never bite her, even if she begged him, it was difficult to keep his promise. His instinct, the very essence of who he was, demanded that he claim her, mark her as his own. His territorial need to own her was scaring him because he didn't understand it. He had never reacted this way with other vampire lovers. He couldn't think of anything he had heard from his family or friends.

He had almost regained his control when she started to kiss and lick his neck. A growl started deep in his throat, his fangs bearing themselves as he began to grip her tighter. Adina, not understanding what was happening, continued her relentless attack on his neck, not only arousing him, but also causing his animalistic need to grow. When she started nipping the prominent vein on his neck, Jin's mouth opened, his fangs lowered towards the skin of her shoulder.

Suddenly, Adina was knocked off of Jin, falling into the center of the Jacuzzi with such force that she went under for a second. When she came back up she found that she was in the water alone. Wiping the water out of her face, she glanced around, trying to figure out what had happened.

"Jin," she said in a quiet voice, searching for him.

When no answer came, she checked the bathroom and found a towel. Taking it off the hook, she dried herself and wrapped the towel around her body. She walked to the doorway, almost afraid. It was deathly quiet in the apartment and very dark. Adina took a deep breath before calling to him again.

"Jin? Jin, what happened? Where are you? "

Nothing. She didn't know what to think. She did know that she was becoming afraid. She didn't like the feeling of creepiness that seemed to suddenly come about. She didn't understand what made Jin act so crazy. But what was worst was that she didn't know where Jin was and what was wrong with him. She wondered if she needed to worry about her safety around him.

How could it go from being so pleasant and wonderful to crazy and scary so quickly? She wanted to understand, but how could she when Jin was playing hide-and-seek. Adina liked games, but playing hide-and-seek with a vampire? No thank you. Especially not one that had just tweaked out on her.

She stared at the dark hallway, afraid to peek out, but knowing that she had to do it. She took a tentative step into the hallway.

"Jin? What's going on? You're scaring me."

Nothing. Adina licked her lips nervously.

"Don't do that," he hissed.

Adina glanced around but she couldn't place where the sound had come from. She swallowed before asking, "Jin, are you okay?"

"No," he responded in a strained voice. "Stay away from me."

Adina stopped moving. She didn't know what to do. How could she stay away from him when she had no idea where he was?

"Where are you?"

Silence. Adina almost rolled her eyes. This was getting ridiculous. Annoyed, she said so.

"Look, Jin, either you tell me what's going on, or I'll..."

Suddenly he was in front of her, eyes sharp and bright fangs bared, muscles taut in his body. Adina's eyes bugged as she stumbled back from him in fear. He had been standing in front of her the whole time, but she wouldn't have known it, for he had hidden in the shadows. Now, standing naked, his vampirism bared before her in such a primal manner, scared Adina senseless. She moved further into the light, as Jin stepped back from her.

"What's wrong with you, Jin? What is happening to you?"

Jin fought to focus. He needed to control himself. Taking his breath slowly, he calmed, forcing all his instincts down. He knew he was scaring her, but he couldn't comfort her until he could control himself. The beast within him, the primal part of him, was raging that he take her as his own. Shaking his head, he screamed internally that he would never do it. The fight was causing a pain in his head. He crumbled to the floor with a feral growl that turned into an animalistic wail.

Aghast, Adina watched him. She watched him fall to the floor sounding like he was in tremendous pain. She wanted to go to him but something told her to let him handle it alone, that whatever was happening was the result of his need to protect her from himself. Still, she wanted to ease his pain.

"Jin, what's wrong?" she asked again.

"I want to bite you," he panted before crying out again and curling up into a ball. No one had ever told him that something like this could happen, that his need to mark a mate could be so powerful. No one had warned him that fighting the need would hurt so much. His eyes watered as a howl escaped from his lips. He hoped to the Gods that his calls wouldn't attract any supernatural attention. Chances were good that his father had soundproofed the place, but still. Another pain raced through him. It was a demand for him to mark, to conquer, to claim what was rightfully his. His hand balled into a fist and slammed the floor with a loud boom.

Adina sat on the floor, feeling helpless as she watched him writhe in pain. She couldn't believe the need to bite her could be so great. She wondered if he was hungry again, but doubted that.

The only thing that had changed was that they'd had sex. More than once. And now he had developed a need to bite her. But why?

"Why do you want to bite me?" she asked, wishing she didn't have to. He seemed to need his full concentration to control his desires.

Jin didn't answer immediately. He calmed himself further as the pain ebbed. When he had more control, he said, "I want to claim you. I need to mark you as mine."

"Oh. Why do you need to do that?"

He shook his head as he sat up. He still wouldn't look at her for fear of the reaction it might trigger. "I don't know. This has never happened to me before."

"What? You've never been with anyone?"

Jin's chuckle set Adina at ease. If he could laugh, then he must have felt better, she reasoned. She had been afraid that she might have to lock herself in the bathroom.

"I've been with others, yes. But never human. Only other vampires. This has never happened before."

"Okay, wait. I'm your first human?" she asked in amazement.

He laughed outright then. "Well, aren't I your first vampire?"

Adina joined in nervous laughter. "That's true."

She watched Jin stand up, breathing deeply.

"I didn't know vampires could breathe," she remarked.

"Only when we are really excited or exert a lot of energy. It's a mystical thing. We don't have to breathe like you, but we have to take in some air. It's like a balance in our body, just like blood. Residual effects of having human DNA."

Adina stood too. She hoped it was safe now, especially since Jin was speaking in his natural calm, deep voice.

"So are you dead or what?"

He finally looked at her. Though his primal need was calling him, he was able to control it, since the heat of passion had cooled.

"No, I'm not dead. But I'm not alive like you, either."

She nodded then asked, "Are you okay, Jin?"

He pulled her close, letting her know that everything was fine and she had nothing to fear from him. "Everything is okay."

Again, it felt safe to be with him. She had watched him fight his need to bite her and that spoke volumes to her. Going against his instincts so he could protect her, now that was power. But what would happen the next time? Would he still be able to control it?

Chapter 9
No Rest for the Wary

JIN TOOK HER TO the master bedroom. It was grand in scale. The colors were dark, rich red accented by black. The bed had antique head and footboards, and a high mattress. There were two sitting chairs, a grand bureau, and a nightstand on either side of the bed. Jin walked to a closet at the left of the bed. After flicking on a light, he found a shirt that was large enough for Adina to wear like a gown, then he went to the bureau and took out silk pants.

He gave the shirt to Adina and turned his back. He stepped into the pants as she changed into the shirt. When he turned around he found her wearing his father's blue silk shirt and folding the towel.

"He's going to be pissed about it, but that's all there was."

Adina glanced down at the shirt.

"Well, I could sleep in the towel. It is a nice shirt. I don't want to ruin it…"

"Don't worry about it. He'll get over it."

The question was, could Jin sleep in the same room with Adina? No, definitely not.

"You take the bed. I'll sleep on the couch."

Adina didn't like the idea of sleeping in that bed alone, though she understood why it would be best. Still, she hated that after what they had shared, she would sleep in that big bed alone. She tried to smile, but it came off weak and Jin instantly knew why.

"Adina, I don't want to hurt you."

"I know. It's just that after all of this, to be sleeping alone..." She heard herself and thought she sounded really pathetic. "Never mind. Good night, Jin." She turned from him, regretting having started something they both knew couldn't last.

Everything in Jin's mind was telling him not to be a fool, to get the hell out of the room, but he found himself following her. When she reached the bed, he was right behind her.

"Tucking me in?" she asked.

"No. Care if I join you?"

She smiled brightly, even as the voice in her head called her the dumbest broad in town. She piped it down with a "Que sera" response. He hadn't hurt her, yet, and he had been managing to fight his instinct. He said he was okay, so what harm could come from it? She climbed into the bed, sliding over to make room for Jin. Once he was there, she moved close to him.

"You going to be okay?"

When he inhaled her scent, the need became strong, but not overwhelming.

"If I can't be, then I'll leave. For now, just sleep."

Pulling her close, he laid his head down and closed his eyes for some long-awaited rest.

Two hours later, he stilled hadn't slept. The call to mark her was getting increasingly strong. Not only was he trying to figure out how to find his father, he had to figure out how to get Adina to safety, far away from the problems of his world. He couldn't let anyone to know about her.

He kissed her shoulder before disengaging himself and leaving the bed. First, he went to the bathroom, releasing the water in the

Jacuzzi. Then he went into the main room. He cleaned up the mess they had made before going into the room with the elevator. Taking a seat and staring out the window, Jin thought long and hard.

By now, his father's people had to be looking for him. If they discovered the car, they would know the truth about what happened to him. His father would be using his best trackers to look for him and would probably find out something about Jin's fate. He hoped that whoever had sent the hellhounds after him would be sent into hiding. By dawn, he would be able to get Adina to safety.

He was sure there was chaos about his disappearance. His mother would be calling everyone and everything incompetent. She and his father would argue until he was found, then they would go back to their respective worlds. They only met to discuss him and his progress. Other than that, they had no feeling for each other as far as he could tell. But they protected their offspring fiercely. They had too much invested in him for it to be any other way. Jin rolled his eyes in disgust. There was no time for self-pity when so much was happening.

He knew that if the Pinu had spotted him, they would soon sell the information to the highest bidder. In fact, it probably had already happened. The only thing he had to worry about was his family coming into the city and his father using this particular apartment. He probably wouldn't. He had a better one with more sophisticated equipment that he used when there was trouble. Still, Jin needed to stay alert.

The more pressing topic on his mind was Adina and his very strong reaction to her. He needed to know why. What was so special about her that he was reacting so strongly? Yes, he was attracted to her, but he knew his attraction and sexual needs went way beyond having been celibate so long. He couldn't seem to stop touching her, as if he was trying to fulfill a purpose. And his need to mark her was also growing. Right now, he needed to gain knowledge for himself and to help protect Adina. He went to his father's bookshelf in the main room. There was nothing that could help him. Annoyed, he stormed to the kitchen and grabbed another pack of blood from the fridge. He heated it and drank. He wasn't hungry, but he hoped it would give him more control over the beast within. After drinking, he felt like his head was clearer and he was full. He wouldn't be drinking for a while...if he stayed out of fights.

Jin walked back to the woman who was sound asleep in the bed. His eyes flinted with need, making him sigh mentally, but he couldn't help it. He wanted her again, to plunge deep within her heat. Already, he felt himself grow stiff from the very idea of it. Slowly walking towards the bed, he told himself that he couldn't touch her, to remember what almost happened last time. But by the time he crawled into the bed, his pants were in a pile beside it. All rational thoughts escaped him and he was kissing her shoulder intently, his hand moving under her shirt, fondling her breasts. Adina moaned in her sleep, but didn't wake. Jin continued his play, moving from her breast, palming her stomach and pressing his hardness against her. She sighed, grinding against him. He raised her leg over his hip and slipped into her.

Adina woke to feeling her inner walls being stroked by powerful thrusts. She sighed as she reached behind her. She twisted around to kiss Jin fully as he made love to her. He massaged her breast and kissed her deeply. The blood he'd just drunk invigorated him more than before. As he thrust inside her, his fingers found her clitoris and began to rub. Adina broke away from Jin's kiss and covering his hand with hers, stroking until the tension built and snapped. She sighed his name. He pushed her onto her stomach, then raised her until they were both on their knees. Jin held her waist, pulling her into him as he thrust. His strokes were becoming faster and deeper.

Adina was fully awake then. Falling forward, she rested on her elbows to balance. She gave it as good as she got it, meeting his every thrust with her own movement. The sound of flesh meeting flesh echoed in the room, along with their cries of ecstasy. She reached between her legs and fondled her clitoris until they both came hard. Jin ground against her with his eyes closed tightly. When they opened, their green fire was emboldened. He yanked her up by her hair. Adina squealed as he took a handful of braids.

"Jin!" she cried as his lips clamped down on her neck. She tried not to shake but she was afraid.

Jin paused, then let go of her hair. He kissed her neck before slowly lowering them onto the bed. He pulled her close to him.

"Jin?"

"Mine," he responded in a dark voice that she hardly recognized.

She turned in his arms, staring at him. She had shared her body with this vampire, giving herself without thinking of the consequences. Now wanting to understand, she held his illuminated gaze, taking in their inhuman nature. She touched his cheek. "Okay," she said, accepting his need to claim her.

Somehow, that calmed him. He still didn't bite her, though. Jin's eyes dulled as understanding returned to them.

"Sorry," he said.

Drinking the blood had given him more control, but not enough. Her consent though, brought him back to reality, quieting the need for now. But his primal need would demand that he mark her, and soon. He had to get her away from him before then.

"No need to be sorry. I don't understand what is happening either. I've never been this way with a guy before. All I know is that I want you. I love when you touch me, and as crazy as it sounds, I care about you. I know we just met. I keep telling myself that it must be lust but…I think it's more."

Her confusion was driving her crazy. She was addicted to this vampire and couldn't understand why. But she knew that every time she made love to him her connection to him became stronger.

He reached out to caress her cheek. "I don't understand either, Adina. I have never wanted anyone as much as I want you. I can't get enough of you, but it's not just your body. I like having you near me. I want to keep you near me all the time. I want more of you than your body. I desire more, but…" he paused before again spilling the painful truth. "We cannot be together any more than we are now. After tonight, you must get away from here. You must go back to the States."

Adina had known that in her heart but for the first time, she hating the idea of leaving London. Rather, she hated the idea of leaving Jin.

"I know." She sighed before asking, "But what about you? What are you going to do?"

"Don't worry about me. I'll be fine. Really, I'll be safe. But you are my first priority. I will make sure no harm comes to you."

She just nodded before resting her head on his shoulder. Jin let her sleep, taking some much-needed rest himself.

His eyes flew open an hour later. He felt that he had two hours before dawn. Though tired, something had awakened him. A second later, he felt it again. Jin was up and out of the bed. He stepped into his pants, went into his father's closet and removed a broadsword from behind some suits. Slowly, he exited the room, closing the door behind him.

As soon as he entered the main room, he could smell the trash that had tracked him. It was in the elevator, trying to come into the apartment. He walked to the door and waited for it to open. When it did, he had the blade ready at the vampire's neck.

"It took me hours to find you, Sire," he said.

Jin lowered the blade. Fritz was his father's servants, one of his best trackers.

"How did you find me?"

"Your father has us all searching the city. Naturally, he hoped that if you escaped, you would have found your way to one of his residences. After many false starts, I managed to track you here. "

Jin had known of the possibility, but he had hoped it would take longer. He could see Fritz's nostrils flare, then his eyes glinted. Fritz knew his secret.

"Sire must be careful. One would think he is violating Law. "

Jin scrutinized the vampire before him, wondering at his motive for pretending that Jin *hadn't* violated Law.

"I understand. Tell my father that I am safe and will come to him in the morning."

"Why not now, Sire? I have a car ready for your disposal. "

Jin knew that Fritz was looking for a confession, but he wasn't about to give it to him. Instead, he growled at Fritz, letting him know where the power lay.

"I said I'll meet him in the morning. Is there anything else, Fritz?"

The vampire bowed. "No, Sire. I'll inform him."

"Good evening."

Fritz returned the elevator. Jin waited until he couldn't hear it anymore before locking it. Then he hurried back to the bedroom and went straight to the bed.

"Adina," he called. "Adina, love, wake up."

Adina rolled over. Groggily, she said, "What?"

"We have to leave. *Now.* "

* * *

Fritz went back to the car that was a block from his Master's apartment. He opened his phone and pushed a button. A number appeared on the screen, rapidly dialing itself. It rang twice before a clipped voice answered.

"Sire, I have found him. He is alive," replied Fritz

Eldon sighed his relief. His panic had grown the longer Jin was missing.

"Is he injured?"

"Not really, Sire."

"What do you mean 'not really?' He's either injured, or he isn't."

"He seemed to be healing from his injuries. I saw faint marks on his chest..."

"He must have been able to get blood quickly then. Good. Let me speak to my son."

Fritz swallowed, dreading his next statement.

"Sire, he is not with me."

"Why not?" Eldon snapped.

"He refused, Sire. He said to tell you that he will contact you in the morning."

"Excuse me?" Eldon couldn't believe his ears. "Where is my son? I demand to speak to him now!"

Fritz took a deep breath.

"He is still in the apartment. But, sire, there is something else you should know."

"Well. What is it?" Eldon's voice took on a frosty tone.

"He smelled of human. I believe he was hiding a human and that's why he wouldn't come with me."

The silence was deafening. Fritz waited for his words to sink in, grateful that he was nowhere near his Master while making the accusation. After a long pause, he spoke.

"I want to speak to my son." Eldon said coolly.

"Yes, sire. I'll see to it. But what if—" his voice faltered.

"What if, what?!"

"Sire I'm sure he knows that I smelled the human..."

"So?"

"Never mind, Sire. I will retrieve him now."

"If he is not there, check the carpark. I have a Jaguar there. If it's gone, let me know immediately."

"Of course, Sire."

"Contact me when you have him, or failing that, what you found."

"Yes, Sire."

Fritz hung up and went to see about finding the young prince.

Eldon's jaw clenched tightly. Things were getting out of his control, and rapidly. If Jin had a human with him, violating the law... Eldon turned from his library to find his Mate. This news would doubtlessly send her into another fury.

* * *

Prince Lars stared out the window, thinking hard about what he needed to do in the coming days. He had to ensure that Tenhar didn't feel the wrath of the head of the Vampire Tribes. He knew that the Grand Master of Danpe and that High Priestess of a wife would be on the hunt for vengeance. He needed to cover the trail that led to his clan.

Lars already had the Hellhounds destroyed; all who had been involved had been quietly removed. Currently, he had a whisper campaign going, placing all kinds of half-truths on the street about who had attacked the future leader of all vampires. Further, how Tenhar sent their own people to aide in the search for Jin when they heard about it. He made sure that the news reached the Grand Master and his wife by using the network of lesser tribes who would color the actions of Tenhar favorably. All he could do now was wait and hope that he had done enough to protect his neck—and that of his tribe.

His phone rang for the second time since receiving the news about the failed assassination attempt. He flipped it open and waited for the person to speak.

"Sire, we have some news."

"And," he said slowly.

"There is word that Jin has taken refuge with a human. They were spotted together in the tube."

Lars leaned back in his seat. "Interesting. Anyone know where he is?"

"No, Sire, but it's safe to assume that he went to one of his father's safe houses in the city. It is possible that the human is with him."

"I see. Find out. Find out who that human is and the connection to that bastard offspring. Whatever happens tonight, we need to make sure we find out everything about her, starting with how she knows the High Prince."

He hung up the phone, thinking. The human female added a whole new dimension to the equation. This female might be able to do the one thing that Prince Lars could not: She could bring Jin to Tenhar's side and finally end his chances at ever getting his fangs into the throne.

He checked the time, noting that he wouldn't make it to London before morning. He hated not being there to facilitate the search, but on the bright side, he would have an airtight alibi if things got hairy when the vampire council met, and they would meet. Danpe and Hinghou would insist on it in light of the attack on the heir apparent.

Prince Lars couldn't wait to see how it turned out.

Chapter 10
Mating Season

ADINA WAS OUT OF her mind with fatigue. She had been sexed up and scared to death all Friday night long, and all she wanted to do was sleep. But when Jin said they had to go, sleep became another fantasy. She sat up and watched Jin move with superhuman speed. Jin stripped with one motion and within seconds she heard a washing machine running. Within seconds, he was fully dressed and strapped with weapons, while she hadn't even made it out of bed yet. Adina climbed down from the bed, spotting the pants and shirt he had left for her. Feeling the urgency, she dressed as quickly as she could. She walked out of the room to find that he was already waiting for her and holding her bag. *Another reminder that Jin was not human.* She was going to ask why he was running the washer, but he cut her off.

"It is time for you to go home. They know where I am and you cannot be caught with me. They will smell you on me, and that will be trouble enough."

Adina nodded her understanding and took her bag.

"But how am I going to get away and what about the opposite? Will they smell you on me?"

Jin froze. He had forgotten that it was entirely possible after what they had done.

He shook his head and said, "I don't know, but you will be fine. I just need to get you out of here. If I keep you hidden until dawn, you can leave the city and get back home safely. As I told you, vampires can go into the sun, but most of us don't. We like the night, so chances of you meeting one of us during the day are very slim."

"Okay. I've got my passport with me. I figured I wasn't going back to my apartment again."

Jin smiled at her foresight. "Good. I'm glad we don't have to make a stop there." He thought for a moment.

Adina approached him and placed her hand on his chest. She said, "What about us Jin? Was this just a lustful night or something more?"

Jin stared into her eyes. "It was something more that we can never have." He brought her hand to his lips brushing her knuckles with a kiss. "But whatever happens, I'll never forget this night or what you did for me?"

"Yeah, right," she laughed, then said more seriously, "So we need to leave?"

Jin nodded. "Yes, we do."

He turned back towards the bedroom. He walked past its door and turned a corner. Right in front of them was another door.

Frowning, she watched him open the door to a hallway.

"The real door," he explained.

When they left the apartment, they knew they were leaving behind the only place where they could truly be together. Jin took them down the hallway to an elevator. They journeyed in silence to the first floor. They turned down an old but elegant hallway, then moved into a stairwell. Passing the stairs, they walked to a door opposite of the one they had just come through. Jin instructed

Adina to wait as he went through the door, leaving her think about her night of intense passion with a vampire she had saved. Could that have been his way of thanking her? She knew that wasn't true. They were connected and it was more than the sex. She was drawn to him and was going to hate losing him.

Jin came back after he determined that all was clear, which wasn't surprising. It was hardly common knowledge that his father kept a car stashed in the garage. He motioned for Adina to follow him. She quietly followed him to the quiet garage.

They made it to the slick jaguar, a two-seated sports model with tinted windows. Adina was clearly impressed by the vehicle, even as she got in and put on her seatbelt.

"We need to stay hidden until dawn. That's in about two hours. I have an idea of where to go." He mumbled something else about trying to find his way through the bloody streets.

He sped out of the garage, making Adina grip the dashboard and frown at him. Jin didn't notice, grinning wildly. *Men and their machines* she thought. Looking at him like this, he appeared quite young. Jin made a right turn and raced down London's streets.

They cruised through London at 160 km/h. Adina wondered if they would attract the attention of the police, but they didn't. After a few wrong turns, Jin found his bearings.

As they drove over London Bridge to South London, Adina wondered where the hell he was taking her. She knew that they were going towards Brixton, but it didn't seem like Jin would go there, not after she had seen how his father lived. Yet, that was where they ended up, maneuvering through the streets until they found an alley. Jin slowed as he drove through it, then parked.

"Where are we?"

Jin smiled grimly at her. "A place where I can get a favor to protect us...to protect you."

He reached down, pulled up his pants leg and handed a gun to Adina.

"Use it if anyone other than me comes to this car."

Adina shook her head. "Are you crazy? I don't know how to use a gun!"

He cocked his head. "Just point and shoot. Be careful though, there is no safety."

Adina's mouth hung open. He pulled her close, kissing her fully, before getting out of the car. Before Adina could call to him, he was gone.

"What the—" she sat up straighter.

Jin walked to an unlit door in the back of the building. He sniffed before knocking five times in a rhythmic pattern. Tap...tap. Tap...tap...tap. He waited, but nothing happened.

"Shit," he whispered. *He must have already gone.* Jin was about to leave when the door opened. Behind it stood a cream-color male with jet black eyes and pale blond hair. The Vamp curled his lips in a sneer.

"What do you want?"

Jin sneered in return. "To cash in my favor."

The vampire swore and beckoned Jin inside. He closed the door and walked past Jin, but stopped suddenly.

He sniffed. His eyes got bigger.

"Have you been playing naughty games with a human?" he asked.

Jin didn't like the foul smile he saw, but it wouldn't help his cause to knock it off.

"Shut up, Flaxon," Jin said instead. "We need to talk."

Flaxon laughed. "You did not bite...ugh, ugh."

Jin had Flaxon's neck in his grip.

"Don't piss me off, Flaxon. I need your help, and you owe me. So shut up and listen."

Flaxon fell in a crumple when he was released.

"You were always a bastard, Jin."

"Save it. Someone tried to kill me tonight."

"I know. Word hit the streets hours ago. Some thought you were dead. If only we could be so lucky."

Jin scoffed. "Well, we both know there's no love lost between us."

"Too true. But you lived, so why aren't you with daddy?"

"It's complicated."

"Human complicated," Flaxon laughed.

Jin swallowed his annoyance. He needed Flaxon, and could only push him so far.

"She helped me. I was desperate and she saved me. Now I need her protected until she can get out of town."

Flaxon sniffed him again. "I'll bet she helped you." He shook his head before mocking seriousness when he said, "You know better. Revealing yourself to a human is against Law, punishable by death. No exceptions."

"So is selling drugs. Drugs that are so addictive that the human consumers would be your slaves and kill for—"

Flaxon sneered. "Hey, a vamp's got to make a living. Not all of us are born into wealth."

Jin rolled his eyes.

"Look. She helped me. I need to help her. Whatever happens to me is fine, but she need not die for being good enough to save a vampire in trouble. And just think, I can keep ignoring your disrespect to my father's city, you know, the dealing, gun running…"

Flaxon raised his hand. "Alright. Fine. But I ain't dying for this, man."

"You're already cutting the line really thin. So much human contact. It can be argued that they know exactly what you are."

The men glared at each other, then Flaxon nodded.

"Fine. I'll hide you both. Where the bloody hell is she?"

Jin walked back out the door.

Adina sat in the dark alley, thinking the whole time that she had to be the biggest idiot in all of London. No woman in her right mind would sit in dark alleys in the middle of the night, with or without a gun. Yet there she was, eyes darting back and forth, every sound making her jump two feet off her seat.

"Dammit Jin, where are you?" she said through gritted teeth. *Okay, Adina, come back to earth. This is unreasonable. Everything you have done tonight is unreasonable. You are making a fool out of yourself and tomorrow morning your face will be splattered on the front pages of every paper. Headline: Idiot Black Female, American, crossed the Pond to be murdered in a dark alley, something she could have done back home.*

She heard the ground crunching and extended the weapon. Counting to ten, she put her finger on the trigger and prepared to squeeze when Jin opened the door.

"Come on. Get out."

Adina followed him. She had to run a few steps to catch up, but she caught him before he reached the door.

"This is a vampire's lair. Touch nothing. He is a criminal but he owes me. I didn't want to use him, but the other place was compromised. He'll keep his mouth shut because I have too much over him. He'll gain nothing by betraying me but tell him nothing."

"Okay. But what if he speaks to me? "

The growl that came from the back of his throat told her all she needed to know.

Jin secured the door behind them. They walked through the dark hallway to a second door. Opening it, they found themselves in a room filled with boxes and papers. Against one wall was a lot of electronic equipment. Against another, a huge calendar was marked in red and black with appointments. In the middle of the room was a beat-up brown couch with a stained coffee table in front of it. To the right was an open door leading further into the building. A second later, a vampire was leaning in the frame, studying her. Jin growled and the vampire's hands went up.

"I got to hand it to you, Jin, you picked a cute one."

His devilish smile revealed sharp fangs that seem to glisten in the semi-lit room. Adina smiled at him, not sure what else to do. She didn't like the idea of another vampire knowing about her after all that Jin had told her, but he must have been desperate.

Jin glared at Flaxon before looking around.

Flaxon said, "Sit wherever. Sorry 'bout the mess. Wasn't expecting company."

Jin and Adina sat on the couch, though Adina worried that she might catch something from it. Flaxon leaned against the wall and observed them both. When he licked his fang, Jin's eyes glinted in a deadly manner. Flaxon laughed.

"You know why they banned human contact, don't you, Jin? I mean the future High Prince has to know the consequences of having…" a nasty smile formed on his lips, "…special relationships with humans."

Jin could feel his temper flaring more and more by the second, but he bit his tongue, in part because he hoped that Flaxon would tell him. Flaxon had already lived two-hundred ten years, so he might remember the old ways.

Adina looked back and forth between the men, not understanding their pissing contest. It was obvious that they didn't care for each other, yet, she sensed a degree of respect. Adina didn't have long to ponder the thought because Flaxon's stare, so intent, was making her uncomfortable. It was like he knew exactly what she and Jin had been doing.

When Jin said nothing, Flaxon asked, "How the hell did you escape? Word is that Hellhounds were out, by the way those humans were torn apart."

Adina paled, a feat for a dark brown woman. She noticed Jin clenching his jaw.

"I morphed," he hissed.

Flaxon smirked. "Really? Must be nice."

"Still jealous that you won't ever have my skills, Flaxon?"

"No. Just thinking of how your morphing could lead to breaking Law."

"Later," Jin growled.

"No. Now. Everyone in this room has a death mark on their head for your stupidity, so out with it."

Jin shot up. He and Flaxon growled at each other.

"You're not High Prince yet, Jin. Your actions can stop that from happening real quick," Flaxon said in a low voice.

Jin glowered at him before turning to Adina.

"Excuse me. I must talk with Flaxon."

Adina thought to protest but from the way the vampires glared at each other, she could feel a fight coming on and really didn't want to be in the middle of it. She figured she'd give them a few minutes before suggesting that they leave.

"Okay. Is it safe here?" she asked.

"Yes, human!" Flaxon snapped.

Jin eyes flared and he snarled. "Speak to her again! See what happens!"

Flaxon looked into Jin's eyes then stepped back. Sniffing again, he shook his head.

"Idiot!" he hissed and stormed away.

Jin was close behind. Adina stared at the archway, wondering if one of them would end up dead.

Flaxon was in the lobby of his club. The tables had been pushed against the walls with their chairs on top. The hardwood floor echoed frantic footsteps. Jin stood by the bar, watching Flaxon like he was a fool.

"Need a fix, Flaxon?"

Flaxon stopped abruptly.

"No, but you do. Do you know what you have done?!"

"What?"

"You slept with that human!"

Jin, though annoyed, was embarrassed. Not because he had slept with her, but because he knew he shouldn't have.

"It just happened. She helped me, I liked her, we talked, and I just felt so drawn to her…"

"Don't those fucked-up parents of yours tell you anything?! Anything worthwhile?! You can't fuck humans when you are in heat. Hell, you can't fuck vampires either!"

Jin frowned, walking deeper into the room.

"What the hell are you talking about? I've slept with vampires before this. This never happened before."

"I saw the scar on her wrist. Did you drink her blood? "

Jin looked away. He took a deep breath before confessing.

"She gave me a little when I was weak. She mixed it with animal blood in a cup. I drank it without knowing what she had done."

Flaxon shook his head then snapped out a brutal, humorless laugh.

"My god. And where did you bite her?"

Jin whipped around.

"I didn't. I fought the urge, but it's getting harder. That's why I brought her here, hoping to protect her."

"You just made it worse. Why do you think you keep hissing at me?"

"Because I don't like you," Jin replied snidely.

"If only it was just that," mumbled Flaxon.

He walked past Jin to his bar. He grabbed two glasses from the ceiling rack and a bottle of vodka from the back shelf. He poured into both glasses and slid one towards Jin before tossing his own drink down his throat.

Jin took a seat on a stool and sipped.

"Say what you will. I don't like leaving her long."

"I'll bet you don't," Flaxon said.

He poured another drink and tossed it back with a grimace.

"Jin, do you know where your father was having you driven to?"

Jin shrugged. "There was some party out at his estate north of the city. Whatever. Just another meet and greet."

"Meet and greet, my arse." He regarded Jin in disbelief. "You really don't know. Now it makes sense."

Jin sighed. "Look, Flaxon. Tell me what you know, and quick."

Flaxon almost felt bad for Jin. He had heard that they kept many secrets from him, but something like this was unbelievable.

"Jin, your father was having a party with a few choice female vampires. These females had good backgrounds and genes. They are able to create a very strong heir to the throne. You catching my drift? It was the reason your parents didn't want you with the Tenhar daughter. It's mating season for you.

"When the Tenhar couldn't get you to mate with their daughter, they decided to kill you outright. But you fooled them all. You mated with a human! Ha ha ha ha!! Oh boy, this will rock the halls!"

He took another drink.

Jin felt his face fall, then denial set in.

"No, that's not possible. I would know if I was in heat."

"Then you drank her blood? Man, double whammy. Not only are you bonded to her, you unwittingly have done the Kaher Blood Exchange. Man, oh man!"

Flaxon actually felt very sick. Things were going to get dangerous very soon.

"I don't understand. This hasn't happened before."

"Jin, when was the last time you were with someone?"

"Fifteen years ago. I've been living with the monks, training, learning..."

"...and kept under wraps until it was decided who would be presented to you as a mate. Why do you think they kept you surrounded by all those males? For jokes? They were taking away all temptations while you were in heat. The bastards had you hidden away because they didn't want you 'accidentally' breeding with the wrong vampire. You were brought here because the negotiations were finished."

"No. They would have told me."

"Apparently not. And for good reason. Everyone says you're nothing but a lapdog for your parents. At least Tenhar says it."

Jin snarled. "I'm no one's lapdog."

Flaxon backed up when he saw Jin's hackles raised.

"Sorry."

Jin released his anger. Thinking hard, he put the pieces together. He remembered his father saying he was too wild and free and it was time for him to live with the monks before he made a terrible mistake that would ruin everything. Now he understood what his father was trying to prevent, but only with another vampire. The idea of a human threat never entered his father's mind.

"Damn. I didn't understand. No one ever told me."

"How the hell didn't you know? Didn't feel it?"

Jin thought back, remembering a discussion in which his mother told him the strange urge to possess someone was just a transformation and the monks would teach him about his new strengths.

"My mother lied to me. She told me that I was just coming into more power. No one discussed mating with me. Why would they do that?"

"Because maybe you're easier to control when you're kept ignorant. You're an alpha male. It's the only way to control you. Anyway, mating just is not a proper topic for discussion. It reminds us how close to the beast we are, and many vampires don't like to be in touch with their...baser instincts."

They were quiet. Then Flaxon asked, "What would you have done if you had known?"

"Known what?"

"That it was time to have a mate."

Jin frowned. "I would have chosen one."

Flaxon nodded. "And they couldn't have that. What if Tenhar sneaked a girl in? Hell, giving them any chance at power would be too much. They would change our lives *and* bring hell and destruction on humans."

Jin started to walk away, trying to digest all that had happened. More than that, he still felt the urge to claim Adina. He stopped to ask Flaxon about it.

"You mated with her. You tasted her blood. With humans, man, mating season takes on a whole new slant. Humans are addictive. Their life force is so powerful it gets you high. A few drops of human blood can have you stronger than any vampire sipping animal blood. By drinking her blood, you now believe that she deemed you worthy. Your need to bite her is based on you deeming her worthy, too. If you didn't think so, you would not want to bite her."

Jin was thinking hard, but said nothing. Finally, he asked Flaxon, "Can I resist the urge to mark her?"

Flaxon smiled.

"Mate, hell no. You will keep coming for her until you claim her. Bloody priceless. The only way to stop it is to get away from her, far away until the need dies. And it will take a long time. It won't happen overnight."

Jin nodded. "Last question. Has this ever happened before?"

Jin didn't notice when Flaxon's face turned to stone.

"No."

"Okay." He started for the door, then stopped. "I need you to protect her from me until dawn, then get her to the airport."

"What?! I can't stay with her!"

"Why not?" Jin asked through his teeth.

"You're her mate. You wouldn't even let me speak to her without wanting to bite my head off. You want to claim her before I do, even if I'm not interested. What makes you think you can walk away and leave her with me? How does the idea make you feel?"

Jin bared his teeth before storming out of the bar.

"I thought so." Flaxon said, returning to his drink.

When he finished drinking, he went over to an old-fashioned cash register and banged on the side twice. The drawer slid open. He took out a phone and an address book and began to dial. He had several calls to make.

Chapter 11
Resistance is Futile
or The Beginning

ADINA SAT ON THE couch feeling lost. It was too quiet in the room, and silence was not her favorite thing right now. Going over the night in her head, she found that she had made some really crazy decisions. Now she wondered if she would regret any of them. She stood up and walked around, inspecting boxes and papers. It seemed that Flaxon was some sort of businessman. From what she could tell, most of it was illegal. But the only thing she really wanted to find was a restroom.

Through the archway, there was a grimy, white kitchen. Empty blood packs and moldy pizza crusts were on the counter. The floor held onto her shoes. She noticed another hallway, leading to a closed door straight ahead. She took a couple of steps and found a room to her right. She stepped in, turned on a light, and found an immaculate bedroom. She stepped in and looked around, liking the black motif and silk sheets on the queen-sized bed. But no restroom.

She backed out of the room into the hallway. A little further down, she opened another door and found the bathroom. Thankful, she hoped it didn't look too scummy and turned on the light. The brightened room was a stark contrast to the man's kitchen. That was until she pulled back the shower curtain. Disgusted, she closed the bathroom door and took care of business. Afterwards, she retraced her steps and was just about to reach the bedroom when she felt Jin.

He leaned over, his hair brushing her neck.

"What are you doing?"

"Just using the bathroom."

She sighed as his hands moved under her shirt, rubbing her stomach. Swallowing, she asked, "Is everything alright?"

He licked her neck and kissed it. "Yes. It is."

Forcing himself to step away from her he said, "We'll leave soon."

She faced him with a sad smile. "Then what?"

"Then you'll be safe."

"And you'll be gone," she whispered.

Jin said nothing, just watched her turn away. Adina licked her lips and took a deep breath. Then she faced Jin's penetrating stare.

"Jin, what happened tonight? I know you talked to that vampire about it. You planning on telling me?"

Jin appraised her slowly, his eyes moving up her body until they met hers.

"I have to leave you alone. We shouldn't—I shouldn't have done this to you."

She tilted her head. "Done what?"

Jin looked away. Adina knew what he meant and it hurt her. She said, "I know we just met, but, but do you regret what we did? Do you regret touching me, a human?"

Jin said nothing. What could he say? How could he tell her why it had happened? He couldn't think of a way to tell it without insulting her. The fact was that he did like her, in spite of his need. He liked her a lot.

"I see," she said. "Fine. We had fun. I helped you, you paid me back. And when I get on the plane, you're just a memory. It's over."

Her cold voice felt like rejection to him. He couldn't allow it. She already owned him and he had to claim her. With a quickness that startled her, he spun her around.

"It was not about fun. It was more than fun. You are mine. You belong to me and I will be more than just a memory. I am your mate."

Adina's mouth came open and Jin's tongue went into it. He kissed her frantically, barely letting her catch her breath. He pushed her against the door behind her. It gave way and they were in Flaxon's bedroom.

Jin picked her and pulled her legs around his waist. He carried her to the bed and laid her beneath him. Jin kissed her neck and her face urgently. He ripped open her shirt, sucking and nipping her breast roughly. She cried out. His hand slid into her jeans, popping the buttons. He stroked her folds roughly, using his thumb to apply pressure to her clitoris.

Adina panted as her body wanted more. Jin removed his hand, then his shirt. His feral eyes were bright with animalistic need. He pulled away her jeans before climbing back onto her, grinding against her pelvis. She wore no underwear; it had been tore to tatters and left behind. He inhaled her scent before taking out his erection and slipping into her.

He moved in her rapidly, setting a pace that Adina could barely match. A tingle started in the pit of her stomach and grew with each passing second. Her nails dug into his flesh, driving him mad, as she gripped his back. He forced her legs wider, pumping harder and harder. Adina's cries carried throughout the building until she came with a force that nearly made her pass out. Jin stroked a few more times before bursting, dying inside of her. He pumped until every drop of his seed filled her. His cry came with it and his fangs elongated. He pulled her up, ready to bury his fangs into her.

"Do it," she said.

"No," he said, fighting his instinct.

Adina lowered his head and whispered, "It's okay. I am your mate."

Jin struggled, but her words sent him over the edge. He sank his fangs just above her collarbone on her left side.

Adina's eyes rolled back images flashed between them. She felt herself spasm and come again, a euphoria feeling coursing through her body until she passed into nothingness.

Jin pulled away breathing hard, with blood dribbling from the corner of his mouth.

Flaxon stood at the bar sipping his drink and trying to think of how to help the man he now wanted as his High Prince. When he finished the drink, he left the bar and locked the door that separated it from the rest of the space.

He walked slowly down the hallway, observing the High Prince splayed across his bed breathing heavily. The human female was naked on her back, no doubt equally taxed by the High Prince's energy. There was blood on her neck. Flaxon shook his head before going on take his own chance at sleep. Tomorrow was going to be a long day.

* * *

Adina woke with a start over cool sheets. A soundly sleeping Jin had his heavy arm draped over her. She watched him briefly, noting that his face had an innocence that she had never seen when he was awake. She turned away, feeling the pain near her neck. Her shoulder felt puffy there and her fingers were wet with blood. The memory of last night came rushing back to her, including the bite. But then other images invaded her mind, making her blink rapidly.

She had let Jin bite her. He had said he wouldn't even if she begged, but he did. She wasn't mad, it had been hurting him not to bite her. But she still didn't understand the implications of the bite. *Time to seek out a certain blond vampire.*

She gently moved his arm and got up. Finding her clothes, she realized the shirt was ruined and took his sweater instead. She padded barefoot into the hallway, looking both ways before deciding to go back to the messy living room.

It was as dark as a tomb. She was feeling the wall for a light switch when a voice said, "Don't."

She looked out and saw illuminating gold eyes. She leaned against the doorframe as he had once done.

"What is it you want, human?"

She sighed. She knew that Jin had told her not to talk to the vampire, but she needed answers.

"I think you know what is going on with Jin, and why he needed to bite me."

"I'd bite you too, human. Human blood is good, especially from pretty girls like you."

She shook her head, imagining the smile on the vampire's face.

"Oh, please. Look, I just found Jin sleeping like a log, when before he couldn't sleep at all for needing to bite me. Why was biting me so important? Why does he think I'm his mate?"

Flaxon was determining what he could tell her without pissing Jin off or scaring her.

"You are a human. He needed to own you. Back in the old days, when vampires could play with humans, we marked them to know who belong to who. That was his problem."

"Bull-shit. Tell me the truth," she demanded.

"Ask him," he fired back.

Adina was frustrated. She wanted to know what was going on before she got on the plane.

"Adina," said Flaxon softly, "you could do worse. Believe me. After all that has happened, that bite is the best thing that could have happened to you."

"Why?"

She felt, more than saw Flaxon get up. A moment later, he was standing before her, shirtless. *Damn, are all vampires fine?* Flaxon was ripped, his creamy color a soft light brown paled by his DNA. His pants hung low on his waist, giving her a nice view of the trail of hair and muscles of his lower stomach. His body was very nice, but not as nice as Jin's. Flaxon enjoyed being inspected. But she was officially off limits. She belonged to Jin, lucky bastard. Smirking he said, "He'll always know where you are."

He walked past her down the hall. Adina knew the conversation was over. Turning, she went back to the bedroom and watched Jin sleep.

Jin had never been so tired in his life. The sleep was good, as were the dreams. Adina stayed in his mind most of the time until he woke to her fingers playing in his hair. He smiled, until his eyes landed on his bite mark.

He jerked upright, startling Adina. Running his fingers through his hair, he closed his eyes angrily.

"Jin?"

He felt her hand rest on his shoulder. After a pause, he placed his on hand over hers.

"I'm sorry, Adina." Turning towards her, he said, "I'm so sorry."

Jin's look was that of pure agony.

"Hey. It's okay," she soothed.

He jumped up.

"No, it's not. I gave my word and—"

"I let you. You fought it and I told you it was okay. I know what you said before, but…look, just tell me that you won't turn me into a mind-controlled slave or something."

He snorted. "No. I won't. I would never do that to you."

"Good." She paused as she thought of how to word her next question. Coming up with nothing, she just said, "I keep getting flashes of images. I don't understand. Why?"

"It is because of the bite. You received some of my memories, the important ones of who I am, my secrets. I have some of yours, too. It binds us."

"So will I know where you are because of this bite?"

"No. But I will always know where you are."

"So you can stalk me?"

Jin laughed. "No. But I will know where to find you if I seek you."

"Okay, then," she said, standing. "One more thing."

He frowned. "What?"

She walked up to him, removing her shirt and taking off the pants. Jin's mouth began to water, his eyes glinted.

"Tell me you wanted me. Tell me you didn't just make love to me to fulfill some need to claim a mate."

A deep rumble came from him.

"Oh, I want you. Making you my mate means no one will ever, ever take your place."

She smiled.

* * *

Twenty minutes and many loud passionate moans later, Flaxon banged on the door.

"Hey, dammit! Time to fucking go!"

He walked away but stopped to say, "And someone owes me for me bleedin' sheets!"

He stormed away, mumbling that the future High Prince needed to learn some manners.

* * *

They stood outside in the alley. Flaxon was dressed in a black suit, with a white shirt and dark shades. Adina was in Jin's shirt, with her pants fastened by safety pins. Jin wore one of Flaxon's skull-and-bones T-shirts and jeans. Flaxon stood off to the side while Adina stared at Jin with watery eyes.

She plastered on a fake smile to ask, "Are you going to be okay?"

He just watched her.

"What?" she queried.

"I'll miss you."

"Right. But you'll always know where I am, unlike me…"

"It's not the same," he whispered.

"I know. I wish we had more time to understand what we've started. I wish we had more time to…to understand why leaving you after only one night breaks my heart."

A tear fell from her eye. She rubbed it away harshly.

"I'm being so stupid," she said quickly.

"Don't ever call yourself that again," he said, stepping closer. "You are perfect. You are the most wonderful person I have ever met. Don't forget that. I won't."

Adina nodded, then taking a handful of his shirt, she pulled him and kissed him. His arms went around to hug her tightly. Then he released her and stepped away.

"We have to go," said Flaxon, turning towards his own car.

Adina headed towards it and got in. Flaxon closed the door behind her. He looked at Jin, nodded, and got into his car. He was just about to pull off when Adina threw the door open and ran to kiss Jin again. She then pulled the ribbing of his shirt down and bit his collarbone. She didn't break the skin, but left a good sized mark.

"Now we're even," she said, choking out a laugh. "Please take care of yourself."

With a tender smile, she climbed back into Flaxon's car and they pulled off. Jin left ten minutes later as planned.

* * *

Jin was sitting in his father's manor being called every kind of fool. He had better hope no one found out about his latest indiscretion, his father warned. Jin's cell phone rang.

"She's gone. Safe."

Jin smiled. He had felt in his heart and mind that she was safe, but it was nice to hear.

"Make sure it stays that way."

"Yeah sure," Flaxon responded and closed the phone.

Flaxon waited on the next flight to New York. Jin didn't know it, but Flaxon had the child of the future High Prince to protect. What Jin didn't know would make everyone involved safer.

* * *

Adina sat on the plane sipping her Coke. She didn't know what to think about her experience or Jin, but she knew in her bones that he was safe and part of him would always be with her. She would just have to take that to heart.

She closed her eyes, images of a younger Jin hiking through tall grass weaving through her mind. The image calmed her and lulled her to sleep.

* * *

Eldon stood in the solarium of his manor staring out of tinted windows. The room was filled with various ferns and flowers, two antique love seat benches and a small table with a glass globe in its center. He was still heated from the discussion with his son. There had to be a way out of this mess, but so far he hadn't come up with a plan. He knew the human had been whisked out of the country, but he had no idea where.

He sensed the vampire's approach. Fritz stepped next to the Grand Master, a vampire he was proud to have served for the past hundred years.

"What did you find?"

"Nothing much was left, sire. It seems your son removed all traces of the human's presence."

Eldon sneered. "What of the building where the humans were attacked by hellhounds?"

Fritz smiled drably.

"We did find something of interest there. It seemed that it may be the place where your son first picked up the human. Someone is asking questions, as we speak. But sire, Ten—"

"I know. Tenhar probably had the place searched thoroughly."

"Not only that. The police have been there, too."

Eldon nodded. "Of that, I am not surprised. Contact our connections with the police. They may also be of use."

He turned towards Fritz and said, "I want this human found. Do what you have to do. Money is no object, but discretion must be maintained. No one is to know that we are searching for her."

"No will know, Sire. Fredon, Cheryl, and Mikhail are on it."

"As soon as she is located—" he paused and leaned in before finishing, "—make it look like an accident. She is not to suffer, and her family will be well-compensated."

Fritz was a little shocked. "Sire?"

"Do not question me. Just do what needs to be done, and fast."

He turned away from Fritz. Knowing he had been dismissed, Fritz left.

Eldon stared out the window, shaking his head. Jin had created the worst kind of crisis and his mother was livid. She hadn't said much since his arrival. But after they left Jin to stew in his rooms, they discussed what needed to be done. Both agreed that the human had to die, even if she had saved their son's life. But Eldon would be damned if he stood by and let Jin get executed. He just hoped that when the deed was done, his son would forgive him. If he had gone to so much trouble to hide her, she probably meant something to him and her harm most definitely would not be taken well.

Part Two

The Hunting of Adina

Chapter 12

Safe

NEW YORK'S WEATHER COULD be weird in November. Some days the air stayed cool, on others it heated up dramatically. On this particular day, it was cool, but slowly warming. By 10 a.m., most people were already at work, and the streets—especially the Upper West Side's side streets—were far less crowded. Adina trudged to work, her body weighed down by fatigue. She pulled the light jacket tighter around herself, hoping it would provide a sense of security. She sighed heavily before turning the corner.

She'd been working at a clothing boutique, Haute Fashions, for two months. When she first got back from London, she went home to her parents in Kansas City, Missouri. They were as happy to see her as they were angry with her. She was only able to tolerate them for a month before getting in touch with her friend, Carol in New York City. Carol helped set her up with a job and her boss there knew some property owners who could rent to her on the cheap.

The store loomed ahead at the corner of a quiet intersection. It was a somewhat exclusive shop with a lot of high-end clients, but it still catered to locals with inexpensive knock-offs of runway items. Adina was fine with being a cashier. She wasn't interested in trying to sell anything to anyone and frankly, her fashion sense wasn't that great, anyway.

Adina opened the door slowly, not really wanting to be in the store. She maneuvered around the clothing racks and headed to the back office and employee rooms. A little nausea crept into her throat, but she swallowed it. She hadn't been feeling right for weeks, but she was too afraid to go to the free clinic and take the test that might confirm her worst fears. Yet, she knew that she had to. She was so sick last night that she barely slept. Worse, she had actually grabbed a small steak from the refrigerator and eaten it raw. The thought disgusted her now, making her stomach flop again. Taking another deep breath, she went to do her job, already counting the hours until she could leave.

Carol was back in the storeroom opening boxes of socks. She watched a sickly pale Adina walk in, looking weak as she removed her coat and hung it with shaky hands. Suddenly, Adina was doubled over.

"Dina!" Carol shouted. She rushed over.

Adina squeezed her eyes tightly, trying to hold back the nausea. Finally, it passed and she slowly stood. She leaned against Carol, sighing heavily. Then she let her friend guide her to one of the chairs in the nearby break room. Carol went to the water cooler and got a cup of water for Adina. She took it and slowly emptied it, then placed it on the table. Lifting her eyes, she caught Carol's concerned gaze. Feeling tired and a little embarrassed, she looked away.

"What's going on Adina? You've been acting strange for the past couple of weeks." Carol took a deep breath for courage, then asked, "Are you pregnant?"

Adina snapped her head towards her friend, then her eyes started to water. Turning away, she nodded quickly, then buried her face in her hands. "I think so."

Carol reached out and stroked her back. Adina let a pitiful laugh escape.

"Carol, I don't know what to do. I can't…I can't deal right now and…I just…I just don't know what to do."

Carol sat quietly for a moment then asked, "How far along are you?"

"I don't know. I haven't taken a test to prove that I really am pregnant but I haven't had a period in three months, so—"

"Adina, my God! Why…why didn't you say something?"

Adina reacted to her friend's shock.

"Say what?! There was nothing I could say. I wasn't sure and now… You just don't understand. This is not a good thing. I could—" she stopped.

How could she explain to Carol that being pregnant was tantamount to suicide? If *they* found out, she was as sure as dead. It was bad enough that she'd made love to the most incredible, powerful being she had ever met, a man she would never forget. Even now, part of her was shredding at the thought of never seeing him again.

Leaving him was so hard that two days later, she'd been ready to buy a ticket back. She was going to hunt him down and demand that he explain what he had done to have such a hold on her life. But she didn't. She'd left him with the understanding that she needed to stay hidden from those that would kill her on sight, or at least make her one of them, then kill him. It had to be done, but now, now this. And to make it worse, she could tell that this pregnancy was different…not just because she'd eaten raw steak just that morning. There was something more.

Carol shook her head.

"You're right, I don't understand. Why didn't you tell me this sooner?" Carol checked her anger. Her friend didn't need that now. Adina was clearly upset and very sick.

"You need to see a doctor," she advised.

Adina jumped up then, suddenly energized.

"Oh no! I can't! I can't go to a doctor! If they—"

Carol was looking at her like she was crazy. Adina calmed and said, "Carol, it's really complicated, okay? Trust me."

Adina had started to pace. Carol glanced at the door before whispering, "Who's the father?"

Adina froze as an image of Jin leapt into her mind. She remembered his flowing, black hair, intense green eyes, charming smile. Her breath quickened at the thought of him. Longing set into her heart, then the fear of knowing that she could never tell anyone that a man like him exists.

"No," she mumbled sadly. "I can't tell him either. His family wouldn't approve. They would do everything in their power to hurt me if I came to them with something like this."

It was a vague explanation but it was true. Trying to find Jin would be a suicide mission. She had realized that a long time ago.

Carol snorted. "Bullshit! Dina, you cannot do this alone. He should know. He has a right to know and if his family can't handle it, screw them!"

"Carol, no! You don't understand—"

Carol jumped up and closed the door. With wide eyes, she said, "I don't understand everything, but I understand this: you're scared and you need help. No, Adina, I don't know what's going on, but as your friend I will not stand by and let you suffer alone. So tell me what's keeping you from seeing a doctor or talking to the baby's father."

Adina stared for moment before turning away, blinking back tears. She couldn't tell Carol anything without endangering her, but she was right. She couldn't handle this situation alone. She was so very scared. She couldn't contact Jin because it could get them both killed. Tired, she sagged back in her seat and dropped her head on the table. She couldn't let herself freak out. A second later, she felt Carol's hand on her back.

"I didn't mean to yell, Adina. I'm just so worried about you. Look, if you won't see a doctor, let's at least get a pregnancy test and verify that you are pregnant. Then we can talk about what to do after that, okay?"

Adina looked up and nodded.

"Thanks Carol. Thanks for being a friend."

"Don't think I don't want answers, Dina. But I guess now isn't the time. In a minute, the store will be opening and the ole boss is going to wonder why we aren't on the floor yet."

She stroked Adina's hair. "Are you going to be okay?" she asked.

"Yeah," she said sullenly. "Thanks."

* * *

Adina leaned on a stool behind the cash register, trying her best to keep a smile on. Every so often, Carol would come by with a glass of water to check on her. Adina thanked God that her friend Carol was there, because she didn't think she could have managed without her. Carol had initially been annoyed at Adina's flightiness in running off to London, but she was a very forgiving friend. Adina swore to be a better friend in return.

Being a delivery day, it seemed like everyone in town had shown up to check out the latest clothes. At the end of it all, the store would be in a shambles, but the racks would be a lot thinner and the salesclerks' pockets would be a lot fatter.

Adina had just rung up a customer when a hum vibrated through her. She placed her hand over her stomach as the feeling increased. Something was setting her child on edge. She felt its fear and curiosity.

Adina was more than mildly shocked by the feeling. It seemed to be happening more often. She didn't understand it fully, but she knew enough to know that her child had grown with an ability to communicate. When she sang at home, she could sense her child's pleasure. If she was upset, she felt her child being upset with her. This morning, it had taken all her power not to talk to her stomach or let Carol see her trying to comfort her baby. She and the baby were very sensitive to each other's feelings. Right now, her child sensed something familiar. Something that it recognized... Adina was confused until a very pale woman came to the cash register and the terrifying realization hit her. There was a vampire in the store. Sensing her fear, the baby also became afraid. Adina almost hissed, but remembered not to. She tried to think of what to do and touched Jin's bite on her shoulder, pulling her shirt to make sure that it was covered.

Adina looked at the woman at the register with a faint smile. Calming herself and desperately calming her child, she inspected the vampire. The woman had long, light hair that smelled like it had just been done. She stood pretty tall, about five feet nine. She had a lean model's figure and wore a light sweater over a pale rose shirt and jeans. Her shades were probably necessary to protect her eyes from the unusual brightness of the fall sun. She wore light makeup with small earrings and a simple chain around her neck. Her nails were manicured, and on her left middle finger, she wore a ring with an intricate design on the band and amber in the center. It reminded Adina of Jin's ring. She wondered if it was a symbol for the elite of a tribe.

The woman smiled and placed several items on the counter. Adina returned the smile nervously, mumbling a greeting then busying herself with the merchandise. The whole time she worked, the woman's gaze was boring a hole through her. It felt like the baby was doing flips in her stomach, but she suppressed the sick feeling as much as possible. She couldn't give anything away.

"Are you alright?"

It was a light, friendly voice, yet Adina sensed deeper meaning to the question. Adina took a deep breath, then pressed an even bigger smile onto her face.

"Sure, thanks for asking. So, um, who helped you, if anyone?"

The woman tilted her head, then slowly took off her glasses. Her blues eyes had an unearthly glint as they scrutinized Adina's face. Adina ignored the challenge in the look, although her child wanted her to take the dare. The vampire studied her a little longer before replacing the shades. "A young woman named Carol," she finally said.

"Thank you."

Adina fought the urged to sigh in relief as she entered Carol's code. She just continued as if nothing had happened, even though she knew that something major had. She wasn't sure if she had done enough to stave off the vampire's challenge. Carefully, she folded and wrapped everything, and happily dismissed the woman.

"Thanks for coming to Haute Fashions. Please come again."

The vampire regarded her a little longer before turning and walking away. Only then did Adina release her breath and wait on the next. But when she looked up again, the vampire was staring at her. A bad feeling went through Adina.

* * *

Adina and Carol left around six and went to a diner. The store was too hectic for them to have eaten much at lunchtime, so they planned to make up for it at dinner.

But first, Carol insisted that they stop at a drugstore and buy several pregnancy tests. Adina wasn't worried about having the test confirm what she already knew; she was nervous about the vampire she had seen. What if that vampire knew that Adina could tell what she was? What if the vampire told others? The very thought of it had her scared silly, not just for herself but for Carol. She wanted to get to a place where she could see better and not have anyone creep up on them.

When they got to the diner, Adina sat with her back to wall, where she had a clear view of the window. She kept a menu in hand, but looked up every time someone outside walked past. In the meantime, she had an indescribable craving. She read the menu four times trying to figure it out. Finally, she just ordered without thinking.

"Can I have a T-bone steak, please? Very rare."

Carol stared at her friend like she had grown a third eye. After giving her own order, she leaned forward and asked, "Since when do you eat raw meat?"

Adina looked away without saying anything. Carol shook her head.

"Something is definitely off with you, Adina. I think it's time for you to tell me what the hell happened in London."

Adina snapped her head in Carol's direction. "What makes you think that something happened in London?"

"Because I know you weren't with a guy in Kansas City or you would have told me, and I know you aren't with anyone now, so the guy who knocked you up must have been in London with you. So talk, and I mean it, Adina. I can't help you if I don't know what's going on."

Adina turned away again.

"Carol, I can't. Not without placing you in the same situation that I'm in—"

"Telling me will make me pregnant?"

Adina snorted a laugh. "No. But look, you don't need to know—"

"Dammit, I do. Now come on, Adina. I swear if you don't tell me now, I will call your folks—"

"Carol!"

"No. You need help and something is obviously wrong. If you won't let me help you, maybe your parents can talk some sense into you."

Adina sighed, thinking hard.

"Okay. But you have to make me a promise. You can't breathe a word to anyone and you have to accept what I give you for answers. No questions. Okay?"

Carol thought to refuse, but she recognized the stubborn look on Adina's face. Carol had pushed as far as she could.

"Fine. What's going on?"

Adina paused for a long time. When she looked up she told Carol, without any names or too many details, what happened on that fateful night in London. She watched Carol's expression change from shock to disbelief. Finally, her face became hard.

"Adina, that's the biggest bunch of bull—"

"See? You wanted me to tell and now you don't believe me."

Adina looked around and pulled her sweater down slightly, showing Carol the distinctive bite mark between her shoulder and neck. Carol stared in horror then shook her head.

"No. No. This is crazy. There is no such thing as—"

The food arrived and they waited until the waitress left before Carol spoke again.

"—vampires. He was just some per-vert."

Carol's eyes grew large as she watched her friend pick up the plate and slurp down the blood. But what scared her even more was the weird glint that came into Adina's eye, like something wild. Carol leaned back, not believing her eyes.

Adina blinked a few times before she focused on her friend. Carol seemed a little ill. Adina grabbed her napkin and wiped her mouth, coming away with blood. She sat waiting, until the silence became unbearable.

"Sorry. I didn't mean to freak you out."

Carol just pushed her plate away. What could she say? She had just watched her friend drink blood like it was the tastiest thing in the world. She saw Adina's worried expression and realized that she needed to react in some way.

"Adina, I don't know what's up with that guy, but you need to seek some help."

Adina sagged in her seat. She knew that Carol was right, but she was helpless to do anything about it. Going to doctors would be very dangerous. They would know something was different about her pregnancy. She couldn't risk it. Her hearing faded out as Carol spoke and all Adina thought about was how far she could run before they found her and her baby.

Soon, Carol packed up her food and they left. As they walked, Carol found her voice.

"Adina, I don't know what's wrong with you, but that guy may have given you a freaky disease and—"

"I don't have a disease. I'm just pregnant with, you know..."

"There's no such thing, and if there is we need to go to the clinic and take care of it, like right now."

"No!" Adina snapped, her eyes glowing with a fierceness that made Carol back away.

A fury rose in Adina at the suggestion of taking her baby away. She knew that it was partly her child's reaction.

Carol swallowed in fear. Something had definitely affected Adina's mind. Adina would never look at her like she wanted to rip her apart. A second later, a hot tear ran down her cheek. She wiped it away quickly.

Adina's anger faded as quickly as it had arrived when she saw the tears. Sagging, she rested against the nearest building.

"I'm so sorry. I don't know what came over me. It's just the idea...God, what is wrong me! Sometimes it feels like I have no control over myself."

Carol shook her head. "Adina, whoever this guy was, he screwed you up pretty bad. We have to get you to a doctor."

"Dammit, Carol! I told you I can't!"

She pushed off the wall, wrapping her arms around herself, and started walking. A second later, Carol followed.

"Adina, do you expect me to believe this vampire story? Okay, let's say it is true. Why in the hell would you screw a vampire? They are blood-sucking, half-dead beasts!"

"Keep it down," Adina whispered. "And I told you what happened. I can't change it, okay? I just—"

Adina felt the hum again, but now it was stronger. This time she knew she was in danger. She saw several people in the distance, but none coming down the same street as Carol and her. At first, she didn't know where to focus, but then her eyes caught him. A tall, dark man with short hair, wearing a light jacket, dark jeans and boots, was just around the far corner. His eyes glinted as he stared directly at her. In that moment, she had the sick feeling of recognition. Her child was screaming as it sensed her fear.

Carol sensed her fear too, and quieted down. Carol looked around, but only saw people walking. Then she noticed a man approaching. There was something off about him.

Adina slipped her arm through Carol's, pulling her close.

"Let's cross the street," she whispered.

Carol stepped off the sidewalk with Adina right behind her. Adina walked stiffly, hoping the vampire would leave them alone. But she felt him directing his energy towards her. He was waiting for the right moment. She felt the challenge he was throwing at her. Her baby mentally screamed and Adina turned without thinking. She bared her teeth and growled with surprising fierceness.

"Adina?"

Adina blinked, realizing what she had done. When she looked back at the vampire, he had bared his teeth at her. Turning, she ran, pulling Carol with her.

"Adina!"

But Adina didn't stop. She understood what had just happened and what she needed to do.

The vampire flexed his shoulders with a smile. The hunt was about to begin. Stepping forward, he made ready to run down the human. But he sensed another vampire— a powerful one, though he couldn't discern the tribe. Just as he turned to look, he felt a sharp pain at his neck. The vampire blinked a few times before his head came off.

A six-foot tall vampire dressed in black stepped out of the shadows. His platinum blonde hair was a severe contrast. He watched the blood drain from the headless vampire. Then he reached over his left shoulder to sheath the weapon. He looked down the street to ensure that it was empty, then lifted out a small bottle from his pocket and poured its contents over the corpse. He struck a match and dropped it on the body, then stepped back and watched it burn. With one last look at the dusty remains, Flaxon walked in Adina's direction.

Chapter 13
Family Tension

ELDON, GRAND MASTER AND Prince of the Danpe Tribe, gave his wife a look of pure annoyance. Xiu, High Priestess of Hinghou, stood before him in an elegant full-length red dress. It was skintight and left one shoulder and arm exposed. Her jet-black hair was slicked back into a tight braid and coiled into a bun. Her dangling earrings shimmered every time she moved. A piece of jade set in gold hung around her neck. Her full lips were a deep red and her eyes a golden brown. At that moment, those wonderful lips (that he sometimes had the pleasure of teasing) were moving a mile a minute in a hot tirade about the upcoming council meeting.

Though a petite woman of five foot two, Xiu was not one to trifle with. She had taken down her fair share of vampires, and most knew of her ability to make a vampire know pain before dying. It was one of the reasons that Eldon respected his wife. She wasn't weak in any sense of the word, but when she was pissed, she made sure everyone else suffered. Right now, she was pissed. With good reason, though. Jin had put them both in a very difficult situation.

Eldon's son sat on the other side of the room with a blank expression. Jin's hair was also pulled into a tight braid, but he let it hang behind him. He wore a metallic dark blue shirt under a black suit jacket and black slacks. His hands were folded in his lap while his eyes followed his mother's movements. He hadn't said much to his parents in the past three months, equally annoyed with them for having kept him so ignorant about himself. Eldon had no intentions of apologizing. Jin's ignorance was for the best at the time, but not anymore.

Xiu stopped speaking to glare at her husband, but stopped short of baring her teeth. She knew that he had zoned her out. Eldon was good for that. It was bad enough that Jin had gotten them into this mess, but they didn't need to fight, not now. She watched her husband walked to the bar and pour himself a drink. His pale hand picked up the brandy glasses and extended one to her. Xiu snatched it away.

Xiu drank slowly, studying Eldon. He was wearing a light shirt and dark slacks. His dark-brown hair was slicked back and his green eyes glinted her way in amusement. *Cheeky bastard.* Her unhappiness seemed to amuse him at times. She noticed that he had a shadow on his face. *I would be forced to mate with the one vampire that can actually grow facial hair, but refuses to shave it.* She set the glass down before speaking again.

"What do you suggest we do?" she asked with a light accent.

Eldon finished his drink then said, "I don't know what we can do besides try to find a way to get Jin matched with a mate, and soon. We have tried to link the attack to Tenhar, but so far the proof is not there."

"Not there?" Xiu did bare her teeth this time. "Are you telling me we are going to let that filthy tribe get away with attacking our son and the heir to the throne?!"

Eldon counted to ten before glaring at his wife. "We cannot act outside the council, not with our little human problem that we are trying to keep covered." He spoke through his teeth to keep from yelling.

"Hmm. And why do we have that, but for your stupid guards inability to do a simple task."

"Back off, Xiu. I am *not* in the mood."

She stepped closer to him. "Well get in the mood. If we do nothing, they will see us as weak."

"And if we act without proof, we will be seen as tyrants."

They faced each other with cool expressions. A moment later, both turned and faced their son, who was standing now. Jin glared at both of them.

"Please don't stop on my account."

He walked past them and poured himself a drink. It was maddening to be treated as if he had no say in the matters before them.

Xiu stepped around her husband and faced her son. "You must know what you have done to us, to what the Elders were trying to accomplish."

"You remind me of it constantly, mother."

"And I'll keep reminding you!" she snapped, her eyes glinting harshly. "You broke the damn law, a law, by the way, that you advocated for the most! And here we are trying to diminish it and—"

"Forget it," Jin hissed, walking away. He heard his father growl and turned with hardened eyes. "We had this discussion. I will not help you kill her."

His mother joined his father and their combined glare turned the room to ice. They were unified in a way that Jin had rarely seen. When he came back home and told his father what had happened, leaving out a few key points like Adina's name, whereabouts and Flaxon's involvement, things hit the fan. His father was already pissed when Jin arrived because the tracker had already brought news of Jin's indiscretion. Then Jin came and confirmed it, refusing to tell anything about the human that had saved his life.

When his mother found out, she slapped Jin so hard that he slammed into a wall. He had never experienced his mother's strength before. If she was that powerful, he knew that he must have even more strength that they had kept hidden from him. Though he was angry, he knew better than to raise his hackles with his mother. Not just out of respect, but because he still feared his parents as much as he cared for them. Some might consider him weak, but he thought it smart. One of the first things he had learned was not to underestimate anyone—they might surprise you. Jin knew that his parents sat on a great deal of knowledge that they could use to hurt him.

But one thing he would not do was put Adina in danger. There was no way he was going to help them find and kill her. They'd said they wouldn't harm her, just hide her from vampires and protect her. But Jin was no fool. Protecting him meant more to them than the life a human.

Eldon understood Jin better than his mother did. She couldn't deal with humans unless they were spiritual leaders, but Eldon, who interacted with them regularly for business, was a little more sympathetic to Jin's feelings. Both his parents were grateful for what Adina had done. When they knew that Jin didn't buy their argument about protecting her, Xiu promised that Adina's death would be quick. Jin walked away in disgust.

They kept at him and he kept his resolve. He knew that his mother had tricks to get into his mind, but she hadn't counted on him learning to block them. When he decided to take responsibility for his life and destiny, he read all the ancient texts he could find to learn to focus his skills and mind. It took him no time to gain mastery. When his mother realized what had happened, her eyes flashed in fury. Soon thereafter, the library was off limits to him.

Jin had to find other resources then. He contacted his two closest friends, Komi and Jode, for help. They came through with more information, linking him up to the V.O.L.S. (Vampire Online Library Source) through his PDA. The V.O.L.S. was created by vampires that wanted to use the Internet without human interference or curiosity. It was double encrypted with passwords in languages that had faded from human consciousness.

From there, he gathered information about different vampire powers, skills and abilities. He also learned more about mating. He found that the bond he had created with Adina would be next to impossible to break, especially because he cared so deeply for her. Whenever feelings were involved in the Kaher Blood exchange, it meant that the bond was for a lifetime, not just for mating. Jin knew with his entire being that Adina owned him and he couldn't mate with anyone else.

What he couldn't find out was how mating with a human worked, or if it ever happened before. Nothing had been written that could help him with his connection to the human, and there was no one he could ask without giving himself away. He wanted to tell his parents, but that would only make them more relentless in their hunt for Adina. So he resolved to keep his mouth shut while he tried to figure out how to get his mate back... without bringing down the whole vampire empire.

His mother thought him a fool, but Jin wasn't. He knew what was at stake. Vampires needed to unite to insure their continued existence. Tenhar could not be allowed to lead, or it would be bad for vampires and humans alike. Not only did Tenhar have a bloodlust, but their need for power was poisonous. They were the main culprits in half of the conflicts between vampires. Something in their past was so dark that no other tribe would ally with them. But time moved on and things changed. Tenhar was no longer the hated tribe that others united against. People forget, new vampires were born, and the history was purged so that only a small elite knew the mistakes of the past. Jin wanted to change all of that and more.

He turned from his parents, sipping his drink and walking back to his seat. Their eyes followed him the whole time, but he gave nothing away. Though he longed to touch Adina's mind, to feel some connection to her, he knew that doing it around his mother would be the same as telling them where she was. He knew that she was New York, but he sensed that she was not okay. He wanted to go to her, but couldn't. He wanted to connect with her, but didn't dare. So all he could do was hope that sometime soon he'd be able to link with his lover, and find out why she was so troubled.

Jin didn't expect the pain and sadness he felt for the loss of Adina. Every day was a struggle for him to stay in London and not go to her. Every night, he scoured his mind for every memory of her. He struggled to remember her scent, shopping for products that mimicked her spicy, musk fragrance. Every day he was away from her, a part of him came undone. For the first time in his life, he *needed* someone. He needed Adina. He wanted her by his side. She was the one person that he truly trusted. If someone had told him that he would care and trust a human female more than any of his own kind, he would have laughed them from the room. He remembered the day that it hit him. The feeling he had might be *love*.

The realization made him take a breath. The feeling was so different, so unique. It made him sit and watch the sun rise in wonder. He knew nothing about the feeling of love. Love had always been taught to be a human emotion, one that vampires didn't acknowledge or need. Although he cared about his parents, he didn't *love* them. But Adina was different. It took everything in him not to attack his parents when they mentioned her death. Even now, his heart was twisting from the pain of not having her. He loved her too much to have her taken from him by anyone, even his parents.

Eldon and Xiu stared at their son with one mind. Jin wasn't telling them everything about the human that saved him. They feared that the truth would end the delicate truce of the last hundred and fifty years. Both had their agents out seeking the human, but so far they had come up empty. The time for finding the woman and controlling Jin was growing short.

Eldon walked to Jin, staring at a son who favored his mother more than him. If it weren't for his eyes, he would have sworn that Xiu had mated with another male. When he stopped in front of him, his face was hard.

"Jin, a time will come when we can't protect you. You must know that there are those that want to see you dead and end the peace your forefathers risked all to have. Do you think this human is worth all that we will lose if others find out about her?"

Jin looked directly in his father's eye and said, "Yes."

Xiu shook her head in disgust. "Jin, there is much you don't understand."

"Whose fault is that," he snapped, jumping up. "You told me only what you wanted me to know. My ignorance is a product of your choices, not mine!"

Jin flew back, crashing into his chair and tipping it over. He rolled onto his feet, baring his teeth with eyes glinting at his father. Xiu wanted to step forward, but Eldon held her back. This Jin was not the same young vampire they had known before the attack. By the way his muscles tensed, Eldon knew that his son had attained another level of power. He could feel it emanating from Jin. What he didn't feel was the fear that Jin once had of them. He was starting to come into his own, and on the subject of the human, his parents held nothing over him.

They watched their son's right hand curl into a fist and penetrate the solid stone wall with ease. He was breathing heavily, as if fighting for control. Slowly, he removed his hand and shook off the dust. When he looked at his parents again, his eyes were cool.

"I apologize for my anger," he said in an equally cool voice.

Xiu glanced at Eldon, her expression neutral though she was alarmed. Eldon's face reflected nothing as he stepped forward and placed a hand on his son's shoulder. *Time for a different approach.*

"Jin, you have great power within you. You will be the strongest of all vampires, but your one flaw is your compassion. It is our fault.

We raised you to have feelings that most vampires are taught are useless. The elders believed it would make you a better leader, one that would understand compromise, one that knew pity, one that respected all life. We were too good at our teachings. As a result, you don't see things clearly now."

Eldon stepped away.

"You're right. We have kept you ignorant, but for good reason. It was the only way to keep you from abusing the abilities you have now, and will have in the future. But maybe we miscalculated. Maybe it's is time your mother and I let you see the consequences of your decision."

Xiu and Eldon looked at each other. He nodded. After a moment, she nodded back.

"You will come to the council meeting. We have kept you from them long enough. It is time we stopped treating you like a child. It is time for you to really see your responsibilities." Xiu said. She stepped forward and placed her hand on Jin's cheek.

Jin looked from one of his parents to the other. They were hoping that he was about to see something that would persuade him that they were right about Adina.

* * *

Jin sat on his throne at the head of the table, his mouth sealed by fear. He looked around the oval at the princes/princess' and elders on the vampire council. The throne was elevated, so he had to look down at all of them. His father was on his left, his mother on his right, and the other vampires were giving him looks that ranged from envy to pure hatred.

The council had been arguing for an hour, their disputes ranging from territorial claims to the impropriety of vampires working in other locals. Some were asking for the right to kill visitors who didn't pay proper respect to the ruling Clan. Others wanted a share of the profits made in the area. It was quickly deteriorating into a crazed shouting match that was just seconds from turning physical.

Jin felt like he was about to inherit a monster. He watched his parents adeptly engineer agreements between tribes, sometimes through compromise, at other times with threats. All the while, he could feel the fragility of the peace alliance; they still hadn't gotten to the heart of the tension.

Then the Prince of the Ba'Sheeni tribe stood up. . He wore a simple light shirt and dark blazer. His skin was a dusky color, and jet black hair flowed in a wave around his face. His eyes were a golden brown. He led the pack that wanted to know when Jin would choose a mate. But first, the Elder of Hinghou wanted justice for the attack on Jin. This caused an uproar until the Tenhar Prince spoke over everyone with the question of whether their future High Prince had violated Law.

All eyes in the room turned to Jin. The issue of the human law was a still a sore one for many, as they did business with humans and had to use extra care in their dealings. Others were angry about being denied a chance to taste human blood. Jin was the main proponent of the law, so his violation would be significant. Jin knew that a lie would be just as bad as to tell the truth, so he dodged the question before his parent's could answer.

"And what makes you question my honor?" Jin kept his voice low and hard, hoping to hide his fear.

The room somehow became quieter. No one had expected to hear his voice at all, so now they were waiting to see who would survive the confrontation.

The Prince of Tenhar was dressed in his usual seventeenth century white ruffled shirt and velvet jacket. His blond hair was tied back by a ribbon. Tonight his diamond earrings were catching the light. *He's 313 years old and a conniving bastard* thought Jin. His blue eyes were cold, calculating. The heavy emerald ring on his left index finger lightly tapped the table to an unheard rhythm. He'd been on the council for one hundred years and he'd been the loudest opponent to Jin's ascension to the throne. He had objected to the peace accord for excluding certain tribes and argued that the compromise was blatantly unfair. This chance to have Jin dethroned, or at least embarrassed, was something the Tenhar Prince relished.

Lars had a nasty smile on his face. He glanced at some of his colleagues before saying, "I would never question your honor, High Prince."

"Then unless you have proof, I suggest you withhold your accusation," Jin hissed.

"It is not I who has made the accusation, Prince. It is simply what is being said," Lars replied.

Jin sat up straighter. "It is also being said that Tenhar sent the hellhounds after me, but I don't fling that rumor around as fact."

Xiu smiled wickedly, impressed by Jin's temerity. Her son was holding up quite well, considering this was his first time being around all the vultures of the council. His voice was strong and his expression gave nothing away.

After a moment of tense silence, the Prince of Ba'Sheeni stood again. His tribe was generally loyal to the Hinghou tribe, so they have been lobbying heavily to have their females presented to Jin.

"I would like to know High Prince, when you will be choosing a Mate. We all understand the delay until this point, but I no longer think caution is an issue."

Jin didn't know what to say. He was glad to have the subject changed, but this topic was no better than the last. What should he say? He hoped his parents would intervene, but their blank faces offered nothing. He was on his own. And that was the reason they brought him to the meeting in the first place, to force his hand.

He shifted in his seat. He hoped his answer would quell discussion.

Finally, he spoke. "It will be arranged in the coming weeks. My parents and I are working on the arrangement and will have set the date by the end of this weekend."

The Prince nodded, satisfied. But Lars smirked and asked, "Will all tribes get to participate or will they be 'forgotten' when the invitations are sent out."

"The nerve!" hissed Xiu. "We made it a point to pick only the finest for our son!"

"Well, since he is sitting on the throne, I assumed you will have nothing to do with this process any longer. I mean, I'm sure the Prince is anxious to begin mating. It has to be very difficult to function when in heat." Lars sneered at him. "Unless the Prince has already found a mate, in which case he can sit very calmly and preside over a council meeting."

The blood froze in Jin's veins. When he glared at Lars, he knew that Lars and Tenhar didn't just suspect, they knew he had done more than just hide a human. There was a challenge in the vampire's eyes. Jin bared a fang, licking it slowly as a sign of disrespect.

"I am calm because as an Alpha, I don't have the weaknesses of some lesser tribes, whose manners are as lacking as their skills."

Lars sneered at Jin, fire in his blue eyes. Vampires at the table began to mutter, glancing at Jin warily.

Finally Lars said, "Yes. An Alpha whose ignorance is legendary."

There were gasps at the Tenhar Prince's insolence. Jin could feel his parents' anger, but while he sat at the throne, he had to respond to the insult or appear weak.

Jin laughed. The room quieted. Even the Tenhar Prince was shocked. Then Jin leapt onto the table with imperceptible speed, landing in front of the Tenhar Prince. Jin's eyes glinted a fierce green. In that moment, eye to eye, each sensed the other's secrets.

"My ignorance of my attackers is the only thing that keeps you alive. Keep talking, and my ignorance clears," Jin said so that only the Tenhar Prince could hear him.

Lars glared at Jin as he slowly backed away. He strolled back to his seat, but didn't sit.

"Get used to me. I am the High Prince. I am the leader of *all* vampires. If you think you can challenge me, then bring it. Until that time, this meeting is adjourned."

Jin jumped down and walked out without a look back. Soon, his parents followed.

"What the hell was that display?" Eldon snapped.

"Power," said Jin.

"Power? That was a blatant challenge. You've given Tenhar more ammunition to attack your rule."

Jin studied his father before saying, "I know, Father. But I hope I also gave them enough rope to hang themselves."

Xiu and Eldon looked at each other, then looked at Jin again.

"Son, all you did was piss them off. Now it's even more imperative that we find the human."

"No, Father."

Jin headed for his quarters.

Eldon growled. Xiu just shook her head.

"Something else is wrong here. He can't be that attached to the woman. I mean, why is he protecting her so? It's almost as if—"

Xiu stopped, horrified.

"You don't think?" she asked.

Before Eldon could respond, he received a phone call. He answered his cell, and for a long time didn't speak.

"I want it taken care of now. And find out who did it!"

He snapped his phone shut, shaking in anger.

"What!"

Eldon looked at his wife. "You asked what I think. Well, I know. He mated with that human. She is pregnant."

For the first time in her 261 years, Xiu felt like she was going to faint. She stumbled to a chair.

"No," she whispered.

Eldon clenched his jaw before saying, "Oh, yes. And not only that, someone has killed Fredon."

Xiu's head snapped up. "What?! He was one of your best."

"I know. He was tracking the human when he was killed."

"Was it Tenhar? If it was them—"

Eldon shook his head. "It is not known for sure. All that is known is that someone else is out there that knows about that human. We must get her now," he said through his teeth.

"Jin will never help us," growled Xiu.

"I know. Look, I'll find out about this killer and the human. You must prepare to mitigate this damage if it does get out."

"There is only one way to do so, Eldon."

"Find another way, woman!"

Xiu flew up, stopping inches from Eldon. Their eyes glinted.

"Do not speak to me that way again," Xiu hissed.

Eldon's nostrils flared, but he backed away. Xiu then backed away.

"Fighting between us must stop until we solve this crisis," said Xiu.

"Agreed."

They went back to talking about a course of action, so lost in their discussion that they didn't notice the shadows shift and disappear. Jin walked away, his face a mix of anger and worry. His parents' spies had identified Adina, and another tribe was out there hunting her and killing off his father's people. Jin had to act. He needed help, and fast.

When he reached his room, he snatched up his phone and dialed a number that he hadn't used in three months. It no longer worked. He didn't know why he had expected anything different. He dialed another number. It rang twice.

"Komi?"

A heavily accented female voice answered. "Jin. What do you want?"

He smiled. Komi was no non-sense. "I need your help."

"That I know. You never call to talk anymore. I'll get Jode. I'm fixing a weapon."

A moment later, a deep, male voice asked, "What do you need?"

"Where are you located..."

Chapter 14

TRUST HIM?

ADINA PEEKED INTO HER apartment as if she expected something to come out. She flicked on the light switch and entered her living room. Her apartment was slightly bigger than the one she'd had in London. The only difference was the short hallway before the living room with its big windows. Immediately to the right was her kitchen, separated by an attached bar. Past her kitchen was the door to the bedroom.

The place was rent-controlled and off the beaten path, otherwise she never would have been able to afford it. Carol had helped her get some furniture and her parents helped her get the rest. She promised to go to graduate school or some school as part of the deal. She walked to her couch, a beige thing with a throw cover over the back. She tossed her bag on top of a pile of college brochures and sat. She leaned forward to calm her racing heart, subconsciously stroking her stomach.

After Adina felt that it was safe, she took the pharmacy bag from Carol and sent her the few blocks home. She wanted to stay with Adina, but Adina was adamant.

"Carol, please. It's not safe."

Carol crossed her arms. "All the more reason for me to stay with you."

Adina glared at her and said, "Look, go home. I'm fine and I'll call you with the results."

"No."

"Yes! Carol, I'm serious. I am fine and can deal with this, but right now I want to be alone. Please respect that."

Carol scrutinized Adina before finally relenting.

"I just don't understand you. I'm only trying to help."

"I know. But right now, I just want to go home and sleep, okay? Really, it's just—I'll be fine."

Carol walked away but she kept turning back to look at Adina. Adina watched her friend get to her apartment, then she went in the opposite direction to the subway station.

Adina rode different trains for an hour. Not only did she hope her tracker would lose her scent, but she just wasn't ready to go home. The truth was, she wasn't okay. She did want Carol to come over, but if there was going be trouble, she didn't want to get Carol involved. She prayed that no one would find out where Carol lived as a result of knowing her.

So by nine o'clock, she managed to find her way home, where she sat on the couch wondering what do. There was no doubt that the vampires had found her. She knew in her heart that Jin hadn't betrayed her, but she probably had betrayed herself. The vampire who had visited her in the shop must have known about her. Now she would be hunted forever. There was nowhere she could go without endangering the people she loved.

She wanted Jin. She wanted to feel his arms holding her close, telling her that everything would be alright and nothing in the world would harm her as long as he lived. Sometimes, when she was just on the edge of sleep, she could feel him touching her mind. Always, she tried to strengthen the connection, but he always pulled away. Her child also tried to connect but failed. Adina felt its sadness and confusion at being denied. The baby constantly questioned Adina for that reason. Adina just let her child feel her love and never explained. All that she knew was that wallowing in self-pity wasn't going to get the job done.

A knock at the door made her jump. Her breathing quickened when she felt it, the hum, the vibe that let her know a vampire was near. The feeling was duller than it had been before, but it was enough to frighten her. But the baby was calm, almost elated. It was as though the child connected to the vampire, like it was a familiar. Adina frowned at the thought. What was a familiar? She didn't know, but that was the term that came to mind.

The tapping came again and the child wanted her to open the door. She, however, was afraid. She didn't trust any vampires, even if her baby insisted that she trust the one outside of her door. She went to the closet and found a heavy umbrella. It might not be much help, but it made her feel better.

She backed away from the door, waiting. If she stayed quiet, maybe the vampire would think she wasn't there. *Not likely, considering you can feel its presence. It probably could at least sense her baby.*

"Let me in," said a familiar voice.

Adina tried to remember exactly where she had heard that voice before. She got close enough to shout through the door.

"Go away. I don't know who you are, but leave me alone."

The door was silent. Adina began to worry. What if the vampire knocked the door off its hinges? She backed away, still ignoring her child's pleas to open the door.

"Adina, let me in," the voice said again.

"There's no Adina here, so fuck off!"

The door banged again.

"Bloody hell, woman. I'm here to help you. Let me in!"

"Flaxon?"

It couldn't be. She hadn't seen Flaxon in months, not since he'd left her at Heathrow airport with a ticket and three hundred

American dollars. At the time, he'd seemed annoyed by working so hard for Jin. But what if it was him?

"Flaxon?" She asked again.

"Yes, now open the damn door," he growled.

Adina still hesitated. Could she trust Flaxon?

"How can I be sure?"

"I had to buy new bed sheets. As a matter of fact, I tossed the whole mattress."

Adina flushed in embarrassment. Taking a deep breath, she went to the door and looked through the peephole. She jumped at the dark eye that glinted back at her. Calming, she returned to the peephole and found Flaxon leaning on the opposite wall of her door. Adina unlocked her door. Flaxon stepped in without comment. When Adina turned from locking the door, Flaxon had disappeared.

She got to the living room and saw Flaxon's head in her refrigerator. He came up with orange juice, cold cuts, mayonnaise, and a tomato. He dumped it all on the counter and began to make himself a huge sandwich. Adina's arms fell to her sides and her mouth fell open. When Flaxon finished, he poured a tall glass of orange juice. Finally, he grabbed the sandwich and took a large bite.

Adina stomped over to him and ripped the sandwich from his hands. Flaxon stared at her, but never stopped chewing. He took a gulp of juice, then wiped his mouth with the back of his hand.

"Can I have my sandwich back?" he asked calmly.

"Since when do vampires eat?"

Flaxon arched an eyebrow. Adina noticed that it was dark brown, unlike his platinum blonde hair. Her eyes traveled to the dark roots before meeting his eyes. Then Adina did something weird. She leaned forward and inhaled Flaxon's scent deeply. When she realized how close she was to him, she jumped back, dropping the sandwich.

Flaxon's pupils dilated as understanding reached him. Adina sat on the couch patting her stomach again. He retrieved the sandwich from the counter and took another bite. *Things are more complicated,* he thought warily. He had reached her just in time.

Adina was frowning. She didn't understand what was happening to her. Being pregnant with Jin's baby was affecting her in many ways. She could sense vampires, she had a strong desire for bloody food, and she growled when she felt threatened, as if she could back up a threat against a vampire. Now Flaxon was in her apartment eating a sandwich and she is sniffing on him like she was a poodle or something.

Her breath became shallow as tears of desperation came to her eyes. She shut them tight. When she opened them, Flaxon was squatting in front of her analyzing her like a lab specimen. He reached for her face, but Adina slid to the far corner of the couch. He simply rose and sat on the couch, but not too close. She was thankful for that, because his male presence was starting to make her horny.

Flaxon watched Adina carefully. She was near the breaking point, and he had to help her until he could get her to his people. It had been a while for him, but he recognized the signs. Her baby was fully aware and soon it would be feeding on her blood. Her belly would swell and the child would be screaming for contact with its father. Flaxon had to get her to one of his midwives so they could help her through the demands of the last two months of the pregnancy. He also had to get to Jin because the baby needed him.

When it looked like Adina was more comfortable in his presence, he spoke.

"Adina, I am here to help you."

Adina shook her head. "Why are you trying to help me?"

Flaxon turned away. What could he say without scaring her silly?

"Well?"

Flaxon's lips tightened as he leaned back.

"Adina, I know you're pregnant. I know—"

Adina shook her head. "How do you know?"

Flaxon looked at her fully. "I've known the whole time. You were pregnant when you left London."

Adina sank back, watching him warily. Then she got angry.

"You knew? You knew, and said nothing to me. Does that mean Jin knew too? You both knew what he had done and said nothing. What are you trying to do to me! What's happening to me?!" Adina was downright hysterical.

Obviously not the time to share everything, he thought. Flaxon ran his hand roughly through his hair. It was his impulse to be brash, cold to everyone, but right now, he couldn't. He had to get through to Adina. He needed her to trust him, and quick. He had to get her out of town before the rest of the vampires converged on her. It was going to be hard enough to keep her safe in the apartment until the morning.

He turned and spoke in a voice that he hadn't used in over hundred years. It was a tender voice, reserved for a person from another time and place.

"Adina, I mean you no harm. Yes, I knew that you were pregnant, but Jin did not. His parents kept him too ignorant for him to have known. I, on the other hand, knew a few more things about the world."

He leaned closer to her to continue.

"I have been tracking you since you got here to make sure that you were okay. I knew that Jin's family would hunt you down because they cannot allow you to live. They need to protect Jin and the promise of peace that his reign may bring. For the factions who want to see the agreement fail, your existence would provide all the excuse they need."

Adina looked away. "I don't understand. If you knew, why didn't you tell Jin? And how could I hurt anyone? I haven't told anyone—"

"—except your friend."

"How...how do you know?"

Flaxon smirked. "I have a few tricks up my sleeve."

"But I would—"

"You would have known. No. I can control the ability of awareness. If I don't want you to know I'm around, I can hide my signature."

Adina just stared. She wouldn't have thought that was possible, but then again, what did she know? She felt Flaxon come closer and looked up.

"You didn't answer me."

Flaxon frowned.

"Why didn't you tell Jin?" she repeated.

Flaxon's jaw clenched. "Because it was too dangerous for him to know. If he knew, he would have made things worse for both of you."

"How do you mean?"

"It doesn't matter."

"It matters to me!!"

"Dammit," Flaxon swore under his breath. "Adina, he never would have left you alone, and as your mate, he shouldn't. But he needed to go home so he could deal with his family and you could escape. Jin must become High Prince. Nothing can stop that."

"Not even his own child?!"

"It's *because* you carry his child that he must become High Prince. Only then can he protect you and your child."

"How?"

"Power. As the chosen High Prince, he could order others to leave you alone. That's why I followed you."

Adina was confused. "But didn't he send you?"

"No. I came because it was my duty to protect you. Not because of him."

"Duty? Why is it your duty?"

Flaxon's eyes went unfocused. He turned away, trying to think of how much to tell her.

"There are things you don't understand, Adina, and it would take too long to explain it all." He looked back at her. "I am here because I understand what is happening to you and I want to help you through it. I'm here to make sure nothing bad happens to you. Isn't that enough?"

She laughed mirthlessly. Shaking her head she said, "No. When I met you, I saw a criminal. A bastard that treated me like a burden. In fact, you acted like you hated every minute of being with me at the airport. Jin didn't trust you one bit. I thought you two hated each other. He even had to blackmail you into helping us. How can I trust you now?"

Flaxon clenched his hands into fists before standing abruptly. He walked around the table to pace. Adina was too lost in her own thoughts to watch him. But she was finally able to ask him something in a whisper.

"What's a familiar?"

Her voice stopped Flaxon cold. He almost wondered what made her ask that before realizing that it was something she must have learned intuitively from her child. Vampire children had a basic understanding of their breed and culture, even in the womb. It was how they connected with their parents. The connection was supposed to get stronger during the pregnancy and after the birth.

Blinking slowly, he answered, "It means that we are kin. When you sniffed me, you were affirming that I was truly of your kind. At least, your baby was."

Something about what he said didn't ring completely true to Adina. She felt her child's almost complete deference to Flaxon. The only other person that would get that would be Jin, she knew. There was something about Flaxon that her child respected implicitly.

"What aren't you telling me, Flaxon?"

Flaxon turned his back, walking to the big bay window. He looked out before drawing the curtain close.

Adina stood and walked to the dining room table in front of the same window. She sat on one of the four chairs and faced his back.

"How can I trust you when you won't tell me the truth? I can tell you're keeping something from me, and if you want to help, then help by being honest with me."

"I am being honest," he whispered.

"No, you're not."

Flaxon turned and took a seat himself.

"Adina, there are some things that you are not ready to learn yet. But, there is something you must know. Jin once asked me if vampires had ever mated with humans. I said it had never happened, but that was a lie."

Anxiety was etched in Adina's face. "What...you mean that vampires have done this before?"

Flaxon nodded. "Yes. It was a long time ago...before Jin was born. One tribe in particular, Tenhar, went around jumping on anything that moved, and humans were their specialty. In less than a hundred years, they had two generations of mixed breeds running around the planet."

"What happened to them? Why doesn't Jin know about them?"

Flaxon's face hardened. "They were systematically hunted down after one of the mixed breeds started killing off vampires. To save their tribe from annihilation, Tenhar created hunters that killed the mixed breeds in what they called rebellion. They had the blessing of every tribe to do so. 'Til this day they hunt, but now it's done underground by a group whose mission is so secret that only a few vampires know about it."

Adina stared at him. "How do you know about it?"

She watched Flaxon's jaw tighten and face become even harder.

"I know because it's my job to know."

Understanding dawned on Adina's face. "You're a mixed breed," she said.

Flaxon's head snapped. "I'm not a damn mutt! I'm vampire! But because one fourth of my bloodline is pure human, I can never truly be a part of my kind." He got up and stomped away from the table. He stood in the middle of living room.

Adina sat, astonished by his confession. Then she got up and approached him slowly.

"So why do care what happens to me or my baby? It doesn't sound like you're too fond of... mixed breeds anyway."

His head turned slightly. He said, "I don't hate myself. I hate what has been done to us."

Adina's eyes widened. "There are more?"

Flaxon smirked sarcastically. "What? You thought I was the only one?"

"I don't know what to think," she admitted, shrugging.

"There are more of us. Not as many as there once were, and most are more human than vampire. But we all swore to look out for each other. And since your child is like us, that duty transfers to you."

"Oh."

"Trust me now?"

Adina rolled her eyes. She didn't know what to make of all that he said, but she knew that most of it was true. In the end, she realized that she had no choice because Flaxon's help was better than no help at all. She was being hunted, and for once she agreed with her child. Flaxon would protect her even if it was about more than his "duty." She would let him do it until she could get to Jin, and damn the consequences. She needed Jin back, but until that time, she had to play nice with Flaxon.

With a faint smile on her face, she answered, "Hell no. But I don't distrust you either."

Flaxon nodded. "Fair enough."

Chapter 15
Lustful Thoughts and Needs

JIN WALKED TO THE bathing room, a large heated pool with a sauna on the left and changing rooms on the right. He needed to relax and that was one of the few places he would have the privacy to do it. As he stripped, he reflected on the conversation with Jode.

"*I need you to get me as much information as you can about Fredon's death. Then I need you to track someone for me.*"

"*Why?*"

"*Fredon was hunting someone that I don't want harmed. He got killed by someone else, and I need to know who and why before my parents do.*"

Jode was silent for a long time before asking, "Does the tracking have something to do with the rumor that you broke law with a human?"

"*Yes.*"

Jin had already decided that he would tell Jode and Komi a little of the truth. Although he didn't trust any vampire very much, he trusted them almost completely. The three of them shared many secrets and Jin knew that neither Komi nor Jode would sell him out. Most didn't know about their closeness; they were like family. Each, then both, had been his lovers before. Though he hadn't talked much to them in twenty years, he knew that he could call them at a moment's notice, just as he would do the same for them.

"I see. And where would you like this to begin?"

"New York."

"It's done. We'll report back when we have something."

Jin took a few steps into the warm pool before diving deeply and swimming. By now, his friends were off searching for information. He hoped they would bring him a good report. He sensed that Adina was okay, but still stressed. He felt that something was calming her considerably.

During most of the meeting earlier, her fear was screaming at the edge of his consciousness, demanding his full concentration to push it back. Luckily, his mother was still too angry with him to notice, but he knew his luck could run out quick. He couldn't risk having anyone sense his connection if he was going to protect her.

He swam to the farthest corner of the pool, looking at the whole room while hiding in the shadows. He chose to keep the lights dim for that reason. He dunked himself again, then rested his arms on the edge of the pool and let his eyes slide shut.

His mind traveled. Memories of Adina filled the darkness until there was an image of her lying on the bed in his Paris condo. The gold top sheet lay discarded on the floor. Adina was in a black thong and bra, twisting as if she were having a nightmare. Jin climbed up beside her, clad only in loose pants. Something was different about her, but when he enclosed her in his arms, all he felt was contentment. He moved the hair from her face before kissing her cheek. Adina sighed and rolled over, opening her eyes to him.

"Jin, you're here."

He smiled at her. "Are you okay?"

She shook her head. "I'm so afraid, Jin. I want you here so bad."

He held her closer. "I wish I could be. You don't know how much I want to be with you."

Adina rested her cheek against his bare chest. "Why can't you come to me? I need you. I really need you."

"I know," he whispered, kissing the top of her head.

She looked up at him, their eyes meeting. A moment later, he captured her lips, kissing softly at first then with more passion. His tongue danced with hers, exploring the depths of her mouth. Adina moaned as he rolled her onto her back. Moving from her lips, he kissed her neck, licking the jugular vein, then kissed the length of her neck to find the mark he had left. He inhaled deeply and so did Adina.

Jin kissed the mark, then sucked it hard, listening to her moan. Adina's hands went into his silky hair, massaging his head as he dragged his tongue over her breasts. He pushed her breasts up to his mouth as she continued to play in his hair.

"God, I missed you Jin. I missed the way you make me feel," she sighed.

Her hands slid down his shoulders and over his chest, her short nails digging in a little. Jin's eyes glinted and a low growl formed in his throat. Then he took her lips with force, needing to feel every contour of her mouth. He brought her hands over her head and held them there until she was breathless from their kiss.

Adina watched Jin intently, then felt her arm jerk. Before she knew what was happening, Jin had her tied up. Her eyes widen in anticipation, not fear.

"Trust me?"

Adina smiled. "Yes."

Jin got off the bed, stepping out of the pants. He went around the bed, taking her legs and tying each to a post. When she was spread eagle on the bed, Jin crawled between her legs, dipping his head low and taking in her scent. He got closer to lick her inner thigh, caressing her legs. When he reached her apex, he gripped her waist. His fingers curled around her panties. He pulled, then ripped them off. He smiled seductively when he heard her gasp. He moved in with his mouth, taking her clitoris and sucking while he massaged her thighs. Slowly he moved down, licking her folds up and down. Adina's hips moved up and down with him.

Jin palmed her stomach to hold her down before inserting his tongue deep within her. He then wrapped both his arms under her thighs and locked her against his face as he ravaged her vagina, his ears perking from her cries of pleasure. Adina clasped the binding that held her wrists as her back arched. A tingling developed in her belly and spread through body and she was coming to brink of ecstasy, only to have the feeling snatched away. Her eyes had been squeezed tight, but popped open to find Jin smirking above her.

He claimed her lips again to let her taste herself. He kneaded her breast, molding with his hands until she whimpered. He lessened the pressure when he saw the pain on her face. He kissed them both before taking her right breast in his mouth, tugging and pulling at the taut nipple. Then he went to the left, encouraged by Adina's cries. Moving back up, he kissed the jugular vein, sucking it as he entered her.

Jin moved excruciatingly slow. He pulled out and pushed in hard. Adina moved her hips to meet each thrust, lifting herself off the bed. Jin growled, moving faster, holding her already bound legs open wider. Adina breathed more rapidly as pleasure consumed her and she could focus on only him. Her cries echoed and blended with his gasps.

"Adina, Adina," he chanted.

"Jin," she sang, feeling her breaking point coming near.

Jin's eyes glinted. He pushed harder into her, making her moved as much as she could and took her breath away with a searing kiss. Adina choked out a scream. Her legs and arms wanted to hold Jin tighter, but he had all the control. When he sensed that she was close again, he pulled out, leaving her panting with need.

"Jin," she begged.

Her vagina clenched with need, but Jin just lifted up and flipped her over. He lifted her up until her butt was pressed against his penis, then slid it up and down.

He bent over her and whispered, "Can I take you there?"

"Yes," she panted.

Jin inserted two fingers into her vagina, taking a little taste before gliding them over her anus. Adina gasped from the pressure of his fingers entering her. His other hand rubbed her clitoris. Adina moaned for more and Jin gave it to her. He slipped his slick penis into her anus slowly. A deep cry came from Adina, but soon the pain became a tingling pleasure. Her back curved while his arms encircled her. His fingers still worked her clitoris and vagina.

Adina mewled as she came closer to release. He pushed back then slid forward so his fingers dragged her folds. Both were moaning loudly and Jin was feeling the pressure himself. He pulled Adina's hair softly to bring her into a position that heightened the feeling, but made her concerned.

"Jin, careful."

She placed his hand over her stomach. At that moment, Jin sensed another. Someone was trying to communicate, but he hadn't heard, so focused on Adina. But now that she had drawn his attention to it, he sensed—

"Jin!"

Jin snapped out of his thoughts, but his brightened and glazed green eyes were slow to open. When they did, he saw his father in the distance.

"What?" Jin said lethargically.

His father's eyes glinted when he said, "Quit mind-fucking your human and come with me. We have to talk."

Jin glared at his father's back, but got out of the pool. He needed a moment to compose himself. As he walked, though, his father's words began to register. He just might know more about Adina than Jin wanted him to know.

＊ ＊ ＊

Flaxon could smell Adina's arousal, especially with her door open. In the background, soft music played to help her sleep. Flaxon could have lived without that drivel, but now...if only that was the least of his problems. Adina's arousal and occasional moans were driving him mad. He'd had to shift in his seat more than once, adjusting his pants as he became increasingly hard.

He walked over to the bay windows, moved the curtains, and opened the window to let in some air. He checked the street to make sure no vampires were in the vicinity. So far, so good. But it was only a matter of time.

By now, Jin's father would know that one of his best was dead and would have the rest of his warriors on the warpath, but that wasn't his concern either. Flaxon knew for a fact that Tenhar was also on the hunt for Adina. They had to avoid that tribe at all costs because they controlled quite a few clans in the States as well as the mixed-breed hunting army. If they found Adina, then Flaxon would have to call for reinforcements, exposing more of his already diminished tribe. And that was something hoped he absolutely wouldn't have to do.

He told her to get some rest and that they would talk in the morning. He avoided fighting with her all night by holding off on telling her that he was taking her out of town. He just said that he would stay with her and make sure that no one who might harm her came by. Now he wished he had just stayed in the shadows and watched from afar.

He let the curtain fall and moved away from the window. As he walked back, he passed Adina's door just when she gasped Jin's name. He paused long enough to make sure she was fine. When she didn't make another sound, he went to the kitchen.

Flaxon searched the cabinets for alcohol and came up empty. Closing the last one in disgust, he walked back to the living room and flopped on the couch. He reached over and found the remote on an end table. He flipped through the channels one time, then turned the TV off. Throwing his head back, he closed his eyes and tried to ignore Adina's spicy essence filtering through his nose.

He heard her move, but didn't sense fear so he didn't react. She was probably just going to the bathroom, he figured. But then he heard her approaching him. He opened his eyes to find her walking towards him in a tiny T-shirt and girl's boxers. He took in her round thighs, her long legs, and the curve of her hips. Her breasts were loose under the shirt and moved slightly as she approached. Adina came around the table until she was in front of him. That's when he noticed her eyes. They glinted like those of a female vampire in heat.

Flaxon sat up straighter. He watched Adina move closer to him and climb onto his lap. She lowered herself and started grinding against his thigh, making him even harder. Flaxon's eyes glinted a feral gold, but he controlled himself. There would be consequences if he touched her. Besides, Adina wasn't herself. Jin must have contacted Adina in a dream, a very sexual one, and wasn't giving her the release she sought. It usually took awhile for humans to come down from the high of the experience...especially when release didn't happen. Obviously, Adina's fantasy had been cut short. Her eyes still smoldered with desire. It didn't matter because Flaxon's huge ego would not let him sex up a woman without her knowing that it had been him and no one else.

Adina leaned forward to lick his lips and test his restraint. She palmed his thigh stroking his straining hardness through the cloth. Flaxon breathed as his eyes rolled back. Adina smiled wickedly at him, then a second later, her lips crash against his. She grabbed his face, trying to puller him closer. Her kiss was desperately hungry. Her breasts rubbed against his chest so he could feel the hardened peaks. His hands were aching to rub them until she cried out, but he kept his arms out and away from her with his hands as tight fists. Her tongue invaded his mouth when he opened it to talk to her.

It took all his control not to respond to her kiss. He couldn't just throw her off without hurting her, but if he touched her... He didn't fully trust himself to touch her. He had to let the thought repeat that she didn't want him. He had almost gained some control when she started grinding again, her wetness penetrating his pants and making his penis twitch with need. *Damn*, he shuddered. When she did it again, his hands flew up to capture her face.

"Adina, look at me," Flaxon ordered.

"I am looking at you," she said huskily.

She pushed her breasts harder against his chest. Her hands were in his hair, massaging his scalp.

"No, you're—" he growled, but couldn't finish because she kissed him again.

This time it was too much for him. His senses were in overload and demanded relief. Instinct overtook him and he kissed her back furiously, attacking her lips with the expertise of a man who lived long enough to know a few tricks. Their tongues clashed briefly as Flaxon's hands came up to grip her waist. She moved in time with him, scrambling to open his shirt.

"God, yes. I need you, Jin. Please..." she begged against his lips.

Hearing the name made Flaxon pull away. He was still breathing heavily but he sobered.

"You don't need me," he rasped, annoyed by the sound of his own voice. He had been taking advantage of her, knowing that she didn't even see him. It wasn't so much about Jin as it was the guilt that Adina would have if they had sex. And that's all it would be, because she didn't give a damn about him, and the feeling was mostly mutual. Yet, his body still pressed against her even though his mind was screaming to push her off.

Adina smiled perversely. "Yes I do. And you want me too."

She took his hand and placed it over her breast. Flaxon's breath caught. The situation got worse when she lifted her T-shirt to expose her bare chest to him. He took an eyeful of forbidden beauty. He wanted it. When she leaned forward, the tip of his tongue touched her hard nipple, making her moan softly.

Flaxon bared his teeth, growling softly before pulling her down to kiss her neck. Then his eyes landed on the mark, the symbol that she belonged to someone else. He froze. If he continued what he was doing, he would ruin all his plans, and very likely get killed. He needed to stop thinking with his dick and recognize that he was there to protect Adina and her child. Anything that compromised the ultimate goal was unacceptable. He took a deep breath, grabbed Adina by the waist, and picked her up. Then he stood and dumped her on the couch.

"No," she moaned as he tried to walk away. She went behind him and rested her face against his back while she stroked his thighs. Flaxon was panting with the desire to take her. He couldn't take much more of her touching him so intimately. He had to do something. He spun around with vampire speed, ending up in her arms. Adina tried to pull him into a kiss but he held himself ridged, arms stiff at his sides. Before she could kiss him, he jerked away.

"ADINA!"

"What!" she growled back.

"Look at ME! Who am I?"

Adina's brow furrowed. She didn't understand the question. When he was distracted, she pushed him into a chair. Flaxon barely kept himself from falling over. Seconds later, she was on him, her lips covering his, her hand ripping his shirt open to expose his hard, pale chest. She dragged her nails over his nipples while biting his lip.

The growl reverberated through Flaxon and touched Adina's fingertips. Flaxon gripped the bottom of the chair firmly. Adina kept whimpering, rolling her hips, grinding against his groin in a way that had him shaking. If he didn't stop her soon, he wouldn't be able to stop himself. The wood on the chair was cracking under his grip. *No wonder Jin couldn't keep his hands off of her*, he thought. He hadn't experienced the feeling of warm flesh against his cool body in a long time. Her smell was intoxicating, and she was beautiful, too. Her life force called him like nothing else. For the briefest moment, he envied Jin.

She licked his neck, making him quiver and whisper her name. But when her teeth grazed his flesh, his eyes flew open. He could *not* let her do that. Jin would have his head before he let that claim stick. He took her face in his hands, staring into her. There was a feral need in her eyes. But what jolted him was the child's need for her to bond with him. The child preferred its own father, but it would accept Flaxon instead. *Definitely need to get Jin here.* A second later, he heard her frustrated plea. "I need you."

"Who do you want?" he asked, leaning in closer. If she said that she needed him, he would take her, damning the consequences.

"Jin," she moaned, trying to kiss him again.

"Do I look like Jin?" he snapped, finding control through his anger.

Adina stared in confusion. Then confusion slipped away and realization set in.

"Flaxon?"

"Yes. Get the bloody hell off of me," he growled.

Adina jumped back. "Oh my...oh my god," she muttered, covering her mouth. She bumped into the coffee table. When she realized her state of undress, she ran to her clothes and pulled them on before stumbling to the couch.

"What's wrong with me?" she wailed, burying her face into a pillow.

Flaxon gathered himself. He noticed that his shirt was in tatters and pulled it off, leaving a heap on the table. He walked towards her bedroom. Behind him, she was berating herself. She must have been coming down from her high. He smelled her arousal ebbing, but his had reached a peak. He needed relief.

Just before entering her room, he said over his shoulder, "It's not your fault."

She mumbled something he didn't understand.

"What?"

"I said I can't believe this. I was dreaming about Jin and it felt so good..."

"I don't want to hear this," Flaxon muttered, placing his hand on the door frame.

"...and the next thing I know, I'm trying to have sex with you. Even now, I want to because I'm so damn horny."

Flaxon shook his head. *I swear the Prince is an idiot!*

"Then I suggest you take care of yourself," he said, stepping into her room.

She frowned at him. "Where are you going?"

He glanced over his shoulder, letting her see the golden fire in his eyes.

"To have a good wank in your shower."

Adina frowned. "Yuck."

He said nothing, but walked away. As soon as he was gone, Adina squeezed her legs together and tried to control her thoughts. She couldn't think about how Jin had felt between her legs, or the fact that she had tried to screw a vampire that he despised. But when she heard the shower come on, her mind wandered. The sound of splashing water brought about images of Flaxon's wet, taut body. The thought made her wiggle. Slowly, she rose and walked into her bedroom. Just before she reached the bathroom, she heard the smacking of wet feet, then the slamming of the bathroom door.

"Urgh," she sighed, diving onto her bed.

She climbed under the covers and tried to ignore her need. Then she closed her eyes and forced herself to sleep.

Chapter 16
Knowledge is Power?

JIN WALKED INTO HIS father's private office. The interior was light oak with white curtains over the huge window. His father's place was on seventeen acres of trees and rolling greens. The Office was on the top floor with the windows curved for a panoramic effect. The room was bright during the day, (by vampire standards) but his father loved the beauty of nature and felt the view should always be displayed.

But his desk faced the door and his back was to the window. Glass had been installed on the opposite walls so the view could be reflected. Light oak bookshelves with attached ladders filled the space from floor to ceiling. The carpet was pale and lush. The desk was the only dark fixture in the room. On it was a closed notebook, and a simple desk lamp. Everything else was filed away inside the desk.

Eldon stood by his window, gazing out at the night. His arms were behind his back and he seemed very tense. Jin stepped closer to him and after a pause, Eldon faced his son. They stared at each

other a long time before Eldon directed Jin to sit. He sat on one of
the plush chairs in front of his father's desk, struggling to control
his expression.

On his way to see his father, the most disturbing feelings
came from Adina. It felt like a very intense sexual encounter
with someone else. Then he felt her profound embarrassment.
He had a needling feeling that the "someone else" was a vampire.
He almost reached further to find out for sure, but thought of his
mother and stopped. He couldn't afford to let her get wind of his
thoughts.

Eldon stared at his son coolly. Inside, he was worried sick. Jin
was in a lot of trouble. Everyone was, because a failed assassination
attempt had created an opportunity for something worse to happen.
If this had happened to anyone else, Eldon would be in hysterics.
But it had happened to his son, and he didn't know if he could
protect him from the consequences…or stop the possible break of
the vampire allegiance.

Eldon walked over to the other chair in front of his desk. He
leaned on the back of it, breathing heavily. Finally, he glanced at
Jin.

"You mated with that human."

Jin didn't respond. It wasn't a question, but a statement of fact.

"You got a human pregnant!" his father hissed.

Jin didn't respond outwardly. Inside, he was shocked. He had
felt that something was different, but now he knew what Adina was
trying to tell him. Now he understood the feeling that someone
was close to Adina, trying to connect with him. *What have I done?*
He let her go, thinking he had made her safe, only to find out that
not only was she in danger, but she was carrying his child.

Eldon shook his head, then snapped. "Answer me!"

Jin turned coolly towards his father. Both men's eyes blazed
with fire.

"What would you like me to say? You seem to know everything."

"Don't get smart with me, boy! Do you understand what you've done? You have not only sealed your own death, but you threaten the existence of your tribes."

"Melodrama, Father? I would expect this from Mother, but not you."

His father bared his teeth, his eyes blazing in a fury that had never been directed at Jin. Seeing murder in his father's eyes made him pause.

"I'm sorry, Father," Jin said.

He knew it was a serious situation, but he was slowly beginning to understand how bad it was. Eldon just glared at his son, trying not to beat him within an inch of his life.

"You'd better be. Your mother and I have indulged your imprudence in keeping that human alive. One of my best fighters was killed, and you dare get nasty with me! You have no idea—"

Jin jumped up. "You're right! I don't! But we've had this discussion already, haven't we, Father? It benefited you to keep me ignorant, and you're pissed at me for acting in ignorance."

"Have you mated with that human?" Eldon shouted, also standing.

"Yes! I did, though it was not my intention. And I will not let her be harmed because of my ignorance. I will not let anyone hurt her or my child." Jin's eyes glinted dangerously.

Eldon held his son's gaze. The tension between them was thick. Jin sensed his father's wish that his mother was there to pick his brain. She used to be very good at it, but Jin had become better at protecting himself from prodding. He watched his father assessing him, probably trying to find out how serious he was. In his father's eyes, Jin saw doubt.

Eldon turned and went to the bookshelf on the right. He scanned the shelves until he found the right book and pulled it out. Eldon tossed the book to Jin, who caught it with one hand. The book's cover showed its age. It was leather, with strange writing etched in gold. When Jin opened it, the paper felt like a cloth. He saw a name on the page. Al-Jahir Ibn Zizi. Jin looked up in wonder. Eldon placed his hands behind his back and began to pace.

"That book is one of the few true accounts of why you exist."

"What?"

Eldon sighed. "I'm not even supposed to have it, but my Mother, like all in our tribe, took pride in truth. She couldn't bear to have all knowledge taken out of the hands of Danpe." He turned to his son. "Jin, there is a reason that knowledge is allowed to fall out of existence. Some things are just not meant to be remembered, some would argue. Even my father, who prided himself on knowing everything and anything about the world, believed this when it came to the truth contained in that book."

"What's it about?"

"What do you know of the vampire wars?"

Jin shook his head a little. "Nothing but what you told me."

"Tell me that."

Jin stared at his father, then sat. He said, "Vampires were feuding, killing each other off over a dispute that had been long forgotten. They didn't see themselves as one race with many different cultures, but still one race was bringing the end to itself. Some tribes were interacting with humans in such a barbaric fashion that they were making it unsafe for vampires everywhere. They were being hunted. So eventually, a group of elders and royals united to create a solution. The two larger tribes, Danpe and Hinghou would merge—"

"Why those two?"

Jin shrugged slightly. "Because...because those two tribes had the most affiliations."

"Tenhar didn't?"

"Tenhar refused to deal at first. So the other tribes banded against them so forcefully that they eventually fell into the fold."

"And where do you fit into this?"

"I was born to represent the union of the two tribes because I would be both and favor neither. I am to govern until death and during my tenure, I would must produce an heir whose ancestry will represent yet another tribe."

Eldon nodded. "Is that it?"

"Basically, I mean there are some little nuances that I left out. But yeah, that's it."

Eldon laughed, confusing Jin.

"What's so funny, Father?"

"Do you really believe that vague account?"

Jin leaned back in his seat.

"If you're asking if I thought there was more to the story, then I can tell you that I always thought there was. It's only logical, because so much of what happened was suppressed with almost religious zeal. I figured that the situation was darker than I was told."

"You were never curious about knowing more?"

Jin rolled his eyes. "Yes, but I figured I would learn soon enough."

His father snorted. "I see. Thought you had all the time in the world, did you?"

Jin faced the window. "Yeah. But now I realize that I don't."

"No, you don't. In fact, all of our days are numbered and that's why it is time for you to learn some hard truths."

"Truth," he said, turning his back to the window. "This ought to be interesting. How much truth are you going to tell me now, Father? Just enough to make me change my mind about my mate?"

Eldon's face was passive, then he smiled deviously. "You will know it all, then you will understand."

"Understand what?" Jin asked, looking up.

"That sometimes we have to make sacrifices, no matter how painful, for the larger picture."

"Right." Jin shook his head.

"In your hands is the truth about the past. I do not lie about that. I'll tell you most of it, but that book will give all the rest. The fact is son, you have placed us right back where we were when vampires were on the brink of annihilation."

"How?" Jin snapped.

"You're an Alpha that mated with a human. That was the beginning and the end of the old ways. That caused vampires to kill each other in droves. That union was how many vampires were killed, period."

Jin became wary. "What? You mean that vampires bred with humans before?"

"Yes, but not all vampires. Mostly just one tribe. Tenhar."

But Jin barely heard his father. He was remembering when he had asked Flaxon the same thing. "How long ago?"

"How long ago? It started well over three-hundred years ago and has never really stopped. The offspring of mixed breeds are still breeding, although it is believed that the most powerful mixed breeds are dead. The weaker ones may still be around, but no one knows for sure"

Jin's couldn't believe it. "Mixed breeds?"

Eldon sat on the edge of his desk. "Yes, that's what they were called. Jin, a long time ago, not only were there mixed breeds, but there were male and female Alphas. About four hundred years ago, the Alphas were the rulers of their respective clans, but they became more and more corrupt. Petty arguments led to unnecessary wars. They stole territory from each other, creating all types of disputes. Some Alphas treated their own like slaves, the tribe's only existing to serve them. But that would have resolved itself if the power-lusting Alphas of Tenhar hadn't started the abomination of breeding with humans, then using the offspring to fight their wars and feed their bellies."

Eldon started pacing again. Jin tracked his movement, hanging on every word.

"Tenhar in effect, tripled the size of their tribe by having mix-breed slaves. Those poor creatures were treated worse than dogs. They had no rights, no freedom, their sole purpose was to please Tenhar. Somehow, Tenhar discovered that while vampires were fertile, they could breed with humans and vampires alike. The trick was to insure that a bonding with a human never happened. That was especially easy for Tenhar, since their mating never involved strong feelings. They would bond to a vampire female, impregnate her, and create an heir. Then afterwards, while still fertile, they could copulate with humans without worry of bonding.

"This went on for many years. The Alphas condoned it, much to everyone's displeasure. After awhile, a few other tribes wanted in on that neat, little trick. Alphas from other tribes saw that they were losing resources and vampires because Tenhar had literally created a disposable army. So Alphas in other tribes ordered some from their clans to do the same, opening up harems, if you will, for that very purpose. It was outrageous what vampires did to humans so we could have the numbers to fight the stupid ego wars of the Alphas."

"I don't understand," Jin said, standing. "Why would the Alphas create such a situation?"

"Because they had been insulated for so long. They were a tribe unto themselves and we were merely their puppets. Don't get me wrong, Son. Not all of the Alphas felt that way. But they were quickly silenced when many of them turned up dead."

Jin looked at his father then looked away. He turned back and asked, "How many Alphas were there?"

"Over a hundred. They were very powerful, smart, and strong. But many were just damn evil."

"Evil," Jin snorted.

Eldon stopped pacing to face his son, a cold smile gracing his lips. "Yes. Evil. They care for nothing but the baser things in life. Most were completely drunk and corrupted by the power we gave them. Many walked around believing they were living gods. According to my father, it was a living hell."

Jin digested what his father said. Then he asked, "What about the humans?"

"The humans?"

"Yes. The Mixed Breeds."

Eldon laughed. "Ah, yes. Them. In a way, vampires owe them."

"Why?"

"There was a group of vampires that wanted to kill off those rouge Alphas. In fact, there were a few Alphas that wanted to help. They understood their true calling and were disgusted by the other Alphas. But there were only a few of them. The main problem was that too many other vampires were attached to the old ways. Although their Alphas were destroying everything we valued, they still refused to release their 'God.' Fools. But one day, an Alpha female went too far.

"Her name was Aluna. She was from the Tenhar tribe. She became so enamored with a human male that she made him a personal slave. Eventually, when she was in heat, she became pregnant by this human, angering her mate, Dracula."

"Dracula?"

Eldon nodded, "Yes. That bloody tyrant was creating havoc all over the place. His personal horde of Mixed Breeds were driving the people in Transylvania mad. Dracula threatened Aluna after she became pregnant, promising to kill her and the child. Well, Aluna didn't care, thinking she had what she wanted. That was until she found out that her human loved another. She had him and his love killed, sending his head to Dracula as a gift. My father told me that Dracula had the man's head mounted as a trophy."

Eldon sneered. "But they forgot about the mixed breed child… the son of Aluna and the human Abraham Van Helsing."

Jin froze, his eyes wide. "Van Helsing was a Mixed Breed?"

"Yes," his father said through his teeth. "And a powerful one, at that. I know you've heard the other stories. They were written by one of his human followers. The real story has faded from memory, as the myth was easier to accept than the truth.

"His mother was an Alpha and that endowed him with the strength of most vampires. He was eight when his father died, but he remembered it well and he swore revenge. Aluna didn't care about the boy. She only kept him to make her human lover happy.

But when that didn't happen, she killed the boy's father and shipped the boy off to be Dracula's slave. Dracula did unspeakable things to him before he escaped."

Eldon fell silent and Jin wondered if his father was telling the truth. He decided that he probably was. What Jin had learned was appalling. He was an Alpha, and his legacy was one of corruption, greed, and pain.

"Father—"

"Van Helsing grew up bitter and angry. He lived for his revenge and he finally got it. He killed Dracula and Aluna. He started a war, rallying the Mixed Breeds to throw off the shackles of their oppressors and fight. Many Mixed Breeds joined him by killing their masters as they slept and taking their heads.

"Certain humans were also tired of the relentless assault by tribes like Tenhar, and they got involved, too. After that war started, the Alphas fought and blamed each other for the mess they had created. All the vampires were fighting multiple enemies until many of them realized that vampires' problems were two-fold. Alphas and one particular tribe, Tenhar." Eldon paused to collect his thoughts. He hated to talk about that time, but recognized the need to do so.

"The fear of the Mixed Breeds created by Tenhar, and the outrageous behavior of the Alphas, lead to a coalition of tribes that first fought off the Alphas. Many of our kind died to get rid of those bastards. By the time it was over, only three Alpha's lived, and only because they sided with us. They were locked away in the tombs of Re'tenadom. There, they are only visited for insight and wisdom. They are part of the inner circle of wisdom and we now refer to them as The Three."

"Why?"

"Because they were the wisest, the bravest and the truest of the Alphas. They understood that for now their time had passed and we needed to rebuild our tribes in a way that would make us all accountable for our destinies. For far too long, no one checked their power. We needed to learn that treating them as gods nearly destroyed us. So they removed the temptation to ever believe that way again.

"After we took care of that, we went after Tenhar and the Mixed Breeds. We threatened to destroy Tenhar. Tenhar blamed their Alphas, saying that they'd been forced just like everyone else. It was crap, but most tribes used that excuse, so it was accepted on a condition. Tenhar was given two years to clean up and stop the Mixed Breed mess. They managed to bring the head of Van Helsing within the year. After a time they were let into the fold because they helped us hunt the Mixed Breeds down and kill them. But that didn't bring peace amongst the tribes."

"Wait. Why would you kill the Breeds? Why not deal with them?"

It seemed absurd to kill the very people that they claim provided the vampires with the initiative to try and stop the Alphas.

Eldon sighed. "It was believed that no one could negotiate with them. Especially not when Van Helsing was running around. Most vampires didn't trust Mixed Breeds, anyway. Many thought it would be easier to just 'put them out of their misery.' And we had so many other problems. There were territorial disputes and power struggles and so much more.

"For a few years, everyone tried to live peaceably. But conflicts arose and they were only resolved through fighting and assassinations. We were disjointed. Many tribes didn't know how to fend for themselves without an Alpha. It became a mess.

After a time, several elders went to the Re'Tenadom to see The Three. They didn't want to help at the start, thinking more harm than good would come of it. The delegation tried in vain for three months while things worsened."

Eldon went to his chair and sat down with a wry grin. "We were doomed to fail. What was worse, the Mixed Breeds had a new leader from Tenhar. He swore that he would protect the Mixed Breed from all of their enemies. Alonzo was a vampire of great power, intelligence, and cunning. He gave Tenhar fits, ran circles around their defenses, and generally made fools of us all. Fear that the Mixed Breeds would regain their strength caused a panic."

Jin sat down and leaned back, contemplating what he had heard. He asked, "What happened?"

"Something unexpected. Out of nowhere, the council got a message from The Three. It was addressed to all the tribes, an outlined a plan for our peaceful future. They knew that some tribes would only accept the authority of an Alpha, and other tribes wouldn't recognize anyone's authority. They told us that we needed to have a single Alpha for all Tribes. Since most tribes are derived from Danpe and Hinghou, those two houses would join to make the one. Your mother and I were required to combine our genes to create an Alpha.

"You were to be raised among all the vampires, to learn the ways of all tribes, to be taught compassion, forgiveness, the responsibility of power. You were to embody all that was good about vampires, about Alphas. Further, there was to be a council to make the laws for all vampires. All the tribes would submit to these laws and it would be your duty to see that they were followed.

"That was the main reason for your ignorance. We didn't want you to feel entitled. Many tribes raised you so that you would feel loyal to all of us, not just Danpe and Hinghou. You were taught by the finest scholars in each."

"Except Tenhar."

Eldon sneered. "Yes. Except them. They never wanted to see Alphas again. They were used to doing whatever they wanted without a leader, or a leader that was too powerful to overthrow. But the main reason they didn't want the alliance was the Mixed Breeds. The Three stated we had to bring them into the fold. We had created them and we needed to stop destroying them if they were going to stop destroying us. Tenhar seethed and they were not alone. Many tribes despised the Mixed Breeds. They were livid about the rebellion and disgusted by the idea of Mixed Breeds as equals. Worse, one of their own was leading the resurgence. No." Eldon shook his head. "They wouldn't have it."

"So how did the agreement come about?"

Eldon shrugged. "Like I said, the Mixed Breeds, rather Alonzo, helped. Vampires were tired of war and they saw an out, but Tenhar raised a valid complaint. No one wanted Mixed Breeds around. For months, the process was stalled. Elders went to The Three to beg for something different, but they insisted it had to be this way. If Mixed Breeds were not included, the peace wouldn't be sustained."

Eldon leaned closer to say, "Then Alonzo asked to come before the council. Of course, they agreed. No one was going to pass up a chance to kill the leader of the Mixed Breeds. But Alonzo was smart. He gave himself all the advantages. The meeting was held at high noon in a building and town that he knew best. He was ready for them and they knew it.

He told them he was willing to go along with the plan. He would sacrifice himself and call off any further attacks on vampires, but we had to leave the remaining Mixed Breeds alone."

Jin sat forward. "Did they take the offer?"

"There were doubts initially, with Tenhar screaming the loudest. But then we thought about it. If he complied with the plan of The Three and surrendered himself, we could convince the others to accept the rest of it. So we made an agreement. Five days later, he was executed."

"So what happened?"

"Nothing happened. The attacks stopped. For the last 136 years, the Mixed Breeds have been silent, as Alonzo promised. A new law barred anyone from revealing himself to humans, even though we still had close contact with them. Tenhar hated that. Dining on and abusing humans was their specialty, but even they complied.

"It all seemed to be working, and that's why Tenhar wants to ruin it now. They swore that you would be just like the Alphas of old. But when you didn't show any signs of malevolence, they came up with other plans. They tried and failed for a long time to corrupt the council. But the mating issue brought the politics of division back. They were able to stir up the storm again."

Jin looked away from his father. His eyes drifted to the book he had left on the desk. What he had just learned was unbelievable. Nor could he believe what it meant.

"The tribes will demand that she die, won't they?" he whispered.

"Yes, son they will. The idea of another Mixed Breed being born from an Alpha could destroy the council. The elders will fear the possibility—"

"But I would not raise my child to hate vampires! He would know that we are not an enemy—"

"Take your head out of the sand, Jin! No one likes Mixed Breeds. Many think they are born crazy. Worst, it might start that terrible cycle again. Tenhar would love nothing more than to enslave humans..."

"Then we make it against the law to do so!"

"It *is* against the law. You broke the law."

"I broke the law seeking help and she gave it. She doesn't deserve to die, nor does my child!"

"If you hadn't mated with her, maybe we could have worked something out. But Jin, there cannot be one set of laws for you and another for everyone else!"

Jin stomped to the window, shaking in frustration. Then he felt a chill in his spine. The fear was still there and getting worse. Adina was in trouble.

"Don't think about it," Eldon grumbled.

Jin stiffened. "Don't think about what?"

"I sense your connection to her. Every day, you're getting sloppier with hiding her."

Jin turned slowly. "Is that a threat?"

"No, it's a fact. It's happening because she's your mate. As her mate, you have a biological imperative to protect her and your child. Any time she is threatened, you will know."

Jin's eyes darted back and forth then he shook his head.

"I will not let any harm come to her."

Eldon rose slowly.

"Didn't you hear anything I just said? You cannot value her more than what we have at stake here! She must die!"

"No!" Jin roared.

Eldon gritted his teeth, then released a long breath. "Jin, I know you care for her. I hate that you are presented with this choice. I am not an unfeeling—"

"Oh, please! You and Mother have no concept of what I feel! You two hate each other's guts!"

"Impetuous child! Whatever your mother and I feel for each other, we are united in one thing: You are our son and we will not allow anything to happen to you. Why do you think we have stayed together this long? You are the most important thing in the world to us. We will not let you be killed!"

"Nor will I allow Adina to be killed! Father, I fought it. I fought it with all my strength. I didn't want to mate with her, but I couldn't help it. I never known anyone like her, human or vampire. I care for her, Father. And the thought of someone harming her, harming the life that grows inside her, tears me apart!" Jin's hands clenched. "I'm dying inside. Every moment I'm away from her, a part of me comes apart." Jin turned away.

Jin. Jin. Please, Jin, I need you. Jin...

He shook his head, covering his ears. Her fear throbbed in his veins. Just when he couldn't stand any more, the child called for him. Jin gasped. He lost himself in the contact, not caring if his father sensed it, too.

Refocusing, he turned around with determination in his eyes. He felt his father trying to pick his mind, but Jin protected his connection to Adina. All his father felt was her fear.

"I have to go to her. I must protect her. Father, you have to understand. She is my *mate*. I will not let her die."

Eldon shook his head and walked away. He stopped in the middle of his office, his back still turned. Finally, he turned back.

"Son, do you know what you are asking of me, of your mother?"

"Yes. I'm asking you not to treat me like a tool against a bunch of opportunistic vampires. I'm asking you to act like a father and help me. Help me protect my mate, my child."

"Jin, you have a destiny. You have responsibilities beyond your own—"

"I have responsibilities to her!" he shouted back. "If you're asking me to choose, Father, I already have. Either help me or don't."

Eldon returned to his son. "Do you think you're the only one that has suffered for this peace? Many have sacrificed for this and you would make it all for naught. You are the High Prince! You cannot gain anyone's respect when you don't respect their fears or the law!"

Jin raised his hands, stopping his father. "Fine. I'm going."

Eldon grabbed his son's arm.

"Jin, sometimes we have to lose to win."

Jin jerked away. "She will not be the sacrificial lamb in a war she did not ask to join."

"None of us asked, Jin. Do you think your mother and I choose each other? We didn't. We were locked in a room for two months until we mated. Your mother had already chosen a mate. Before they could finalize their bond, she was taken from him. I had a family. My own mate and our daughter were killed during the wars. Oh, yes, I had someone before your mother. I was almost out my heat cycle, but they found a way to keep me in it until I mated with your mother. It can be done. But our personal desires were less important to us than the good of our race. Everyone sacrificed so that you could exist! Now what are you willing to sacrifice? Or are you just like the other Alphas, your needs above all else?!"

"My needs are not about being an Alpha. I didn't ask to be born into this shit!"

"But you were. So what are you going to do, Jin? What do you expect us do?"

Jin looked away. The fact of matter was, he was the High Prince. He was head of the council. He had always known that he was born to rule. He had always felt some pressure, but now it was choking him to death. Hearing about how his parents were forced to create him only made it worse.

"Jin, if this falls apart, more than just the council will suffer. Tenhar will begin the nightmare again. They cannot be in charge because I'll tell you this now, *no one* will be safe, especially your mate."

Eldon touched his son's shoulder. "Son..."

Jin turned with sadness in his eyes. "I won't let her die, Father."

Eldon looked away.

"Please understand, I have to protect her. I promise I will try to make this work for everyone, but I need help. I swear, if she dies by your hand or mother's..." He held his father's stare. "Just don't make me choose."

Eldon dropped his hand and stepped away. His cool eyes revealed nothing, but suddenly flickered. He refocused on the sad, but determined face of his son.

"Your mother's here. I would advise you to withhold your threats."

Eldon turned for the door.

"I'm serious, Father."

"So am I," Eldon said over his shoulder.

Chapter 17
Plots and Escapes

THE PRINCE OF TENHAR sat in the blue, white, and gold lounge of his hotel penthouse. Curved windows offered a view of the city. Two over-sized armchairs, covered in dark royal blue velvet with gold silk cushions, a gold armchair, and an ivory sofa filled the space. There was pale carpet and a coffee table that allowed laptops to be hooked into it, and the wall directly in front of the sofa had a built-in television. To the left was the entrance to the common area, while bedroom doors were on both sides. Straight down a short hallway was the main door. The Prince sipped wine while he stared out the window, waiting. Surprisingly, hip hop music played softly in the background.

Lars' ears perked. He turned as the footsteps came closer to him. An olive-complexioned man came in the room. His fire-engine red hair was spiked on the top, but hung loose on the sides and back. He wore a light shirt and dark slacks. On his right ring finger, was the royal ring, which encased a dark emerald. His eyes were piercing blue, his nose narrow, and his lips unremarkable. He was six-feet tall with a lean build.

"Tobias."

"Lars." Tobias sounded distinctly American.

"Drink?"

"No." He glanced around. "You listen to rap music?"

Lars smiled lazily. "I find some of the songs express my sentiments quite accurately."

He extended the remote to turn the stereo off, then walked over to the blue armchair. "Please, have a seat."

Tobias sat in the other armchair, crossing left leg over right. Lars just stared expectantly.

"We have located her, however, there is a problem."

"Problem?"

"Someone else is after her."

Lars laughed. "Of course someone else is after her. Jin's family is trying to find the sorry little tart, too."

"No. Someone *else*. One of Eldon's best warriors was cut down—"

"So much for his best," Lars smirked.

Tobias tilted his head. "Fredon was pretty good. A vampire got the drop on him, and cut his head off before he had a chance to protect himself."

"So. Is this going to be a problem for you?"

Something about his icy tone made Tobias choose his next words carefully.

"I believe we'll handle any contingency. I just wanted to keep you informed of other forces that may be interfering."

"I see. Fine. Consider me informed. Now what of the human?"

"We have located her apartment. I have sent a few soldiers there. They should be arriving as we speak."

"They understand that I want her alive, right." Lars looked into his drink as he spoke.

"Yes, they do."

Lars looked up. "Good. Because I would hate to reduce our bloodline any further, cousin, because harm befell the human too soon."

Tobias held Lars' eye for a long time before nodding.

"Good. Now let me tell you of the council meeting and the impertinence of the so-called High Prince."

* * *

Flaxon walked the length of Adina's apartment for the seventh time. He glanced at the wall clock to see that it was after one in the morning. Rolling his eyes, he walked back over to the kitchen, opened the fridge, and took out the last of the orange juice. He ignored a glass and drank from the container, tossing the empty carton into the trash. He burped and wiped his mouth on his sleeve.

He left there and stopped in front of Adina's door, where he watched her sleep briefly. He didn't allow himself to think back to what had happened earlier. That would have been the dumbest thing he could ever do. His shirt only had the two bottom buttons left. He smiled a little. Adina could be a little harlot when she needed to.

He was so glad that she was back in bed half-asleep when he got out of the shower. He didn't bother waking her, not wanting to have a conversation about the incident. Instead, Flaxon went to the living room, put on the remains of his shirt, and sat by the window to plan his next move. He had to get Adina out of the city soon, but when? If he left too early, there might still be a vamp walking around. He had no desire to be caught in New York City traffic, either. He decided that before sunrise would be good.

Clear in that decision, Flaxon's thoughts moved to Adina and her child. The baby was aware. He was surprised that it wasn't already draining the life from her. He knew that until he found Jin, he would need to get her enough blood to sustain her and the baby. Her child would not know that its need to drink from her could kill her. Flaxon sighed heavily. Vampire pregnancies were hard on humans. The gestation was shorter, but the vampire needs could be devastating to human females. The baby demanded both food and blood. The problem was that the mother's blood loss could be so great that she became too tired to get the food, then she needed her mate to watch over her. Flaxon had found someone to watch over her, but she still needed Jin's blood.

Jin would be the first pure vampire to father a child with a human in over a hundred and fifty years. The thought both amazed and vexed Flaxon. He was amazed because he thought it would never happen again, but he was pissed because of what it meant for his kind and for Adina. She and her child would forever be hunted. Fear and hatred of Mixed Breeds would only grow with the birth of an Alpha's mixed child.

Flaxon just hoped that his plan worked. He hoped that his faith in the High Prince paid off, because he couldn't afford a repeat of the past. Flaxon never thought he would see the day that he would try to bond with anyone from the family that had destroyed his.

He flushed with anger, remembering his family, especially his father. He had sacrificed everything to protect his kind and ended up dying in vain. They were still being hunted, and their numbers were still shrinking. Tears came to his eyes. He exhaled slowly, trying to find his equilibrium. It was easy for him the fall into despair when he thought about the past.

The past was the reason he changed his image so often. The more he changed himself, the more distant the past became, as if all the tragedies were suffered by someone else. He gritted his teeth to exhale again. A short time later, the person he had become, Flaxon was in control. He couldn't afford to indulge in moments of pity. It had been a long time, and he wasn't the only one who had lost. Everyone in his tribe had stories of tragedy and loss. They needed him to guarantee that it wasn't all for nothing.

After sitting for an uncomfortably long time, he paced, checking on Adina from time to time. It was after three, and soon he would wake her up to leave. He was already dreading the argument that would surely come. The woman was a force to be reckoned with when she was angry or annoyed. He left her room, trying to relax the sore muscles in his neck. He began to shake out his shoulders and froze. His eyes glinted as his lips curled, baring his fangs. *Vampires...*

Tenhar tribe. He would know that hum anywhere. Thankfully, he had been masking his, a trick he learn from an old vampire, Beven. The secret guard had killed Beven more than thirty years ago.

Slowly, he walked to the kitchen and picked up his sword from the other side of the bar. He unsheathed it before creeping to Adina's door, only to find that she was up. She stared at him with wide eyes. Her child must have sensed the vampires, too. *Fascinating. Jin's blood must be powerful for the child to have that type of awareness. Most mixed breed children aren't that aware from the womb.* She stepped forward until she saw the blade. The fear went through her like a jolt of electricity.

"Go back into the room, get some clothes on, and get whatever you're taking. We're leaving."

"What? Why? Who's out there?" Her voice quivered.

Flaxon's head snapped. "Do what I say. Get your ass in gear and be ready to go when I say."

Adina started to protest, but didn't.

"Go!" he hissed.

Adina flitted back to her room, where moonlight was coming through the small window. She struggled into some jogging pants and a sweatshirt and grabbed the familiar backpack from the closet. She snatched up a couple of shirts, some jeans, and nervously opened the dresser as quietly as she could. She took out some socks, some underwear, and jewelry that her mother had given her from the first drawer. From the second one, she pulled the sweater Jin had worn in London. Her hand was on some photos when she heard glass break. She stumbled in fear. She could feel her baby having fits, its fear elevated too. She crouched low by her bed, pressing herself into the shadow. She never liked her bedroom because it had only one small window; now she wished it had none. Adina closed her eyes to calm herself and her child.

Flaxon pressed himself into the shadows when he heard the door open. It was easy to do with the lights off. He lowered his blade so that the moonlight wouldn't reflect. He kept his eyes close and his ears opened. A moment later two elite guards of the secret sect, Uriklo, were in Adina's apartment.

The women, Tia and Mia, moved stealthily towards Adina's bedroom. Both were dressed in black shirts, pants and boots. The blonde's hair was in a single braid and the brunette had her hair short. Flaxon identified them as the Night and Day girls. He had named them that forty years ago in Germany, the first time he saw them fight. They managed to kill two of his foot soldiers. He wanted to take their heads off, but had to get the others to safety.

Mia, the brunette stopped moving. Something was off. She couldn't be sure, but it felt like something was missing. A hand gesture stopped Tia cold. Tia gave a questioning look, but Mia shook her head. Tia stepped back to Mia's side.

"What's the problem?" she whispered, her voice like a feather in the wind.

"Someone or something else is here."

Mia's searched but saw only shadows.

"Who?"

"I don't know, but I tell you something is not right."

Tia had learned long ago to trust Mia's instincts. Slowly, they drew their blades and walked towards Adina's bedroom.

Mia's eye just caught the shift of the shadow just when the blade came across her neck. The only sound was that of her body collapsing into a glass vase. Tia spun her blade around in time to catch Flaxon's. Her eyes widened in white, hot anger. Her teeth bared as she sniffed. She knew what he was.

"Mongrel shit. You'll pay for what you've done."

He allowed himself to come into focus. The nasty grin on his face was enough to set Tia off, but she held her anger. She sensed his power and knew he would not be an easy kill.

They circled each other, blades still touching. This was the closest he had ever seen her. She was deathly pale with eyes a cool blue-green. Her nose was very sharp and her lips a thin line that might just be reflecting the tension of the moment. She was almost as tall as him, lean, but clearly muscular. She sometimes darted forward with superhuman speed, but he matched every move. It made her growl in annoyance. Finally, they both stopped, just waiting.

Flaxon moved first. He kicked Mia's headless body, provoking Tia's scream. She swung her blade, but he knocked it away, spinning and sending his elbow into her chin. She stumbled but recovered in time to block his next attack. She swung left, he swung right, the blades clashing loudly. Flaxon did a sweeping swing that she dodged by swinging her blade low. He leaped back, but he still got cut across his stomach. He growled as Tia laughed.

"Bleed, you Beast! I intend to see you bleed to death before I take your head!"

Flaxon moved into his attack stance, his left leg slightly before the right. The blade was drawn up on his right side, waiting for her. Hers was above her head, but she brought it down. Flaxon crashed his blade into her, knocking it to the left. Drawing his back slightly, then pushing forward, he punctured her throat. Tia froze. Before her shock registered, Flaxon jerked out his blade and swung to take off her head off. She crumbled to the floor. After a deep breath, Flaxon looked up to find a horrified Adina at the door. He studied her before lowering his blade.

"Ready?" he asked.

Her big eyes stared at him. When she first heard the voices, she had moved to the door and watched the end of the fight. Flaxon was cool when the vampire's head came off, though she freaked out. She couldn't move her feet, watching him lay his blade on her dining room table. He shrugged on his jacket, picked up the blade, and winced when he bent to retrieve the sheath. When he stood again, he waited for Adina.

"Well, come on. Others will come."

Shaking her head, she silently begged Jin to help her. For a moment, she felt him.

"Move your arse! We don't have much time!"

She jumped at the harsh sound of his voice but came out with her backpack. She had no choice; it wasn't like she could protect herself if more did come. When she was beside Flaxon, he practically dragged her from the apartment to the elevator.

"Shouldn't...shouldn't we take the steps," she stuttered.

"No. It's faster this way, and they wouldn't expect us to be so bold."

"You mean stupid," she said softly.

He sneered.

When the elevator reached the bottom floor, he moved her behind him. Adina stood against the wall, shaking. *Adina, you did it again. You're in it deep, girl. Real deep.*

The doors opened and he waited before stepping out, ducking as a sword just missed his head. He rolled out onto his feet, raising his blade to block the next blow. The vampire knocked Flaxon back with a kick in the stomach. The other vampire was a male with reddish hair and dark eyes. His black outfit was similar to that of the Night and Day Girls. He didn't recognize him, but in a second it wouldn't matter.

Flaxon dropped to one knee, swinging out his blade. The vampire brought his down to parry Flaxon's. The vampire then lifted his blade, pushing it forward to stab Flaxon in the heart. But Flaxon blocked and counterattacked by moving his blade forward, grazing the vampire's side. The vampire hissed angrily, his blade clashing with Flaxon's again as they engaged in a test of wills. Both strained to hold their ground.

The vampire was pushing Flaxon's blade closer to the top of his head when he stumbled. Flaxon jumped up and brought his blade down on the vampire's neck, taking off his head. He held his pose a moment, then watched Adina put the strap back on her shoulder, having just swung the bag. Seeing Flaxon's glare, she swallowed.

"Who told you to move?"

"I was just...just helping," she said.

"I don't need your help," he snapped.

Adina's lips tightened. "Fine, then. I'll act like the helpless damsel so your balls won't shrivel up."

Flaxon glared at her before switching the blade into his left hand, his right taking hers.

"Let's see if your fat arse can keep up," he muttered.

"Wh...asshole," she whispered at him.

They walked slowly towards the exit, with Flaxon surveying the area. He flicked blood off of his blade then sheath it his side.

"What are you waiting for?" she whispered. "There's no one out—"

He turned his head, his cool gaze quieting her. "I'm sure you think that your new ability to sense vampires is far superior to my skills." He dropped her hand. "Why don't you go out there? Tell me what you see."

Adina took a step back. "That's okay."

"Then shut your gob, human, so I can concentrate."

Adina had grown tired of his nasty remarks. She didn't understand why he was so pissy. All she had done was try to help. He looked like he couldn't sustain the power to block the vampire's blade. She felt she should help so she used her bag and swung hard. The vampire was so focused on Flaxon that he didn't know what hit him until it was too late.

Now Flaxon was acting like the world's biggest asshole over it. She almost wanted to tell him to screw off. But when he grabbed her hand again, she didn't fight him. As much as she hated to admit it, she felt secure with him. If she couldn't have Jin's help, Flaxon would do...until she could figure out just how screwed she was.

He pulled her out and turned left. Adina almost had to jog to match Flaxon's pace. Suddenly, he pulled her up the stairs of a building with a small alcove. He pushed her against the wall in the darkest corner and pressed the length of his body against hers. Adina was confused until she felt it. The hum in her veins that meant another vampire was near. It made her press herself tighter against the wall.

Flaxon stood over her, quietly looking into the street. Adina couldn't see anything, but she could hear. A car was coming. She heard a grinding as the car slowed, then rolled on. Still, Flaxon didn't move. After a long time, he faced her. They held each other's eyes for a long time. Then he raised an eyebrow, looking down, then up at her. She realized that she was gripping his shirt. She released it, slightly embarrassed, and then fully when she saw his smirk. He raised his finger to his lips to hush her.

He stepped back. She started to follow, but he stopped her with his hand. Adina went back to wait in the corner. She watched Flaxon take out his sword and slowly descend the stairs. He looked both ways before waving her to come with him. As she stepped into the moonlight, she noticed a sticky substance on her hands.

Adina gasped. It was blood! Flaxon was frowning at her. He stared at her raised hands before reaching up and taking the left one. They walked briskly down the street. At the first corner, he looked both ways, then they raced across the street. They crossed diagonally towards a sleek black sports car with tinted windows. Flaxon took keys out of his back pants pocket. He pressed a button to unlock the doors, directing Adina to the other side. She scrambled into the car and closed the door quickly. Flaxon tossed his blade on the back seat, then kicked the ignition and made a U-turn.

They drove in silence for twenty minutes, Flaxon glancing at his rear view mirror, then over at Adina. She just stared down at her hands, saying nothing. He knew that something was off with her, but he wasn't sure what.

"You okay, eh?"

Adina swallowed, breathing slowly. Then she whispered. "Are you okay?"

He wasn't okay, but he wasn't bad either. The cut wasn't that deep, but it stung like hell. It had stopped bleeding a while ago, mostly because his shirt sealed it as the blood dried.

"I'm fine..."

"This is your blood?" she asked, raising a blood-glazed hand.

The concern in her eyes made an unexpected flutter go through him.

"Don't worry about me. Answer my question. Are you okay?"

She nodded faintly. "Yeah. Just tired, scared..." Her bottom lip quivered. She took a deep breath. "They were coming to kill me weren't they?"

Flaxon gripped the steering wheel a little tighter. "I don't think so."

"Really?" she said, hopefully. Then she frowned. "So why were they there?"

Flaxon shifted, saying nothing.

"Flaxon," Adina's voice hardened. "Flaxon, tell me why they were there."

He stopped for a light, still looking forward.

"Flaxon!"

He glanced at her briefly before moving the car forward. Her anger was mixed with fear. He was about to speak when she cut him off.

"This is my life. I have a right to know what the hell is happening," she snapped.

Flaxon chuckled. "Right, that's a good one. You lost your bloody rights when you screwed the High Prince."

Adina started to slap him, but he caught her hand. He gripped for a moment before tossing it back.

"You're a bastard," she spat.

"Yeah, maybe I am. But the fact of matter is, there are vampires that want you dead."

"Fine! But what about the ones that came into my apartment!"

He growled at her and Adina felt herself shrink. Then she realized that it was her child. She must have broken a vampire rule or something. Whatever it was, her child seemed to want her to defer. Tears were forming in her eyes. She was tired, just physically and mentally worn out. She didn't have the energy to keep fighting Flaxon. Adina wanted the truth but Flaxon was determined not to give it. She wished again that Jin was there. At least he would answer her questions. Leaning back in the seat, she stared out, watching the traffic roll by.

"Those vampires in your apartment were Tenhar. I don't think they were there to kill you, though." Flaxon said.

"Why?"

Her voice was tired too, like she carried the weight of the world on her shoulders.

"It's just something I feel. When you spend most of your life outrunning your enemies, you learn to trust your gut."

"Whatever," she mumbled.

They both fell silent. After a while, Flaxon looked over and found her sleeping. He reached over, caressed her cheek, and moved her hair behind her ear. His hand dropped to lightly glide down her arm, then touch her stomach. He felt her child reach out to him.

"You have to get your mother to trust me, little one. I promise I will protect you both." He frowned, then answered, "I will find him. I will bring him to you soon. You just have to trust me. Just try to have faith in me."

"I'll try," Adina whispered.

Flaxon's surprised gaze caught her sleepy one. Adina put her hand place over his before letting her eyes close again. He could feel her child resting, too. He felt emotions deep within that he hadn't felt for over a hundred years. And though he knew he shouldn't, he relished the feeling.

Chapter 18

Compromises

JIN STOOD THE SITTING room, where his father was no doubt relaying their conversation to his mother. *Keep your threats to yourself.* The words played over and over again in Jin's head. When he told his father that he didn't want to choose between Adina and them, implying that his parents would lose, the expression on his father's face tore at him. It was the first time he thought that maybe his father did care about him and that his opinion mattered. It was a confusing situation.

Vampires just didn't deal in emotions very much, and then not very well. Most of the time, they were one of three things: angry, bored or amused. Lust was something different entirely. Outside of the main three, everything else was pure nonsense. Yet, Jin felt that his statements hurt his father. Even more surprisingly, he wanted to protect his mother from hearing the threat.

His father must have known that Jin's words would hurt her. Eldon was threatening Jin when he told him not to threaten his mother. In spite everything negative that they had to say about each other, his father really did care about his mother. The idea amazed him, but it gave him a glimmer of hope. If his father could care for and be loyal to his mother, maybe he could be convinced to respect Jin's feelings for Adina. Maybe there was a solution—though Jin doubted it. When it came to vampire politics and the future of the race, it appeared that his father was immovable.

Just before he arrived, his cell phone rang. He excused himself and his father told him he had two minutes. Jin planned to make them count.

"You arrive yet?"

"We just made it," said Komi.

"She has an apartment. I think it's on the upper West side, maybe further north, I believe on 198th Street," Jin whispered.

"We'll find it and have a report to you in an hour."

"Hurry, she was frightened out of her mind. Something has happened."

"Don't worry. We'll be there soon."

"Don't approach her. She won't trust you. Just call me and let me know she's okay."

"All this fuss over a human," Komi laughed.

"A human that belongs to me," he growled.

Komi was silent. "I understand. One hour, two, tops."

"Thank you. I owe you."

"Only the truth when it is all said and done."

Jin snapped the phone closed. Though he wanted to reach for Adina, he decided not to tempt his mother to try and pick his skull. He opened the door to find his mother sitting, with his father standing behind her. Jin walked across the room and stood before them.

Xiu gazed at her son, amazed that she and Eldon had created such a magnificent being in spite of not wanting the pairing. Eldon had told her what had happened. As angry as she was, she admired Jin's determination. He was going to honor his mate and what she had done to save his life by saving hers. She felt Eldon's hand on her shoulder and touched his fingertips. She sensed his anger, his pain and even deeper pride for his son. But she also felt their shared fear that they might lose their son.

Eldon didn't tell Xiu about Jin's threat. He didn't think she needed to know that he valued the human more than them. Besides, she got the point. Jin was determined to save the human and her child. They had to come up with a way to avoid disaster. He felt his mate's touch and brushed her fingers before waving Jin to a seat. He watched his son walk to a chair, sit down, and wait.

"Your father tells me not only do you refuse to help us track this human, but you plan to find her yourself."

"Yes."

"Jin! You cannot do this! Several vampires already seek your death. You will be targeted! You will be tracked!"

"I'm not as helpless as you both think."

Xiu snorted. "This isn't about helplessness. You not only endanger yourself, but that so-called mate of yours. Your father and I are not the only ones who seek her. Other forces hunt her."

"Fine. That does not change my decision."

Xiu threw her hands up, glancing at Eldon. He just stared at Jin. When she realized that Eldon wasn't going to say a word, she turned back to Jin.

"Do you not understand what hell you bring on us by chasing after this trash—"

Jin's fangs elongated. Xiu's glinted in return.

She stopped Eldon from approaching Jin. The room was tense for several seconds, then Jin calmed and bowed his head. Xiu stood and walked over to her son. When Jin looked up, he was slapped soundly across the face. His jaw clenched, but he didn't react any further.

"What is *wrong* with you? Do you not understand that your life is more important than that human! Didn't your father impress upon you the danger we are all in with her running around? Don't you know that if the human is caught by the wrong people…it will cause an uproar that you cannot imagine."

"That's why I must protect her." Jin whispered.

"No, that's why you should tell us where she is so that we can—"

"Don't."

"Don't what?" she asked

Jin stood. "Don't say it. That is not an option."

"Yes, your *mate* is more important than anything else," Xiu snarled.

Jin flexed his hands.

"There is no point to this discussion. You want to let my mate and my child die so I can be a symbol for a peace that doesn't really exist. Well, that's not going to happen. I will *not* give her up for you, or any other vampire."

Eldon stood rigid as Xiu spun around to glare at him. Eldon closed his eyes before nodding faintly. Taking a deep breath that she didn't need, she faced her son again.

"Do you understand that you are High Prince, the Alpha to lead us all?"

"Yes, Mother. I know."

"Then how do you plan to explain breaking the law and keeping this human alive?"

Jin was silent. He had no idea how to broach the issue. His main concern was his Adina. He knew that it was irresponsible of him not to consider everything else, but he could only think about getting back to her.

"You talk a lot about duty and obligation, but you reserve it only for your mate. Damn the rest, my human's in pain. Never mind the hell that will be unleashed when the tribes find out what you did. No matter the consequences of you failing to fulfill your mating duties...duties that were agreed upon over a century ago. Forget that Tenhar is itching to start a war to impose its tyrannical will. Your needs before all others!" she shouted.

Jin shook his head. "I wouldn't be in this mess if it weren't for Tenhar and I wouldn't be here if it weren't for her. She kept me alive when my *vampire* bodyguards *failed*." Jin saw his father's eyes glint.

Xiu stared at her son a moment. She turned away from him as she said, "We cannot allow all the sacrifices of the past to be torn asunder by you're mating—however it happened. Since you are determined to keep this human, you must do whatever it takes to protect what we have built." She faced him then. "Eldon tells me you want our help. What will you do in return?"

Jin's eyes shifted. It didn't bode well for him when his mother was willing to bend.

"What do you want from me?"

Xiu lifted a vial of dark rose liquid. Jin's father wouldn't look at it, his jaw tightening.

"What is that?"

Xiu walked slowly to her son. "The tribes will not accept a human for your mate. It was agreed that you mate with another vampire tribe. This liquid will make that possible."

Jin frowned. "What do you mean?"

"Once you drink this, it will break the bond you have with that human..."

Jin shook his head. "No. No, No..."

"Yes," his mother hissed. "Time for you to grow up, Jin. If you want our help, you will honor our sacrifices to maintain the peace, and help us thwart Tenhar's plans."

"You expect me to take this? You think I will? No way!"

"What? Afraid that the human won't be important to you anymore?"

Jin glared at his mother evil smirk.

"No, Mother."

"You *will* take this Jin. You have a responsibility to something beyond yourself. This liquid will make it possible for you to bond with a vampire, impregnate her, and bring up a new heir."

"And what of my true mate? Do I just forget about her and our child?"

Jin caught her looking at Eldon.

"Why are you looking at Father?"

"Because he knows how it works."

Understanding dawned on Jin. The liquid had been used on him. He looked down a second, then looked up. He was about to speak when his phone vibrated. It couldn't be anybody but Komi and Jode. He didn't take the call.

Eldon gazed at his son for long moment before speaking.

"This will not permanently bond you. It is something that Tenhar has used quite a lot. It just makes it possible for you to breed. You will be able to create a child with a female vampire and move on."

"But didn't you and mother—"

Eldon and Xiu shared a look before Xiu said, "There are still many things you don't understand, Jin. The bonds are formed to insure the survival of the child, or in rare cases, children. Most mated couples don't stay together beyond a certain period and many let the tribe raise the child. But if you are truly connected to this human, nothing can permanently break the link. Maybe you need to determine whether you actually care for this human, or if it's just the mating instinct."

Jin already knew the answer, but he wasn't about to share it with his mother. His father caught his eye, though. Jin knew his father sensed his true feelings. His eyes clouded for a moment, then cleared. He walked to Jin with a stern face.

"You will do this and we will call our people off. We will help build the leverage to protect her. The original agreement stated that Mixed Breeds had to be included. If you take a vampire mate, we, meaning you, may be able to work a deal."

"Me?" Jin asked.

"You are High Prince. We take some responsibility, but you still chose to break law. You have to explain yourself, make people understand your intentions. Let them see that you are fit to rule. We can only set the stage, you have to perform."

Jin stared passively at his parents, though he was stunned. They would help him. Not in the way that he hoped, but it was still help.

Not only that, they had ceded all power to him. They had set him free to face the consequences of his decisions. He could either swim or sink.

"Fine." He turned to go.

"Where are you going?" asked a confused Xiu.

"To secure and protect my mate."

"And what of your duties as High Prince?" Her face was stern as her question.

Jin stiffened. He faced his parents again. "I will do it."

Xiu almost smiled. "Well then let me—"

"—But not now."

She froze, annoyed. "Then when will it happen?"

"After I check on my true mate, make sure that she and our child are safe. When I return, I will take that drink and mate with whomever you choose."

"How long will you be gone?"

However long it takes. "How long do I have?"

Xiu glanced at Eldon before saying, "Two weeks."

"How long does it take for the solution to work?" he whispered sadly.

Xiu waited for Eldon. "It depends on the vampires involved. It could take a day or it could take a month. You're at the height of fertility, so it will be quick," he said.

"Why?" she asked Jin.

"I just wanted to know. Two weeks, then." He felt dead inside. "Before the mating, I want to meet with the council. A few things need to be done before I mate again." *Like demanding that Adina and my child are protected and recognized as part of my clan.*

"It will be arranged," she said. Then Xiu and Eldon did something Jin didn't expect. They bowed to him. "High Prince."

Jin nodded back, and left.

"You have your people in place, Eldon?"

"Yes." He turned to her. "We will find out who else is after her."

"Make sure your people don't expose themselves."

"You just do your part, and I'll do mine."

They stare at each other, then Eldon leaned in to kiss Xiu passionately, surprising her. When he pulled back, he smirked at her flustered form.

"About time you found some maternal instinct."

"That was about survival."

"Sure it was," he said over his shoulder.

She sneered, touching her lips. *Cheeky Bastard.* Then she left as well.

Chapter 19
Strange Discovery

HE'S STILL ISN'T ANSWERING."

Jode glanced at Komi. "He will call."

"Hmm."

She flipped the phone shut.

Komi and Jode took a plane from Chicago after completing one of their projects. They flew in their small Cessna plane, a Citation XII, making record timing to New York. From the airport, they rented a car and drove into the city. Komi called Jin to let them know they were in town and he told them where they should go. Then Komi got in touch with an underground vampire network to find out the word on the street. The best sources came from the Kantal Tribe, who was similar to the Pinu. They knew very little about Fredon. The only story was that someone had gotten the drop on him and burned the body. They only identified him by his ring. But they also learned that vampires were hunting a human in the same location that Jin had given. The rest was up to them.

Komi was a sensitive. Her skill was legendary, even for her tribe, the Asanti. She had the ability to sense a vampire long after it had gone. Her eyes were hyper-sharp; she could see sharply for three miles without any devices. Her sense of smell was even more advanced than most vampires, letting her pick up a scent of blood that was two weeks old. To top it all off, she was a skilled fighter and killer. As a result, she had become an enforcer for hire. She worked primarily for her tribe, but others had used her, too. Komi was an ebony hue that was smooth as midnight. Her hair was cut close and her large brown eyes were bright. For her prey, her broad smile was their last earthly vision.

Jode, her partner, was a natural tracker from the Jufu Tribe. His skin was the color of sand, his hair coal-black. His eyes were darker than Komi's, a deep, soulless black. Once he had a vampire's scent, he could track him for years. The prey could only hope to outrun Jode. He spoke only when necessary. Also a skilled fighter, he specialized in ammunition.

Komi and Jode had been partners for over eighty years. The Jufu and Asanti tribes had always collaborated and traded with each other. They met as children when their respective families came to a celebration of an Asanti Elder's birthday. They started as fierce competitors but became partners when they recognized how well they complemented each other. Soon, they would both be in heat and everyone expected them to mate. They wouldn't believe anyone else was fit for the purpose.

They were only obligated to each other until Jin came along. He was the only one to ever disrupt their partnership. It caused a lot of tension, but it was resolved when Jin decided to be their friends instead of lovers. Over time, the three were nearly inseparable. Jin would tag along with them on many of the non-killing adventures. He backed them up, protecting them. He claimed that he would make them his personal bodyguards. Neither Jode nor Komi believed him. They knew his parents would put the thought out of his mind, but the idea made them happy. Then one day it all ended. Jin had to go away, and the threesome was back down to two.

Hearing from Jin again was a shock. They learned through the grapevine that Jin's abrupt departure was his parents' doing. Later, they found out that he was in heat and about to ascend to his seat of power. They didn't expect to hear from him again—what would the High Prince need with two vampire mercenaries from two inconsequential tribes? Yet, when they got his call, they knew they would help. The High Prince enamored both and he was a good friend as well.

On the way to the human's location, both contemplated what was driving Jin to seek her. It had to be more than just having been rescued by her, which Komi found hard to believe. Jin had broken the law, and with good reason. His current actions, however, made no sense. He should have just left her alone, but he insisted that they check on her.

Now hearing about all the activity, they wondered what was really going on with Jin and the human. How tangled was the web? Would they get caught in an inescapable snare?

"Are we close?"

Jode nodded.

They arrived twenty minutes later at 198th Street. Jode parked the car off of Broadway and 198th. They got out, both dressed like ordinary citizens of New York. Jode wore dark jeans, a dark pullover shirt, and dark boots. Komi wore a dark tank, mini skirt, a long trench coat tied at the waist, and combat boots. They looked in both directions and went right. Five minutes later, Komi picked up the scent. She stopped to take it in before glancing at Jode.

"How many?"

She frowned. "I'm not sure."

Jode looked at her with mild surprise. She had never made such a statement.

"Why?"

Sniff. "I know at least one came in this direction but there is a strange scent too. It's not human, but it's not vampire." She thought about it, then shrugged. "Forget it. Let's move on."

They walked on, Jode following Komi, until they reached a building. She nodded at the door. Jode went to try it, but found the lock was busted. He took out a gun and Komi unbuckled her trench, resting her hand on her sword. Jode pushed open the door and they walked in.

Once again, Komi sensed the vampires that had been there, plus the strange smell of something not quite vampire. Then she spotted it. Blood, though faint, blended with the worn carpet. She checked closely then stood up.

"Someone lost their head here."

Jode frowned. "Do you smell that?"

"Yes. I sensed it before, now I can smell it. What is that?"

Jode shook his head. "The same smell comes from the elevator."

Komi stood and pushed the button. The doors opened instantly and the overpowering stench of death hit them. Both stepped back, expecting to see dead vampires, but found nothing but a pristine elevator. Jode and Komi scanned the box before stepping in to inspect it more thoroughly. Komi looked at the buttons. She leaned in and noticed a fleck of dry blood between two of them. She pushed floors eight and nine.

At the eighth floor, they stuck their heads out. Sensing and smelling nothing, they stepped back into the elevator. When the reached the ninth floor, the smell of rotten corpses hit them again.

"What has Jin gotten us into?" said Jode through his teeth.

Komi didn't respond, instead taking a cautious step out of the elevator. She closed her eyes then opened them. "Come."

They walked past five doors until they reached apartment number 96. Jode reached for the door. He turned the knob, expecting to break the lock, but the door yielded to his touch. Komi pulled out her blade, nodding at Jode. He kicked the door open and stepped through, gun extended. He waited before beckoning for Komi to come through.

They stepped into the apartment, walking and inspecting until Komi sheathed her sword, annoyed.

"Whatever happened here, we missed it," Jode said.

"Yes. It smells like Tenhar has been here." Komi replied. "Not just been here, but died here."

Jode noticed a large, but faint stain on the floor. Then Komi pointed to the wall where spots were shaped like an arch.

Her eyes glinted when she looked at Jode. "Call Jin."

Jode took out his phone.

* * *

Jin picked up the phone on the first ring. He was in the middle of packing some of his weapons when the call came.

"What did you find?"

"Death."

A chill went down Jin's spine. But he opened himself and could feel that Adina was still alive. Jode confirmed it.

"The human..."

"Adina."

Pause. "Adina, is not here but someone else was. They were cut down."

"Who do you think it was?"

"Best guess based on Komi's sense and the scent, Tenhar."

Jin's jaw clenched. "Tenhar."

"Yes, but I doubt they got what they came for. I don't smell human blood."

"I see. Well I'm coming soon—"

"There's something else, Jin."

"What?"

"Something was here, and I believe that's what killed the Tenhar vampires."

Jin went cold. "What do you mean something?"

"I can't place it, but there is some other blood here. Komi can't identify it. It seems to be vampire, but there's something about the smell of it. The scent of the being was all over the house in places that the other vampires weren't. It could only mean—"

"Someone was there when those vampires came." Jin's anger was rising.

"Yes, and if she was here, that being may have taken her."

Jin bared his teeth. Someone was with Adina and he didn't sense that she wasn't afraid of him or her. They might have done something to make her compliant.

"Can you track them?" asked Jin

"Possibly," replied Jode

"I'm coming. When I have more information, I'll let you know," said Jin.

"Fine." Jode hung up.

Jin quivered in anger. Slowly, he went to his armchair and sat. He closed his eyes, not caring about the consequences. Jin let his mind connect to his lover.

Adina. Adina answer me.

Chapter 20
Needs and Sympathy

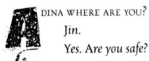DINA WHERE ARE YOU?

Jin.

Yes. Are you safe?

Yes.

Where are you?

I don't know. So tired, Jin. I need you. Come to me. Come to us...

Adina. I'm coming.

Promise.

Promise. Now tell me—

"Jin, your flight is ready."

Jin's eyes slowly opened to look at his father. Swearing softly, he stood and went to his bags.

"Thank you, Father."

He nodded. "Are you packed?"

"Yes," he said. "Don't worry about me. I can take care of myself."

"Of that, I have no doubt. You were trained by the best. We made sure of it."

Eldon walked over to Jin. Jin looked up.

"You understand the arrangement?"

"Yes." Jin clenched his jaw.

"Good. Then take care of this...situation, but keep it as quiet as possible."

"Of course," he whispered.

Eldon turned to leave, but instead, closed the bedroom door. The look on his face made Jin pause.

"What is it, Father?"

"You think I don't understand, but I do. When I was forced to mate with your mother, I felt that I was betraying Enua, my first mate. Danpe does not believe in breaking mating bonds. That was a Tenhar barbarism. To us, it's tremendously disrespectful. You picked a mate and stayed with them until the mating bond faded or you choose to continue it. The choice was taken from me anyway, since my mate was dead. There was no disrespect and duty had to come first, it was said.

I fought the serum for a long time, causing myself great pain. I was determined not to let a new mating to happen. Your mother helped me through it. We talked to each other about the unfairness of it all, how we were just puppets. In the end, we became more than mated, and that's what sustains us. It is the reason I let go of my fight. It is the reason you are here and why we are together today."

Eldon stepped closer to his son. "But I never forgot Enua or my daughter. Nothing could change the way I feel about them."

Jin stared at his father before asking, "Did you love her?"

Eldon's smirked. "I don't know about love. That's a human emotion that I never learned. But I do know that I lost something important when she was taken from me. That's the only reason I am going along with this plan of yours. I hope she is worth it, as much as I hope you will fulfill your obligations here."

He squeezed his son's shoulder before walking away.

"Don't forget the book. The truth has a way of helping solve many problems, especially when people don't want the truth known." Eldon said at the door.

Jin smiled faintly. "Thanks father."

"Two weeks," was his father's stern reply.

* * *

"Jin," she whispered.

Flaxon glanced at her, but she stayed quiet after whispering Jin's name. He shook his head, still amazed that things had gotten so far out of hand. He turned back to driving. They had a long way to go.

Flaxon had a stronghold upstate in the Adirondack Mountains. It had taken him thirty years to set it up. It was one of the few places his kind could live because of its isolation. He hadn't been there in seven years, having left a very capable Mixed Breed in charge. That was Sashi. Currently, she was thoroughly pissed at him, but that couldn't be helped. He remembered that he needed to ask her to prepare the place for Adina's arrive.

Flaxon slowed so that he could grab his phone from the glove compartment. He flipped it open, dialed rapidly with his thumb, and listened. He drove faster. After four rings, someone answered.

"Castille Lodge, how may I help you?"

Flaxon's lodge accommodated real guests, too. It made what they were doing there less conspicuous and drew income for supplies. It was a good place for skiers in the winter, and summer brought family vacationers, campers and those who wanted to trek through the mountains.

"This is John Prince. Connect me to Tina Red."

If a mixed breed ran the desk, they would know the code names, and the occasional human employee wouldn't be any the wiser.

"One moment, sir."

He waited for the three clicks. The voice that answered was wary, annoyed, and waiting.

"Yes, Sire?" Her coldness did not go unnoticed by Flaxon.

"I'm on my way up. Are things ready?"

"Yes. A midwife was driven in yesterday. The room is set up as you both advised. We have plenty of stock for the human as well."

"Good. I'll be there in less than three hours."

"Fine."

Sensing her attitude, he asked, "Something you want to say?"

There was silence. She said, "No, Sire. I believe that if there is anything left to be said, it can wait for your arrival."

"There is nothing left to say," Flaxon answered.

Pause. "As you wish. Is there anything else?"

"Just have the back entrance ready."

He hung up. Sashi was strong-willed and determined. That was one reason he liked having her for a soldier. The only problem was that she'd been his lover once. That ended twenty-five years earlier when she realized that he would only give her his body every once in a while. Even more, she didn't like what he did for money. She figured there was a more dignified way to do it. He said he didn't care what she thought and she walked out. It just made him respect her more.

He put the phone in a small compartment below the heat controls. Sashi was going to have a major attitude and there was no way to placate her. *Whatever. I know what doing is right and it will work. It has to...* He was thinking about his next move when a thought occurred to him. He had to keep Jin from finding Adina until he could control the location.

The Prince didn't know exactly where she was, but if he put his mind to it, he could track her anywhere in the world. Flaxon was betting on Jin not knowing how to do that yet, but with all that had happened... It had to gotten back to Jin that vampires were after Adina. Jin's parents could do only so much to stop him from coming for Adina. And he would come. Not just because Adina was his mate, either.

Flaxon had seen the interaction between Adina and Jin, and what Jin felt for her went beyond mating. Flaxon also figured that Jin knew about his child, and that would probably light a fire under him. Flaxon would have to contact the Prince soon, probably right after he got Adina set up. He didn't want compromise that safe house just for Adina. Too many Breeds counted on it. But he just might have to, because he couldn't keep moving her around. Soon she would have a constant need for blood.

He had driven another hour and a half when he sensed something…not right. He frowned, then glanced at Adina. She was deathly pale, as if she was being drained. He touched her neck and barely felt a pulse.

"Shit!"

He pulled off at the next rest stop and hastily parked the car in a secluded place. He touched her face and neck, feeling the coolness of her skin. He shook her gently.

"Adina. Come on, Adina wake up," he said, to no avail. She was slipping away, her pulse getting even slower.

"Dammit," Flaxon said.

He pushed the button for the trunk and jumped out. He searched the truck but came up empty. Flaxon ran his hand through his hair. Adina needed blood and he didn't have any to give, except his. If he gave her his blood, there was a good chance that Jin's child would get addicted and bond to him because of it. If that happened, Jin would surely want his head. But he had to do something. Adina was dying!

"Oh, fuck it."

He slammed the trunk shut and climbed back into the car. Reaching under the driver's seat, he pulled out an eight-inch knife with a jeweled handle. Without flinching, Flaxon cut his left wrist lengthwise. The blood came out quickly and he put it to Adina's mouth.

"Come on, baby, drink," he whispered, rubbing his bloody wrist against her still lips.

It took some coaxing. Flaxon was close to soaking her mouth before her lips parted. Adina bit down and drank deeply, causing him to breathe heavily. Adina pulled the arm closer and Flaxon leaned into her.

Drinking his blood was affecting the child. He felt it when he rested his head against hers. Her baby was connecting with him. Focusing, Flaxon let the child know that he was only helping his mother until his father came. But the child continued to connect anyway. Flaxon was being drained, and fast. He needed to pull back or he would be in no condition to drive, let alone defend against any enemies.

"That's it. Now let go," he rasped.

But Adina held tighter. Flaxon was near a euphoric state, as blood exchanges could be quite erotic. They were both aroused. Again, he tried to pull away, but couldn't.

"Adina!" he growled

Flaxon didn't want to hurt her, but he couldn't take much more. He was fighting for his blood and to keep the baby at bay. Making a decision, he used his right hand to pinch her nose. When she gasped, he jerked his arm away from her. Adina whimpered, leaning over to get to his arm.

"No. That's enough. It's gonna have to be."

He licked up his arm, then ripped his shirt, wrapping the ragged piece over his wound.

"I'm so hungry," she whined. Rather, her child whined through her.

"I know. I'll get you some blood soon, but you have to slow down or you'll hurt your mother."

"What?"

Adina was coming back to her senses, her eyes half-open and glazed. She raised them to meet his when she growled in a strange voice.

"Who are you?"

Flaxon leaned close to her face. His eyes glinted in amusement.

"It's me, Prince."

Chapter 21

Indignities of Failure and Truthful Surprises

JIN SHIFTED IN HIS seat, his anger almost at the boiling point. He had been in flight for two hours when he sensed that something was very wrong with Adina. She felt like the life was being sucked out of her. Closing his eyes, he tried to connect with her but got only a weak response. The more he tried, the less her felt of her. He panicked, pushing deeper into her mind. As he did, he began to feel the presence of another, then recognized it as his child. He gasped in awe. He basked in the feel of its spirit, letting it touch him, feeling the connection between them grow. It was a glorious moment that briefly made him forget about Adina.

The feelings faded as he felt that something was wrong. He felt his child's hunger for his blood and its mother. It was then that Jin realized what was happening. Adina's life was fading as the child took it from her. An image came to mind of their child suckling her breast while Adina smiled faintly. But her color was fading, her vitality draining.

Adina...

Her head slowly rose. Her smile, though happy, was a struggle.

Jin.

He went to her and touched his child's head. Adina gasped faintly and sagged even further. He touched her cheek.

Baby, you can't keep doing this...

She tilted her head at him.

"What am I to do? Our baby needs blood...I can only give it."

"I know. But—"

She smiled again. "But nothing. Nothing can be done."

Jin's heart beat faster. He watched in horror as her eyes closed and he felt her life and the child's fading.

"Adina!" *he mentally shouted.*

She was going to die. He wouldn't reach her in time. As his heart was breaking from his failure, he felt another presence. Through her, he smelled blood. He heard someone begging her to drink it.

"No," *he heard her whisper. He knew she was doing it because of him but at the moment he didn't care who was offering the blood. He wanted her alive. He embraced her leaning over to whisper in her ear.*

"Drink, baby. Take all you need. You have to. Drink so that you will live and I can find you."

She refused for a second, but the instinct to protect and feed her child made her respond. She was thrown back against him. His connection to her broke.

Jin slammed back into his seat, breathing deeply. When he tried to connect to Adina again, he couldn't. It was like a force was blocking their connection. Jin was confused until he thought that it had to do with the blood she was drinking. Drinking another's blood was a powerful experience that forged a connection. A chill went down Jin's back. He wondered if the person giving her blood was doing so to deliberately create a bond.

He tried again to enter her mind. This time he felt his child begging for more blood. The baby turned its pleas to its father. Jin let the child know he was coming, that he would be there soon. He could feel that Adina was exhausted and she would need more blood very soon. Jin needed to know who was with her. He demanded without thinking that Adina ask.

It's me, Prince. Flaxon's image flashed through Adina's mind before he was pushed out. Angered, he tried to enter her mind and found that she was in such a deep sleep that it might hurt her to push her awake. A couple of minutes later, his airphone rang.

He stared at it before picking it up.

"Yes."

"I said I'd keep your mate safe."

Jin sneered. "Flaxon. How did you get this number?"

"None other, and don't worry about the phone. I have my ways. Neat trick there talking through her. I didn't think you would know how to do it."

"I can do a lot of things that you don't know about."

"I'm sure."

They were both quiet, then Jin warned, "You harm her, you die."

"The only person that has harmed her is you. I'm just helping you clean up the mess."

"Mess? Adina's no one's mess. Why do you have her?"

"I'm trying to protect her, Prince. Her and your child."

Jin growled. Composing himself, he asked, "Where are you taking her?"

"Someplace safe. I'll contact you soon."

"What have you done to her?!"

"What do you mean?"

"You know what I mean! She's practically comatose, you tosser!"

"I've just given her a mild sedative. She needs rest."

"Really? Why don't you tell me where you are," Jin growled, his voice dropping to a darker tone.

"Soon."

The phone went dead. Jin bared his teeth before pushing the intercom above his head.

"Yes, Sire."

"Make this hunk of junk go faster."

"Yes, Sire."

Jin gripped the arm of the chair so tightly that it broke off when he stood up.

* * *

Flaxon crashed against the wall near the vending machines. It had taken all of his power to keep a strong voice while talking to Jin. Now he could give in to the weakness. Adina had taken more than he realized. Flaxon slid down the wall to the floor. A couple walked past looking concerned; he knew he was a sight to behold. He was pale, sweaty and if not for his jacket, they would see his torn, bloody shirt. The woman looked like she was about to ask him if he needed help, but the man pulled her away.

Flaxon took another deep breath and stood up, leaning against one of the machines. Slowly, he produced five singles from the wallet in his back pocket and rolled himself in front of the vending machine. Dizziness passed through him. He rested his forehead against the plastic case, his eyes fluttering. When the spell passed, he stood straighter.

He fumbled with the money and the machine's thin dollar slit. As his frustration grew, he considered just smashing the glass. *Yeah, like you need the attention*, he thought. Finally, the dollar caught, disappearing into the machine. His hand slid down to slam the orange juice button. He heard the bottled being pulled and fall down. Flaxon squatted down, grabbed the bottle, and drank it all. It wasn't enough, but it was a start.

Flaxon bought two more and a small bag of muffins, then headed back to his car sluggishly. He almost collapsed against the car. He drank more juice before getting in and tossing the empty container into the backseat. Once he settled, he glanced over at Adina. She was out cold, but her color had returned. But she would need more blood soon. He had to make up the time he lost on the stop.

He turned on the car and backed out, hitting the parking lot at sixty. By the time he had gone a mile, he was up to eighty. He flipped on his radar to detect police activity within thirty miles. It was a rare product that he'd had the pleasure of selling for over $50,000. Flaxon used his teeth to rip open the bag of muffins, then stuffed his mouth. They tasted stale, but he needed all the energy he could get.

＊ *＊* *＊*

Lars sat at the dining table in his hotel suite, drinking an excellent glass of blood. It was relatively fresh human blood. Lars never believed in the synthetic and animal crap that the others used. There was a secret supply that he and his kind used when away from other vampires, so no one would suspect that he was violating law. Away from them, he drank heartily.

Three generations of Lars' family sat at the table. There was Deka, his daughter, who was close to 160 years old. She was as blond as her father with same eye color and facial structure, and the worst kind of attitude. At the moment, her thirty-year-old child, Dirk, who still acted like an infant, was magnifying it. Dirk was dark-blond, four inches taller than his mother, and lanky.

Dirk played with a portable game console constantly, forever distracted from what he really needed to be doing. Lars attributed Dirk's stupidity to the bad choice his daughter made in a mate. Lars thought that executing the vampire would derail any further influence from the male, but stupidity must have been in his genes. Lars would have taken his grandson's head, but stayed his hand for his daughter's sake. Thankfully, Lars had two children, and his daughter Muriel's offspring had sense. Too bad she wasn't there with him. She could also hold a very intelligent conversation, unlike Deka, who complained endlessly.

Just when Lars was about to tell Dirk to put the game away, there was a knock at his door.

"Enter."

Tobias walked in like a dark cloud, instantly putting Lars on alert. Deka smirked as Tobias passed, but he only nodded respectfully, ignoring her lecherous grin. Lars sighed inwardly about his daughter's ridiculousness. The woman was always seeking male attention. He never understood her need to have one with her at all times. Tobias made it to Lars and whispered in his ear. Lars stood.

"Meet me in the lounge."

Tobias nodded, walking away. When he was gone, Lars walked over to the small bar against the right wall, where he removed an elegant saber. The blade was slightly curved and the handle was gold-encrusted with embedded blue sapphires.

"Excuse me." He started to walk away, but stopped. "If I return and have to take that game, boy, your head will be next."

Dirk paled then looked at his mother.

"You heard your lord. Put it away and try reading a book for a change."

Lars entered the room to find Tobias facing the window, blade drawn. Lars almost smiled at his cousin's boldness. He went to the center of the room.

"Explain your failure."

Tobias turned slowly, his face devoid of expression.

"We went for a breach and three of the best were killed."

"Who?"

"Mia, Tia and Dorian."

Lars' eyes flickered. Even he was surprised by that news. He had expected Tobias to report that some weak vampires had gone after the human, but he had sent the best and they still failed.

"How did this happen? How could the human escape?"

"She is being protected."

"By whom?!" growled Lars impatiently.

"By a breed."

"A breed! A sorry breed! You're telling me that a breed got the advantage over your best guards?!"

Tobias glared at him. "This breed wasn't some weak-blooded human vampire. The analysis of the blood on Mia's blade indicates that this breed was more than three-fourths vampire..."

Lars froze. "What a minute. I thought we destroyed all Breeds like that over a hundred years ago."

"Apparently not."

A thought hit Lars then. "Why was this breed around the human? In fact, how would he even know about her?"

Tobias frowned. He hadn't thought about that himself. He watched the Prince think. A second later, a weird smile turned up on his face.

"That's it! That's how that idiot Prince was able to hide all those months ago. He must have had help from the breed!"

"How's that?"

"Think about it. No breed would come out of hiding to help any human. We assumed they wouldn't even know about Jin's predicament, because they stay away from all things vampire. Yet, you have a powerful breed helping this human—a powerful breed we knew nothing of until now, which means it was hiding all those years, eluding us. And the breed was interacting with vampires. It had to be for that fool Prince to have known it.

"More than three months ago, that bastard Jin evaded our attack. We heard nothing of him until we found the apartment, then word came out that he was with a human. He disappeared again, only to be spotted with a human in the subway of all places. Then he disappeared again.

"Later that night, our spies tell us that he went to his father's flat, but disappeared when his father tried to retrieve him. Likely, it was because he still had that human with him. There aren't too many places that he could hide with a human tagging along, so what happened? He got help from the breed, probably someone he had dealings with in the past."

"But how would he know about breeds? Breeds don't exactly advertise."

"Idiot. He didn't know it was a breed. A breed that's more vampire than human is hard to detect. Unless you have been exposed to those types of breeds and their scent, you'll never understand what makes them feel…different. A vampire would tend to dismiss it. The Prince has no concept of breeds and wouldn't have known he was with one." Lars smiled coldly. "The Prince was in heat at the time, and the breed must have understood what was going on with the Prince. So…"

Tobias nodded in realization. "So it helps the Prince, then follows the human once they separate. But why?"

Lars rolled his eyes. "Think fool. The breed must have figured that the future High Prince had his way with the human and impregnated her. Jin, the prat, probably didn't know he could do that, but the breed did. So it tracks her. It knows more knowledgeable parties than Jin would want the human dead for a range of reasons. The breed figures that if it finds and protects her, it can parley favors for the other breeds' protection."

Tobias was quiet for a long time before saying, "So this breed has her and plans to use her to blackmail the High Prince."

Lars nodded. "Indeed. And I'm beginning to think we can use this to our advantage."

"How?"

Lars glared at him. "Don't you worry about it. You failed me. I don't like failure."

Tobias stilled. He knew his cousin had a short fuse and he had to be ready for anything.

"However, I still need you. It will be your job to personally track this breed. I want it, and the human found. Don't bother to come back if you fail…unless you're ready to lose your head."

Tobias nodded without expression, then said, "There's more."

Lars leaned back expectantly.

"I just heard that the High Prince is no longer in the city, and his parents are going to choose a mate for him in two weeks."

Lars leaned forward, his mood brightening. "Really? Who told you?"

"I learned from one of our sources that Eldon's personal Concorde has left the country."

"Then I'd advise you to find out where that plane is landing."

Tobias ran his tongue over his teeth, annoyed. "I already have. It's landing in New York within the next hour. I have some of my people there to track him once he's off."

"Not kill him?" Lars asked quietly.

"He would be hard to kill, landing in an international airport. We would all be exposed. Considering the amount of suspicion on us already, I didn't think it prudent to try again, especially there."

"Fine. Besides he might lead us to the human. Make sure your people don't lose him." Lars tilted his head thoughtfully. "So they are seeking mates for Jin. But...maybe he didn't get that far with the human."

Tobias watched Lars mumble to himself. Tobias was really sick of working under the Prince of Tenhar. The vampire was a callous jerk with no regard for anything or anyone that didn't serve his own ends. Tobias knew that his time on earth was being measured by his cousin's patience. As much as he resented it, he understood his goal. Tenhar ranked lower than Danpe and Hinghou, when in fact they were equals, or so Tobias believed.

"You still here?"

Lars' voice jerked Tobias out of his thoughts. "You didn't dismiss me, milord."

Lars sneered. "Dismissed."

Tobias bowed slightly with an eye on Lars, then backed towards the door. A second after turning his back, Tobias was pinned to the wall with a violent force. He grunted softly. Pain radiating through him when the blade was pulled from his back. Lars' hot breath was on his ear.

"Don't fail me again, cousin, or the pain you suffer will have you begging me to take your head."

Blood pooled in the back of Tobias' mouth but he swallowed it. Lars grabbed the back of his shirt and dragged him, tossing him near the exit. Tobias picked himself up again, holding his stomach.

"Get a move on," Lars said, taking the cloth from a small table and wiping off the wall.

Tobias left without a comment.

"Deka!" snapped Lars.

His daughter's heels clicked on the floor until she reached the carpeted area of the room.

"Yes, Father."

"Do you know anyone who's in heat? I have a need for them."

Chapter 22
Double Surprise

THE DRIVE TOWARDS THE lodge became increasingly difficult as Flaxon's strength ebbed. He wove through the light traffic with the skill of a racecar driver, but it was starting to take more concentration. His foot was practically through the floor, trying to get to the safe house. Taking a ragged breath, he pressed past six cars.

Just when he thought the exit would never come, a sign announced that it was less than two miles away. After taking the exit, he went so fast that he had to stamp the brake while turning the wheel. The car spun wildly before facing the right direction. Cursing himself, he glanced over to Adina, who seemed not to notice how close they had come to flipping over. After calming himself, he took a winding road to a mountainous area. He found relief on the familiar road, though he hadn't been there in a long time.

He usually stayed away from the place, mostly because of Sashi. He wasn't avoiding her as much as he was their inevitable fighting.

He hoped she wouldn't give him a hard time when he arrived, though he knew that was just wishful thinking. Sashi's mouth would probably be on full blast and he would have to pull rank to shut her up. He doubted that would work, as strong-willed as she was. It was something he both loved and hated about her. Shaking his head, he refocused and continued to drive to the secret road that led to the lodge. It was between two trees and branches hung low in the overgrown drive. It wasn't a road that would be found by mistake.

He stopped on the road across from it. No one was coming they probably wouldn't in the next minute. He reached into the compartment between the two front seats and pulled out a pencil-sized metal cylinder; a Photolight Key, or P-Key. He raised it to his eye and pushed a little node in the middle of it. A soft red light came on, scanning his eye, while projecting a signal to an unseen lock in the trees. A second later, the light turned green.

Flaxon swung the car to the left, driving off the road slowly. A sharp decline curved to the right. He saw the faint lines of security snapping back in place in the rearview mirror. Any unauthorized person who crossed that barrier would suffer an electromagnetic shutdown of the car and get their brain a little cooked. The alarms at the lodge would go off, giving his people time to escape. It had cost Flaxon a hefty amount, but it was worth it. All safe houses had similar security for the secret routes.

He drove slowly, the road narrowing as it went down a steep slope. After about five miles, the road curved back through thick foliage. In minutes, he came up behind the lodge. He took out his P-Key and let it scan his eye again. The light turned green and he went through in the small employee parking lot.

The lodge stood six stories from the back, four on the main road. The lower two levels were base operations for Flaxon's people. On the lowest level were a well insulated communications center, training room, blood storage facility, and a garage. The sleeping area, cafeteria, and storage were on the next level. The top four levels were the business, guest rooms, and entertainment for guests of Castille Lodge. It was rustic, made of wood and surrounded by lots of trees and shrubbery. It was nestled on the side of a rather large hill, with a hiking trail that connected with others in the region. Flaxon required anyone hiding out at the Lodge to know the trails to the point that he could send them out blindfolded or at night. As a result, his Lodge had never lost a guest on the trails.

The garage door slowly opened as his car approached. He eased into an empty slot behind a dark jeep. He turned off the ignition and leaned back, exhausted. He took a few long breaths, then opened the door. He stepped out, inhaling the crisp air that filled the space before the doors closed. It was a struggle to keep focus after the blood loss. His body felt like lead, like he could just sleep for days. Finally, he pushed off the car and walked around to Adina's door. He made sure she wasn't leaning on it before opening it.

He picked her up gingerly. She felt heavier than she would have if he wasn't so weak. Flaxon adjusted her in his arms, resting her head in the crook of his neck. He kicked the door shut and walked to the door straight ahead then on the left. He kicked twice, paused, then three times more. He then dipped so he could twist the doorknob. The door opened slowly and Flaxon stepped through.

Flaxon entered the dim hallway, wondering why the light bulbs hadn't been changed. He closed the door behind him. When he looked up, there stood a short woman with reddish black hair, of Inuit and Puerto Rican descent. Her eyes were a slate gray that turned metallic in moments of anger. Sashi Velas, his former lover. She was dressed in jeans, a loose T-shirt, and work boots.

Sashi had a gun pointed at him, but not the same gun the others used. It was a laser gun, capable of burning a hole through the flesh, and had been perfected by one of youth in the tribe. Flaxon was good at finding inventive and creative youths.

They stared at each other. Flaxon smirked faintly, but Sashi remained cool. Finally, she lowered her weapon.

"This way," she said in a soft, neutral voice.

Flaxon followed her down a corridor. She whispered into the microphone on her collar and the lights gradually brightened. By the time they reached the elevators, normal lighting had been restored. The area had elevators on both walls and steel doors next to electronic panels. The security code was based a voice and eye scan identification. Straight-ahead was another hallway with doors on either side. Sashi pushed the "up" button, keeping her back to Flaxon. They waited in silence.

When the doors opened, she stepped in, holding the button until Flaxon stepped through. When she released the button, she took out her key and put it in another lock, turned it, and pushed a button twice, then took the key out. The elevator ascended quietly. Flaxon had just leaned back when the doors opened. Sashi held them open again to let him exit first. They stepped into a foyer and turned left. It was painted dark green, but brightly lit. A door directly ahead allowed access to the public part of the facility, but it also had an eye and voice identification pad.

Sashi walked to the first door on the left. After her eye was scanned, she said her name.

"Sashi Velas. 34667879."

After a click, Sashi opened the door to a living space. It was a posh living room, with dark sofas, a big screen television, and coffee tables. The floors were carpeted and the walls a pale yellow. The space was devoid of anything living. Flaxon assumed Sashi had the area cleared out so that no one would see Adina's arrival. They walked across the room to an archway. Down the hallway was several doors, most of them to bedrooms. They passed a second archway that led to more quarters and the kitchen. They reached another door and Sashi held it open for him.

The room was cream-colored. A king-size bed with pastel sheets and a warm, sand comforter was in the center of the room. Medical equipment and a small refrigerator were on the right. On the left, a nightstand bore a few books and a remote control for the TV on the dresser across from the foot of the bed. The bathroom was just beyond it. To right of the bedroom door was a low bookshelf that was decorated by ornaments of woodland animals. A window near the bookshelf provided a breathtaking view of the landscape.

Flaxon gently laid Adina on the bed and checked her pulse. It was steady, but slowing. When he turned, Sashi had gone. He walked to the fridge and opened it. It was stocked with blood and plasma. He frowned, but took two blood packs. He was about to bite one when he heard a soft voice.

"Where are we?" Adina whispered.

Her eyes were opened and she was trying to sit up.

"At a safe place."

He put down the blood pack to walk to her. He sat on the edge of the bed, touched her forehead, then stroked it.

"Relax. It's safe here. There's nothing to worry about."

Adina felt herself falling back to sleep but she fought it.

"Jin... Flaxon, I want..."

She passed out again, but he continued rubbing her temples, only stopping when he heard the door open.

A woman entered, Maggie Free Bird. She was 3/8 vampire and descended from an Indian tribe in the American west. Two jet-black plaits hung on the front sides of her face; two more hung in the back. She had brown eyes, a sharp nose, and stern lips. Her 5'9" frame was stout, and her long, delicate fingers were expert for healing. She wore a pale yellow tunic, dark pants and mules. On her right index finger, a small turquoise stone was set in sterling silver ring. With one hundred forty-five years of experience, she was the head midwife for all Mixed Breed

Maggie bowed. "My Prince. I am here to serve."

Her voice was soft and soothing. Maggie never spoke loudly. She preferred to let her presence speak for her.

Flaxon stood, noticing that Sashi was with her. He dipped his head in acknowledgment. Maggie walked to the bed, sat down, and touched Adina's forehead.

"What was done for her, Sire?"

Flaxon hesitated to say, "I put her to sleep."

"With what?"

"Massage technique. Before that, she had lost too much blood... so I gave her mine."

Maggie turned slowly. "Sire?"

"What was I to do? She was dying. I didn't expect her to lose blood so fast."

Maggie continued to stare, but he held her gaze. Finally, she nodded.

"You need blood, Sire. Take both of those packs for yourself. Is your wound serious?"

Flaxon looked at his stomach. "No."

"Then let me do what is necessary to stabilize her."

"I'll return in an hour, and I want a thorough report."

"Yes, Sire."

Flaxon grabbed the packs and left the room, brushing past Sashi. She watched his back until Maggie called her.

"Yes?"

"Please prepare a large salad, a glass of whole milk, a rare steak, and a roll for our guest."

Sashi frowned. "Me? I can't cook."

"Then find someone who can. She needs food."

Sashi sighed but went to complete the task.

Maggie began to examine Adina. Her pulse was slow, but steady. Maggie sat back and stared at her. She had the ability to measure anyone's blood flow by simply focusing on them, the method she had just used on Flaxon. Maggie determined that Adina would need another bag within the hour. But something wasn't right. In all the pregnancies she had seen, a human female had never lost blood so fast.

She hadn't believed Sashi when the girl told her what Flaxon had. A human pregnant by a vampire? That simply wasn't done anymore. The law forbade them to make themselves known to humans. The only contact a human might have with a vampire was through the breeds, but even they mated within the tribe. Mating with humans only happened after being screened by the council and approved by the Prince.

Maggie wanted to know more about the human and the mating, but Sashi was evasive, so Maggie let it go. When the Prince wanted her to know more, he would tell her. She gathered her supplies and came to the lodge. She thought one of her other midwives could have cared for the human, but she understood why Flaxon wanted her. It was more difficult for a human to carry the seed of a pure vampire than a mixed breed. Now, she wished she had questioned more, because the woman in front of her was very slowly dying. She needed her mate for her child to develop properly. It would also help her produce and keep her own blood, as vampire blood would do more to satisfy a growing child.

The woman's face was wane, but she looked as peaceful as she did lovely. Maggie could see why a vampire would admire her beauty. The Prince couldn't hide his mild attraction to the human, either. She shook her head and continued her examination.

She slipped her hand under Adina's shirt and felt the heaviness of her breast. Already, the young woman was developing milk for the child. Maggie lifted the bottom of the sweater to feel the slight swell of her stomach. Soon, it would be twice as big. Vampire babies grew rapidly. She felt around to sense the child within. Closing her eyes, Maggie linked to the baby to assess its health. She felt the rhythmic patterns of the child's heart, but something was off. Inhaling deeper, she focused more.

Hello, little one. Don't be afraid of me. I am here to help you and your mother.

Hungry

I know, but you've had plenty to eat. You need to slow down so your mother can better sustain you.

Hungry ...hungry.

Maggie's eyes flew open. She turned to the sleeping Adina. There were two voices. The second wasn't as strong as the first. Closing her eyes, she connected again. But the child drew away.

Little one...what are you hiding?

The child refused to speak, amazing Maggie with its strength. The child's awareness in the womb depended on the amount of vampire blood in the system. Adina was pregnant by a pure breed, so her child would be able to communicate to their mother and manifest their strengths through her. Adina's child seemed stronger than most though. It was suppressing something.

Maggie placed both hands on Adina's stomach and let herself relax. She opened her awareness, listening to all that came to her.

Hungry.

It was faint, but she caught it. The dominant child realized what had happened and panicked, pushed her away, and broke the connection. Surprise and wonder filled her when she opened her eyes. Adina seemed agitated, her breath quickening. Maggie sent the children feelings of calm through her hands.

You have nothing to fear, little ones. I will not harm you. You need not hide from me.

She felt them calm. After a moment of accessing, she stood up and set up the IV line. Now that she understood the situation, she needed to talk to the Prince. Those children would need their father, and fast.

* * *

Flaxon stood under the water, trying to relax his tense muscles. The bathroom was completely steamy, but he didn't care. He put his head back under the water. It darkened as the rest of the dye went down the drain. After five more minutes, he stepped out and toweled off. He then used the towel to wipe the foggy mirror and check out his hair. His natural dark brown had been replaced by midnight-black. He turned his head to make sure the blond was all gone. It was. He used his fingers to comb back the wavy, shoulder-length hair.

He left the bathroom, drying his hair with the towel, and stepped into the bedroom. The bed had been made with black sheets and four black silk pillows, a contrast to the stark white walls. Behind the bed was a mural of the landscape of a place he had lived a hundred years ago. A lush dark carpet covered the floor. Flaxon walked to his bed and put on the black pants and white tank top he had laid out, then he grabbed a blood-red shirt. He had just partly slipped it on when he heard the knock.

"Enter."

Sashi came in and closed the door behind her. Her heart thumped hard at the sight of Flaxon. He always had that effect on her. He excited her as much as he infuriated her. When he turned to face her, she took note of the way his arm flexed before disappearing into the sleeve. His eyes caught hers and held them. She knew she could get lost in their depths, just as she had many times in the past. They were timeless, reflecting nothing most of the time, but so much when he let them.

"What?" he asked.

Sashi stepped closer, determined to confront him like no one in the tribe would.

"You fed that woman your blood. Are you crazy?"

Flaxon glared. "I'm going to pretend you didn't speak to me as if I answer to you."

"You do answer to me, to all of us. Your actions affect us all. And feeding the High Prince's mate your blood, possibly bonding his child to you was the dumbest thing you could have done. You have to be crazy!"

His lips twisted into a nasty sneer. "Are you finished?"

Sashi stepped even closer. "No. What makes you think this plan of yours will work? Vampires never cared about us. His tribal ancestors betrayed us and you want to put your faith in him, a Prince you've said was a spoiled brat with no idea of the world. You are risking yourself, our only real power, on the hope that he cares one shred for that human. Why?"

Flaxon silently gazed at her, taking in her lips, the way her hair framed her face. If she were anyone else, she would be dead, but Sashi held a special place in his heart, even if she didn't know it. It is the only reason he hadn't already snapped her neck. However, he couldn't let her get away with her insolence. He jerked her forward by her shoulders. She didn't flinch or look away.

"You must learn your place. I am Prince and I make the decisions..."

"Maybe. But when you place yourself in danger, you place us all in danger. We are not as strong as you. We need you. You have no right to endanger yourself. Your father—"

He gripped her tighter. "—My father was a fool, but I'm not. I know what I'm doing! I have no intention of getting my head removed from my neck." He released her.

Sashi flexed her shoulders. "Oh. And what do you think will happen when the High Prince finds out that you gave his mate your blood?"

He smiled coldly. "He'll be grateful that she's alive, that's what."

She shook her head. "Whatever. Just...forget it. I have to work."

She turned to leave but stopped. "You know he'll be able to track her here."

He didn't respond. She was about to face him again when she heard him move like the wind. He was right behind her. Flaxon leaning forward to smell her hair, stroking it as he did. It reminded him of lilacs on a cool summer day. He had always loved that smell on her. He stroked her neck, sliding down her arms, moving to her waist, encircling her in his arms.

"I like that you still worry about me," he whispered in her ear, then kissed her neck. He hadn't seen her in years and he really had missed her. Having her close reminded him of what he had lost when she walked away...someone who cared about him more than just as the Prince.

"You're my Prince. It's my duty."

Her voice hitched as his hands moved under her shirt to clasp her breasts. He smiled against her neck. She was only trying to put him off with that response.

"What else is your duty?" he asked.

She leaned against him, betraying herself. She knew she should push him away, but... She gasped as his hand slid into her pants. Her hips rocked with the motion of his hand, grinding against it. When his teeth grazed her neck, an involuntary moan slipped through her lips. She wanted him. She always wanted him. His touch sent fire through her veins and she had missed it so much.

"Alphonso," she whispered when his thumb glided over her clitoris.

Sashi was one of the few people that knew his real name, and he loved to hear it flow from her lips in the throes of passion. He turned her head to capture her lips in a searing kiss. That kiss conveyed so many things—his need, how he had missed her, and in a small way, how much he cared for her. Sashi reached back to slide her fingers through his drying hair, pulling him deeper into the kiss.

When it ended, Sashi was breathless. He attacked her neck again, nibbling at the pulsing vein. She stroked his strong thighs as he opened her jeans to discover a black thong. He hooked his thumbs through the thin bands on the sides and slowly moved them down. Sashi saw herself in front of the floor-length mirror. Her face was flushed, her petite frame engulfed in Flaxon's embrace. It made her feel safe, but it also reminded her that she wanted to feel this way all the time. What he—what they were about to do was not enough for her. She loved him and he was only offering lust. She closed her eyes to savor his touch, then put her hands over his.

"We can't do this," she whispered.

"We can't?" he said in a low voice, his fingertips raking across her belly.

She grabbed his hand again. "I can't." She stepped away from him, buttoning her jeans. "I can't...no."

Flaxon watched her stammer to herself, denying the way he made her feel, denying herself his touch. That was the way it always happened, but he liked to see if he could change her mind. Sashi was one of the few women who always kept him intrigued. If things had been different, he would have claimed her a long time ago. It was the things she wanted that kept them from being together now.

She wanted to live the way some humans did, with a family, a home, stability... but she would have settled for just him. She understood his role and was willing to forgo all her other dreams just to be with him. All she needed was his commitment. Twenty-five years earlier, Sashi realized that he was never going to commit to her or anyone. He said that he couldn't. He was the Prince and he didn't have time for it. He had told her the deal from the beginning, so what did she expect?

Yet, she knew that it had very little to do with being Prince. He just didn't want the responsibility of caring for someone. Something tragic happened to him before her time, and since then his heart was sealed against anything but anger and pleasure. She tried to find out what it was, but he never really told her. The more she pushed, the more he pulled away. Soon, they couldn't talk at all. He thought she left because of his nasty business practices, but it was the fact he was emotionally unavailable. Sashi left because she needed more. She loved him. She loved him still, but she couldn't let him use her just for a night. His touch meant much more than that to her.

Once she had herself together, she faced him again. Her face was still flushed, but she was in control. When she glanced at him, she caught an unguarded smile. She had seen real smiles from him on rare occasions, but it had been a long time. It disappeared quickly, though, his face becoming stoic.

They stared at each other quietly. She watched him slowly licked each finger, his eyes glinting. Just watching his tongue almost made her moan. She always loved to see him like this.

Flaxon could never get enough of the spicy taste that was only Sashi. As he tasted her, he envisioned her writhing under him. When he finished, he winked at her. He walked past her to his boots, next to the door.

"I believe we have business to attend to."

Sashi took deep breath. "Yes, Prince."

* * *

Maggie had just finished cleaning and dressing Adina when there was a knock on the door. Flaxon came in. Maggie stood, bowing.

Flaxon saw that Adina was on the IV and had been changed into a simple nightgown. Color was returning to her face and her breathing seemed better. He swallowed a relieved sigh, not wanting Maggie to know that he'd been the slightest bit worried. The pregnancy was taking a serious toll on Adina and he knew it. As much as he needed her for his own gain, he didn't want anything bad to happen to her. He saw Maggie fiddling with a few things and decided to wait before discussing Adina's condition. He went to look out the window.

He liked the quiet and solitude of the mountains. They gave him peace. But that would soon be gone. Right now, his people were packing to leave Castille Lodge. Too much heat would be coming, and he couldn't endanger them all on his gamble. Sashi had been told to get everyone ready to leave. After he ensured that Adina was okay, he was going to meet with some of his Breed guardians to discuss his plan further.

He turned back to Maggie, who was standing behind him, waiting. He respected Maggie a lot. She was the best midwife in his tribe. She was also skillful with a sword. It was for that reason that he enjoyed engaging her in practice.

"Is she going to be okay?"

"Yes. She will be fine. She'll need blood every hour."

Flaxon frowned. "Why is that? It's not normal, is it?"

Maggie tilted her head slightly. "It is normal when there are twice as many children to feed."

Flaxon froze. "What?"

Maggie looked him directly in the eye. "She is carrying twins, Sire. That's the reason she was losing blood so fast, and at this rate, she will need the blood of their father very soon. If not, Sire's blood will be sufficient."

"No, it won't." he snapped. "I gave her blood to keep her alive long enough to make it here. That was the only reason. She'll get the rest from her lover."

"May I ask who her lover is? I can't think of any vampire that wouldn't leave her this way, not caring if she lived or died, not to mention the children."

"Her lover is Jin, the future High Prince."

Maggie actually gasped. "No...no. You've got to be kidding..."

Flaxon shook his head. "No, I'm not. He came to me three months ago with her in tow. She saved his life and he was trying to protect her. He was also in heat. He struggled not to brand her with his mark, but they'd already had sex. Biting her just sealed their fate."

"I saw it. You know he'll be able to find her once she comes out of that deep slumber. If he's in the country, that won't even matter."

"I know. He is very protective of her..."

"Are you sure he's not just making sure that she won't surface and ruin his ascent as High Prince?"

Flaxon stared at Adina. "I saw him with her. I saw the way he wanted to protect her. No. If he wanted to destroy her, she would be dead. He is attached to her. Very attached."

"Then you know how he'll react to his mate having received your blood."

Flaxon snickered. "Whatever. I can handle that. Don't worry. Besides the children didn't bond to me."

"Yes, they did. Not completely, but enough to anger the High Prince. I felt it when I was hooking Adina up to the IV. They were trying to find you for more sustenance. I told them they had to wait for their father and they were content, but they wondered why you aren't their father..."

Maggie quieted when she saw Flaxon pale, his eyes turning to stone. "Flaxon.... You did what you had to, I know, but this is serious. He might kill you for this. He might kill you once he knows who you are."

He nodded. "I know. I know the stakes, Maggie. But the fact of the matter is, this is our best chance at insuring our survival."

"I've heard that before," she whispered.

"Do you lack faith in me, Maggie?" he growled.

"No, Sire," she murmured. "I lack of faith in them. I meant no disrespect."

She turned to check on Adina with Flaxon following. Maggie stared and Flaxon sat next to her. He reached out to touch her hair.

He whispered, "I have no love for them either, Maggie. They have taken so much from me. But I have faith in her because she has faith in him. My father once told me that my mother was the reason he knew love. She inspired him to fight for all of us. He sacrificed himself for that reason. Adina is the reason I believe Jin will finally honor the promise made to my father. To condemn us, would be to condemn her, and I believe that she will be the reason that he will do what is right."

"And if he doesn't?" Maggie asked.

Flaxon looked up from Adina and studied Maggie long and hard.

"Then you're in charge of protecting the tribe."

For the second time in Maggie's life, she gasped in shock.

Chapter 23
Confrontation

JIN LOOKED CALM WHEN he stepped off the plane, but he felt like taking someone's head off. He had been trying and failing miserably to connect with Adina. She was knocked out, too tired to tell him anything or let him know exactly where she was. All he knew was that she wasn't dead and that Flaxon must have done something to her to make her so unresponsive. Jin wanted to know what and why.

Once he reached the terminal, he went through the security. They scanned him and asked him a barrage of questions that ate up more of his precious time. By the time they released him his anger was past the boiling point. He went to the private luggage claim, grabbed his stuff, and walked outside.

The sky was brightening in the brisk November air. It was just after seven in the morning. He hadn't been to New York City since the original *Studio 54* closed and the idea of coming to the States was refreshing after having been in Europe for so long. *Studio 54* was the place he had first met Flaxon to start their turbulent relationship. Now that he was back, the city didn't bring a smile to his face.

He looked around for the taxi station. Waving his hand to the attendant, he walked over just as a cab pulled up. Jin slapped a twenty in the attendant's hand and climbed into the cab.

"Take me to Riverdale, please."

"Where in Riverdale?" asked the cabbie.

Jin's voice became hypnotic. "Take me to 225th street in Riverdale, the house facing the water. You hear nothing and only see the path that will get you there."

The cab driver's eyes glazed over and he nodded obediently. They sped off and Jin took out his phone. He was just about to dial the number when he felt a pull in his mind.

Adina.

He sensed her. Although she was still unable to communicate with him fully, he sensed her strongly. He knew she wasn't in the city or close by. She was north of him. Closing his eyes, he followed that feeling, applying it to the mental map of New York that he studied on the plane. *North...north. Past the suburbs, past the Catskills... past the capital... north.* He couldn't put his finger on it, but he knew that she was upstate. Quickly, he dialed the number and called Jode.

"Have you arrived, Jin?"

"Yes, Jode. I'm on my way to the rendezvous point. When I get there, I want to leave immediately. Wait."

Jin lowered the phone, a humming coming over him. *Tenhar.* He casually glanced at the traffic beside the cab, but saw nothing suspicious. He slowly turned his head towards the back window. Before he had turned completely, a tan Volvo to the right caught his eye. The windows were tinted, but Jin could see the driver through the glass. He wore shades and seemed to have light hair.

"Let me call you back, Jode."

Jin snapped the phone shut. He leaned close to the driver.

"Speed up."

The driver pressed the gas and the cab jetted through the traffic. The Volvo continued to follow the flow of traffic in its lane, so Jin told the driver to slow down. But then the Volvo started weaving through traffic to catch up. It had a clear path to pass them if it wanted to, but didn't. He thought for a moment, then redialed Jode's number.

"Jode, we have company. Change of plans."

"What do you want us to do Jin?"

Jin smiled. Finally, here was a chance to release some aggression. He relayed his plan.

* * *

Komi and Jode sat in the backyard of a large house in Riverdale. Sitting on a hill, it provided a view of the Hudson River and New Jersey. Some of the original trees were still rooted in the yard. The house itself was an old stone manor, bought by Eldon's people at the turn of the century when surrounding area was mostly farms. The manor and the land behind it was the only thing the family owned, the rest having been sold over the years.

Komi glanced at Jode as he took out his guns. He checked that each was loaded. Then he screwed on the silencers. Komi shook her head and continued to polish the blade.

"You know once we do this, we will become the enemies of Tenhar," he said softly.

Komi shrugged. "We have lots of enemies already. What's one more?"

"Tenhar is known for its vindictiveness. It's one thing to be hunted by a few vampires that are angry about a colleague's death. Anyway, we were protected. The tribe itself had sanctioned it. It's another thing to anger the tribe we know is trying to start a war. What if they attack our tribes? They're not above it." He turned and pointed his gun at an invisible target.

Komi stopped cleaning her blade. She hadn't thought about it. She glanced up at Jode.

"You want to call Jin? Tell him we can't do it?"

Jode snorted, but said nothing else. He completed taking care of his guns and turned to see if Komi was had done the same, only to find her staring intensely at him. She seemed to be memorizing every part of him. She put her blade down and stepped closer to him.

"We have been through a lot together. Fought many battles, gotten many scars. We've always entered head first. But you're right. This is different. Jin has us mixed up in something far more deadly. We may not come out of this the same. The consequences are far-reaching, as you said."

Jode faced her fully. "What are you saying?"

"I'm saying once we go down this path, there's no turning back. So I'm asking if you think this is a path we should follow."

Jode stared into her eyes. They eyes reflected nothing.

"Why are you leaving this decision to me?"

"I'm not. I want to know what you think."

"I think we know too much already to back out of this. More importantly, he is our High Prince. He asked for our help, and we must respond."

Komi smiled coolly. "So this is part of our duty to the High Prince?"

"I do it because Jin is my friend."

"I agree. So I guess you can come out of the shadows, Jin. You know you can't hide that scent from me."

Jin stepped into the open area with a cold smile on his face. He stopped in front of them, glancing at both before speaking.

"I'm glad you've decided to assist your *friend*. It would have been awkward to have demanded your service because I'm the High Prince."

Komi arched an eyebrow. "Really?"

Mirth danced in Jin's eyes. "Yes really. You ready?"

"We're always ready."

They walked further onto the property, taking the slope towards a wall at the property's edge. From the low vantage point, the view of the river was obscured, but that made it easier to fight because the trees provided cover.

"How long?"

Jin said, "Less than ten minutes."

The Volvo that followed Jin deliberately overshot him to seem like it was going elsewhere. Jin stopped the cab two blocks from his true destination, not only to throw the Volvo off, but to give him and his friends time to move into position. Jin stood beside a tree with his long blade flat against his leg. He watched as Jode climbed a tree and Komi moved to another just a few feet from Jin.

Five minutes later, they heard and felt them approaching. Jin tilted his head slightly, trying to assess how many were approaching. Komi who raised three fingers to him. Jin nodded slightly. He counted to thirty twice, before stepping from behind the tree.

Ahead of him, a vampire was dressed in a pale gray suit. He wore black gloves and held a broadsword. When he saw Jin, he moved into attack position.

"Why are you here? Do you not know who I am?"

The vampire sneered and said, "I heard you violated law, Jin." He had deliberately ignored Jin's title and spoken to him as a common familiar.

Jin flexed his grip on his sword. He rolled his shoulders before glaring back at him.

"Attacking me on my property? That's grounds for death. You better think about it."

"There's nothing to think about, Jinny," the vampire smirked. "Where's the human? Hiding her around here? Give her up and we'll act like you deserve to be called High Prince."

Jin couldn't believe the fool standing in front of him. He wondered where the vampire had gotten his confidence. He must have believed that Jin had been overly sheltered. What many vampires failed to realize was that Jin had trained to fight his whole life to fight. His mother wouldn't have had it any other way; she believed in training the body to be a weapon. In addition to martial arts, he had been trained with swords and archery. His father had trained his mind to be another weapon. It was true that his parents had kept him ignorant about many things, but defending himself wasn't one of them.

"So be it. Come get me."

The vampire scowled, then stepped forward. The chaos that ensued was brief, but bloody. From his perch in the tree, Jode took aim at a vampire trying to creeping three feet behind Jin. Jode waited until the vampire just passed him before firing at his head. The vampire stumbled forward, then had his head removed by Komi's blade. Jin swung his blade once and charged forward. Three cuts followed: One slash across the vampire's chest, another to cut off his hand, and the final slicing off his head. It happened so fast that the vampire was still blinking when his head hit the ground. Jin stepped around him, walking slowly towards a vampire in the distance.

Jode had shot the vampire twice, placing a bullet in each leg. He had crumpled to the ground, but was trying to get up. In a blink, Jin was pulling him up by his light brown hair, stretching his neck severely.

"Who do you think you're dealing with?" Jin hissed.

The vampire quivered beneath him. He saw how fast the High Prince moved. He had hear the myths about the Alpha's abilities, but seeing it himself made him realize that they should have heeded Tobias's warnings not to engage Jin. But Barry didn't think Jin would know how to use his power. Now Barry was dead, sliced to pieces.

Jin jerked his neck again, making the vampire's voice strained as he begged.

"Mercy, High Prince. I was just following my orders..."

"You were ordered to attack your High Prince? Who would be stupid enough to order that?"

"B...Barry. He wanted to attack you, High Prince, I swear."

Jin stared at the blubbering fool below him. He raised his blade, then brought it down just short of the vampire's neck. But he pressed against it hard enough to draw blood.

"I could kill you now, but I think I'll let you live. I want you to get those carcasses off my property. You can deliver them to your Prince with a little message from me. If someone else from his clan gets stupid enough to challenge me, right after I take their head, I'm coming for his."

He tossed the vampire aside. As he walked away, he nodded and he heard the zip of a gunshot that hit the vampire between the eyes. It wouldn't kill him, but it would slow him down considerably. It would give Jin and his friends time to leave town.

The vampire remained on the ground for over an hour while his body tried to heal. He faintly heard someone walking towards him, as a hum vibrated through his nerves. *Danpe* he thought. He opened his eyes to slits. A tall, blond woman stood above him. She wore tight, white leather pants and a bustier with a white leather jacket. Her sword was drawn, its hilt an elegant ivory with intricate designs. By then, the vampire had managed to open one eye fully, the other too crusted over by blood.

"Cheryl...what are you doing here?" he rasped.

She tilted her head at the mess Jin had left behind. She smiled coldly. "Levi. You were never too bright." She saw the corpses to her right. She laughed harshly as she raised her sword.

"No," he gurgled. She arched an eyebrow, questioning.

"The High Prince spared me..."

She shrugged and brought her blade down swiftly.

"I'm not the High Prince. Neither is he...yet."

She turned on her heels and walked back to her car. Snapping up her phone, she called the clean-up crew. Afterwards, she pulled a computer from the dashboard. She tapped a few buttons and the screen brightened to a GPS map. On it, a dot moved north of the city. She opened the phone.

"Sire, I have him heading to upstate New York."

"Stay back. Since we can track him, let him have a two-hour lead. I want you to make sure you gather evidence against Tenhar."

"You want the heads?"

Eldon lifted his drink and gazed out at the foggy courtyard behind his manor.

"Yes, send them to me on ice. There's a Prince that I want to see them."

"Yes, Sire."

* * *

Jin sat in the backseat, concentrating on feeling Adina. He was pulling an invisible rope towards his goal. When he tried to contact her, all he got were faint murmurs of being tired or the child said it was hungry and wanted him to come.

"This is this right direction," he said to Jode, who was driving.

"What the hell is somebody like Flaxon doing out here?" Komi asked, frowning at nature.

Most of the trees still had their leaves, rich shades of brown, gold, and orange. She couldn't believe that Flaxon would be able to tolerate this much nature, but then again, she didn't really know anything about him. They met him occasionally to buy guns, having met him through Jin. Komi always thought the fact that Jin knew someone like Flaxon was odd but it also was made her like Jin so much. No one could pigeonhole his virtues based on his associations.

Jin told them what had happened three months earlier in London, and that Flaxon had his mate. He told them that Flaxon had taken her to upstate New York or maybe even further. They wouldn't know until they got there. Jin thought he would have heard from Flaxon already, but there was nothing yet.

"I don't know. I just know that's where she is."

"Is she alive?" Komi said, turning slightly to stare into Jin's glazed eyes.

"Yes," he said, as if he was in a trance. Then his head snapped back.

"Adina..." he whispered.

Adina woke in a strange bed. She raised her head a little too quickly, causing a dizzy spell to come over her. She pressed her eyes closed to try to stop the spinning. She heard the door open and slowly opening her eyes. The strong sound of Jin's voice invaded her mind.

Maggie walked to the equipment, checking that the blood was flowing quickly enough for the children. She decided to open the valve a little more. Maggie noticed that Adina was watching her steadily. She smiled faintly at her.

"How are you feeling? Think you can eat?" Maggie asked.

Adina said nothing. Her eyes glinted slightly when Maggie sat next to her and touched her forehead. She still said nothing. Adina looked around the room, then out of the window. Maggie noted her fierce concentration. Then it dawned on it what was happening. She rocked back, got up, and pushed a button to make the blinds close.

"Why are you doing that?" Adina asked menacingly.

Maggie smiled coolly. "I have your attention now."

She walked back to Adina, who was now glaring at her. She started to place her hands on Adina's stomach, but hesitated when Adina hissed at her.

"I'm just checking on the children. I'm a midwife. May I?"

She took Adina's silence as consent. She laid her hands on her stomach and sensed the children calming and connecting with their father. She looked up at Adina.

"The High Prince should know that possessing his mate's mind will tire her. You can speak to me without controlling her. No harm has come to her and none will, but as a human, it would stress her too much for you to continue."

Maggie waited. Adina stared at her for a moment longer before blinking rapidly. Her face turned into an angry scowl before she rolled her eyes. She focused on Maggie again.

"Where am I?"

"In a safe house."

"But where? How did I get here? Where's Flaxon?"

"He'll be joining us shortly. He can explain everything."

"Bring him to me now," she growled in an ethereal voice.

Adina blinked rapidly. Then she said, "Hey. He's pissed and he really wants to talk with Flaxon now."

Maggie nodded and stood.

"Wait a second. Did you say children?"

Maggie nodded back. She watched Adina's eyes grow large as the young woman began to rub her stomach.

"I'm going to have twins?"

"Yes. They were trying to hide the truth from you, from everyone."

"Why?" she asked, half-speaking to her children. She waited before looking at Maggie. "They didn't want to scare me. Hmm. It's so weird to be able to hear them...communicate with them." She was contemplative for a moment. Suddenly, a rumbling sound permeated the room. Adina smiled shyly. "You know, I am hungry. I hope the offer for food still stands."

"Of course. I'll just—" Maggie started.

The door opened and Flaxon walked in. At least, Adina thought it was Flaxon. She hardly recognized him with his darkly dyed hair. She had to notice that his skin color was not as light as she had thought; he was a pale olive. He looked more sinister, older, but still cocky. He walked over to her after nodding at Maggie.

"How are you feeling?" he asked, sitting next to her on the bed.

"I'm fine. Why did you change your hair?" she asked.

He smirked. "It was time. I think my presence was requested. I know your is mate floating around in your head, growling about all the different ways he's going to kill me."

Adina glared. "Flaxon, where the hell are we?"

Flaxon stood, arms outstretched. "This is one of my many homes—a home away from home type of thing." He backed away from the bed smiling smugly.

"And exactly where are we?"

Flaxon walked to her. He leaned down, a mocking smile on his face. "Wouldn't you like to know...Jin."

Adina growled and Flaxon took out his phone. "Tell your Prince to pay attention. My phone number is 914-555-0916. He should give me call and give you a rest."

Adina stared at him before closing her eyes. Then she opened them again, annoyed.

"Why must you two be in this constant pissing contest? And with me in the center of it."

"It's not me feeling inadequate. You should rest, but when your mate contacts you again, let him know that I have kept you safe."

Adina studied him a moment before laughing.

"What?" Flaxon asked glaring at her.

"You're afraid he's gonna beat your ass. Now you finally want the girl with the fat ass's help."

He sneered just as his phone rang. Adina continued to giggle as he answered.

"What?"

"This is the person that will take your head unless you can tell me in the next minute why I shouldn't," snapped Jin.

"Cut the bullshit threats, High Prince. Your mate is safe. I made sure of it. She is secure, getting blood, and eager for you to sweep her of her feet again. I think I've earned the right to a few requests. You know our—"

"Oh...My..God!"

Flaxon nearly dropped the phone.

"What happened?"

"Look how big I am!"

Flaxon frowned at her. "What do you mean?"

"*Flaxon!*"

Jin was shouting his name. He put the phone back to his ear.

"Hold a sec. Your mate is going through the 'I'm as big as a house' phase."

"What!" Jin snapped.

Komi wondered why he was so riled. Jin just shook his head, then he heard Flaxon snarling at Adina. He growled into the phone and Flaxon growled back.

"The sooner you get to your mate, the better off I'll be," Flaxon said.

"You should have left her where she was," replied Jin.

"You would prefer her to be in the hands of your enemies? I didn't think you would."

"I'm not certain that you're not my enemy," Jin snapped.

Flaxon stunned Jin with his next words.

"I chose to help her partly because I wish to serve you, High Prince."

Jin was silent, then he said, "Fine. Tell where you are."

"Meet me at Coleman's Lodge. You'll see the sign for it. Before I bring you here, we need to discuss some things."

"No. I want to see her, then we can talk."

"High Prince, we need to discuss a few things. I told you that I have other reasons for wanting to protect Adina."

"Does it have anything to do with the Mixed Breeds?"

Again, Flaxon was silent. After a pause, he said, "So you took the time to learn some history. It's a wonder. I always thought the history of Mixed Breeds was suppressed."

"Not for me. I made it a point to learn the past, and one thing I learned was that breeds like killing vampires."

"Not as much as your kind likes killing us. As I said, we have much to discuss, or my people will take you on a wild goose chase around this country in search of your mate."

"Do you dare threaten to keep me from my mate?"

"I will do what I must. But all I ask is that we meet. After that meeting, I will take you straight to her."

Jin thought for a moment, then let himself connect with Adina. When he entered her mind, he sensed her anguish.

What is wrong? Are you being harmed?

I'm so big. When I went to sleep, my stomach was flat. Now it's almost the size of a basketball! What the hell is happening to me? This isn't natural. Jin, what is happening?

It's okay. You're okay. You're not in pain, are you?

No, but I look...

You look beautiful.

How can you know? You haven't seen me.

I don't need to. You're always going to be beautiful to me.

Really?

Don't ever doubt it.

There was a pause as Adina thought about something. She thought to Jin, *He's a bastard, but...I trust him. You aren't mad are you?*

Of course he was mad. But what could he say? Flaxon had a point. He had protected her and kept her safe. He couldn't fault her for trusting the vampire, breed, or whatever Flaxon was. He sighed before speaking into the phone again.

"Fine, Flaxon. But you will ride with me back to where ever you have Adina."

"Fine. I'll be there waiting for your arrival."

Jin hung up. He told Komi and Jode about Flaxon's request.

"We're not going to meet him, are we?" asked Komi.

"Yes, we are."

Komi and Jode looked at each other. Komi looked back at Jin, frowning.

Jin smiled. "I know that I could just go to her, but he helped her when he didn't have to, and she is safe. What's the harm in indulging him a little? He knows that if he screws me over, I'll take his head."

"I guess. I still don't understand why he took her if not to sell her to the highest bidder."

"I don't know, but it has something to do with Breeds."

"I still can't believe they exist."

Jin faced the window. "They do, and Flaxon's tied to them. That's another reason I'm meeting him. I want to know his connection to them that he would willingly use my mate against me."

"Are you going to let him get away with it?" asked Jode, glancing at Jin in the rearview mirror.

Jin smiled coldly in response.

* * *

Flaxon stared at Adina, who was looking on in misery at her very swollen stomach. He was surprised that she hadn't noticed it sooner. Then he remembered that her mate's mental communication had probably distracted her. A comment was on his lips when Maggie entered with a plate of food.

Adina perked up at the smell. Maggie nodded to Flaxon before going to Adina and setting the plate on the table.

"Let me help you up," she said.

Adina nodded and watched Maggie pick up a pillow to place behind her, then adjust the IV. A tray came out from between the nightstand and the bed, which Maggie placed on Adina's lap. Next, she put the hot plate on the tray, arranged the silverware, and set up a drink. Adina smiled at Maggie.

"Thanks," she said.

Maggie nodded before turning to Flaxon, who was leaning against the wall. She walked over to him.

"She gonna be alright?" he asked.

"Yes, Prince. She'll be fine. The food will help her create more blood, making her stronger, but—" She leaned closer to Flaxon. "She'll need the blood of her mate soon. The children are developing fast. They need their father's blood to develop properly."

"He'll be here soon enough. I'm stepping out. Be ready to do what is necessary if you get the signal."

"Yes, Prince."

"Give us a moment."

Maggie nodded and left the room. Flaxon faced Adina, who was eating her bloody steak with a satisfied smile. She looked up at him momentarily before returning to her steak.

"'Prince' is not the name I would use to identify you. How are you a Prince?"

Flaxon stared at her. "Don't worry about it," he answered.

Adina snorted. "Why won't you answer any of my questions?"

"Because I don't want your mate knowing anything before I'm ready to tell him. And right now it seems like he has mastered getting into your head."

Adina rolled her eyes before taking another bite of steak. She chewed slowly, glaring at Flaxon as she did. Then she sneered.

"I guess you don't want Jin to know how you conned these people into calling a thief like you a Prince."

"Yeah, your Prince wouldn't like to hear the story of how I *earned* the right to be called 'Prince.' Unlike him, I wasn't designated because of who my mummy and daddy are."

She rolled her eyes. "Whatever. Your jealousy of Jin sounds petty to me. People can't help who they are born to. It is what they do after they are born that should be the measure of their character. Jin's character lets me know that he more than deserves to be High Prince. You, on the other hand, have the character of a snake."

"A snake?"

"Yes. You slither to whatever position makes it easiest for you get what you want. Everything you do is ultimately for your own benefit. You only helped me because it serves you in some way, and I knew that way before your conversation with Jin. I'm not a fool, Flaxon. I know there is more going on than you wanting to protect me.

"But I know something else. As much as you dislike Jin, you respect him and need him, and that's what you hate. You're using me because deep in the back of your mind, you believe in Jin's good character, too. That just chaps your ass, doesn't it?"

Adina laughed slightly before returning to her food. But Flaxon growled at the truthfulness of her words.

"You'd better hope that you're right about your mate's character, because if you're wrong, there'll be a heavy price to pay."

She looked at him, taking note of the strange expression on his face. It disappeared so quickly that she wondered if she had seen it at all. For a moment, it appeared to be sadness.

Curious, she asked, "If you hate him so much, why protect me? Why are you willing to face the consequences for taking me?"

He looked down at nothing before responding. "If it wasn't for his family, I wouldn't be who I am today," he whispered. "His clan, vampires, betrayed us, the Mixed Breeds. We've paid a heavy price for trusting them before..."

"Why trust him now?"

Flaxon looked up, holding her eyes. "Because I will not live forever, and like it or not, I need your mate." His voice dripped with disgust.

Adina thought before saying, "He's different. You can trust him. Despite your motives, Flaxon, he'll know that you protected me. That means something to him. He's a good man—I mean, vampire."

Flaxon went and sat next to her. She tried to ignore his stare, but after a while, she looked up at him again. Their eyes locked for a moment. She titled her head.

"What?" she asked.

"He doesn't deserve you."

Adina frowned uncomfortably. "Why not?"

He smiled a deep, genuine smile. It faded too soon and his face became stolid. He said, "Maggie will take care of you. No harm will come to you while you are here."

"I know," she replied softly.

Then he ran his index finger along her cheek, his eyes hooded in deep thought. Adina was wondering about the gesture while her children reached for him psychically. But he withdrew, standing up before they could connect. Flaxon looked at her one time with soft eyes. Then he walked out the room, leaving Adina in her confusion. She felt her children's confusion, too, and stroked her stomach. It still amazed her to know that two children were growing in her womb. She hummed softly to them as she finished eating.

* * *

Flaxon was almost at the car, but he was still thinking about the conversation with Adina. Out of nowhere, Sashi stepped in front of him. He stopped mid-stride. He had trained her too well. She had actually caught him off guard.

"Are you sure about this?" she asked.

"Are we having this conversation again?"

"What did the council say?"

His eyes glinted, but Sashi stood her ground. She needed to know if they approved of Flaxon's suicide mission. Her arms were tense at her sides as she waited for him to answer.

He eyed her a long time, then smirked. "Of course they went along with it."

"How many heads did you threaten to take in order to have your way?"

He stepped towards her. Immediately, her hand moved to her back. He darted forward in a blindingly fast motion, but Sashi tracked him. She almost managed to whip out her tranq gun, but he stopped her, pinning her arm behind her back. She didn't bother to struggle. She felt him snatch the gun from her waistband. He held it in front of her.

"What's this?" he growled.

"It's a method to protect you. The High Prince will kill you for taking his mate. You can't possibly trust him not to take your head after what his clan did to your fath—"

"I'm keenly aware of what they did to my father," he hissed in her ear. "But the last time I checked, I was fucking in charge and I don't like people going behind my back."

He released her quickly, making her stumble into a wall. When she turned, she watched mutely as he took the gun apart with rapid precision. He tossed all the parts to the floor and started for the garage door, but Sashi blocked him.

"That is not a place you want to be right now."

His face was flushed, a human trait that showed itself in moments of rage. Sashi didn't care. She had to protect him at all costs, and if he took her head for it, at least she'd die trying to do her job.

"Move," he hissed.

They glared at each other before Sashi conceded and stepped out of his way. They both walked to the garage in silence. When they arrived, Flaxon was surprised to see that Nathan wasn't waiting for him as he had asked. He started to turn back, but Sashi stopped him.

"I told Nathan to stand guard here."

Flaxon's expression went blank. *What the fuck?! It's like I'm not in charge here.* "Why?" he asked, feigning calmness.

"Because you need someone who really knows you to watch your back. You need the best, and I am the best."

"You told him to disobey me and he listened?"

That was amazing enough, but then he thought about what she had said. She thought she was his best? She thought she knew him? It was weird that anyone would claim to know him. Hell, he had changed so much, sometimes he didn't even know himself.

"I told him that he'd better. You only blow in once in a while, but he deals with me everyday. Don't blame him, blame me. The fact is, you know I'm right. I'm the best and the strongest here, other than Maggie. So let's cut the crap and get a move on, since you're determined to make this crazy gamble."

Flaxon hid his amusement as she pushed past him, no longer feeling angry. She was right. Sashi was the best guard in the facility besides Maggie. Many people thought that her small stature made her a weak opponent, but it actually gave her an advantage. She was quick, flexible, and quite fierce. Sashi could fight with the best of them and usually came away the least bloody. On top of that, she was very intelligent, and had phenomenal hearing. Not even Flaxon could sneak up on her. It was a gift that he had relied on in the past. But he didn't want her there.

If things went badly, he didn't want her to be a witness. She might end up doing something stupid—not because he was her Prince, but because she loved him. He'd just been reminded of it in the hallway. She would die trying to protect him and would make it her life's mission to kill anyone that harmed him. Her loyalty was a good quality, but it might be her undoing. Right now, she was all business—face hard as stone. But he sensed fear, worry. There was nothing he could do about that. His path had already been chosen.

Flaxon walked over to a slick, black motorcycle. He grabbed one of the helmets and tossed it to Sashi, who had finished arming herself. She caught it and put it on. Flaxon climbed onto the bike and waited for Sashi to get on behind him. Her arms slipped firmly around his waist. Flaxon kick-started the motorcycle and roared out of the garage.

Chapter 24
Meeting of the Minds

TOBIAS GOT OFF THE plane, irritated beyond belief. His back and stomach still hurt from having been stabbed by his cousin. Then he'd had to sit on the plane for over five hours after a hasty patch job, and it was enough to push him over the edge. He walked through security with a face so contorted, it made the guards wary. They delayed him for another ten minutes before they were sure that he wasn't a threat to anyone. He stormed out of the airport to flag down a cab. Tobias tossed his bag into the backseat and slammed the door behind him.

"78 W. 207th Street."

The cab pulled off just as Tobias' phone rang. He flipped it open.

"Yes?"

"*Barry's dead. So are Levi and Jas.*"

Tobias clenched his jaw, the muscle jumping for a second.

"Why are they dead?"

"*Because Barry was killed by Jin...*"

"Who the hell told that idiot to go after Jin, when I explicitly said to wait for me?"

The voice on the other line hesitated. "I..He got a call, then he left with Levi and Jas."

"Who called?"

"Well...we thought it was you. Barry said that you gave the order and—"

"I never called Barry." Tobias frowned. He wondered who had called Barry and why.

"Do you have Barry's phone?"

"No, sir. It was taken along with their heads. We only found the bodies...what was left of them."

"What?"

"Someone burned the bodies and took the heads?"

"Jin?"

"I don't think so, sir. We can't prove that he didn't, but we don't believe so."

Tobias steamed. If Lars found out about this latest debacle, he would surely take Tobias' head. Someone out there was trying to sabotage him, and Tobias needed to find out who.

"I'll be at the rendezvous point in about twenty minutes. I want an update on everything you know. Is someone tracking the High Prince?"

"Yes, sir."

"Fine. Make sure everyone is ready to leave after I'm updated."

Tobias closed his phone, thinking hard. *Something is not right.* He couldn't believe that three of his people had been killed. Who the hell would tell them to attack the High Prince? Jin was an Alpha, and contrary to rumors, he'd been well-trained. If anything, Tobias would have chosen to fight Jin only after he'd been heavily sedated. He considered contacting Lars, but dismissed the thought quickly. That would only invite more trouble. He called someone else instead.

The phone rang three times before it was answered by a voice. that caressed his ear like velvet.

"Baby, I *didn't think you'd call*."

"Chelina, I need you."

"*I see. You need me. How do you need me?*"

"Business."

There was silence.

"*When do you need me?*" she continued.

"Now. Meet me at 78 W. 207th Street. It's very important. Come packing."

"I *always do*."

The call ended. He let go of a breath that he'd been holding. He didn't want to involve Chelina, but it couldn't be helped. He just hoped that he could keep her under control. She was the best muscle he had alive and nearby, and he needed all the help he could get.

*　*　*

The owner of the restaurant came to the window where orders are served up. His waitress, Sally, had come to him, wary about a customer. After thirty-seven years, Mike had learned to trust her instincts. Sally had been with him for most of those years and was usually spot on when it came to troublemakers.

Sally pointed to a man in his mid-thirties who was sitting at a booth in a dark red shirt over a white tank. He had light, dusky skin with very dark eyes and dark, wavy hair. Most of it was off his face, though a long strand flopped forward. Many of the women noticed his Adonis-like features, apparent even though he was clearly tense about something. He wasn't being obvious, but Mike knew that he was looking out the window for something.

Just looking at the man gave Mike the creeps, but he'd only minded his own business. So far. Mike gave a faint nod to Sally, acknowledging that he had an eye on the man, then went back to cooking. Ten minutes later, Sally was back and looking scared, but this time Mike caught the source of her nervousness.

A tall, young Asian man had come in. Behind him was a man who looked distinctly Arab, with a dark-skinned black woman.

The Asian man stood at least 6'4", was broad-shouldered, and had long, jet-black hair pulled into a loose ponytail. He wore a simple dark pullover and leather pants. The Arab man stood six feet tall and wore a light jacket with dark slacks and white shirt. His hair was cut short with thin sideburns. The female, 5'7", was dressed in a mini-skirt, dark top, and a long trench coat.

The Arab male and the female stood back as the Asian male walked to the man in the red shirt. At that same moment, Mike went for his rifle. Nothing about this situation felt right. He wasn't going to throw them out, but he would be ready for anything.

Flaxon barely looked up when Jin came in the restaurant, although he did notice that Jin had come with his friends, Komi and Jode. He remembered meeting them years ago, when Jin spent most of his time partying across the globe. He had sold them some of the best weapons that he carried for commercial purchase. They were very good customers.

Flaxon grabbed the salt, lightly sprinkling his vegetables, then did the same with the pepper. He picked up his knife and fork, proceeding to cut into the steak. He forked up a nice chunk and stuffed his mouth just as Jin arrived at his table. Flaxon chewed slowly, letting his eyes slowly rise to meet Jin's. He noticed the Prince's cool gaze. Flaxon waved his hand, offering Jin a seat.

Jin sat slowly, taking in the sight of Flaxon eating *food*. Vampires rarely ate because it did nothing for them. They only did it for the sake of appearances. But Flaxon seemed to be really enjoying the steak. Jin rested his hands on the table, clasping them together. He waited until Flaxon finishing chewing before he spoke.

"Why?"

Flaxon lifted a glass of water to take a huge gulp before saying, "Why, what?"

"Why shouldn't I just take your head now and save myself the trouble of taking it later?"

Flaxon smirked. "Think you can take my head that easily?"

Jin stared coldly. "You want to test me?"

Flaxon shook his head slightly. He cut into his steak again. "Spare me the threats, High Prince. We are here to make arrangements."

Jin noted that Flaxon had used his new title, and had even used a respectful tone. He leaned forward and asked, "Why?"

Flaxon stopped cutting and stared at him. "Because, Jin, you need a lot of help and I'm the only one who can provide it."

Jin leaned back. "Really? I can find her without your help..."

"That's not what I'm talking about and you know it. You have no idea what's coming, especially with Adina..."

Jin bared his teeth, barely managing to contain the snarl. He was just about to speak again when the waitress came over.

"What can I get you?" she said. Her voice squeaked at the end. Jin noted the fear, looked up at her nervous smile, then said, "Coffee, please. Two creams, no sugar."

Flaxon snorted. "Thought you would like it black."

"Ha, ha," replied Jin.

The woman was still there. Jin turned back to her. She cleared her throat before asking, "Anything else?"

"No. Nothing else."

The waitress nodded and quickly left. Jin nodded again and his partners took a booth behind him.

Flaxon continued eating and Jin waited for him to speak. A while later, Jin's coffee was in front of him. He poured in the two creams and stirred.

"How can you eat that mess?" Jin sneered.

"I know," Flaxon replied. He picked up another piece of steak and inspected it. "This meat is far from the best, but what can you expect up in the mountains? Now the venison, that's good meat." He plopped it in his mouth.

Jin's lip curled in disgust as he looked away.

"Flaxon, you've got two minutes to explain why you are relevant to me." Jin's voice was low and menacing.

Flaxon stopped eating and stared at Jin. He placed the utensils on the plate then pushed it away. He stared at him a moment longer before speaking.

"Know your history, Prince?"

Jin scowled. "I know that as a Breed, you are violating your truce by taking my mate."

Flaxon laughed, shaking his head. "I violated the truce? By taking the human Mate that shouldn't exist because it's against vampire law? Yeah, I broke the truce."

"You lied to me, Flaxon. You knew the truth when I asked you in London."

"Yes, I knew the truth. At the time I didn't think you could deal with it."

Jin snorted. "Well, isn't that something? I was already arse-deep in trouble and you thought that I couldn't handle knowing that humans and vampires mated. That's rich. Real funny, considering the way things turned out.

"You knew the truth and kept it hidden because you wanted to use my mate as some form of collateral. Flaxon, your time is running out." Jin ended with a fiery glare.

Flaxon leaned forward. "I'm not afraid of you, Jin. Your kind has been hunting us for centuries."

"My kind hasn't been hunting anyone."

"Yes...They...Have. Your tribe publicly endorsed the truce then secretly created a militia to continue hunting and killing my kind."

"Bollocks!" snapped Jin.

"Bollocks? What the hell do you know about it? You've had an insular life. The only real truth you've had to deal with is that you are to become High Prince. The fact is that Tenhar created special ops to kill off Breeds with the blessing of your grandfather and elders from both sides of your family."

"You dare scandalize my family's name!" Jin hissed.

"It's not a dare, it's a fact." Flaxon snapped back.

They both bared their teeth, eyes flickering. Unspoken threats passed between them, and neither would back down. Jin saw fury in Flaxon's eyes, their intensity making Jin pause. In all their years of baiting each other, Jin knew that Flaxon would die for his truth this time. The vampires had violated the truce. For the first time ever, Jin deferred to Flaxon.

Flaxon saw Jin back away, giving a slight nod. That was as close as he would ever get to an apology. Flaxon concealed his shock with a nasty smirk. Jin leaned back, ignoring it.

"Is that why you took her?"

Flaxon also leaned back. He looked out at the reflection of mid-morning light. He had lost his calm a minute ago, almost ruining his plans. If it hadn't been for Jin's deference, Flaxon might have lost his chance to help his people. The fact that Jin was letting him explain himself strengthened his belief that he made the right choice in trying to talk to the new High Prince. He faced Jin calmly.

"I took her for two reasons. One, because it wasn't safe for her. Two, because I needed to get to you."

"Why? You had my number. Why didn't you just call me—"

"—and tell you what? That she was pregnant? You would have come blazing into this without thinking, and that wouldn't have helped anyone. I needed you to become High Prince. She needed you to become High Prince. Only as High Prince would you have the power to protect her. Only as High Prince can you make laws and enforce them. You could influence the Council and make them live up to their duties and respect the existence of Mixed Breed."

Jin studied Flaxon impassively. He recognized a fundamental flaw in Flaxon's thinking: his idea of Jin's authority. Jin might be High Prince, but he had to work with the council, not lord over them. Yes, he was to provide guidance and enforce the rules as the final arbitrator, but he wouldn't be the one making the rules. That would be done by a council whose main concern was keeping the in-fighting to a minimum.

But he'd had a point about Adina. Jin never would have left her if he had known that she was pregnant, and that would have been bad. He would still be hunted, nothing would be resolved, and he would have had an even harder time trying to come into power. In two weeks, he would need to make a forceful speech about leaving Adina and his offspring alone. He might have a bargaining chip, though. If, indeed, vampires were in violation of the truce with the mixed breeds, Jin could hold that over the council. But he needed to know something first.

"My understanding is that the Breed could have one representative on the council..."

Flaxon laughed. "You're kidding, right? You're not bloody serious. I told you, we are being systematically killed off—"

"Why not come to the council?"

"Because vampires on the council knew this already and they would have us killed rather than let that fact be known."

Jin nodded. Then he stood. Behind the counter, he noticed the male cook tense.

"Fine. We'll discuss what you want in the car."

"What?"

"It's time to go. I want to see her and I'm tired of being this exposed. We have too many eyes here and though I know why you brought me here, you have nothing to fear from me...unless I learn something different from her."

Flaxon gave Jin a perplexed look. He couldn't believe that it had been that easy. But the glint in Jin's eye was a promise for retribution yet to come, in spite of all that had been said. Flaxon knew he had to be prepared for it.

Flaxon tossed a few dollars on the table as he slid out of the seat. He smiled slightly at the waitress and grinned at the frightened owner. He heard the gun un-cock.

Flaxon got in the car on the right side, Jin on the left. Jode drove with Komi sitting beside him. The car pulled out of the lot slowly, but joined the highway traffic quickly.

They drove in silence for a couple of miles. Jin was testing whether Flaxon was leading him away from the intense connection he felt to Adina. When he felt it growing stronger, he decided it was time to get to the heart of Flaxon's need to kidnap his mate.

As he turned to Flaxon, he heard a distant motorcycle accelerating behind them. Jin looked back to see the bike and its petite rider catch up with them, slow, then zoom past. A very faint hum passed through Jin, but he thought nothing of it. It didn't feel dangerous. Besides, there was a larger issue sitting right next to him. He glanced at Flaxon, who was perfectly alert. *Probably waiting for the other shoe to drop,* Jin thought.

"Flaxon, how are you connected to the mixed breeds? I thought you were a vampire."

Flaxon cocked an eyebrow. "What do you know about Mixed Breeds?"

"Not much. I just know they existed, they were part of the reason the war started, and there was a truce between the Breeds and the vampires. Not much beyond that."

Flaxon almost rolled his eyes. He had a sneaking suspicion that Jin knew more than what he was admitting, but decided to play along.

"Well, I guess that's all a vampire would know at this point. There has been a concerted effort by elder vampires and princes to make sure the past stays in the past. At the rate they are hunting down breeds, it will get a lot easier." He paused to take a breath before speaking again.

"A little over a hundred and thirty-five years ago, the tribes made a deal with the Breeds that allowed them to live in peace. Alonzo, then the Prince of the breeds, heard about the counsel The Three gave to the vampires and believed that he could reason with them based on that declaration. He was dumb enough to think that the tribes would respect the truce, that they would keep their word. So he sacrificed himself. He allowed his head to be taken for the safety of all Breeds. And for a time, we were at peace."

Flaxon looked out of his window without really seeing anything. The trees, rocks, and traffic blended into an image from the past of a young man out in the frontier with a woman, whose flowing dark brown hair lifted as she twirled her daughter. His hand reached for the image, but it faded and all he saw was his own bitter reflection.

"That was all the vampires needed. Seven months after the truce was signed, they began hunting, quietly killing off the strongest breeds, whose blood heritage was closer to vampire than human. The Great Secret Purge. The first wave lasted five months. By the end of it, the vampires had wiped out more than three-quarters of the strongest in the line. It was easy. They knew where we were because we usually lived in packs to protect the weak.

Once we realized what was happening, a few approached the vampire council. Breeds were entitled to a seat even though we didn't care to use it. But after the killings, they went to the council, hoping for justice. They wanted to go through the proper channels, not start another war. They were greeted by the Elders and a few Princes who called them liars and had them executed."

Jin stared at Flaxon, watching his hostility grow by the second. Flaxon was so tense he quivered. Jin still hadn't heard Flaxon confirm his suspicions. Jin wondered how all of this happened without his parents' knowledge. Then he remembered that they were probably locked up somewhere, being forced to mate with each other. He stopped himself from grimacing and tried to focus. He had to keep his head straight.

"How do you know anything about it? Were you there?"

Flaxon gave Jin the don't-be-stupid look. Closing his eyes to keep from rolling them, he said, "We had spies, some vampires who were sympathetic to us. One of the aids to an elder witnessed what happened at the meeting. He became an ally to the Breeds, unbeknownst to his elder. But don't worry, he was killed as a traitor by the Secret Sect, The Uriklo. Needless to say, we got the word and had to go into hiding. Not long after that, the Second Purge began and has been going on ever since."

Jin regarded Flaxon thoughtfully. "I still haven't heard how you became responsible for the fate of the Mixed Breeds, or why you didn't fight."

"Not enough of us were trained to fight. Like I said, the strongest ones were killed first when we were just walking around freely. Because of the lies told to us, they were sitting ducks. Those who weren't killed were called to protect the weaker members of the tribe. We went into hiding, thinking if we just stayed away from vampires altogether, they would leave us alone. A lot of good that did." Flaxon's jaw clenched briefly. "We used to be over three thousand, now we are fewer than nine hundred."

Jin stared at him then asked, "And you?"

Flaxon snorted. *Cold-hearted bastard.* He started to give a smart-ass reply, but thought better of it.

"I'm the strongest alive now, making me the Prince according to our Hierarchy. I'm charged with making sure no more of my kind is exterminated by vampires."

Jin felt Flaxon's anger constricting him. He had never seen such controlled fury. Based on the book his father, Prince Eldon, had given him, Jin knew that the promise had been broken. But the book didn't go into much detail and ended abruptly. He reasoned that somebody must have caught the author working on the forbidden book…but that didn't make sense, because the book would've been destroyed. Maybe the author panicked because someone found out about what he was doing. Regardless, Jin had a gut feeling that Flaxon was telling the truth. Flaxon was a lot of things, but he wasn't a liar. Not about this, anyway.

He couldn't imagine Flaxon a Prince, either. It wasn't as crazy as it seemed. Some of his anger towards Flaxon dissipated. Jin needed to know one more thing before everything could make sense.

"So, Flaxon, why did you take my mate? What could you possibly hope to gain by taking her?"

"I didn't take your Mate. I protected her like you asked," Flaxon snarled.

"I asked you to take her to the airport," Jin growled in response.

"You should be thankful that I didn't just leave her at the airport. Or should I have left her to deal with likes of Tenhar on her own?"

Jin's growls rumbled through the car, forcing Flaxon to respond with just as much force. He heard the intense protective growls from Jin's friends in the front of the car. Flaxon grudgingly backed down.

"Didn't you threaten to keep my mate from me if I didn't assist you?"

Flaxon sighed and turned from Jin. "I'm taking you to her now, aren't I? And by the way, take the next exit."

Jin's eyes glinted before he turned away. "You'd better be." After cooling down, he said, "But you still haven't answered my question. What do you want, or better yet, what do you think you're going to get from me?"

Flaxon's lips curled, his fangs slightly elongated. He wanted to rip Jin's neck out. The High Prince was such an ass. He mentally counted to ten before saying the words that were like ash in his mouth.

"Protection."

Jin almost laughed.

"Protection. You want protection from me?"

"Not for me," Flaxon hissed harshly. "For my kind, your children's kind…"

"My children are not your kind," Jin roared, shocking his bodyguards who had never heard him yell before.

Flaxon didn't blink. He yelled back. "The hell they aren't! They are Mixed Breeds, powerful ones, too, because of who you are. They deserve to be respected regardless of their bloodline, as do all Mixed Breeds." Flaxon took a moment to control himself.

"I'm asking you as High Prince, to fucking do your duty and enforce the treaty. Just like I said in the diner. The Three ordained the treaty and your kind subscribed to it. Honor the truce, stop killing Mixed Breeds. Allow our representatives on the council."

Jin looked at Flaxon, unimpressed by his passion. But he respected the demand. He hadn't asked anything for himself, just what was owed to his kind.

Crossing his arms, he held Flaxon's eyes with a steady gaze. "So why didn't you just say all of this in London before putting Adina on the plane?"

Flaxon took a deep breath. This was a test question. He sucked it up, knowing he was going have to delve further into some personal truth.

"Because you didn't...I didn't think you would care unless you had something invested in it yourself."

Jin glared at him before turning away. Both men sat in silence, Flaxon breaking it only to give more directions to the Lodge.

* * *

Adina sat on her bed thinking hard. She could sense the tension in Jin, but she kept sending him reassurances to calm him. She looked around the room for the first time with her own eyes. It was a nice room, comfortable, but plain. She wished she could see out of the window, but the blinds were sealed shut. The remote was next to the television. She sighed and leaned back onto the pillows.

She was in deep. She never imagined in all her wildest dreams that she would be in a situation as crazy as the one she was in now. Pregnant with twins by a powerful vampire, whose tribe made it a point to kill anything that wasn't pure. Someone who she had thought of as a thief-con-man-vampire had kidnapped her, but now she discovered that the con-man was a Prince over a group called Mixed Breeds. It was still mystifying.

Flaxon disturbed her. His emotional displays were usually limited to anger or disgust, so when he smiled at her, she didn't know what to think. It was actually a really nice smile; it softened his face and made him seem more human. She wondered what he could have been thinking about when he did it.

He cares about you

She rubbed her stomach slowly. "Is that what you think? Hmm. I think he just needed bait for your father."

He cares for you

Her children were insistent little tikes. She felt the conviction in their voices. She also felt the small bond they had developed to him. She was a little worried that Jin wouldn't appreciate it.

Why?

She kept forgetting that her children were connected to her thoughts, and like all kids they heard too much.

"He's just not fond of him, but I'm sure that he'll come to understand that Flaxon—"

She didn't know how to finish the sentence. What would Jin understand? He didn't like Flaxon. And Flaxon taking her from him probably would not help matters. Shaking her head, she just kept rubbing her stomach until she heard the door open to her room. The tall woman named Maggie came in smiling.

"How was the meal?"

"It was fine, thank you."

Adina turned to lift the tray, but Maggie waved her away. Maggie picked it up and set it next to the TV stand, then she stooped to take some blood out of the fridge. She set it on top of a movable shelf while she replaced the bag on the IV. Adina watched Maggie in silence. Maggie worked with professional efficiency and finished quickly. She nodded at Adina before turning to leave.

"Is Flaxon really your Prince?"

Maggie froze before turning back.

"Yes, he is. And he's a damn good one." Her voice was filled with unguarded passion.

Maggie's words sent a chill down Adina's back. From the look she gave, Adina felt like she had to watch what she said around the woman.

"I was just asking. I don't know what the hell I just put myself into, but I know that it's major. I just…I just want to know the sides in this. So I'm sorry if you feel offended that I question your Prince—"

"He is also your Prince," Maggie snapped.

Adina arched an eyebrow. "I think the High Prince will have something to say about that. Aside from the fact that I am not a servant to anyone!"

Maggie worked her mouth a moment before bowing. "Good afternoon, Miss Adina." She turned to leave again.

Adina wanted to throw up her hands. "Just tell me what the hell is going on here, Maggie! I'm pregnant, but I know this is not normal. I'm bigger than I should be for three months, even with twins. I need blood transfusions to stay alive, I can hear my kids talking to me, and I know I'm being used as a political football. So could you be a sistah and talk to me?"

"I'm not in a position to answer your main question. It is not my right." After taking a deep breath, she turned around. "But you are right. You should understand how this pregnancy will affect you."

She walked back and sat next to Adina. Maggie looked at her with steady eyes.

"I heard about how you became involved with the High Prince. It was quite admirable of you to help him when he was hurt. Your connection to him is deep, but it was made deeper because you carry his children. He has marked you as his mate so he will protect you at all costs. At least that is what is said."

Adina frowned. "What do you mean?"

Maggie tilted her head. "In the past, Vampires mated with humans without any regard for what it would do to them, especially the females. Many didn't survive. Those that did could not have children again. Carrying a vampire child to term wreaks havoc on the human body. The gestation period is shorter, the baby grows faster, and they constantly drain the mother of blood. Most of the time, vampire fathers had nothing to do with human women, except on rare occasions when he would provide his blood."

"Oh…so mating doesn't mean anything?"

Maggie shook her head rapidly. "No, that's not what I'm saying. I'm saying that your case is different because the High Prince seems to care about you and wants to protect you. He sees you as his mate, an equal. In fact, the Prince thinks the High Prince considers you more than a Mate."

"And he's counting on that to make Jin do what he wants."

Maggie said nothing, but smiled softly.

"So what's going to happen to me?"

"Well, in three months or a little less, you will give birth. As you see, I have to keep you on an IV because you're feeding more than one life. However, when the High Prince arrives, his blood will sustain the children better and give your body the opportunity to heal from the strain of creating so much blood so fast."

Maggie rested her hand on Adina's. "Giving birth is going to be rough. I won't lie to you about it. Women have died from it." Maggie grabbed Adina's hand when she pulled back. Fear was prominent on Adina's face, but Maggie gave her a reassuring smile. "But as difficult as it will be, my Prince made sure you would have the best care. He contacted me because he knew I understood how to deal with this situation. I have been doing this for a very long time. I know what to do and why."

Adina searched her eyes. Her conviction did not waver.

"How bad is it?" Adina whispered.

"The blood loss is the problem. Although the womb is filled with the usual human fluid, it is also filled with blood that the children are siphoning off of you. There is a chance that you'll lose too much blood, but we took every precaution against that. We have enough supplemental blood to keep you alive."

But Adina could almost hear the 'I hope' in Maggie's tone. Adina took a deep breath, worried. She could feel her children worry that they might hurt her. She rubbed her stomach reassuringly. Taking a deep breath, she faced Maggie again.

"Maggie, why is this happening?"

Maggie frowned at her. "Why is what happening?"

"Why does he think I can influence Jin when I...I barely know him."

Stating the truth that way stung, but she had to face it. She didn't know him that well. She didn't understand how vampires operated. Her heart wanted to believe that what they shared was real, that it was love, but even Jin had told her that vampires didn't feel the same ways as humans. Adina knew that Flaxon was hanging a lot of hope on her relationship with Jin. But how could he, when she wasn't sure of it herself?

Maggie watched the young woman fighting to be brave in a world that she knew nothing about. Adina was looking for more than an answer to Flaxon's need, but also reassurance as to what she had with the High Prince.

"The Prince believes that for you, the High Prince will be more than helpful. I cannot tell you because I did not see what the Prince saw to make him believe it would be so. I only know that the High Prince went out his way to make sure you were safe after helping him. That action is a whole lot different from the behavior of most other vampires." She patted Adina's knee before standing. "Get some rest."

Adina nodded, feeling lost, but shaking it off. In a little while, Jin would be with her. She felt his presence nearing, no doubt another gift from her children.

Chapter 25
Plotting and Insecurities

TOBIAS COULD ALREADY FEEL the nervous hum of the vampires within when the cab stopped in front of the building. Sneering, he gave the cabbie a generous tip and got out. The cab had disappeared from sight before Tobias walked towards the building. It was a walk-up with a dark green exterior, twelve windows visible in the front, and alternating windows connecting to a metallic fire escape.

He was about to go to the door, but he sensed *her* coming. He turned to his right and watched the woman approach. Her strawberry blond hair hung bone straight, dark shades covered her eyes, and her skin was porcelain white. Her fire-engine red lips curved in a funky smile. She wore a white trench coat that stopped just above her knees, her pants were silver, and her boots, also white, were mid-calf stilettos.

She stopped in front of him, waiting. Tobias stared at her a moment before he saw the clear strap across her chest. It was attached to a white case that held the sword she had named Ivy. Tobias nodded at her and started walking towards the door.

"I expected a better reception than that," she said in her smooth voice.

"Hi, Chelina," Tobias said over his shoulder.

He heard her snort and rolled his eyes. Dealing with Chelina was such a chore. She had a sketchy personality and was flamboyant beyond belief, but she had always been that way. Tobias first met her forty-one years ago, in the sixties, when she'd been running around, getting high as a kite, and acting like a hired gun in the Los Angeles. He was hunting a particularly cunning Mixed Breed who had been evading him for twelve years. The Breed managed to get the drop on him and Tobias was about to lose his head, but a gunshot out of nowhere stopped the Breed cold. When Tobias got up, there stood Chelina (Abby then) with the smoking gun.

From then on, Tobias and Chelina would work together at times. She would join him for the sheer thrill of the hunt; but her propensity to create chaos was unprecedented. She had no problem shooting into crowds, taking her blade out, literally roaring as she ran down an opponent. She liked to party hard and drink even harder. She consorted with humans like they were worthy of her time and she lived in a haze of counterculture, constantly hanging with the fringes of society.

She was the most unconventional vampire he had ever met, and she gave off a weird vibe. It was only later that he figured out that her signature was a cross of Pinu and Danpe. Danpe didn't believe in mixing with lower castes and Pinu was at the bottom of the barrel. One of Chelina's parents must have seriously fallen from grace for that to have happened, but she never said. In fact, he hardly knew anything about her except that she hated Danpe with the fire of a thousand suns.

Some thought that they were lovers, but that was never the case. Chelina wasn't interested in him that way, and he knew instinctively that she was not one to take lightly. She had too many issues. Sometimes he could see a berserker-type zeal in her eyes when they spoke or fought and it frightened him. That said a lot, because very little scared him. But she was good muscle—when he could control her—and one hell of a fighter. He never knew why she took up fighting with him or why she had saved him that day. He just knew that if he needed her, she would help him again. She had always said so.

As they walked up the stairs, he winced. The pain was kicking in again. He swore silently.

"What happened to you?" the soft voice said behind him. He continued up the stairs.

"Nothing."

"It doesn't seem like nothing."

He kept climbing. When he reached the right floor, he started walking towards the door at the end of a short hallway. Chelina caught his hand, pulling him gently. He winced again.

"You're bleeding, Tobias," she said coldly.

He turned, noting that she had taken off her sunglasses. Her light blue eyes stared coolly.

"I'll patch it up when—"

"What the hell is going on here, Tobias? Why are you bleeding?"

He pulled his wrist away from her. "I'll explain it later."

"Explain it now. You are obviously hurt and if you're calling me, something big must be going down. The word on the street is that the High Prince is in town, and you're here meeting some of your little peons. No. I think I want to hear it now."

Tobias stared at her, then walked back the way they had come. But he didn't go down the stairs. He beckoned her. When she got closer, he noticed a light, floral scent.

"The long and short of it is Lars wants the High Prince's mate. The High Prince mated with a human, we tried to grab her, but my best agents were killed by what I believe was a powerful Breed. Lars was pissed and acted in his usual way of inflicting pain. Before I called you, someone told three of my people to face the High Prince alone and all that's left of them is their ashes. Any questions?"

She stared calmly, twisting her lips. Then she laughed out loud. Tobias frowned.

"What's so funny?"

"Are you seriously trying to take the High Prince's mate from him?"

Tobias didn't answer. He headed to the apartment door, even as he heard giggling behind him. Just before he knocked, she spoke.

"You're going to get killed fucking around with that asshole Prince of yours."

Tobias glanced over his shoulder. "I'm so glad you care, but it's my duty to the tribe—"

"Bullshit. This little war that Prince Lars is trying to wage is going cost Tenhar a lot, and he's making you a sacrificial lamb. Hell, he probably was the one who sent those fools over to the High Prince. Bet you ain't called him about their deaths, have you? Probably because you suspect that Lars got his nasty little hands in it. You need—"

Tobias growled, silencing her. "You need not worry about what my Prince is demanding of me or what he is doing. Just be ready to fight when I say so. If you can't handle that, then leave."

She stared back in amusement. Finally, shaking her head, she said, "You're a fool, Tobias, but I got your back."

"Good," he snapped, turning to knock on the door.

The greeting in the apartment was brief. Of the wary team of vampires, all dressed in black, four stared back at him. After one look at Chelina, they frowned at Tobias. But he ignored them and headed straight to the bathroom, dropping his bag along the way. When he got there, he checked his wound and noticed that indeed, he was bleeding again, though not badly. He cleaned himself up by taking a towel and pressing it against the wound. He winced, raising his head slowly to stare in the mirror. His reflection was tired and drawn. He realized that he'd probably look a lot worst when it was all over. He removed the towel and tossed it in the tub.

Tobias rinsed the blood out of his shirt before putting it back on and slipping on his jacket.

He stepped out to find that Chelina had taken up post against the wall by the door. She looked bored out of her head. The other vampires were huddled around a couple of laptops, a few glancing furtively at Chelina. Tobias stopped in the middle of the mostly empty room. It was furnished only with the desk and the laptops, a couple of chairs, and a beat-up couch. On the right wall was a dry easel and a map of upstate New York.

"Attention, people!" said Tobias.

Everyone turned expectantly, if not a little tense. Tobias looked into the eyes of the vampires there, the oldest being the grey-haired Freda, a female with dark green eyes, a hooknose, and thin lips. She was the brain of the operation more than anything else. The youngest was the vampire named Charlie. His red hair stood spiky on his head, freckles covered his face and his blue eyes were eager. Tobias instantly knew he wasn't about to have that kid in the fight because his head would be removed within the first ten minutes.

He directed his eyes to Mort. Mort was a curly brown-haired male, standing over six feet with brown eyes and pale skin. He had full lips, a sharp nose and several ear piercings. Tobias noticed the fool swallow slightly and almost rolled his eyes. Mort was way too twitchy when not in action. Once the fighting started though, he was able to recalibrate and focus on the goal at hand.

"Who found the bodies?" Tobias asked quietly.

"I did, sir," said Harold. He was blond with dark blue eyes, a pointy nose and a full bottom lip. With his features evenly spaced on a round face, he looked more like the Tenhar Vampires from Northern Europe.

"What reason did you have for going out there?" Tobias asked.

"When we hadn't heard from Barry, Freda told me to check out what happened. We arrived at the house and it was quiet. We sensed no one. We walked around the property until we found the bodies. Rather, what was left of them," said Harold.

Tobias stared at him before looking to Mort.

"Were their weapons found?"

Mort walked around the desk. He picked up the blades of his fallen comrades and took them to Tobias. Tobias inspected each for authenticity before handing them back.

"Make sure they get back to their families," Tobias told Mort.

Mort nodded once and stepped back.

Tobias felt anger enter his heart. The deaths of those three didn't have to happen and what Chelina had said in the hallway was true—he was being set up for failure. But he didn't have time for self-pity or remorse. He had to prevail in spite of the pitfalls. He had no doubt that Lars would make good on his promise, and Tobias had heirs to protect.

"I don't know how this latest screw-up happened, but now that I'm here, that should be the end of it. Since we lost three vampires, I hired some help." He waved his arm to his left. "This is Chelina. I've worked with her before and she knows how to handle herself. She will be fighting specifically with me.

"You know the mission. We have to get the human that the High Prince saw fit to make his mate. The problem is that he is here, and I have reason to believe that the human has a very powerful Breed protecting her until the High Prince arrives to claim her. It's going to be our mission to track them down and get this human at all costs. Our Prince has demanded this. He wants it done as soon as possible.

But the fact of the matter is, we aren't the only ones looking for her. The High Prince's clan will be seeking her, too, and others, who just want some bargaining power. In addition, take note of the fact that we lost three people, who thought facing the High Prince would be a cakewalk. The simple fact is, Jin is an Alpha, and none of you will be able to take him, at least not in a head-on confrontation. So as we travel, we need to come up with a plan to disable the High Prince so that we can get his mate.

"But let me make this clear. No one is to act unless I say so and only if it's confirmed by Freda in my absence. Understood?"

Everyone nodded and Tobias went into the plan. Twenty minutes later, they were packing up to leave when Chelina stepped in front of him.

"You can't take on the High Prince, either. You're no match for him. None of you are."

He glared at her briefly. Keeping a hushed tone, he said, "I know that. Hence my plan..."

Chelina rolled her eyes. "Screw your plan. Let me handle the High Prince, and you take care of getting his mate."

"You? Are you barking mad, Chelina?" he asked through his teeth.

She smirked. "There are things you don't know about me, Tobias, and be grateful for that. Just let me handle the High Prince and you worry about his mate." She walked away and Tobias watched her leave.

What does she mean by that? he wondered.

* * *

Adina hated feeling helpless. She was completely at the mercy of vampires or Breeds or whatever, with their own agendas. Even though she could feel Jin coming closer with each passing second, it didn't stop her from recognizing the obvious.

She was in over her head. Again.

There was nothing about the situation that she controlled. To make matters worse, her twins were slowly killing her because of their vampire half. She didn't resent her children, she blamed herself for having been so silly. She didn't have to make love to Jin without a condom. *Do vampires even use condoms?* Adina shrugged off the thought. She didn't have to attach herself to Jin like she did, either. But she did, and now here she was.

Do you regret our meeting?

She sighed upon hearing his voice in her head. Truth be told, sometimes she did regret it, but then she remembered how she felt with him, how they connected beyond the sexual, how he wanted nothing more than to protect her for helping him. When she remembered that connection, her answer was clear.

No.

She rubbed her belly to soothe the children. They were worried about her, worried that they were hurting their mother. She assured them that she would be fine. She closed her eyes and embraced the feeling of Jin coming closer, but still her mind wandered to the conversation with Maggie. She didn't really know Jin. She had flashes of images of him. Sometimes she dreamed about places she had never been or seen, but in her heart, she knew they were real. She knew it was a result of her connection with him. Yet, it wasn't enough. As sleep started to overtake her, she wondered how much more her life was going to change.

As Jin sat in the car, he was thinking hard, though his face revealed nothing. He was aware of Adina's concerns and her doubts. The doubts bothered him more than anything. She didn't think she knew him, and that meant there was an underlying mistrust. She doubted that what they had was real, thinking it was just some lustful misadventure. Knowing that she felt that way stung him. He knew, for his part, that what he felt for her was real. He felt it every day since leaving her. He knew it wasn't the magnetism of just being bonded to her. He had felt pulled to her before then.

He glanced at Flaxon, who gazed stoically out the window. That vampire was an enigma wrapped in a mystery. A part of Jin wanted to snap Flaxon's neck for having taken Adina and lying about what he knew. But the fact was he understood Flaxon more than he cared to admit. Flaxon had a duty to protect his clan, and like any other Prince, he did what he needed to ensure its survival. Still, Jin had a hard time picturing Flaxon as the Prince of anything or being responsible for anyone. Jin wondered what other secrets Flaxon was harboring and how they might come back to haunt him.

He tried to send reassurances to Adina, who had just told him to hurry up. He smiled as a rustic lodge came into view. Flaxon's attention went towards it.

"Just park in the front," Flaxon said.

"I don't particularly like this idea, High Prince," said Jode.

Jin glanced at Flaxon. "Don't you have a less conspicuous place?"

Flaxon sneered before saying, "Go to the front. Don't worry, no one will notice the car. Leave the keys in the ignition. My people will secure it."

"You expect me to leave my car with 'your people'? I don't think so Flaxon."

Flaxon snorted. "What? You think we want this piece of shit you're driving? Please. The fact is we need to dump this car because it's probably being traced. We can leave it here and take a different way, or you can take this car to my place, leading them straight to your mate. So what will it be, High Prince?"

Jin studied him, then nodded at Jode. He drove the car to the front of the lodge and parked. As Flaxon was getting out, Jin grabbed a bunch of his shirt.

"If this is a trick, I'll make sure that you beg long and hard for death," he hissed.

Flaxon glared at him before jerking himself loose. Everyone got out of the car warily. Flaxon looked both ways before walking across the street. Jin and his bodyguards followed him into the woods. Half a mile in, Flaxon stepped in front of four motorcycles.

He turned to Jin, smirking. "Do you and your friends know how to ride bikes?"

Jin stared at Flaxon like he had asked if vampires drink blood, then looked to Komi and Jode. They nodded and Jin faced Flaxon again.

"Then hop on. The keys are in the ignition. We are not that far from where we need go, just about four miles," Flaxon said.

Each one climbed on a motorcycle. Flaxon slipped a pair of shades over his eyes. He kick-started his motorcycle and listened for the others to do the same behind him. He turned to find them waiting. Flaxon's back tire kicked up dirt and leaves, but he righted it, racing through the trees on a vague path. Jin followed, with Komi and Jode close behind. They raced through the woods at breakneck speeds until they hopped out onto a two lane road. Jin rode on Flaxon's right side, tracking Flaxon's every move as they sped closer to Adina.

I'm almost there, baby, Jin thought.

I know, Adina answered.

* * *

Sashi walked into the building, barking orders to the vampires that were still there. Once she gave the last one, she sought out Maggie. She found the woman in the kitchen sipping coffee and looking irritated. Sashi had never seen Maggie look so tired and *pissed*, but there Maggie sat, swearing softly and sipping her coffee.

"Are you going to stand there all day, Sashi?" Maggie asked without looking at her.

Sashi walked into the kitchen, taking a seat at the table across from Maggie. Maggie looked up, smiling wryly.

"How did it go, Sashi?" Maggie asked softly.

"He didn't look like he was in danger. I guess it went smoothly. I had the boys send out four bikes and they should be here at any moment."

Maggie stared at her cup before saying, "Things have changed and I don't know if it's for the better or the worse."

Sashi looked away from Maggie, having the same thought herself. She sank back into the chair and felt the weight of the world on her back. She hated what was happening. She was terrified for Flaxon's safety. And now they had a woman in their midst that was bonded to the High Prince, of all people. Sashi knew in her heart that the High Prince was going to make Flaxon pay dearly for taking her.

"What are you thinking about, Sashi?"

Sashi looked at Maggie. "He's trying to kill himself, isn't he?"

"Who?"

"Alphon—Flaxon. He has to be, to think of this harebrain scheme. Do you think that the High Prince will let him get away with taking his mate? What's going to prevent the High Prince from ordering all of our deaths? Yet, he leads him to us."

"Stop, Sashi!" ordered Maggie. "He is your Prince and you will not talk as though you have no faith in him, not in front of me. You don't know what he has endured, so you can't possibly understand the sacrifice—"

"Oh, please! You think I don't want to understand him? You think I don't have faith in him? I damn well do, but this is still crazy and you know it. Flaxon could have thought of something else, but he'd rather do this suicide mission than—"

"Than what?" growled Maggie, her eyes glowing intensely. "You may think you know him because you slept with him a few times, but you really don't. You're a child trying to understand an adult game, and you're too stupid to realize that he's trying to save us all and protect you. You need to grow up, Sashi. Flaxon is not some idiot. He knows damn well how this game is played. He is a vampire. The human blood in him means nothing. He has lived as a vampire most of his life, and every decision he makes is based on the power and rule of vampires. So you can take your whining someplace else, because right now I'm too tired to hear it."

Sashi glared at Maggie, then rose slowly. She wanted to take out her gun and shoot the woman between the eyes, but instead, she turned and walked away.

Maggie watched Sashi go, feeling a little sad that she had spoken so harshly, but the girl needed to be prepared for the inevitable. Sashi was right. Jin was going to make Flaxon pay, and Flaxon knew that, too. The punishment was coming and there was nothing anyone could do about it. Maggie also knew that her frustration wasn't with Sashi as much as it was with Adina. The scale of Adina's ignorance irritated her, even though Maggie knew it wasn't her fault. Before she could think any further of it, a powerful hum passed through her. She sat up straight to let the feeling flow through her. Then she pushed the cup away because she knew that the most powerful vampire alive had just walked into the building.

Chapter 26

Reunited with Painful Revelations

ADINA'S EYES FLEW OPEN. Jin had arrived; she felt it. His presence was like a vibration in her mind, on her skin. It wasn't an uncomfortable feeling, but it was weird.

What surprised her more was the fact that she knew what it meant. She knew distinctly that it was *his* signature. Her heart quickened as she called him to her.

It seemed like an eternity before the door opened, though it had probably been just minutes. When the door opened, she held her breath. Jin stepped inside. He was dressed in dark clothes and had his hair bound behind him. He looked healthy, more alive than the last time she had seen him. He faced her, his cool jade eyes taking in the surroundings before he focused on her again. Adina lay on the bed in a light blue gown, opened slightly in the front, revealing her swollen breasts. Her face was flushed with expectancy and her hair hung natural and loose, thick with curls. His eyes followed her hands. She was absently rubbing her stomach while she watched him.

He could hear his children calling him.

"Jin?"

Hastily, he closed the door, climbed onto the bed, and pulled her into an intense kiss, flooding Adina's senses. There hadn't even been time to blink before his mouth was against hers, their tongues dancing in delight. It was the most welcoming feeling in the world. His strong hands held her face, his thumbs stroking her cheek. Adina's knuckles glided across his cheek, then her hand opened to let her fingers slide through his hair. She sighed in happiness of having him near again. Jin let one hand slide down her arm until it reached the hand resting on her pregnant belly. Instantly, he connected with his children.

He let them explore his mind and soul. They felt bonded to him, but still they reached for more. Adina was nibbling his lip as they held each other. Jin rested his forehead against hers, his eyes closed, speaking to her in her mind.

I missed you.

Me too, Jin. I'm glad you're here.

Are you?

Adina frowned and opened her eyes. His were now the color of dark jade. *What are you asking me?*

Jin broke his connection with her and the children long enough to remove his jacket. He tossed it to the floor, kicked off his boots, and moved closer to her. His arm went around her shoulders and he connected with her and their children again, satisfying their longing. He smiled.

"I sensed you doubting that what we shared was real...that what I feel for you isn't real." His lips brushed her neck. "That you don't know me."

Jin inhaled her scent, claiming it as his own. He would never confuse it for anyone or anything else. Adina reciprocated the gesture, amazed that she could really smell him, not just the soap he used. She tried to think of terms that would best describe Jin's scent, but the words that came to mind were strange. Ancient, powerful, earth, intelligent, perfection, love, strength, courage, endurance, stability, passionate. Those words were unexpected, but that was what she felt as she bonded with her mate.

They moved away from each other again. Jin stared in her eyes and asked, "Do you doubt me?"

Adina looked away. Jin gently placed a finger under her chin, turning her face to his. "Do you trust me?"

Adina let herself get lost in the brilliance of his eyes. She almost wanted to lie, but he would know instantly if she did.

"I do, but—" she started.

"But what?" he asked softly.

"Jin, I feel so overwhelmed. Things have gotten way out of control and I really don't understand what I got myself further into by—" She almost blushed. "—by getting so intimate with you. Now I'm pregnant with twins by what everyone is telling me is the most powerful vampire on earth. You have this ability to control me completely if you choose to, and I find myself behaving in ways and knowing things that vampires do. So do I trust you? I trust that you really mean you want to keep me safe, but despite all that you told me, I don't know you."

Jin's expression was neutral as he watched Adina. She held his gaze, not wanting to back down. As she stared at him, she felt her vision change. She heard thumping and her eyes were drawn to the blood coursing through the veins in Jin's neck. Then just as quickly, her vision cleared, the sound faded, and she was left frowning, a little freaked out by the experience.

"Adina!"

Jin's voice sounded like a blast, making her jump. She was looking at worried eyes. She closed hers and took a deep breath, but she felt the tingle, the need beginning to push through her mind.

When her eyes opened again, she noticed that Jin was talking to her but she only heard a rushing sound. She was watching his lips move but couldn't help thinking about his neck.

Jin was worried about Adina until he saw her eyes glint, to his disbelief. Jin watched her eyes focus on his neck and he knew instantly that she and her children had connected. The children were unconsciously influencing her actions. Jin was talking to Adina to see if she was okay, but he stopped talking, just to see what she would do. Though he knew that they needed to discuss her concerns, their children had more pressing concerns.

"Adina, what do our children need?" Jin asked.

Her eyes slowly met his. They glinted again as she leaned closer. She whispered "*hungry*" before kissing him. A sharp tooth pierced his lip, followed by Adina sucking the blood. Just that little action was enough the electrify him. He grabbed her face, kissing her more deeply, feeling her bite and suck his tongue. Jin growled deeply and kissed her a little longer before pulling away. Adina tried to kiss him again, but then decided to nip at his chin and work her way to his neck. He knew once she reached it, she would bite him, and he could not allow that to happen, not yet. Adina was his mate and that gave her the right to take from him wherever she chose, but he needed to convince the council to accept her before she could exercise obvious dominion over him.

Jin pulled away quickly, removing his shirt. He leaned in, kissing her neck and the tops of her breasts as he gently removed the needle from her arm. Just as he was coming up, he felt her bite into his left shoulder. Jin gasped as she drank deeply from him. He felt his own fangs elongate, causing him to take her wrist and lick it before biting into it.

Adina moaned as she disengaged from Jin's shoulder. Blood ran from his wound, and her tongue wove intricate patterns in it. Aroused, she twisted on the bed, even as the children begged for more of their father.

Jin released her wrist and sat up. His own eyes burned with desire and need to bond again with his mate and now with his children. Jin brought his lips to hers in a fiery kiss, his left hand cupping her neck as his right slid up her leg moving the gown and exposing her soft skin. Adina's fingers dragged across his chest to leave faint scratches. When he broke off the kiss, he gazed into her eyes as his hand, for the first time, touched her bare stomach to feel his children rest within.

The feeling was overwhelming. The magnitude of what was about to happen humbled him. In his heart, he knew what he was doing to protect her was right, but at that moment, the imperative became real. He stared in awe, knowing that he was on the verge of breaking his promise to his parents, because at that moment, he wanted to be with his mate and no one else.

He lifted her to his lap with ease, surprising her again with his strength and speed. Jin used the ends of the gown to pull it off, leaving Adina fully exposed and leaving him at a loss. At that moment, he was looking at the human woman whose swollen belly carried his children. He reached out to trace her body, memorizing every curve and dimple. She stared back at him confidently, and he smirked back. A sense of pride sweep through him. *She belongs to me. She is my mate carrying my children* he thought.

His hands reached her face. His left knuckles brushed her cheek as his right thumb traced her lip. Adina took his thumb in her mouth, sucking on it slowly, letting her tongue twirl around it, before biting it. She watched his eyes glint as he rose, wrapping his arm around her waist. She released his thumb as he brought his lips to hers.

Mine, he claimed to her mentally.

Mine, she replied.

They kissed long and hard. Adina became more aware of herself, even as she recognized that her children needed more from their father. She pulled away, smiling softly at him.

"Is this what you want?" she asked quietly, staring in his eyes.

He tilted his head slightly. "What do you mean?"

She thought a moment before saying, "I don't... I'm not sure how to describe it, but...I feel as though you're seeing me and what has happened for the first time. I just want to know if I'm really what you want?"

He smiled at her, his hand on her belly a moment before hugging her close.

"Yes. You are what I want. You are my mate, but more than that, you—" he hesitated then said, "—you mean so much more than that to me. I look at you, heavy with my children, and I can't image anything more perfect." He moved a little so that he could gaze into her eyes.

"I am yours, Adina. Nothing will ever change that," he said, knowing in his heart that it was true. Nothing could break their bond because what he felt was beyond just being mated to her. He was connected to her and as long as she lived, his life would belong to her.

Adina didn't know how to respond. Jin had just admitted that he was in love with her, in so many words. As she stared into his eyes, she saw sincerity laced with the utter shock of its truth. She almost frowned until she saw the sexy smile touch his lips. She smiled back before gently kissing him again. As they kissed, she bit his lip again. Jin moaned, sliding his hand behind her head to her neck. He slowly massaged it until she drew away, her own eyes glistening with need.

Jin kissed her neck as one hand skimmed over her skin, stopping to gently knead her breast. Adina sighed, arching her neck for his tongue to glide along its length, nibbling, but never breaking the skin. She dropped head, bucking slightly against him. Jin moved with her arousing them both.

"I want you, Jin," Adina said in a husky voice.

Jin responded by kissing the nape of her neck. He leaned her back so that he could kiss lower, his mouth taking in her left breast and suckling it. Adina gasped, her fingers once again finding his hair. She gripped it tightly when she felt his sharp fang graze her nipple, making it instantly taut.

"Jin," she moaned, her head resting on top of his.

Jin lowered his head to kiss her stomach, connecting strongly with his children. He rested there momentarily, speaking to them, letting them know how much he cared about them and who they were to the world. He promised to protect them and keep their mother safe. After a few minutes, he felt Adina quivering. He moved then, kissing his way back up until he licked under her chin, then claimed her mouth again. He pulled away to see desire burning in her eyes.

He cupped her face and they held each other's eyes. No words were said; none needed to be said. They bared they souls and knew that they cared deeply for each other. Any doubts Adina had slipped in that moment of seeing him look at her so openly. She trusted him in spite of knowing so little about him, because in that moment, it didn't matter. She knew that what they had would keep him with her for as long as she lived. She still had questions about her situation, but she no longer doubted him.

Jin must have sensed it because he whispered, "Thank you."

"What?" she asked.

"Thank you for trusting me. You don't know how much it hurt to have my mate doubt me, our bond, what you mean to me."

She tilted her head, smiling slightly. She said, "You could show your appreciation by finishing what you started, followed by helping me feed our children."

He smiled brightly at her. "We have to hold off on the first thing…"

"Why?" Adina asked with a frown.

He leaned close to her ear and said, "Because when I take you, you won't be able to move for a long time, and neither will I."

His voice was low and seductive, making her shift against him. Then his nibbles on her ear made her sigh.

"Gonna fuck me senseless, hmm?" she whispered back to him.

"Damn right," he said. He placed a kiss under her ear before moving back to look at her. "Besides, I still don't trust this situation here."

Adina started to say something, but thought better of it when she saw how hard Jin clenched his jaw. She asked, "Well, what about our babies?"

He noted her hesitation, but let it go. Jin leaned back, taking her with him. He saw the mark on his left shoulder and said, "Take what you need."

Her eyes glinted. A part of him enjoyed seeing her eyes behave like vampire eyes. He wouldn't have expected to like it, but he did. He gasped when she bit into his shoulder again. He felt his fangs elongate with the need to reciprocate, but he didn't. She needed his blood more than he needed hers. So he just rested his head against hers, letting their thoughts blend as she fed their children.

Jin got flashes of her life, images of her as a child playing, of her family at a picnic and on holidays. He began to see her world, her very human world, knowing that she could never go back to it. He held that thought back from her, but she was too focused on the children to notice. He knew he would have to talk to her about very soon. He had to take her away from her family, not only for her protection but for theirs.

The memories flashed forward to when they first met. Jin experienced her conflict about whether to help him. He sensed her curiosity and then almost laughed out loud at her first impression of him when he woke. *Silly,* she thought to him. He smiled against her neck as he relived their passionate night until parting. He felt her pain at leaving him.

I'm sorry I let you go, he thought.

She slowly withdrew from his shoulder, turning to look at him. His eyes were clouded with thought. She sat back, studying him, then asked, "Why are you sorry?"

He shook his head feeling a little angry, a little helpless, and finally like the fool. When he brought his eyes back to hers, he saw acceptance and warmth. He almost didn't want her to be so forgiving.

Adina could sense his self-deprecation. Feeling that the children were content for the moment, she slipped on her gown while Jin watched her. She shifted in his lap, turning so her back rested against his chest. She leaned her head back onto his right shoulder, taking his hands and placing them on her swollen stomach. Once she was comfortable, she spoke.

"You have nothing to be sorry for, Jin. What happened, happened."

He sighed, inhaling her scent. The smell intoxicated him, reminding him of home, of being where he belonged, of comfort and caring. But he also felt that he had failed his mate. He failed to protect her and his children and as a result, she was caught in the middle of a lot of damn bullshit.

Adina started laughing. Jin frowned at her.

"Why are you laughing?" he asked.

"I like to hear you curse," she replied.

"I didn't…" he started, but then realized that she had been listening to his thoughts. It amazed him that she could without him initiating the connection. He tilted his head to look at her. She turned to catch his eye.

"Blame your children. It seems they are making me into a vampire."

Though her voice was steady, he heard the faint tremor of fear at the idea. He wanted to be hurt by her rejecting the possibility of being a vampire, but how could he when he didn't want that for her either. He liked that she was human. It let him experience feelings that he would never know with a vampire mate. But her humanity scared him, too. He would never admit his fear to her, but she wouldn't live as long as him, and she was so fragile! He wanted the mother of his children to be with him in all her youthful vibrancy. He didn't want to watch her grow old, her body breaking down until death finally took her forever.

Jin swallowed the thought when he felt Adina sensing his distress. Refocusing himself, he decided to deal with the now, beginning with telling her why he was sorry.

"I placed you in such an awful position that day. I should have never come to you—"

Adina rolled her eyes. "But you did, and like I said before, I don't regret it." She hesitated before adding, "I didn't think you regretted it. I mean earlier you said—"

He held her closer, kissing her temple. "No. I don't regret us. But I do regret leaving you like that. I regret not knowing enough about myself and my abilities to prevent you from becoming a pawn in this mess, caught between so many. I introduced you to a criminal who kidnapped you for his own gain."

A faint smile touched her lips. "He wasn't *so* bad. I mean, he kept me safe."

Jin sneered. His ears hurt from hearing her defend the waste of flesh named Flaxon. Something in her tone bothered him, but he let it go…for now.

"Yes, I can see that, but he betrayed me, lied to me, and used you to get to me. Forgive me if I have no liking for the bastard."

Adina chuckled. "It's okay, Jin. I understand. I'm just saying…"

"Please say no more about it."

She stiffened at his tone. Releasing his tension he said, "I'm sorry. I just hate that I wasn't there for you when you needed me. I hated that I couldn't come without leading half the vampires in the world straight to you." He laid his hand over hers. "Tell me what happened, how did he come to find you?"

"He didn't tell you?"

"No," he said. "But even if he did, I would still want to hear what happened from you. Tell me, please."

"Okay," she said, sliding a little to get more comfortable. "Well, I got back…"

He smiled. "No. Use your mind. It's faster. Besides if you can communicate with me mentally, then you should practice so that you can control it and use it better. Think about what you want to tell me, but focus. It's easy to let things come out in a jumble. I usually don't mind, but the more focused you are, the more information I can get about what happened to you, okay?"

She nodded feeling a little nervous. "I think I can do it."

"I know you can. Close your eyes, it might help."

She closes her eyes and thinks back to the point when she returns home. She shows him how she came home to a family pissed at her for running off like a fool. Then he sees their concern for her when she tells them she got dump in London and watched as they became angry again when she didn't call them for help.

The memories flew by until she left for New York City to get away from her overbearing parents. She was starting to suspect that she was pregnant. As she worried, she got a job working with a friend. Then the memories came of that fateful day when she confided in her friend about her situation and her encounter with a vampire.

Wait, he thought, stopping her. She sensed him reviewing the memory of the vampire, as if he was walking in her memory, trying to memorize the image.

Do you know who she is? she asked.

No. But she's from the Tribe of Yan, a derivative of Tenhar. They tend to be apolitical, but that doesn't mean she wouldn't tell what she saw. She would have a duty to do so.

Instantly Adina's memory went to the vampire she confronted and her actions towards him. Jin felt himself wanting to growl at the vampire that dared threaten her. Then he recognized him. It was one of his father's people, not Tenhar. The shock felt heavy. His father was so close to attaining her and if Fredon had captured her, he would have killed her, of that Jin was sure.

Did he chase you? What happened?

Adina showed him how she and her friend ran, how she took the train and went home, where she heard a knock at the door. He saw how she eventually let Flaxon into her life, the argument they had, and then… Just as he was getting a glimpse of something very provocative, she skipped over it, going to the fight she had witnessed. Jin felt her awe and respect for Flaxon grow has he battled the vampires. Her pride in the other vampire fueled his ire, but he still wondered what she was hiding from him.

The images in her head shifted to escape. He took some humor in her attitude towards Flaxon, felt his own failure as he watched her grow weak to the point where she had to take blood from someone he barely respected, let alone trusted. The very idea of it set his teeth on edge. As she drank his blood, he felt his children form a light bond with Flaxon.

Second Father, they whispered fondly. He was pissed enough to snap his contact with Adina abruptly.

"Ouch! God, that hurt. What did you do?"

Jin rubbed her temples, easing her pain.

"I'm sorry. I…I broke our connection a little too quickly. Does it feel better now?"

She let out a shallow breath. "It's a little better. Why did you cut me off? I didn't show you the rest of what happened."

Jin's jaw clenched tightly. How dare that insolent Breed bond with his children?! The rational part of him knew that it might have been out of Flaxon's hands, but what of Adina's admiration and respect for the charlatan? Was that an accident too? Did she not see him as more worthy than Flaxon? Jin closed his eyes because his irrational thoughts were driving him crazy. He remembered the quick glimpse of interaction between Adina and Flaxon that she had blocked from him. Now he really wanted to know what she was hiding.

"Adina, tell me why you are hiding things from me," he said a low cool voice.

Something about the way he spoke put Adina on alert. She twisted as much as she could so that she could see him. His jade eyes were dark, but bright spots expanded in them as she watched. He was trying to stay calm, but he was far from happy.

"It was nothing, Jin, really." She lightly ran her fingers across his cheek.

He was calm as he said, "If it was nothing, then what happened?"

She let her hand drop, as well as her head. She felt his finger under chin, slowly raising her head so that their eyes could meet. "What did he do to you?"

Adina sighed. "Nothing," she said, exasperated. "It was just embarrassing, that's all, and I'd rather forget it."

"But it's okay for him to know, and not me?" he growled.

They held each other's stares. Finally, she relented.

"Just let it go, Jin. It's not important. It doesn't matter, okay?"

"Stop saying that!" he snapped. "It is important because you're hiding it! Is it because you have a need to protect him? Have your feelings shifted?"

"Is that what this is all about? I can't believe you! Jin, Flaxon means nothing to me. You are my mate. We are together. Nothing Flaxon can do will change that." She kissed the corner of his mouth. When he didn't respond, she rolled her eyes and turned away.

They sat in silence. Jin stared at her in anger and Adina wondered why she wouldn't just say it, knowing the answer but afraid to admit it to herself. Resigned, she asked, "Why don't you just look for yourself? You can go into my mind, so why don't you?"

Jin softened slightly, pulling her closer.

"I cannot disrespect you like that. If you choose to keep things from me, I will not just take them from you. There would be a loss of trust and respect. I care about you. I would not take from you what you will not give freely. So if you don't want to tell me…I'll let it go."

Adina turned to him. His eyes reflected his sincerity, but there was an underlying emotion she couldn't identify.

Don't believe him, Mama. He's very angry. Very Angry. He won't forget it.

Her kids had surprised her. She looked at Jin to see if he had heard them too, but he was gazing out the windows, expression neutral. Way too neutral. She thought about what he had said and wondered if she was missing something innate to vampires, a pecking order, some type of respect between mates. Her thoughts turned to Flaxon. Jin was going to make him pay for taking her, but what else would he do?

"Jin?"

He turned his handsome face back to her, staring calmly.

She took a deep breath before asking. "Are you going to force Flaxon to tell you what happened?"

His eyes glinted, then clouded over. He traced her face with a finger and asked, "Why?"

"Jin, what happened was my fault. He didn't do anything except stop me."

Jin's finger stilled. "What the hell are you talking about, Adina? Stop you from doing what?"

Adina wanted to cry at that moment. She was going to have to show him how scandalous she had acted with Flaxon. She couldn't have Jin blaming him or thinking the worst.

Her tear set off an internal alarm. He swept it away with his thumb, cradling her jaw. Shaking his head he said, "What has happened that upsets you so? What do you think you've done that's bad enough to make me look at you differently?"

She shrugged, then laughed sadly. "I just...whatever. Look, Jin, I woke from a dream about you, and I was getting hot and heavy but I didn't wake fully, so I..." she blushed fiercely, "I tried to finish the dream with Flaxon, thinking he was you. I basically jumped his bones with him trying the whole to time wake me up and see who he really was. Eventually, he woke me up. I was embarrassed, he was embarrassed...I'm sorry," she ended in a whisper.

Jin stared at her, his mouth agape. He forced himself to close it, but frowned. Then he looked at her and said, "Adina, you have nothing to be embarrassed about. I understand what happened."

Adina shook her head. "No. If you saw what I was doing."

"Then show me," he replied calmly.

No, Mama. Don't.

It's okay, little ones. Your father will understand.

She showed Jin what transpired that night, not realizing that his hostility was growing by the second. By the time she reached the end he was ready to snap both her and Flaxon's necks, though the desire to hurt Flaxon was stronger.

Adina opened her eyes to Jin's fangs. She moved back, but he gripped her arm. She swallowed as she watched him calm himself, his eyes still glowing hotly. He was the picture of tranquility when he looked at her again, but her gut and her children were telling her otherwise.

"Are you mad, Jin?"

"No. Just a little upset that I put you in such a state. I shouldn't have started something I couldn't finish."

"Now you know why I didn't want to tell you. I feel so silly…"

"No, baby," he said bringing her close. "You have no reason to feel that way. Don't worry about it. I understand."

Jin massaged her temples, saying soothing words to her. Adina tried to fight the sudden drowsiness, but she drifted into sleep anyway. The last thing she remembered hearing was her children telling her that their father was livid.

Jin gently laid Adina down, kissing her brow and getting out of the bed. He ripped the bedroom door open. When his bodyguards saw him, both wanted to flee, but held their ground. Jin's eyes were aglow, his fangs shining just as brightly.

"Find me the Prince of the Breeds, NOW!" he roared before slamming the door shut.

Komi and Jode looked at each other. They had never seen Jin so pissed in their lives. Komi nodded at Jode and he left to deliver the message, only to return a moment later. Komi frowned at him.

"What gives?"

"Someone said he will be there shortly. He needed to talk with Jin anyway."

Komi shook her head. "I hope they have a replacement for him, because I don't think he'll have a head after this."

Jode nodded in agreement.

Chapter 27

Misunderstandings Reclaiming and New Alliances

FLAXON WALKED THE HALLS at a leisurely pace. He had been dreading this talk with the High Prince since their arrival.

Jin had something up his sleeve, but Flaxon hoped that seeing Adina would curb his desire for revenge. *Probably not, the tosser. His kind always finds an excuse to mete out their idea of justice,* he thought.

When he reached the hallway housing Adina and her Alpha-blooded mate, he felt the tension there. Standing outside the door were Jin's two buddies, who faced him as he approached. When he reached the door, they blocked his path.

"What?" he asked, annoyed.

"Weapons?" asked Komi.

Flaxon screwed up his face. Shaking his head, he held out his arms, watching her as he did. She stared back, waiting.

"What's the matter, Komi? Not gonna search me? Think you might enjoy it too much?"

He was slammed into the wall by Jode, barely managing to throw out his hands in time to protect his head. He laughed while the vampire searched him, roughly jerking him back around. Jode glared at Flaxon, who just sneered back. Finally, Jode waved him to the door.

Flaxon entered the room after throwing one last snarl at the vampires at the door. He closed the door behind him, looking around for Jin. Adina was asleep on the bed, but no Jin. Just as he was about call him, he felt a hand on his throat. Flaxon was lifted from the floor and carried a couple of steps before being tossed into the corner, a bookshelf coming down with him. Flaxon coughed, still seeing stars from the chokehold. Jin was standing over him, baring his fangs and growling heavily.

So this is it, Flaxon thought, standing slowly. He rolled his shoulders, getting himself into a fight stance.

Jin walked towards Flaxon, anger coming off of him in waves.

"You dare touch my mate," he hissed.

"I didn't do anything but protect her," said Flaxon.

"Liar!" When he reached Flaxon, he swung out.

But Flaxon ducked, bringing his fist up to connect with Jin's chin. Then he brought his knee into Jin's abdomen. Jin's fang sliced his lip and the knee knocked him off balance, but not enough to keep him from stopping Flaxon's next punch.

Jin caught Flaxon's punch with his left hand, and with rapid precision, landed a hard right in his ribs. He was deliberate in pulling his punch just before impact. He only meant to *crack* his ribs, not kill him.

A blinding pain exploded in Flaxon that made him coughed blood. He was wheezing when the next punch, on his jaw, sent him staggering for the wall. It took all his effort not to scream out in pain when he collided with it. In his haze, he saw Jin coming for him again, so he used one of his more advance vampire skills, speed. He quickly grabbed a book and flung it fast enough to hit Jin in spite of his reflexes. The book cut Jin above his left eye.

Jin was incensed. Flaxon was proving to be a little too resilient. But it was time to end this and show who was superior. In a blink, Jin was in front of Flaxon pummeling him, cracking the ribs even further, punching his face a couple of times, before landing a heavy blow to his stomach. When Jin stepped back, Flaxon fell face down to the floor. Jin grabbed Flaxon by his hair and pulled him up.

"You never should have touched my mate, bastard."

"So I guess this is the punishment?" mumbled Flaxon. He glanced up at Jin. "Do what you will, but remember I did what I did to protect my people."

"What?! You put your fuckin' lips on my mate for your people?! You tried to screw her to protect them?!"

Flaxon's face turned stone as Jin jerked him to his feet. Jin's face inches from Flaxon's.

"It was bad enough that you took her, but then you tried to take advantage of her. I could kill you for what you did," he whispered harshly.

Flaxon glared back. "You've *got* to be fucking kidding. You get your mate all hot and bothered, and it's my fault that she sought me to satisfy her needs. Don't blame me for putting her in that state. That was all you, High Prince."

Jin growled at him, baring his teeth, and Flaxon responded in kind. Quickly, Jin let go of Flaxon's hair and used the other hand to grip his throat. Flaxon refused to let Jin see the effect the lack of air was having. He continued to glare even as his vision faded.

"Jin! Stop it!"

He froze before turning slowly to see an irate, not scared Adina. Her eyes glinted fiercely as she rose from the bed. Jin growled at her and was mildly surprised when she bared her small fangs, growling in kind. They stared at each other menacingly before he released Flaxon. Flaxon fell to his knees. One hand held his throat while he tried to catch his breath.

"Stay out of this Adina," snapped Jin.

"Don't tell me to stay out this. What the hell do you think you're doing, beating him to death in *my* fucking room?"

Jin's fist curled and tightened. She was trying to sit taller on the bed, one hand rubbing her stomach, as if trying to reassure her children. Even with the distance between them, he sensed his children's anxiety. Their concern that he might fatally harm Flaxon only fueled his ire. His fangs were bared in rage when he saw Flaxon picking himself up.

"See what you've done?" Jin hissed, reaching for Flaxon again.

"Don't ignore me!" Adina yelled behind him.

Jin clenched his jaw, then turned sideways so that he could keep his eye on Flaxon. "Adina," he growled.

"You tell me why you're fighting him! I told you, it wasn't his fault—"

"It was his choice to take you!" he raged. "He had no right to go near you without my consent. He had no right to place his filthy lips on you, to take pleasure from you when you were weak."

"You know what, Jin? It all happened because you *weren't there!*" she hollered back. "He protected me when you didn't come, no matter how I begged you, and don't tell me you didn't know I was scared, you fucking had to know. I could feel you in my head!"

"What do you think? That I didn't want to protect you? That I could come here without anyone hunting you? Do you think I wanted all this to happen?" he hollered back.

Adina's face hardened. "So because you were *busy* I was left unprotected, but the one person who took the time to do your job, you want to beat to death. When were you going to make time for me? When there was nothing left but a body to collect?"

Jin's eyes darkened to a midnight color. "Do you think he came out some noble need to protect you? He used you, took advantage of you—"

"Jin, he didn't."

"Why are you so sure he didn't?" Jin said through his teeth. "Or are you just trying to protect him?"

"Jin, she doesn't understand," Flaxon choked out.

"Shut up," Jin snapped at him before returning his glare to her. Adina glared right back, lips pressed tightly together.

"I don't understand what you're saying. Of course he was using of me! But that's not the point. He was there when—"

"Don't say it again! You would honor and protect a liar! Don't you remember what he did to you? Don't you know he threatened to keep you from me if I refused to meet with him on his terms? This thing you would protect from me, your mate, as if I have no right to be angry. What do you want of me?"

She stared at him steadily. "Spare him. I do remember what he did but in the end he stopped himself and me. What happened, happened. There's no need for all this fighting. Let him go."

He turned away, coolly regarding Flaxon. There was a pain in his chest that he couldn't describe but he knew why it was there. The betrayal was burning a hole in him. His jaw tightened, then relaxed. He looked down at Flaxon with eyes devoid of emotion. Flaxon shook his head mumbling, "She doesn't understand."

"Understand what," Adina asked, annoyed. "Don't pretend I'm not in this room. I can still hear."

"You don't understand what you chose."

Jin watched Flaxon roll his eyes. "High Prince, she's human. Keep that in mind when—"

"If you love your life, you will not speak to me until you show me my due respect. You want my help, and it seems my *mate* wishes for me to give it. Your actions need to reflect that."

It was Flaxon's turn to tighten his jaw.

"Jin—" Adina started, but fell silent when he glared at her fiercely.

* * *

Sashi walked towards the room when she heard the yelling. Her heart jumped into her throat, making her even more nervous than she already was. She rolled back her shoulders, held her head high, and walked towards the vampires by *the door*. They instantly turned to her, and from their stance, they weren't planning to let her through.

She stopped a few paces before them. Her eyes darted back and forth as she tried to determine exactly what she could say and just how twitchy they were.

"I need to speak with Flaxon," she said.

"No one enters," said the female coolly.

"I think I will be entering. I need to see my Prince," Sashi snapped back.

The male showed off a fang before curling his lips into a sneer. Just as Sashi was about to speak again, she smelled blood. Her eyes enlarged as she stepped forward, only to be blocked by a blade that came within inches of her face.

"No one enters," said Komi.

Sashi's left hand whipped behind her just as the male vampire went for his guns. Everyone's eyes glinted, the two vampires showing a flicker of surprise as well. Sashi sneered. *I guess they didn't think I could do that,* she thought, hand resting on her gun as she crouched.

The tension lasted a few minutes before they all heard Jin's voice.

"Let her in," he said.

The male vampire flexed his shoulders, causing his jacket to adjust over his weapons. But the female vampire didn't move.

"Relinquish your guns," she said.

Sashi said, "No."

The vampire bared her teeth before grinding out, "You will not enter unless you leave your weapons behind."

"I don't think so, vampire," she replied calmly. "I will enter with my gun. If you want it, come take it."

The woman's eyes danced in amusement. "You think you can take me, mongrel?"

"Don't underestimate me, blood-sucker. Many have and their last wish was that they hadn't."

The vampire lowered her head as the smile developed on her face. The male vampire took a step back to let the female adjust her stance. Sashi felt a tingling go through her, her fingers flexing as she began to control her breathing. Just as the spring was about snap, a deep voice growled in the room.

"Enough! Let her in, now!"

The woman scowled, but took a step back as Sashi stood straighter. The male vampire opened the door. She kept her back against the wall, sliding into the room and waiting for the door to close. Only then did she let her eyes register the scene around her.

Adina sat on the bed glowering and wincing as she rubbed her belly. The High Prince stood in all his breathtaking splendor, some of his dark hair loose from the braid. His eyes were a very dark green and his face hard, but it didn't hide his good looks. He was tall, lean and even through his loose shirt she could tell his was very muscular. Her eyes traveled to her Prince, who was down on one knee, his head bowed. She could just make out the bruises on his face.

Sashi swallowed, blinking slowly. She stared at her Prince, humbled before the High Prince. Her ears perked up to the sound of his labored breathing that he was trying to hide. When she noticed the sheen of sweat on his face, her heart turned to stone. Flaxon was hurt, seriously hurt. She almost stepped towards him, but the High Prince's voice halted her movements.

"What is it that you want?" he asked.

Sashi stood frozen, not knowing what she was supposed to do. Should she curtsy, bow, or address him as 'Sire'? She looked to her Prince for help, but he kept his eyes turned to the floor.

The silence extended until everyone in the room began to forget about Sashi altogether. Jin turned towards her, his piercing gaze holding her eyes. It felt like he could see into the depths of her soul with the intensity of his gaze. She wished she could run out of the room, but she controlled herself.

"What was so important that you just *had* to see Flaxon right now?"

Sashi dragged her eyes from the High Prince's back to Flaxon, whose head was still bowed. A part of her was willing him to speak, to get up and show his usual defiance, but he didn't. If anything, his head sagged lower. Seeing Flaxon this way broke something in Sashi and brought forth her anger. She hated vampires, the way they lived what the represented. At that moment, she wanted nothing more than to melt the High Prince's head off his shoulders.

When she looked back at the High Prince, he was smirking at her as if he'd heard every thought in her head. A second later, she was sure of it. She knew some vampires had that ability and it would only make sense that the High Prince could hear thoughts.

"Especially when you're yelling them at me," he said.

Sashi's face lost color and her heart raced. What would happen to her now? The High Prince had to know that she wanted him dead. She decided that if she was going to die, it would be on her terms. Standing even straighter, she held the High Prince's eyes.

"My message is for my Prince," she stated.

"Really?" Jin tilted his head. "There he is. Give him your message."

"It's private," she replied through her teeth.

"Nothing is private when it concerns me and I *know* it concerns me. So what has happened," he growled out the last part, making her jump. Again, she looked at Flaxon.

"Look at me," snapped Jin. When he had her attention, he said, "My patience is almost gone. If you are worried that I have taken your Prince's tongue, then I shall assure you, I haven't. Ask her what she wants."

"What do you have to report?" asked Flaxon quietly.

Sashi stood in horror. The High Prince had spoken to Flaxon like he wasn't a person he needed bother to respect. Her face flushed, anger shaking her to her toes. But she refused to pity him. Flaxon would hate that more than anything.

"Sire," she said in a formal tone, "we have hidden the car, but we have spotted a car in the vicinity. Our cameras weren't able to pick up the image of the individuals in the car. However, we were able to get the license plate number and it has been traced to Morgan Ward of the Danpe Tribe."

Sashi took small pleasure at seeing Jin's face register a surprise.

"Are you sure?" Jin asked.

"Yes, High Prince," she snapped. "We are very good at what we do. We have to be, dealing with your fuckin' kind!"

"Sashi!"

Flaxon's voice reverberated through the room. The High Prince looked down on him in amusement, Adina's ears perked with curiosity, and Sashi's flushed cheeks became darker. Her eyes lowered before she bowed. She had rarely heard him use that voice, a sound too ancient, deadly and decidedly vampire. She knew then that she had crossed a dangerous line that might put the whole tribe at greater risk.

"My apologies, High Prince. That was rude and inappropriate," she said dully.

"But it was the truth."

She rose slowly to see him staring at her intently.

"You are angry because of what you see here, but remember that this is no concern of yours. I assure you that your Prince will walk out of here and I will learn all I need to know from him. Now I must ask you to leave. Your Prince will be with you shortly."

He bowed to her, showing her a small amount of respect.

For a brief moment, Sashi thought she was in an alternate universe, but her brain finally caught up. She hesitated, but noticed that Flaxon was looking at her. His eyes were pleading with her to leave. His look made her feet move, even if her mind was screaming to stay. But she was quickly out of the room, standing with the two bodyguards. They all glared at each other before she turned to go back to the command center.

* * *

Jin stared down at Flaxon, then took a couple of steps back.

"Get up, Flaxon."

Flaxon rose slowly, lifting his head. Jin sensed that Flaxon was badly in need of blood, but he also knew the Breed's pride. Flaxon wouldn't take a drink from him now to save his life. Jin respected that. Flaxon looked at him with eyes that showed he had not been defeated.

"You came between me and my mate. I don't care the reason. However, you protected her from danger. For that reason alone, you are alive. Just know that if you come between us again, I will take your head."

He could see the nasty retort forming on Flaxon's lips, but the Breed just huffed and bowed slightly.

"I will not dare to insult you or your mate in such a manner again, my Prince," he said tightly.

"Good. Let's cut the bullshit Flaxon. I need to trust you and you need to trust me. We both have something important at stake. No more lies. When I ask a question, I want the truth no matter how brutal, painful, or obvious it may seem to you. I have to know there is someone with knowledge about the past that I can trust to get an honest answer. And I need loyalty, not just from you, but your entire tribe."

Flaxon tilted his head. "Loyalty goes both ways, High Prince. My people have no reason to trust vampires."

"I don't care if they trust all vampires, I need them to trust me. It is something that I intend to earn, but I cannot do it as long as their Prince thinks that loyalty to me is a fools deal."

They held each other's gaze, assessing each other.

Jin said, "We'll talk later. Thank you for your time, Prince Alphonso."

He gave Flaxon a clipped nod of respect, then waited for him to leave.

Jin saw Flaxon swallow the surprise upon hearing his real name. Jin had acquired it from Sashi when she was panicking over her Prince. He bowed deeply, showing Jin his due respect, then without a word he left.

Chapter 28
Healing the Pain

EXHALING TO RELAX HIMSELF, he turned to his mate. She had cut him deeply by defending Flaxon. He knew that Flaxon had been right, that Adina didn't understand what she had done, but Jin wasn't any less hurt by it. It felt to the core of his being that his mate respected and preferred Flaxon over him. His rational mind knew she that she probably didn't see it that way, but his primal instinct is screaming to reclaim her, to make her know that he was the only one. His eyes glinted a dangerous green before he turned to face her.

A tinge of anger was still on Adina's face. In spite of the anger, she looked pale. Jin rolled up his sleeve as he walked over to the bed. He sat, extending his forearm to her.

"Drink," he said.

Adina looked like she wanted to smack him, but took his arm, raising it to her mouth. She kept her eyes on him when she bit. He watched her small fangs pierce his skin but closed his eyes while she drank. His children felt satisfied and warm as their mother fed them. Adina wanted to take his other hand, but he kept it from her.

Before they could bond any further, they needed to have a serious talk.

A few minutes later, she let go with a fiery glint in her eye. Jin would never get used to seeing Adina with vampire abilities. He was getting increasingly worried that her humanity, the thing that drew him to her, was being lost. His thoughts halted when he felt her tongue flicking around the bite wound. He closed his eyes to savor the feeling. When he gathered himself, he slowly twisted his arm away, almost laughing when she growled softly.

She sighed warily, rubbing her belly slowly. Pained was etched in her face and in that instant, he felt it, too. His children were kicking because they were unnerved by Jin's anger. He placed his hand over hers, letting them feel his caring for their mother, in spite of his anger. They calmed a little. He sent them soothing thoughts while gazing into his mate's eyes. Her face softened with the connection, lips forming a little smile. She looked at their intertwined fingers and rested her head under his chin, bewildering Jin.

Why was she acting as if nothing had happened, like she wasn't just growling at him in anger?

I'm not angry with you, Jin.

Jin leaned back so that their eyes could meet.

"Why are you so angry with me?" she asked.

The question hung in the air for some time before he responded.

"You interfered. You chose him over me."

He watched her face register shock, then confusion, then finally settled on downright annoyance. Pulling away, she sighed heavily.

"I didn't choose him over you. I just stopped you from killing him."

"Why would you care if I killed your kidnapper?"

Adina's shoulders fell. She leaned back in frustration until the pillows caught her. Sighing deeply, she looked at him with tired eyes.

"Jin, I understand what he did, but that beating you gave him wasn't about me, not most of it anyway."

"Really?" he said coolly.

"Dammit Jin," she snapped, slapping her hand on the bed. "I just didn't want you beating his ass for what happened."

"And why shouldn't I? Why just forget what happened?" he snapped right back. "He took you when he could have easily called me. Then while he held you, he took advantage of when you were weakest."

"No, he didn't!" she protested.

"Yes, he did!' he hissed. "Or have you forgotten that he kissed you, placed his wretched lips on your breast when he never should have touched you at all."

"Well then, I guess you're going to whip my ass too for rubbing up on him, hmm?"

"Adina!" Jin shouted, jumping up. "Why would you even say that? Don't you understand? I am the High Prince. You are my mate. How do you think it looks that I wasn't able to protect you from the likes of him, to know that I left you vulnerable to his lecherous behavior? I cannot let him think that he could do such a thing and walk away untouched."

"Oh, I see. So beating him up was your way of proving you are the biggest, baddest of all vampires. If that's the case, why am I hiding in the woods with these folks? Why are we here at all?"

"We are here because he brought you here," he growled, his frustration mounting. "But that's not the point. Why do you persist in defending him, even now?"

"Because I'm pissed!" she fired back. She slid off the bed and stepped in front of him. "You put me to sleep on purpose, after telling me that everything was cool. You did it because didn't want me to see you beating him to within an inch of his life over something that doesn't matter—"

"But it does matter," he shouted back, making her stumble away from the force of his voice. He reached for her arm to steady her.

"Don't you get it? You belong to me. No one has the right to touch you, to take you, to try and keep me from you. By rights I can kill whoever would dare do it!"

Adina tried to jerk away, but he held tight. She growled at him and he growled back. When she bared her teeth, surprising him with the fierceness of her expression, he let go. Though her fangs were tiny, her anger was clear.

"I don't care what rights you *think* you have! You gave them up when you let me go! You gave them up by leaving me alone! He was there for me when you *weren't,* and you have the nerve to be pissed at him. Thank God he kidnapped me, or else I would have been dead or worse if he hadn't come along. Instead of just calling it even, you're going to beat him for doing your damn job!" She was hysterical by then.

Jin's jaws clenched tightly. "So, I failed you? Is that it, then? After telling me that I hadn't, that you forgave me for not being there, the truth comes out. You hate me for failing you. You prefer him now because he was there, is that it?"

"No! Dammit, Jin," she shouted, tears forming in her eyes. Her hand went to her stomach as she winced. "That's not it! I'm not saying that! I'm saying—, I'm saying—"

She doubled over as a sharp pain pierced her.

Jin's anger evaporated when he saw her about to collapse. Her flailing hands tried to wave him off, but he caught them. As soon as they touched, he felt his children scream in terror and anger. Jin picked Adina up and carried her back to the bed.

She was breathing harshly, tired from arguing. Jin laid her on her side and he lay behind her, holding her close. She felt one hand in her hair as the other slowly rubbed her stomach, still reassuring their children. It took some time, but they eventually fell asleep, in turn making her drowsy. But she kept her eyes opened and placed her hand over his.

"I'm sorry," he whispered against her hair. "I'm such an arse, upsetting you that way. Forgive me."

She heard the pain in his voice and knew that he felt like he had failed her again. She was glad that he felt bad for upsetting her, but didn't like his sense of failure. She moved his hand from her stomach to her lips. She kissed his knuckles lightly before placing his hand over her heart.

"Jin," she said softly.

"Yes?"

She sighed. What could she say to him? She didn't know because she didn't understand his anger, well, not completely. She understood why he was angry at Flaxon's actions, but she didn't understand the need for so much violence. She abhorred violence and watching Jin's anger manifest itself so viciously scared her. She didn't like that look on him. And then his jealousy over Flaxon was just ridiculous. She thought back to what Flaxon said to Jin about her being human and not understanding. Again, she considered that she was missing something. Maybe now was time for her to find out what. But she needed to tell him something first.

Adina let go of his hand and rolled over. He slid away to give her room. When she was comfortable facing him, he moved close enough to slip his arm around her waist and return his other hand to stroking her hair. They held an intimate gaze. Adina reached forward to touch his cheek. His jaw clenched briefly and his eyes closed. She leaned forward and kissed his lips lightly. Disappointed by the lack of response, she started to pull away. But he moved forward to deepen the kiss. When she looked into his eyes again, they looked heated but guarded.

She rested her forehead against his for a second, returning again to his eyes. She smiled and ran the back of her hand against his cheek.

"I love you, Jin," she said softly. She saw his eyes flicker for an instant before becoming guarded again. She shook her head. "But you don't know what that means."

He was silent, taking her hand from his cheek and kissing the palm. He said, "No, I don't. Not really. But I know what you mean to me, and what happened, what you said, hurt. It makes me feel like you don't want our bond to last. I feel like I'm competing for my mate…because I failed you."

"No, Jin," she said forcefully, gripping his hand. "You aren't in competition with anyone. I'm sorry I said those things to you. I was angry. When you lied to me, it hurt me because I trust you the most. You said you understood. Then you put me to sleep because you really were angry and lied to me about it."

"Adina—" he started.

"Do you how I woke up? Our children woke me up. They felt your anger and Flaxon's pain. They were begging me to stop you two from fighting. They were kicking the crap out of me."

She saw shock register in Jin's eyes, followed by a cool anger, probably at the knowledge that his children gave a hoot about what happened to Flaxon. Adina took her hand from his and cupped his face.

"Jin, I don't understand all of this. I need you to explain it to me. I'm missing something significant, I know. But you have to understand that there is nothing you can do about what happened between Flaxon and me now. Whatever his reason, he did keep me safe and he brought you to me. He gave me blood to keep me alive until you got here. I don't hate him. That doesn't mean he will ever take your place, he can't. Am I a little fond of him? Yes, but he is not you. You are my mate. Please believe that."

He stared deeply into her eyes for a long time, then leaned forward to kiss her deeply. Images, thoughts, and feelings began flooding her mind. His pain when she accused him of failing her, his betrayal when she defended Flaxon, his need to reclaim what was his, and finally, the feeling of peace. Their problem, she decided, was that they were of two different species.

As a vampire with primal instincts, he had territorial needs and his reactions were based on protecting his claim. Where she thought he was overacting, he was remarking his territory. When she understood that, she knew that Flaxon's connection to their children would always bother him. It was the reason he was so angry with Flaxon's indulgence, however slight. It was an insult that Flaxon would touch his mate when the bite mark was apparent. She realized that Jin never planned to kill Flaxon, only punish him.

Why punish him?

Like I told you before, I had to. As the High Prince, I must show that no one can touch or harm anything of mine. To let it pass would be a sign of weakness. It was also for your honor. Taking you was not just an offense to me, but to you. I had to do it for you even if you didn't wish it, because as your mate, it's my job to protect you.

Adina pulled back, catching her breath. Her eyes slowly opened to Jin's blazing jade eyes and she knew that the most primal part of him was staring back at her. He was letting her see all of him again. She realized that she never really understood what she saw before. Now he was presenting himself to see if she would *really* accept him.

"Mine," she whispered.

His eyes slowly closed. When they opened again, they were a little duller.

"Really?" he asked.

"Always," she responded. Then she yawned, her eyes fluttering closed.

He smiled, pulling her head against his chest.

"Sleep, my love," he whispered.

Adina went to sleep in Jin's arms. For the first time in a long while, Jin felt content. He savored that feeling, knowing that soon, it would be gone.

* * *

Flaxon's hands shook violently as he tried to open the storage case of blood in the med lab. He pulled, but the door wouldn't budge. Flaxon cleared his blurry vision and looked at the glass door again. There was a lock on it. He nearly fell when he reached down and unlocked it. Then he pulled out a couple of packs and slammed the door shut. He plunged his fangs into the pack and drank quickly.

Sashi came in as Flaxon was leaning against a bed, trying to take off his shirt but gasping in pain. She rushed over to him, but the anger in his eyes made her step back. She noted the sweat trickling down his brow. His lips were tight with pain and he was quivering. He looked down, trying to focus on removing his shirt. Sashi took a tentative step forward, but his growl stopped her. She watched him fail again to take the shirt off. His hand was shaking badly and his breathing was labored. That was all Sashi needed to stop hesitating and go to him.

"Leave me alone, Sashi," he rasped.

"No. You need help and I intend to help my Prince," she stated firmly, reaching for him.

He grabbed her wrist with surprising strength. She waited for his next move, but he simply let her go.

"Please, leave."

His voice was cool, but there was something else to it. His cheeks were flushed and he was avoiding eye contact. It dawned on her that Flaxon was embarrassed at her having seen him weak. He was humiliated by the fact that she saw him beaten to his knees by the High Prince. It had been the worst moment in her life to see him that way, but it had to be even more painful for him. Flaxon was trying to preserve what little pride he had left.

Sashi thought to leave, but her love for him made her stay. She reached out again, not saying a word, and began trying to take off his shirt. Flaxon jerked away.

"Isn't it enough that you saw me on my knees? Leave me alone! I don't need your pity!"

"Who the hell pities you?" she retorted, grabbing his shirt jerking it down his arm. He started to fight her, but pain and exhaustion made it impossible. She went to the other arm, pulling down the sleeve and noticing the bruises on his arm.

"Please, go. I hate having you see me like this," he whispered shakily.

She stopped and placed her hands on his face, slowly lifting his head. His eyes were red- rimmed as he fought to keep his composure. Sashi felt her heart breaking from seeing him like this, but she kept it to herself. If she showed that she was upset, he would push her away.

"Why not me, Prince? You did what you thought was right to save us all. You have nothing to be ashamed about," she said sternly. Then she moved closer to him, standing on her tiptoes. "Besides, I love you, Alphonso. I will not sit idly by while you're hurt to suffer alone." She let her lips touch his softly, but moved away quickly, not allowing him to react one way or the other.

"So on the bed, Prince, and let's get you patched up." She placed her hands on her hips waiting for him.

He climbed up on the bed and let Sashi help him out his shirt, then they both got him out of his tank top. She controlled her reaction to the bruises along his ribs, knowing that he would be watching for any sign of her becoming upset. She had to be strong for him, not show any empathy or sympathy because all he was feeling right then was low. He would take it as a sign that he was weak, no matter how contrary the belief.

She went to the supply drawer and retrieved band aids, tape, gauze, and alcohol, taking all the supplies over to the bed. She cleaned him up and began wrapping his ribs. He gritted his teeth but made no sound. She finished and pinned it up, but blood would help him to heal faster.

She glanced at the empty packs on the counter. They were all drinking the weak, synthetic crap because the good stuff was being given to the High Prince's mate. Sashi thought a moment. She knew they were going to have a battle ahead. The vampires tracking the High Prince would find them soon. If Flaxon was to be in full strength, he would need more potent blood.

"You need blood," she said.

"I know," he answered, speaking for the first time since she had started to treat him.

Sashi grabbed the bottom of her shirt, pulling it up and over her head leaving her clad only in a bra. She tossed it next to Flaxon, who was watching her intently.

"What are you doing?" he asked.

"What do you think?"

She climbed on the bed next to him, swung a leg over his lap, and carefully straddled him. She gazed into his eyes, nodding as she turned to expose more of her neck.

"Drink," she murmured.

Flaxon shook his head weakly.

"No. I could hurt you. Just get me the synthetic."

She rolled her eyes. "Don't be dumb. You know this way is better."

He growled softly. "I said no."

She faced him again, determined. "And I said yes. I'm doing this of my own free will."

"That doesn't matter. I need you strong—"

"No, we need you strong. You are going to serve the High Prince now, and his enemies are about to become ours. You need to be strong to protect us. So please drink, Sire."

"As your Prince, I'm telling you that you don't have to do this," he said coldly.

"I don't do this because you're my Prince. I do it because it's you. Don't you know that?" she whispered, her eyes reflecting love.

Flaxon didn't move for a long time, just studying her. His dark eyes were devoid of emotion, his face blank. But underneath his cool exterior was a raging battle. A part of him wanted nothing more than to let Sashi into his heart, finally. He missed having someone who took care of him just because it was him, not a duty. He missed feeling close to someone. This woman was offering him the very thing he craved—companionship—and he knew he wasn't going to accept it. The sad part was that she knew it, too. Yet, she was going to let him take her blood, knowing that he still wouldn't be hers. He had never felt bad about being such a bastard until today. He began to lift her up off his lap, but she leaned forward to kiss him.

Flaxon tasted blood in that kiss. He instantly reacted the way she had expected when she bit her tongue. He sucked on it hungrily before pulling back. She kept her hands firmly on his head and slowly brought it down to her neck.

"For you, my love, there is nothing I wouldn't do," she whispered.

"Sashi, I can't…"

"But I can. Please heal yourself, Alphonso."

He swallowed, but his composure slipped. The taste of her and having her so close caused him to let go of his fight. For once, he accepted a gift that was offered freely. He bit into her, drinking heartily.

He wrapped his arms around her letting her warm skin heat his cool chest. He heard her gasp as she rocked against him. He responded by letting his hand slide down her back into her jeans to cup her bottom. He squeezed it as she gripped his hair tighter. Flaxon moved his hand lower and began stroking her. Sashi rested her cheek against his head, inhaling his scent, a faint almond smell. When his fingers dipped into her she cried out.

The intensity of the feeling overwhelmed her. She could feel his desire peak as she felt his hardness. She sighed in ecstasy as she twisted on his three fingers and her clitoris rubbed against the hard ridge in his pants. She finally came, moaning low and long.

Flaxon lifted his head then, dark eyes glinting. He felt the power of her blood healing him. He leaned back down to lick her neck, knowing that the mark would be his claim on her. He also knew that he would regret it later but at that moment, he could not care less. He felt her head fall on his shoulder as her arms slackened. Her temperature dropped almost immediately. Maybe he had taken too much. She needed to rest and get a refill of blood herself.

He cleaned her up, setting up an IV connection to a synthetic blood pack to replace the blood he had taken from her. Flaxon went to the closet, grabbed a blanket, and spread it over her. His hand moved to her face, pushing away a curly lock before he stepped away to grab his shirt. He went to the mirror and gazed at his reflection. The bruises on his face were already fading and his jaw was healed. He twisted and felt his ribs, though still cracked, were well on the mend. He slipped on a shirt. Glancing back at Sashi and clamping down the desire to lay with her until she woke up, he left the room to find out the status of the High Prince's trackers.

Chapter 29
Things get Worse

THERE WAS A KNOCK on the door. Jin's eyes opened slowly. Adina was drinking from his shoulder, even as she slept. He was about to close his eyes, but the tapping persisted.

"Enter," he said faintly.

Komi came into the room with another woman. The woman carried a tray of food and had her head down, but Jin recognized her as the woman that Adina had said helped her. She was the midwife.

"Thank you, Komi. It's fine."

Komi nodded and left as quietly as she had come.

The woman walked further in the room, head bowed. She stopped by the bed, waiting with the tray.

"I prefer for people to look at me, not the floor," Jin said softly.

Maggie raised her eyes to meet the High Prince's. He was a sight to behold. He sat upright on the bed with his mate cradled in his arm. He stroked her back as she fed from him. Maggie was struck by his care and affection for her. The way he held his mate, a human, was not unlike the way a human male would hold his pregnant lover. Maggie never would have believed it possible for a vampire to feel anything for something so different, but today the High Prince had proved her wrong.

She saw him raise his eyebrows in curiosity. Maggie cleared her throat. "High Prince, My name is Maggie. I am here as a midwife for your mate. With your consent, I would like to check on her. I brought her some food. She'll need that in addition to the blood you're giving her."

Jin eyes fluttered, then closed. As Maggie scrutinized him, her expression changed from confusion to understanding.

"Perhaps the High Prince is in need of sustenance," she said, setting the tray on top of the refrigerator. She opened it and took out several packs of blood. She made a lot of noise as she approached Jin, lest he think she was sneaking around him.

His eyes opened to the sight of Maggie offering him blood. He took it from her, immediately draining it and taking another. After the seventh, Jin was starting to feel more like himself. He nodded to Maggie when he was sipping the eighth.

"Thank you," he said.

She nodded. "If I could, I would like to examine her."

Jin finished, then placed the empty pack on the bed.

"What must I do?"

"Let me check her pulse, and the children…" her voice trailed as surprise registered in her eyes. Adina's belly had grown since her last examination. She watched Adina disengage from her lover's shoulder, her eyes glinting before becoming normal again. When she recognized Maggie, she smiled faintly at her.

"How are you?" Maggie asked.

"I'm fine now." Adina replied.

"I need to check you over. I also brought some food."

"Really?" said Adina, excited. She sat up with her back against Jin's chest. He opened his legs so that she could sit between them and wrapped his hands around her waist.

Maggie nodded. "I just need to check on your babies, okay?"

"Sure. What do you need me to do?"

Jin was watching sedately. When he didn't object, Maggie went and leaned over the bed. She placed her hands on Adina's belly. Closing her eyes, she connected with the children, sensing their calmness and delight at having their father there with them and their mother. She felt that both children were healthy, but she was missing something. When she tried to reach deeper, they retreated from her. She waited for a moment, but nothing happened. The feeling left her. Slowly, she opened her eyes and moved her hands away. The High Prince caught one of them.

"Is everything okay?" he asked.

His eyes bored into hers. She looked over to Adina, who was also waiting for an answer. Another thought crossed Maggie's mind suddenly. She controlled her expression to hide her alarm. She nodded and stood straight.

"Yes, they are fine," she said.

"And my Adina?" he asked.

"She's needs to eat."

Maggie waited for him to let go of her hand. He did, but only after studying her for a long time. Maggie turned and picked up the tray. She took it to Adina and placed it across her lap, only to have the High Prince move it to the empty space next to them.

"Adina, let me up," he said softly.

"Where you going? To the bathroom? Vampires use the bathroom?" she asked, half joking, half serious.

Jin missed the humor. "No. I need to check on some things while you're eating."

Maggie watched panic come onto the young woman's face. To her amazement, the High Prince wrapped his arms around her to reassure her. When Adina calmed, he eased her forward so he could get up. Then he returned the tray to her lap.

"I'll be back before you know it." He leaned down and kissed her gently. "I'll still be in this building, okay?"

"Okay. Don't take too long," she replied.

Maggie was about to bow and wait for dismissal when he leaned over her and whispered, "I need to talk to you."

He fixed his shirt as he walked over to the door. Maggie followed him out.

In the hallway, Jin told Komi and Jode to watch over Adina. Komi started to question it, but Jin gave her a look that quieted her. Jin directed Maggie to follow him. They walked slowly down the hallway, turning right at the first corner. He stopped, facing her.

"Where is a private place that we can talk?" Jin asked.

She nodded, walking past him. They went a few doors down, made a left turn at another corner, and stopped in front of some double doors. Maggie pushed one of them open and stepped inside. Jin closed the door behind them, then looked around.

The room had rosewood paneling and bay windows that only reflected one way, no doubt, to show the woods sprawling on the right side of the lodge. A large glass conference table sat in the center of the room atop dark green carpet. It had rosewood legs and was surrounded by black executive chairs. To Jin's left was a wall with a projection screen in place of four panels.

Jin directed Maggie to sit. She was conflicted for a moment, but eventually sat. Her back was stiff as she waited. Jin sat in the chair next to hers, leaning away from her just a little.

They sat in silence for a few minutes. Maggie waited for Jin to speak and Jin hoped that she would just volunteer information. When nothing happened on either front, Jin took the initiative.

"What's happening to my mate?" he asked.

Maggie looked at him calmly. "What do you mean?"

"When you were examining her, I know that you felt something wrong. Your facial expression verified my suspicions. Tell me. Is there something wrong with the pregnancy?"

Maggie cleared her throat, feeling nervous for the first time in her life. The High Prince probably wouldn't react well to anything she told him. He might have been gentle with his mate, but she had seen the damage he'd inflicted on her Prince. What would happen if he thought she hadn't properly cared for his mate?

Maggie almost jumped when she felt his hand on hers. When she looked at him, she saw respect and concern in his eyes.

"Please, I know your kind has no reason to trust me. I don't ask this because I seek to judge. The truth is, I cannot possibly judge you. I have no idea what to expect and you are the only person I can ask. Obviously, there is no love lost between your Prince and me, but since I do business with him from time to time, I know that he always uses the best. If he has you here, it's because you're the best one to care for Adina. So please tell me. Is she going to be alright? Are my children going to be alright?"

Maggie digested what he had said. She decided to trust him a little.

"She is losing blood rapidly. It has slowed down since you've gotten here, but carrying twin breeds is taking a toll on her body. Her organs are suffering from the strain. In addition, she is growing faster than I've seen humans do with vampire pregnancy. I mean that she is bigger than she should be at this particular time. That is also having an adverse effect on her."

Jin leaned back, expressionless. After a pause, he asked, "Is she dying?"

Maggie stood and started to pace. When she spoke again, she ignored his question.

"Then the babies are feeding very fast, but I feel like they are keeping something from me. I can't discern what. You have to understand, High Prince, this just doesn't happen anymore. I mean humans getting pregnant by full-blown vampires, and you're Alpha. I just can't begin to comprehend what that has added to an already complicated and dangerous situation. When it happened in the past, there were so many complications..."

"Is she dying?" he asked again, his voice hard.

Maggie stopped pacing to hold his eyes in an unwavering stare. She nodded slowly. Though fleeting, a shocked, pain-filled expression flitted across his face before it became expressionless again.

"Is there something we can do to prevent it?" he asked softly.

Maggie sighed softly, her head dropping a bit. She hated what she was going to say next, but it had to be said.

"I don't if there is any way that she can stay human and survive." She did not look away to emphasis her point.

Jin stood slowly. He stepped closer to Maggie, his green eyes glinting.

"What do you mean?" he said icily.

Maggie held her head higher and spoke with resignation.

"High Prince, vampire pregnancies are hard on humans. Many females die from them. She is losing blood and she feeding a lot because she carrying twins. She has even been draining you to feed your children. When she gives birth, she will lose a lot of blood. I don't know if we will be able to keep up with her blood loss and save her. The fact is I don't think she can take this pregnancy full term because…" she pressed her eyes closed before finishing, "…her body cannot sustain this much longer. We may have to remove the children early or risk losing them both. Even then, her chances of survival are very slim, as it will be for your children."

He held her eyes for a long time then looked away, but not before she caught the unshed tears in them. Maggie's lips parted in utter shock. Although his back was turned, she knew that he was trying to control his emotions. She reached for him, but he stepped away before she could touch him. Her hand dropped.

Jin's heart pounded in his chest. *What I have done is killing my mate. Not my mate, the woman I'm finally understanding that I love. I came all this way to save her, and now I find that my actions are killing her and maybe our children.* The worst part was that there was nothing he could do about it. He let the pain course through him until he remembered that Maggie mentioned something about her not surviving as a human. *Did she mean…?* His voice was flat when he looked over his shoulder and asked, "What if I turn her?"

Maggie shrugged. "I'm not sure. I'm not that familiar with the process, Sire, but it may help. There are drawbacks, but again, I don't know."

"Then who would know?!" Jin roared.

Maggie took a step back, though the fear never showed in her face. She swallowed and was about to speak when he interrupted again.

"I'm sorry. I just...I just need to know who to ask."

Maggie nodded. "I understand. The only person who might know is my Prince, Flaxon."

Jin shook his head, a mirthless laugh choked out of him. He didn't what to have anything to do with Flaxon so soon, but Fate seemed to have other plans.

"Where is he?" Jin asked.

* * *

Flaxon stood in the terminal watching the monitors. A young Breed tapped away on the keyboard. Then the boy pointed at the screen.

"There. I've tracked this car," he said, flicking the screen, "and this one is coming this way."

Flaxon nodded. He recognized both. Sneering, he stood up. "Alert the others and get the hell out of here. Tell Screech to take everyone to the safehouse in Alaska. I'll meet you there as soon as I can. We are in official stealth mode."

The boy nodded and got up to leave. Flaxon stared at the screen shaking his head.

"Time to go," he whispered to himself. He walked out of the room to inform the Prince and his guards that the enemies had arrived.

* * *

Tobias was tense. He knew they were close after being thrown off track for two hours. He glanced at his crew in the car. All looked as tense as him, except Chelina, who was grinning maniacally. He looked away, thinking instead about the fight to come. He would bet his right arm that the High Prince knew they were coming. All Tobias could hope was that their plan worked and that Chelina turned out to be as good as she thought she was.

* * *

Eldon held the cellphone close to his ear as he listened to the woman on the line. His wife was standing close to him, trying to listen, too.

"I have the heads. They will arrive sometime tonight, Sire," said Cheryl.

"Good. And have you tracked my son?"

"Yes, after going on a wild goose chase. Whoever's helping him knows what they're doing."

"You still haven't established the vampire?"

"No, Sire, but I know this. More of Tobias' minions are coming for him. Right now, I'm thirty minutes behind them. I don't know—"

"No excuses, Cheryl. Get there. I want that Tenhar scum and I want to know who is helping my son, understand."

"Yes, Sire."

* * *

Jin was waiting in the conference room with his head in his hands. Maggie had been gone for ten minutes. He knew he needed to get back to Adina, but he couldn't until he got his emotions in check. The feelings he was suffering were totally unfamiliar. He was scared, upset, sad, but the feeling of utter helplessness was crippling.

He's going to lose her.

The thought played over and over in his head. He felt like a part of him was slowly being ripped out. It made all the fighting, all the planning, and all the promises he'd made to his parents seem surreal. Finally, he raised his head. For the first time in his life, something mattered to him and he had no idea how to protect it. What was worse was the alternative. Taking the chance to turn her was almost as dangerous as the pregnancy itself. She could die before the conversion was completed. Jin was about to slam his hand on the table when he felt Adina's panic.

Jin jumped up and raced for the door, where he was greeted by Jode.

"What happened? Where's Adina?"

"She's with Komi getting ready..." started Jode.

"Getting ready for what?" Jin asked.

"They are coming, Jin. Assassins are coming for you...and her."

Jin's face hardened. "Are they? Well, won't they be surprised."

Jin stepped around Jode and headed to Adina's room. He needed to check on her before he found Flaxon.

End of Book One

CPSIA information can be obtained at www.ICGtesting.com
Printed in the USA
BVOW03s1001230614

357117BV00020B/837/P

9 781439 211847